Rule #1: Trust you[...]

Rule #2: Know y[...]

Rule #3: Lure your enemy to you.

Rule #4: Strike fast, strike first.

Rule #5: When all else fails...
make your own rules.

Quantico Rules

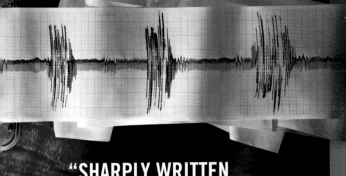

Outstanding Critical Praise for
Quantico Rules

"A must-read, suspense-packed cautionary tale of corruption told by an ex-FBI agent who isn't afraid to show us the ugly stuff on the inside. With this stunning debut novel, Gene Riehl has brought a fresh new voice to the world of crime fiction."

>—Harlan Coben, bestselling author of
>*No Second Chance* and *Gone for Good*

"*Quantico Rules* is my kind of story. It is full of high tension, intrigue, and the details of life as an FBI agent that could only have come from a career agent himself. Gene Riehl has taken his experiences and turned them into a thriller that is good till the last page. But it is more than a page-turner. It is an incisive study of an agent battling the obstacles of bureaucracy to finally make his stand."

>—Michael Connelly, bestselling author of
>*Lost Light* and *City of Bones*

"Stock up your refrigerator. Unplug the telephone. A master spy has arrived, and you're not going to want to leave home until you finish his smart debut thriller. In *Quantico Rules*, former FBI agent Gene Riehl swings wide the doors of Washington's secret back rooms in a search for power gone wrong. Full of authentic detail, bristling with fascinating characters, *Quantico Rules* proves Riehl is a new master of suspense."

>—Gayle Lynds, bestselling author of *Mesmerized* and
>co-author of *Robert Ludlum's The Altman Code*

MORE . . .

QUANTICO RULES

RULES

Gene Riehl

St. Martin's Paperbacks

To Diane Martin Riehl. To Rosemary Kopp Riehl and Eugene M. Riehl.

QUANTICO RULES

Copyright © 2003 by Gene Riehl.
Excerpt from *Sleeper* copyright © 2004 by Gene Riehl.

Library of Congress Catalog Card Number: 2002191967

ISBN: 0-312-98772-2
EAN: 80312-98772-5

Printed in the United States of America

St. Martin's Press hardcover edition / August 2003
St. Martin's Paperbacks edition / July 2004

St. Martin's Paperbacks are published by St. Martin's Press, 175 Fifth Avenue, New York, NY 10010.

10 9 8 7 6 5 4 3 2 1

ACKNOWLEDGMENTS

Authors write alone, but they don't work alone. *Quantico Rules* had lots of help along the way, much of it from author friends like Ken Kuhlken, who read the manuscript more times than anyone should have to; the immensely busy Michael Connelly, who was never too busy to take another look; and Gayle Lynds, who provided expertise and enthusiasm in equal measure; along with Alan Russell and Harlan Coben, who gave me exactly what I needed, exactly when I needed it. I also want to thank Federal Judge Judith Keep for insight into the world of judges and the Supreme Court, and retired FBI agent Clyde Fuller for details of bureau life I may have overlooked. But the most special thanks of all go to my wife, Diane Martin Riehl, expert researcher and story analyst, who read what seemed like millions of words, and displayed the rare ability of knowing which ones to keep.

Others read the work along the way and helped more than they know, including Paul Baerwald, Nancy Grinder Reinman, T. R. Reinman, Gayle Kehrli, Kristina Weller, Sam Weller, Chris Pack, Mike Pack, Pat Greene, Ken Bowman, Joe Ruff, Jaime Liwerant, Elizabeth Bowman, Noreen Mulliken, and Chip Harrison. Also, Brenda Riehl and Matt Riehl, good kids and great friends.

In no way have I been more fortunate than with my professionals. Jean Naggar is simply the best agent in the world, and Jennifer Weltz stands shoulder to shoulder with her. In Hollywood, Jerry Kalajian is both a friend and relentless advocate for my work. At St. Martin's Press, my superb editor, Marc Resnick, not only made the words better, but championed the manuscript in-house every step of the way.

ONE

I WAS A LIAR A LONG TIME BEFORE I HOOKED UP WITH DR. Paul Chen—good enough at it to fool my bosses for years—but now they'd changed the rules. At long last they were getting serious. Now they had a brand-new machine, and suddenly I didn't stand a chance. Or so Dr. Chen was telling me during our regular Monday afternoon session at his biofeedback clinic in Georgetown.

"This is not about self-confidence alone, Mr. Monk," he said. "If it were, you would not need me at all. You have mastered a few tricks to manipulate the polygraph, but that means nothing anymore."

In the darkened office he kept too warm, the doctor sat at his desk-console while I lay in a leather recliner a few feet to his right, my stockinged feet hanging over the end as they always did. Aromatic smoke curled from a smoldering stick of incense in the corner of the room, and a cone of light from the high-intensity lamp on his desk dramatized Chen's gaunt face and the gray chin-whiskers that made him look like Fu Manchu. His hushed voice and stilted Chinese accent added to the illusion.

"Polygraphy," he continued, "is a science of emotion. That is why it is so unreliable, why a strong-willed person such as yourself can be taught to fool it. That is why the technology has moved in a different direction, to cognition instead of emotion. The future is in brain waves, Mr. Monk, not such transient phenomena as blood pressure and galvanic skin response. And now—for you at least—the future appears to have arrived."

I glanced at my watch. What the hell was he talking about? I didn't have time for this today. I turned my head to stare at him.

"What're you saying . . . that you can't help me?"

"I am saying there is no point, not with the same method we have been using at any rate. What use is it to be able to beat a polygraph if the machine no longer exists? Why learn to use a slide rule in an age of computers?"

The back of my neck began to burn. "You wait till now to tell me this?"

"It would have been a waste of time, until I knew you better. If you had not made such progress with the traditional test, there would have been no hope you could beat the new one."

I nodded, but time was wasting, and I didn't give a damn about what he thought I could or couldn't do. Whatever it was, I'd get it done.

"There's no test that can't be beaten," I told him. "I'm paying you to show me how, not to tell me why not."

He smiled, his lips parting a centimeter or so, his uneven teeth gleaming in the weird lighting. "I cannot recall a more determined client, Mr. Monk. I, too, have little interest in excuses. Perhaps we should get started."

"What are we talking about, timewise? I've got a six o'clock flight out of BWI, at least an hour of paperwork to clear up back at the office before I can leave for the airport. I'll only be gone overnight. Maybe it would be better to try this tomorrow when I'm not so pushed."

He shook his head. "You cannot leave. We must not stop just because you are in a hurry, because your level of stress is high. Just the opposite as a matter of fact. If you cannot learn to do this with your stomach clenching and your neck rigid, you will be lost. But once you can, their instruments will be useless against you."

I opened my mouth to argue but closed it again as I admitted he was right, that when it finally happened I'd be grateful for his insistence. I nodded, and Chen seemed to leave his desk and appear next to my recliner without taking a step.

In his hand he carried dozens of thready electric wires—leads similar to those we'd been using with the polygraph—that I could see were connected to the mahogany instrument panel that dominated his desk. He stood over me and began to tape the sensors to my face, scalp, and neck. He kept talking while he worked.

"To lie successfully," he said, "you must first think of the words you are about to say, assess the probability they will be accepted as truthful. Doing so causes a burst of brain-wave activity that is lacking when you tell the truth. Researchers believe human beings are powerless to control such bursts, but my hypothesis is that they are wrong. You first came to me because of the success I have had with others of your colleagues. You people have now become critical to my study."

"What's so special about FBI agents?"

"You are exceptionally authentic liars, Mr. Monk. I am the only researcher in the field fortunate enough to be working with you."

I stared at him and tried to think of a response. *My pleasure* didn't sound right. *Fuck you* didn't either, but before I could think of something better he was talking again.

"For studies like these, authentic liars are almost impossible to recruit. And inducing fake liars to think like real ones is very difficult." His smile was ghastly in the shadows of his face. "The FBI is a rich source of liars, all the way back to Hoover himself. Not in court—not often in court, I should say—but within the bureau itself. Hoover set up a system that required his agents to tell him lies to keep their jobs. The system has never changed."

He bent closer to tape the last two sensors somewhere over my right ear. "Your particular lies are not work-related, you contend, but the bureau would disagree. In fact, they would fire you just for being here. You have been promoted into an assignment you do not like, but to get to the counter-terrorism work you consider more important you must first pass a lie detector test. You are here to learn how to make that happen. I will not send you away until you do."

I nodded, the wires clattering. "Let's get on with it then. Where do we start?"

"We must establish a baseline for you. I will ask very simple questions. You will answer them yes or no, just like you did with the polygraph. The monitor in my console displays information from the sensors attached to your head. The digital input is converted to colors. Blue lines for truth, red lines for the brain-wave bursts that indicate you are lying."

"Do I watch the screen with you?"

"Not today."

I tried to get comfortable, but it wasn't easy. Maybe that was part of the test.

"Are you forty-four years old, Mr. Monk?"

"Yes."

"Are your eyes blue?"

"Yes."

"And your hair is brown?"

"Yes."

"Are you an FBI supervisor in charge of special investigations for the White House?"

"Yes."

"Have you ever lied on an official FBI document?"

"No."

"Do you live in Fredericksburg, Virginia?"

"Yes."

"Do you socialize with known criminals?"

"No."

"Do you work out of the Washington Metropolitan Field Office?"

"Yes."

"Have you ever lied to the FBI about any aspect of your personal life?"

"No."

Dr. Chen stood, came around to the recliner, and began to remove the electrodes.

"How'd I do?" I asked him. "For the first time, I mean."

He looked at me and shook his head slowly. I didn't bother to ask again.

TWO

CROSSTOWN TRAFFIC TOWARD THE WASHINGTON METRO-
politan Field Office on Fourth Street was thick enough to
give me plenty of time to think. Dr. Chen's negativity troubled me until I decided I'd been too distracted by the
prospect of my night in Connecticut to give his newest
gadget a reasonable shot. Next time I'd be ready. If Connecticut worked out the way it should, I might even be able
to pay down some of his bill.

I passed the Hoover Building on Pennsylvania Avenue
and noticed a commotion near the front entrance at the corner of Ninth Street. Blue-and-white Metropolitan P.D. squad
cars lined the curb. A throng of protesters had gotten too
close to the doors again. M.P.D. was shoving them back toward the street, and the crowd didn't like it. They jabbed
their signs at the cops like torch-bearing villagers in a
Frankenstein movie, and I could hear their familiar chant
over the slap-slap of my windshield wipers.

"No more *Carni*-vore!" they shouted, ignoring the fact
that the bureau had long ago changed the name of the con-
troversial e-mail interception program to the less provoca-
tive but pretty much unchantable DCS1000. "No more
Carni-vore!"

They'd be over at WMFO, too, of course, with their

growing outrage over the newest addition to the program, the sci-fi–sounding Magic Lantern that could penetrate a home computer all the way down to the individual keystrokes that send data to the hard drive. Even I realized how spooky that could sound if you thought about the possibilities for abuse, if you pictured an unscrupulous FBI using the program to get around the Fourth Amendment. Hard to blame the protesters for bringing their message directly to us. The legitimate protesters, that is, but the honest ones have never been the problem.

Unfortunately for both sides, there were the others—the hardcore rabble of window-breaking and rock-throwing mouth-breathers who turned out for anything that gave them a chance to indulge their hobby. Today it was Magic Lantern, but before that it was the World Trade Organization. Next month—the way things were going since 9/11—would bring out the Fair Play for Terrorists crowd.

I took the short diagonal on Indiana Avenue and three minutes later saw I'd been right. The down ramp into the bureau garage was blocked by protesters, but there were no cops or GSA guards around. Typical. As long as the Hoover Building was secure, we peons could eat cake. And this bunch was loud, I had to give them that, their message clearly audible over the music from my radio.

"No more *Carni*-vore! . . . No more *Carni*-vore! . . . No more *Carni*-vore!"

I turned down the ramp, eased my Caprice toward them, tapped on the horn a couple of times but kept the big car moving. I didn't get far before I felt a jolt from the rear. I checked my mirror. At the back of the car a bearded man in an army camouflage jacket and black knit watch cap was jumping up and down on my bumper, screaming, his middle finger thrusting at me, his mouth slobbering with rage as he tried to spit on my rear window. I thought about making a federal case out of it, but I didn't have time for the paperwork, so I tapped my brakes instead. Thrown off balance, the idiot toppled forward across my trunk deck then fell off the car. I grinned. The simplest way is always the best.

But it wasn't that simple, I realized an instant later.

The bearded man appeared outside my window, his arm cocked before it flashed forward at me. I turned away reflexively and heard the crack-splat of an egg hitting the window. I turned back, stared at him through the spreading yolk on the glass between us.

I slammed the gear lever into park, hurled the door open, and caught him before he could jump back. He stumbled, fell to the pavement, and I was all over him. I grabbed a handful of the camouflage jacket and jerked him to his feet. His eyes widened, but shouts of rage from the mob emboldened him.

"Just like a pig!" he hollered. "Whattya gonna do, beat me up?"

"Gestapo!" a voice shouted from behind him.

"Nazi!" a second voice added.

A third man moved toward me, his mouth wide open. "Maybe you oughta kill all of us!" he screamed as he got closer.

The crowd began to edge toward me. I dragged Egg Man a few steps in their direction and it confused them into silence.

"Think about it," I said, loud enough for everyone to hear. "A year in jail for assaulting a federal officer . . . ten-thousand dollar fine, minimum, but don't let that stop you. Maybe you can all go to the judge together, get some kind of group discount." I turned back to my prisoner. "I'm going to make you a deal," I told him. "Think of it as a plea bargain."

"What the hell are you talking about?" he muttered. "You crazy or something?"

"Or something," I told him, then pointed at the grocery bag in his left hand. "Got any more eggs in there?"

He appeared lost for words, so I grabbed the bag and checked for myself. Sure enough, there was a fresh carton inside. Grade AA extra large. The only one missing was already hardening on my window.

"What's your name?" I asked my captive.

"I don't have to give you—"

I jerked his jacket so hard his stocking cap fell halfway down his face before he got it back on his head.

"Steve," he mumbled.

"Okay, Steve, here's what we're going to do." I lifted his carton of eggs out of the bag. "Give me your cap."

"No way!" he said. "No goddamned way! You can't make me—"

I reached for the handcuffs attached to my belt. "Fine. It's probably best we do this the right way anyway."

He held up his hand. "Fuck you," he muttered as he dragged the stocking cap off his head and handed it to me.

I emptied the carton into his cap, placed the cap back on his head very carefully, then snugged it down over his ears. He started to shake his head at me, realizing now how this was going to play out. To my credit I didn't make him agonize long over it. Before he could get his hands up to stop me, I used my six-inch height advantage to reach out and clap him right on the top of his pointy head. The soft explosion of collapsing eggshells was clearly audible in what had become an almost surrealistic quiet.

The crowd gasped. Steve's eyes got wide. A yellow curtain of yoke descended from beneath the cap down his forehead and into those eyes. He wiped the worst of the mess away, glared at me with what I guessed were the first seeds of his plans for revenge.

I would watch for him, I told myself as I got back into the car and continued down the ramp into the garage, but I wasn't much worried. His type was no good without a mob, and it would be a while—after word of this passed through Washington's cretin community—before young Steve found another group willing to back him.

Upstairs, I strode through the bullpen toward my office at the rear of the Squad 17 bullpen. Most of the twenty agents assigned to my Special Inquiries Squad—SPIN, in bureau speak—were at their desks, telephones at their ears, pumping the world for information about one or another of the hundreds of applicants and nominees for government positions important enough to merit a White House request for special attention. The cacophony was startling the first time I heard it, but after a while I didn't even notice it. I'd gotten the squad a little over a year ago as my first step up the administrative ladder, but I still had no idea how these people could turn out such high quality of work in such chaotic surroundings.

I stopped at Karen Kilbride's desk. My secretary stared at me.

"I was just about to call you on your cell phone," she said. "The ADIC wants to see you. Didn't sound real happy." Her eyes narrowed with concern. "What have you done now?"

"Not a thing," I told her, but I knew better. Somebody'd seen what happened downstairs, had dropped a dime on me. Or Assistant Director-in-Charge Kevin Finnerty had seen it himself. The ADIC's office overlooked the street, as well as the open down ramp into the garage. He might very well have been watching, and the thought did not please me. The man who ran the Washington Metropolitan Field Office was about as much fun as a visit to the proctologist.

Inside my office I headed for the phone to call him, but Special Agent Lisa Sands sat squarely in the way. I moved past her to the metal coatrack next to my desk, hung up my raincoat, turned and glanced above her head at the schoolroom clock on the wall.

"This'll have to be quick," I told her. "I have a meeting with the ADIC in a few minutes, and I've got to be at BWI in an hour." On the way to my desk I could smell her perfume. Flowery but not sweet, wildflowers maybe, and a big improvement over the stench of underarm sweat I'd brought back with me from the sinister Dr. Chen.

Agent Sands's dark brown eyes jabbed at me. "You're *leaving*? Now? Before we finish the Thompson report?"

I sat behind the desk, reached for the phone, told Kevin Finnerty's secretary I was on my way upstairs, then hung up.

"I'll be back tomorrow morning, Lisa. You told me Friday you were finished with the investigation. That all you have left is the report to dictate."

"That's what I thought on Friday, but I was wrong. I came in Saturday to dictate and that's when I caught the problem. It's a bad one. We can't let it go . . . not after what happened with Grady."

My back teeth began to grind. Christ, I was sick of Supreme Court nominees. The Josephine Grady fiasco hadn't happened on my watch, but it was the reason the supervisor's job was open when it came time to promote me. My predecessor was working out of Butte, Montana, these days, but his failure had stayed behind with the squad I'd inherited. As far as the Hoover Building was concerned, a second Supreme Court disaster would be counted as *my* second failure, and two failures were deadlier than anthrax. I reached for my briefcase and opened it.

"Go ahead," I told Lisa Sands. "I can listen while I get ready to leave."

She shook her shoulder-length brown hair from side to side. "There are twenty days missing, boss"—in the bureau, the term survived despite the PC involved—"and I don't know how to find them."

I looked at her and grunted. You can explain away a day or two, but not twenty of them. Not to the Oval Office you can't. SPIN cases were boring as hell for the most part, but could be fatal when the White House was involved. Suddenly my trip to Connecticut didn't seem like such a hot idea. I glared at Lisa, then reminded myself it wasn't her fault.

"How long ago?" I asked.

"Nineteen seventy-two."

"Seventy-*two*? Thirty *years*?"

My spirits lifted. Maybe my plans for the night weren't ruined after all. I removed an airplane ticket from the briefcase and slipped it into the inside pocket of my suit jacket, lifted my black leather credential case with the imbedded gold badge from my shirt pocket and put it in the briefcase.

Lisa consulted the yellow legal pad in her hands. "Brenda

Thompson graduated Cal-Berkeley, on June 17, 1972. Left the Bay Area immediately, reported to Yale Law School on July 8. But her SF-86 doesn't account for her whereabouts in between."

"Twenty days . . . less than three weeks, three decades ago. That's asking a lot, even for us."

"If it were easy we'd hire ribbon clerks, isn't that what you keep telling me?"

"What I'm saying is that even the bureau can't know everything."

But I was wrong even to think such a thing. Knowing everything is exactly what we do, and the only reason the SPIN Squad exists in the first place. Impossible or not, we're expected to verify every word on the SF-86, the personal security questionnaire each and every nominee submits as part of the investigatory process.

Lisa pulled her chair closer. Her eyes got even darker and more intense. "That's not the worst of it. The problem's not the missing days . . . not exactly anyway." She glanced at the metal coatrack to the right of my desk. "You might want to hang up your suit jacket. This could take a while."

I shook my head. "Finnerty's waiting for me. I don't have a while. Just tell me what's going on as quickly as possible."

"As soon as I discovered the gap," Lisa said, "I called Judge Thompson. At first she said I must be wrong, that she'd gone straight from Berkeley to Yale, but I gave her the same dates I just read to you. Surely, I told her, it couldn't have taken three weeks to get back to law school. She was quiet for a few moments, then laughed. It *had* taken three weeks. She'd stopped on the way in a small town in Virginia—Brookston, Virginia—to care for a dying aunt. Spent two or three weeks with the aunt before the elderly woman died. Never considered it a real residence—still doesn't as a matter of fact—so she didn't include it in her questionnaire."

My fingertips began to drum on the top of the desk as I pictured my waiting boss's face upstairs.

"Lisa, please, if there's a problem, I'm not seeing it. The judge made a mistake on the 86. Happens all the time. Add a paragraph to the administrative section of your report, explain what you just told me. Business as usual."

I opened a second hidden compartment in my briefcase, removed a plain white business envelope half an inch thick, put it next to the wallet in my pocket. I started to get up, to fetch my raincoat, but she stopped me.

"There's more," she said. "Stop trying to get out of here. Wherever you're going, it can wait five minutes."

I stared at her. For an agent not yet finished with her probationary year, Lisa Sands was damned pushy. I remembered something from her personnel file, her interview with the recruiting agents in El Paso, and her audacious statement that she planned to become the first woman director of the FBI. A commendable goal, but someone needed to tell her it would take more than a year to get there.

"I called the Cobb County clerk's office in Brookston," she continued, "to check out the death certificate."

"Same deal," I told her. "Routine business. Have the county clerk send a copy, certified and exemplified. Do an insert for the report, I-A the copy, and attach it to the file."

"Not that simple, I'm afraid. Thompson told me her aunt Sarah Kendall fought the cancer as long as she could but finally died on the second day of July 1972. Thompson left for New Haven the day after the funeral."

"And you verified it, you dictated your report . . . yada, yada, yada."

"Not exactly. The lady died all right, no question about that, but she didn't do it in 1972. Or '73 or '74, either." Lisa smiled, mock sweetly. "Bless her heart, old Sarah Kendall hung on till 1991."

I felt my eyebrows lift.

"And what'd the judge have to say about that?"

"Give me some credit. I wasn't about to go back to her until I talked with you first."

I had to smile. Lisa might be new, but she was a quick study. Presidential appointees are best approached with extreme caution, and not at all when the possibility of lying exists.

"How about the rest of the report? What else did you find?"

"Nothing. Except for her miraculous aunt, Brenda Thompson's about as exciting as Mister Rogers." She glanced at the notebook in her lap, then looked at me again. "I almost wish I hadn't noticed the residency gap. I'll never make the bureau deadline now. Ten days isn't nearly enough time to sort this out."

I nodded. "Prepare a delay letter asking for a new buded"—the acronym for bureau deadline—"and get it ready for me to sign. I'll run what you just told me by the ADIC and we can talk about it again tomorrow morning."

At the door to Assistant Director-in-Charge Kevin Finnerty's outer office on the top floor, I straightened the knot in my tie, pulled the door open and went through. The ADIC was a Hoover man first, last and always, and the retro look of his office had been calculated to make that clear to his visitors. With its museum-quality furniture and musty air of old carpet and velvet draperies, the place reminded me of the set for *The Maltese Falcon*. One of these days, I was sure, Humphrey Bogart would step out from behind the heavy maroon drapes, his fedora pulled low, snub-nose in hand, looking for the fat man.

Finnerty's secretary was the perfect complement. Her mouse-brown bun of hair, crimson smear of lipstick, and high-shouldered floral dress made Betty Swenson look like a Norman Rockwell painting. The last of a long line of bureau old maids stretching back to Hoover's fabled Helen Gandy, Betty was proud as a battleship and tougher than the *Bismarck* to get past in one piece. Her head came up as I approached. She glared at me over the top of her frameless half-glasses.

"He's been waiting for fifteen minutes," she growled. "You better get in there."

I tapped on the door. "Puller Monk," I called, then went through and headed across a dozen yards of gray carpet toward the assistant director in charge, enthroned at the far end of the room behind an aircraft carrier of a desk laden with stacks of files and other paperwork. Flanking him, twin flags stood like sentinels. Behind the ADIC, floor-to-ceiling windows admitted gray light from another in a long series of drizzly January afternoons.

The ADIC's strong chin and clear gray eyes, his perfectly tailored navy blue suit and crimson tie, radiated enough power to light the entire building. Power dangerous enough that I'd made it a point years ago to learn his tell—the nonverbal warning that always preceded his wrath. When he began to straighten up his paperwork, it was time to duck and cover.

I moved to the nearest of the leather chairs in front of his desk and sat. He said nothing, but I didn't expect him to. The bureau is like a dog pound. Everyone knows where he stands, but the top dog is the only one who has to keep proving it. Kevin Finnerty wouldn't acknowledge me until I knew exactly who was in charge. If it weren't for the mess, he'd lift his leg and piddle against the desk to drive home the point. I grinned at the image, and he caught me red-handed.

"Perhaps you'd like to share the joke, Mr. Monk." He glanced toward the window overlooking the street. "Or maybe you're still amused by that display outside."

"That was no joke, boss. I made a very serious point to those people."

"You did nothing of the sort. We have a police department to handle such things. Your job was to arrest the perpetrator and take him to the U.S. Marshal's office. What you chose to do instead—engage in some kind of baggy-pants comedy routine—is not acceptable, not for one of my people, especially not for one of my supervisory staff."

"He'd have been back on the street throwing eggs before I got back upstairs to start the paperwork."

"That's not our concern. You made a fool of yourself, of this office, of me personally. I know you're impatient to get into the counterterrorism program, but an incident like the one I just witnessed is a sure way to kill your chances. You will not get where you want to go by acting like a child. I will not warn you again."

I slid forward in my chair, the back of my neck starting to burn. ADIC or not, he was out of line. I opened my mouth to tell him so, but closed it again. The best I could do was change the subject.

"I'll exercise better judgment next time, Mr. Finnerty, you can count on that, but I do have something else to speak with you about."

He nodded for me to go ahead.

"We have a problem with Brenda Thompson," I told him. "She left out a three-week period of residence between college and law school, and may be lying about it."

"Lying?"

"We went to her when we discovered the residency gap, but what she told us about it appears to be untrue."

"Woman's what, fifty-something? You're talking about a long time ago."

"Fifty-three, and you're right. It was a long time ago."

"What about the roommate, the missing roommate from the University of California? Won't she be able to clear it up?"

I glanced into his eyes. You had to hand it to the man. A few years past the mandatory retirement age of fifty-seven—exempted by special fiat from our director—Kevin Finnerty ran WMFO like an accountant, missed not a single detail of cases he considered essential to rebuilding the bureau's dwindling reputation.

"She might be," I answered, "if we could find her." I caught his scowl, a clear indication of what he thought about my answer. "We ran out of leads on the roommate," I added, "and, to be frank, until this happened I hadn't considered it a high priority to find her."

"But now . . ." he said, leaving the words hanging.

"But now we're looking for her again, of course."

We weren't, but it was the whitest of lies. We sure as hell *would* be the instant I got back downstairs.

"I think that's a good idea," he said in an FBI code that really meant, *If you don't find her, I will personally remove your testicles and watch you eat them.*

"Shall I send the delay letter directly to the Hoover Building," I asked, "or would you prefer to see it first?"

He shook his head. "There will be no delay. The director's deadline is a week from Thursday. That will be sufficient."

"It's a huge report, boss. Take us most of that time to get it through the typing pool, revisions and all. I'm not sure we can—"

I stopped when I saw him reach for his paperwork.

"Ten days, Mr. Monk," he told me. His teeth showed for an instant in what I'm sure he considered a smile. "The whole universe only took six."

At the airport, I shuffled along in the one-hour line through the security-check system and boarded the US Airways jetliner as soon as they'd let me. I sat in the aisle seat of row 14 and tried not to think about Judge Brenda Thompson, even though I knew it was foolish to try. Like the man who was promised a million dollars if he could go thirty seconds without thinking about a hippopotamus, I didn't stand a chance. The stopwatch had barely started when the lumbering beasts began to crowd the periphery of the poor bastard's imagination. Ten seconds later they were tromping through the door like unwelcome relatives, another ten and they had set up housekeeping and ordered cable TV.

So I gave in and started with Josephine Grady. To fully appreciate the Thompson problem, I first had to review the Grady debacle.

Judge Josephine Ellen Grady had been the president's first choice for his history-making appointment of a black woman to the Supreme Court. My predecessor had done a bang-up job of clearing her background—he thought—until the *Washington Post* uncovered the judge's undocumented Guatemalan housekeeper, a housekeeper the SPIN squad had not even thought to ask about. The headlines were brutal. The president had dumped Grady quicker than medical waste, then summoned our director from the Hoover Building and chewed his ass raw. The director wasted not a moment before flinging the blame downward to Finnerty, who turned the bureaucratic double play by hurling the SPIN supervisor out to Butte and promoting me to replace him, then making my mission exquisitely clear: Do not let such a thing happen again. And that brought up a question I couldn't help asking myself.

With the stakes this high, what am I doing going to Connecticut?

I'd told Lisa Sands we couldn't do anything more today about Judge Thompson, but I'd been lying. I could be in the judge's chambers right now, taking care of business, but I was heading for Connecticut instead, and the truth was I was going because I couldn't *not* go. There'd be plenty of time for Brenda Thompson when I got back. No matter what it cost, no matter who might end up paying for it, I wasn't about to cancel what awaited me up north.

And speaking of Lisa Sands, I still didn't quite know what to think about the woman who was the latest addition to my squad.

She was an FOA—a first office agent—but an unusual one. Thirty-five, for starters, at a time when most new agents were ten years younger. She'd been an assistant district attorney in El Paso and knew the law-enforcement ropes pretty much cold before she came to Washington. Sharp as a pit-boss, Lisa didn't need me to hold her hand, but that didn't mean I wouldn't like to. It was a very pretty hand, as was the rest of her. I pictured her long legs and gorgeous smile and felt a twinge of disappointment. We were both single, but I was her boss. In these days of corporate rectitude her magnificent body was a thousand miles off-limits, so I ordered her out of my mind. Like the hippos, however, she loitered, as I tried to concentrate on warming up for Connecticut.

I sank deeper into my seat and began the counting-backward ritual that seemed to work for me. From one hundred by sevens, to start with. One hundred, I mumbled, ninety-three, eighty-six, seventy-nine . . . Then by elevens. One hundred, eighty-nine, seventy-eight . . . Then by fourteens, and so on until my brain felt limber as a gymnast. I laid my head back, closed my eyes, and thought good thoughts until the announcement to buckle up for landing brought me upright again. On the ground in Hartford we rolled to the terminal and hooked up with the flexible tunnel that jutted like an overeager lover toward the plane. I got off and headed for the Avis desk.

"Mr. Bland," the thin woman with the red jacket said as I walked up. "How nice to see you again. Your car is waiting. You can expect the usual discount."

"Thank you, Judy," I told her. "You take very good care of me."

"Same time tomorrow, sir?"

I shook my head. "Earlier. Quick turnaround this trip."

"I'll be on the desk in the morning. See you then."

I scribbled my John Bland on the rental form and headed out the doors to the Avis depot on the left side of the covered parking garage. I could feel Judy watching my back, and my neck began to tingle. Relax, I told myself, she's not working for the bureau. She's just friendly, is all . . . might even have other designs, and why not? I had my own hair and teeth, a decent topspin backhand down the line. Why shouldn't she cop a peek if she wanted to?

In the rental—a blue Ford Taurus that smelled like cigar smoke and Lysol—I followed Connecticut Route 2 south toward Norwich. My wipers swept at the latest rainstorm pounding against the windshield. I drove through grassy expanses green enough to make you blink, past scarlet barns and white farmhouses, and half an hour later crossed the Thames River at Norwich, continued south on 2 for another twenty minutes, through the Pequot reservation and the town of Mashantucket, and pulled up the tree-lined driveway to the Foxwoods Resort and Casino. It sat waiting for me. The twenty-story hotel's central tower looked like a hand raised in welcome, the building's two jutting side wings like arms stretched out to embrace me.

My stomach began to flutter with the rush that kept me coming back to a place where I dared not be seen. I accelerated toward the front doors, pulled up at the valet parking stand. A young man I'd never seen before opened my door, pulled a ticket from under his rain-shiny poncho and handed it to me as I got out of the car. I headed into the palace with the sweeping golden façade. The twenty-foot-tall doors slid open and the casino lay defenseless before me.

I reached into my pocket for my lucky ring, a yellow glob of gold I never go to the tables without, a ring I never wear anywhere else. I slipped it on the pinky finger of my left hand, stepped through the doors, and stood there for a moment.

The noise hit me first, a cacophony of bells and whistles, shrieks of hope and despair, a slap of sound that stopped me in my tracks. Then came the smells—sweat and perfume, whiskey and cigarettes—and finally the stunning spectacle itself. Two and a half green-carpeted acres of self-indulgence ... four thousand slot machines to my right, stretching away into the gloom ... on my left, table after table of blackjack, roulette, baccarat ... all for the taking.

Men and women, fuzzy figures in the half-light, shuffled from machine to machine like acolytes covering the stations of the cross, and the metaphor wasn't a bad one as I thought about it. Religion comes in all shapes and sizes. In here the faithful were every bit as vocal in their petitions to God, just as despairing when he failed to show, but it was counterproductive to think that way, and I warned myself to stop. I'd long ago made a deal with God. Stay out of my business and I'll stay out of yours. So far we had made it work just fine.

Suddenly, standing in that doorway, I felt myself inflate with confidence, as optimistic as an accordion player with a beeper as I strode toward the action. A hostess who used the name Melinda—a gorgeous brunette with legs and breasts and everything—hurried toward me. I stepped forward and offered my hand. Her teeth blazed white. The golden nugget on my pinky finger gleamed in the reflection of her smile.

THREE

Tuesday morning my head hurt. My pride hurt even worse, and my suddenly flattened wallet was really killing me. A handful of aspirin took care of the headache, but the damage to my ego and bank balance from the long night at Foxwoods was going to take a lot longer to mend. I felt like taking the day off, but there was one big reason I couldn't.

The clock on Kevin Finnerty's deadline for the Brenda Thompson investigation was ticking, and Lisa Sands couldn't finish her investigation until I'd talked with the judge again. I was tempted to let Lisa do the interview by herself, but I knew better. That business about the judge's dead aunt still didn't sound right. At the very least it represented an unusual mistake for a federal judge to make, at worst it could be a scandal big enough to ruin the president.

What it meant for sure was that a brand-new agent couldn't be allowed to handle it.

I got a late start from home and didn't bother stopping at the office first. It was after eleven as I mounted the steps of the E. Barrett Prettyman Federal Courts Building at the corner of Third Street and Constitution Avenue. I passed the statue of General George Meade outside the courthouse, pushed through the doors and used the elevator to ascend to United States District Judge Brenda Thompson's courtroom on the sixth floor. The judge didn't know I was coming, of course. In an interview like this you never want to let the other side get prepared. I'd already determined she was on the bench this morning, and I wanted to watch her in action before going after whatever she was trying to hide.

I slipped through the courtroom door and took a seat in the back. It was a drug case—methamphetamines—and had been all over the papers and TV. The defendant was a notorious gangbanger, a coconspirator in a homegrown drug cartel that included most of the really bad guys in the District. Albert Scroggins's street name was "Scum," and from the looks of him it was an apt description. I glanced around. His street gang—the Blades—had packed the courtroom, not wearing their colors, but despite that every bit as ominous. With their long black braids and fierce beards, they looked more like Afghan terrorists than urban Americans.

I watched Judge Thompson closely for her reaction to their unmistakable tactics, by now familiar in gang cases. Things went along fine for about ten minutes of questions and answers, until finally the judge had seen enough.

The assistant United States attorney—a young black woman with a no-nonsense dark suit and matching glare—was interrogating a prosecution witness, another black woman with a short afro and heavy glasses. Midway through the examination, Judge Thompson slammed her gavel hard enough to make my ears ring.

"That's it!" she shouted. "That's the end of this nonsense!" She pointed at a slouching figure in the second row. "You!" she snapped. "Out of here right now!" Her dark eyes blazed. "You will not sit in my courtroom and intimidate a witness! Get out before I have you thrown out!"

Noise erupted. Judge Thompson raised her gavel, pounded the room back into silence. The defense attorney, a short white guy, leaped to his feet, used the thick-framed reading glasses in his hand to punctuate his words.

"How can you *do* that, your honor? My client has every right to be supported by his friends and family. You have no business—"

"Sit down, Counselor! *Now!* Sit down and keep your mouth shut or I'll throw you out as well!"

Now the bangers were all on their feet, shouting and pointing fingers. The judge turned to her bailiff. He touched a button on his desk. The doors behind us opened and U.S. marshals flooded in, grabbing arms, shoving gangstas toward the door. Thirty seconds later the courtroom was pretty damned empty. I glanced around at the wide eyes of those allowed to stay, felt my own eyes widen as well. Whatever else she was, Brenda Thompson knew how to keep order in her courtroom. Seeing her like this—watching her fearless disregard for some truly dangerous people—I reminded myself to tread lightly.

The sound of Judge Thompson's voice interrupted my thoughts as she announced the early recess and ordered the jury to come back at one-thirty. I slipped out of the courtroom and headed for the judge's chambers around the corner.

The judge's clerk, a red-haired young man who looked like he hadn't smiled for a long time, glanced up from his desk as I approached. I flipped open my creds and asked to see his boss.

"Got an appointment?" he wanted to know.

"A couple of minutes," I told him. "That's all I need."

"Her book's full, I'm afraid. She's not even taking phone calls today."

"Busy or not, I've got to see her."

"She left orders, Agent Monk. No one, she said, not until after court this afternoon."

"Call her."

He shook his head. "I told you I can't do—"

His voice died as I lifted the phone from his desk and handed it to him.

"Call her," I repeated. "I'll make sure she knows it wasn't your idea."

His narrow shoulders sagged. He took the phone, pushed a button, mumbled into the receiver, and hung up. He stared at me as the chamber door opened and Judge Thompson came through, her hand stretched out to me.

"Special Agent Monk," she said. Her handshake was firm, but it was a little moist at the same time. Could mean a couple of things, too soon to know for sure what.

"Please come in," she told me.

I followed her and couldn't help admiring her light gray suit, the perfect tailoring that concealed the spreading that comes with age.

"Have a seat," she said when we got to her desk.

I did so, in the closest of the matching crimson leather chairs facing the desk, then waited for her to walk around to her own chair behind the desk. On the way she stopped near the floor-standing American flag to her right, turned toward me for a moment before sitting. Clever woman, I thought. Bill Clinton couldn't have done it any better. Without saying a word, she'd reminded me exactly who she was and what she represented.

Behind her dark cherry desk with its inlaid leather top and intricate detailing, Judge Thompson stared at me for a moment, then smiled. Her teeth contrasted with her light chocolate complexion, her brown eyes and slightly darker hair, which was cut short and styled perfectly for her triangular face.

"What can I do for you?" she asked.

"Before we begin, I have to say I'm impressed. I was in the courtroom. I saw what you just did in there."

She waved her hand in a dismissive gesture. "Those guys? I was dealing with worse garbage than that before I was ten years old."

I nodded. She was right about that. Her file had all the details. Born in the worst part of Washington's black ghetto, a heroin-dealing father who died in prison before she was three. Gangbanging stepbrothers she hasn't seen since she started school. Raised by her grandmother after her mother had OD'd once too often. A dreadful story, even by D.C. standards.

I looked up to see that she was waiting for me to get down to business.

"You spoke with Special Agent Lisa Sands yesterday morning," I said.

Her eyes flickered but stayed directly on mine. "Of course. The mixup over my mistake on the personal security questionnaire—isn't that what you people call it?"

"Yes, your honor. The PSQ. I'm afraid we have a problem with it."

She leaned forward and her eyes did fall this time, but only for an instant before she brought them back up. "A problem? I don't understand. I explained to Agent Sands what happened. Didn't she tell you?"

"She said you stopped in Brookston to care for a dying aunt, that after the funeral you went on to law school at Yale."

Her hand went to her throat, massaging gently before she dropped it back out of my sight.

"Funeral?" she said. "No, there was no funeral. Aunt Sarah didn't die, that was the point. We were told she'd never make it, but she did." The judge cleared her throat. "I was determined to stay for the funeral, but, bless her heart, she refused to die. I hated to leave her, but I just didn't have any other choice. Law school was going to start with me or without me, so I finally drove up to New Haven. I got there . . ." She stared upward, as though she were reading her itinerary off the ceiling. "Must have been a day or two before school started." She looked at me again. "I can't think why I left this off your questionnaire."

"And is she still living, your aunt? Can she verify your stay with her?"

Judge Thompson frowned, reached for a piece of paper on her desk, stared at it for a moment, then grabbed a pen and made a quick note on it.

"Sorry," she said. "This writ should have gone out yesterday." She laid the pen aside. "Did my aunt die, is that what you asked?" I nodded. "Yes, Agent Monk"—she cleared her throat—"yes, she did, a number of years ago."

"What year would that have been? Just for the record, your honor."

"I don't remember. A long time ago, but I'd have to search my files to tell you exactly when."

"Your conversation with Lisa Sands was over the telephone. Perhaps that's why she misunderstood you . . . why we avoid the phone for important interviews."

She nodded. "I told her I *waited* for a funeral, not *went* to one. I thought I was pretty clear about it, but it's been a madhouse around here since my nomination. The truth is I could have said anything." She cleared her throat again. "I hope I haven't caused a problem for you, but isn't this overkill? We're only talking about a few days, thirty years ago. What difference can it possibly make now?"

I stared at her. Surely the judge knew better than to ask such a ridiculous question. I wanted to tell her that, but now wasn't the time. Not while I still needed her help.

"You know the bureau," I told her instead. "A few days, a few years, it's all the same to my masters. I'm sure I don't have to tell you why."

"Of course not, not after Josephine Grady." She smiled. "What you really want to know is whether I was in jail, or in Moscow training with the KGB." She shook her head. "I'm afraid my life's depressingly normal. I was just a college kid blown away by the thought of going to Yale Law School. I did my duty with my aunt, but as soon as I could leave I was on my way again. End of story."

Which left me with nowhere to go with that line of questioning, so I changed directions.

"I have a second problem, your honor. We need to interview your last college roommate, Dalia Hernandez, but we can't find her. You told us you lived off-campus with her for almost nine months, but our agents in Berkeley can't find any way to verify that. Or any records to indicate where she might be now."

"She'd be in student records at Cal, for starters, and pretty easy to track down after that I would imagine."

"Can't get into student records, not for Dalia anyway."

Judge Thompson nodded. "Right. I forgot about the waiver. You've got twenty releases from me, but none from her."

"That's why I'm asking. Maybe you can put your memory to the test."

"That won't be easy, I'm afraid."

The judge cleared her throat again, and when she continued, the timbre of her voice was just the slightest bit higher.

"We didn't part on very good terms, Agent Monk. Both

our names were on the apartment lease and I had to leave before the end of the month, the end of the lease. Dalia thought I was trying to skip out on rent, on cleaning up the place. You know the problem."

"Have you had any contact with her since then?"

"None, I'm sorry to say. I sent her a note with enough money to make sure she didn't get hurt on the lease, but she never replied. The months turned into years." She shrugged. "What can I tell you?" She laid her hands on the desktop, palms down. "I have to ask you again. What could you hope to get from finding Dalia Hernandez now? She didn't like me at the end, probably still doesn't, but so what?"

"You're a Supreme Court nominee. Surely the president warned you about the depth of our investigation."

"Of course he did, Agent Monk, and I don't mean to be so difficult. It's just that my confirmation hearings are coming up soon and even to think about them makes me cranky. I saw the Bork fiasco, what Clarence Thomas went through. Mother Teresa herself would have a tough time, and I'm beginning to understand why."

"If you had to find Dalia Hernandez, really had to find her, where would you start?"

"She was in pre-law with me at Cal. Her home was in Philadelphia." The judge shook her head. "Not much to go on, but I guess I'd check out the law schools in Pennsylvania."

I stared directly into her eyes. "I'm obligated to remind you of something, Judge. If there's something in your personal history that I should know about, now's the time to tell me. It would be a mistake to let me find it first."

"I have never done anything I'm ashamed of."

"With all respect, your honor, that's not responsive to my question."

Her smile died. "Then let me make it clear enough that you and your headquarters can't possibly misunderstand. There is *nothing* in my history that disqualifies me from sitting on the Supreme Court." She lifted her reading glasses from the desk. "And if that's all, I need to get back to work."

• • •

On the way back to my office I considered the two things I'd just learned. One, Judge Thompson never did answer my question—not the way it needed to be answered anyway—and two, she was the most incompetent liar I'd ever interviewed.

Talk about tells, Brenda Thompson had been awash in them.

Overexplaining at the start, repeating far too many times her assertion about her aunt's miraculous survival, clearing her throat repeatedly, then using her hand to massage her throat, as though she could physically squeeze out words she didn't really want to say. Hands in her lap out of sight, and when they weren't, flat on her desk with the palms down. Then that ridiculous business of attending to a piece of unrelated paperwork in the midst of my questioning. And half a dozen other clear indications she was not telling the truth. My stride lengthened as I neared the front doors into WMFO. Suddenly I couldn't wait to find out why.

Back at Squad 17, Lisa was frowning as I approached her desk in the surprisingly quiet bullpen. Most of the desks were unoccupied, and I wondered why until I remembered that most of my squad was scheduled for firearms training this morning.

"Thanks a heap," Lisa said before I could speak.

I stopped at the corner of her desk.

"Kevin Finnerty stopped by," she continued.

I frowned back at her. "The ADIC was down *here*?" I wondered if I'd heard her right. Assistant FBI directors didn't come to middle management, not ever. "What did he want?"

"To know where the hell you were, for starters. Then he tore into me because you were gone." She seemed to read the question on my lips. "No, I didn't. I didn't tell him anything . . . but I feel a little used, Puller. Like you hung me out to dry."

"I had no choice," I said, and it might have been true. At least one person had accused me of that very thing, that my overnight casino runs were no longer under my control.

A stab of pain behind my eyeballs reminded me of my ordeal in Connecticut the night before. I hadn't had a drop to drink in the casino, but the trip had been a disaster, enough disappointment and pain to keep me from my usual nap on the plane coming home. Now it felt like a small cabinetmaker was working inside my skull, sandpapering my eyeballs from the other side. Suddenly I wanted to sit down. I looked around for a chair to drag over, then decided to prop myself against the edge of Lisa's desk instead. She smelled good, I couldn't help noticing, and somehow it made me feel better.

"How's the Thompson report going?" I asked her. "How far along is it?"

"I'm assembling the stuff from the other offices—three hundred and some pages so far—and I should have a rough draft by the end of the week." She stared over my shoulder for a moment before her troubled eyes swung back to me. "But there's still the missing college roommate . . . the unaccounted-for three weeks . . . the not-quite-dead aunt."

I told her what the judge had said, that the aunt had in fact not died while Thompson was in Brookston. "Could you have misunderstood, Lisa? Misread your interview notes?"

"Not a chance."

She opened the file on her desk, then the 1-A section of the file, a manila envelope attached to the inside back cover, used to store documentary evidence too small to be maintained in the vast bulky-exhibit vault on the second floor, as well as original interview notes from the case agent. Lisa pulled out a sheet of lined yellow paper and handed it to me.

"Here they are," she said, "my notes from our conversation. Look for yourself."

I took the paper. Her handwriting was as meticulous as the rest of her work. I didn't expect to find a mistake and I didn't. Halfway down the sheet, the words couldn't have been more clear. *B.T. waited till after S.K. funeral, then left for New Haven.* Then, a bit further down, Lisa's record of her call to the county clerk in Brookston. *Date of death S.K, April 17, 1991.* I read the notes again just to make sure, handed the page back to her.

"I'd say we have a problem," I told her, but just saying the words made my pulse quicken, and the feeling made me wonder about my motives.

As an FBI agent—a pro—I'm expected to examine such lies as Thompson's with the objectivity of a technician in a white lab coat, not as a predator racing to the scent of fresh prey. I should be able to do that, but no one in our type of work does. Firemen's hearts leap at the sound of an alarm bell, policemen rejoice in the sudden bark from the radio that sends them into harm's way. Soldiers would rather jump out of helicopters into blizzards of bullets than go through another goddamned day of training, and FBI agents can't wait to go after the kind of people who claim to be righteous.

"So what now?" Lisa asked as she tugged her straight skirt toward the edge of her knees. "I've been through the file half a dozen times. Where do we start looking for the roommate?"

"You finish dictating the report. Make sure it gets highest priority through the typing pool. I'll take care of the roommate."

I started for my office at the rear of the bullpen, but took only two steps before I turned back to her. She looked at me, her dark eyebrows forming a quizzical arch.

"Thanks," I told her. "Thanks for covering for me with Finnerty."

She nodded and said something that sounded like Spanish, but real Spanish, the kind you learn before you learn English. I headed for my office, but made a mental note to take another look at her personnel file.

At my desk, I turned to the daily paperwork I had to get done before I could even think about solving the intriguing mystery of Brenda Thompson, the routine paper shuffling nobody ever sees in the movies, the everyday tedium no screenwriter would be permitted to include in a script. FBI agents have some incredible adventures, no doubt about it, but for the most part the job consists of filling up reams of paper with reports no one ever reads, compiling massive files that sit around for years until they're finally destroyed to make way for new and equally useless compilations. I've often thought the files could be used for a better purpose. Like making convicted felons wear them around their necks.

My phone rang, a welcome interruption until I heard the voice on the other end. A voice I'd come to despise.

"Mr. Monk, it's Jack Quigley from Pinewood Manor."

My mouth formed an obscenity but I managed to keep it from turning into a word he could hear. "Yes," I said in its place.

"I'm calling about your father's account again. I don't like doing this any more than you like hearing it, but the unpaid balance is simply too large to overlook. Your father's care isn't free, you know, and his condition is getting worse. If you can't do something about this immediately, you're going to have to send him somewhere else."

Somewhere else, my ass. There was no place else, except to live with me.

"You're going to get paid," I told him, "but you'll just have to wait till escrow closes on my house."

His voice brightened. "You found a buyer?"

"Looks that way," I lied. "We just have to iron out a couple of contingencies." Like *actually* finding a buyer, for one. I heard in his voice the sound of his hopes crashing.

"Yeah . . . contingencies . . . right. Forgive my skepticism, but you've been telling me the same thing for months."

"I'm meeting with my realtor just as soon as I get off the phone."

"I'll give you two more weeks," the nursing-home administrator said. "Fourteen days, then you can come and get him."

He hung up before I could answer, which was a good thing, because I didn't have anything more to say. Lies had stopped fooling Quigley six months ago. My father's care was enormously expensive, his monthly keep a significant chunk of my monthly salary. I thought about Connecticut again and felt a surge of resentment toward the casino.

There'd been a time last night—from one-thirty in the morning till almost three—when I could have paid Jack Quigley's overdue balance *and* a hefty chunk toward Pastor Monk's next month's tab. Another hour on that kind of a run and I could have bought the demented old bastard his own wing. It had been that close, but it just didn't happen, not last night anyway. That it would happen someday, someday soon, I took as an article of faith. There was no denying that the last twelve months had been a nightmare, but it would turn for me. Always had, always would. Not that Jonathon Monk knew, or cared. Not that the son of a bitch even knew where he was, or who was paying for it.

Or wasn't paying for it, I guess Jack Quigley would say.

But regardless of what the administrator had said, his call had shattered my already puny resolve about catching up on my stack of files. Just the sound of Quigley's harping made me think about all the years I'd wasted listening to Pastor Monk's mindless rules, made me want to ignore the drudgery of my paperwork. Have some fun for a change. So I pushed the files aside and went to work on finding Brenda Thompson's missing roommate.

But first I left my office, took five minutes to use the bathroom, to splash cold water on my face and run a hand through my hair. The face in the mirror didn't make me happy, the pouches under my eyes, the stubbly shadow of whiskers. I'd seen that face before, I had to admit. Usually in a casino, but attached to *other* people in the casino, to the losers, the "bad beat," as gamblers say. Losing does that to you, beats you up bad, but the good news is that winning reverses the process, and that's why I needed to find the roommate. Some very good FBI agents had tried already and come up losers. By whipping the system until it gave up Brenda Thompson's roommate, I'd be a winner again. Walking around lucky, as they say. I took another look at my tired face. And I'd be beautiful again, as well.

Back at my office door I hung up my DISTURB AND DIE sign, closed and locked the door, grabbed my briefcase and opened my secret stash compartment. Christ, I thought, as I stared at the eight lonely hundred dollar bills that remained after last night's setback. My stomach began to hurt. Eleven thousand dollars gone. The worst night I'd ever had, despite the great start. I'd been at least that far up when it turned on me, far enough ahead to convince myself I couldn't possibly lose, although I no longer thought about gambling in such terms as winning and losing. The eleven large were still mine, I was just letting the Foxwoods Casino hold the money until I got back there to reclaim it. The philosophy is rife with error, of course. Nobody needs to tell me that, but I make it a point not to analyze it too closely. You start to believe the money's gone forever, you can go crazy.

Besides, it isn't about money, not for me anyway. I play for the action, the thrill of fear, the in-your-face belligerence of battling odds I can't possibly beat . . . except that somebody always does, and sometimes it's me. And when it is, I win more than just money. When it's me, I not only beat the odds but everything else my old man taught me to fear, along with a couple of things he made me dread.

At least that's what Dr. Annie Fisher tells me.

I can't tolerate boredom—my now and again lover insists—and that's the whole problem with me. Even worse, I'll do any goddamned thing to avoid it.

Picture life as a spinning pie plate, Annie had told me more than once. Picture yourself riding that spinning plate. There's a pole sticking up out of the exact center of that plate, and holding onto the pole is the only secure perch on the entire plate, the only sure way to keep from being thrown out to the edge, then off the plate altogether. It isn't much fun clutching the pole, but at least you know you'll make it to the end of the ride. Not like the risk-addicted bastards who let go of the pole, who creep toward the edge of the plate, their bodies quivering against the centrifugal monster trying to hurl them into the abyss, their mouths already forming the first faint moans of ecstacy. According to Annie, I'm only happy when I'm out on the edge, even happier when my grip is slipping, and far and away happiest when I'm clinging one-handed to the very lip of the plate, legs extended above the void, eyes wild and throat bulging as I holler for more.

She says that my childhood harnessed to Pastor Jonathon Monk's church of no-matter-what-you-do-you're-fucking-doomed has ruined me for a normal life. That given the choice I'd rather die than be ordinary. I argued with her at first, but we both know she's right.

I shook the negativity from my mind as I prepared to slide a little closer to the edge of Annie's plate.

First I removed two of my remaining hundred-dollar bills—"dimes" in casino speak, the curious vocabulary I find irresistible—and put the rest back into the secret compartment of my briefcase. If I failed to find Thompson's roommate before my five-thirty appointment with Dr. Chen, I'd go down to the street and give the two hundred to the first wide-eyed panhandler I could find. If I located the roommate, I'd win. Not money, of course, but in the only important sense of the word I'd win.

Ready to go, I reached for my in-box and pulled out a sheaf of paperwork, spread it on my desk, and invoked the gods of bureaucracy to speed me along my way. I pulled my briefcase closer, opened it, and retrieved my pinky ring, slid the ring on my finger, then used the same hand to grab the telephone. Before I dialed I took a moment to admit what I was about to do, that I needed to change the rules of the game for the next few minutes. Official bureau rules had not been good enough to find Brenda Thompson's college roommate. Now it was time for Quantico rules.

Like most states, California law forbids its universities from releasing information about students without a signed waiver from the student herself. I had one from Brenda Thompson, but nothing from Dalia Hernandez. To review the woman's file at Cal without her consent I had to break California state law, but I didn't have to search hard for justification. I couldn't possibly harm the roommate, and I'd be clearing up a problem that could delay Judge Thompson's Senate confirmation.

So I punched numbers, and three thousand miles away the switchboard at the Berkeley campus of the University of California answered, then directed my call to the student-records office. I told the woman who answered the phone who I was.

"I'm calling from Washington, D.C.," I said, "and I'm hoping you can help me."

FOUR

"Of course, Agent Monk," the woman at Cal-Berkeley told me. "I'll be happy to help you, if I can."

You can't, I should have told her in the interest of full disclosure. Not unless I can convince you there's no other choice. That we're both better off with Quantico rules.

"I'm doing a routine background investigation," I said, "and I need to verify the attendance of one of your former students. A woman who attended Cal back in the late sixties, graduated in 1972."

"Certainly."

I felt my eyes widen. It couldn't possibly be this easy. Maybe the woman was too new to know better. I reached for my pen as she continued.

"Just send an agent to my office with credentials and a release form. I'll be happy to help."

"There's a time problem, I'm afraid. Can we do it now, over the phone?"

"Surely you know about the Privacy Act here in California. I can't tell you anything about a current or former student without a signed release."

"But I do have a release, ma'am. In fact, I'm looking at one right now."

Which was the truth, albeit slightly modified. My in-box

was filled with signed releases, all kinds of them from all kinds of people. The only one I didn't have was the one she wanted.

"Good," the clerk told me. "Now all you have to do is bring it to me and we can do business."

"But I told you I'm up against a short deadline. There's got to be a way to expedite the process. What if I mail it to you later? Will that do?"

"I'm sorry, we just can't do that."

"Would you mind checking with your supervisor?" It was important in a thing like this to complicate the process as much as possible.

"I guess so . . . but I know what she's gonna say."

"I'll be glad to hold on while you double-check."

I listened to the dead sound of being on hold, thankful that colleges couldn't afford elevator music. She was back in a few moments.

"My boss says if I can verify who you are you can fax me the release."

I smiled to myself. This was more like it. I had my foot in the door, they'd play hell getting rid of me now.

I repeated my name, spelled it carefully, then asked the woman to use directory assistance to get the number at WMFO and call me back. That way, I explained, she would be absolutely sure she was talking to the FBI.

Her voice turned petulant. "Why don't you just give me the number?"

I shook my head at the predictability of her request, then did so. Three minutes later my phone rang.

"Okay, Agent Monk, I'm ready for the fax, but you'll have to be patient. Our machine is at the other end of the office. It'll take me a while to get over there and back."

Of course it would. In a civil service office without concern for efficiency or profit, fax machines were always hard to get to.

"Me, too," I said with a sympathetic chuckle. "In fact, I have to go all the way upstairs to use mine. Give me five minutes. I'll keep this line open."

I laid the phone on my desk with a clunk, rustled several

sheets of blank paper near the mouthpiece, then clomped to the door, opened and shut it loudly enough that she couldn't miss hearing. Then I returned to the desk, sat quietly for four and a half minutes, got up and repeated the door routine, went back to the phone and picked it up. "Hello," I said. "You still there?"

The line was silent for another minute before the woman rejoined me. She sounded a little winded.

"Nothing happened on this end," she said. "I didn't get anything."

"Damn. The machine's been acting up again. It breaks down a lot, so many different people use it."

"Tell me about it."

"I'll send it through again."

I repeated the procedure—rustling paper, deliberate foot-steps, noisy door—this time for six minutes. This time she was wheezing like an asthmatic racehorse when she got back.

"Nothing," she gasped.

"Are you sure? It says 'one page received' in my message window. Problem's got to be on your end. Let's give it one more try. Hold the line." I dropped the phone onto the desk-top, bent to listen.

"No! God almighty, no more!" the woman shouted. "I don't have all morning to screw around with this. At least I know who you are. I'll confirm whatever you already know, but I can't give you anything else."

I glanced at the clutter of papers on my desk. Anything I already know. That'll be a hell of a trick. I started with one of the only two things I *did* know.

"Dalia Hernandez was a student at Cal, graduated in 1972, went from there to law school. Does the computer verify her graduation?"

"I'll pull it up." I heard the sound of keystrokes. "Yes, here it is. 1972. June 14."

"What about requests for transcripts from law schools? See any of those?"

"I told you I can't give you that, Agent Monk. Not unless you already know it."

Jesus Christ, I thought, talk about Catch-22. You'd think the woman had given birth to the damned records.

"I have the law school stuff right here on my desk," I said. "Just give me a moment to find what I need."

I rustled papers close to the phone. "Sorry about this," I mumbled, Colombo-like. "Don't know what's wrong with me today . . . should have been better prepared. It was Philadelphia, I think . . . Philadelphia someplace . . . Temple University, was it? . . . No, that wasn't it . . ." I shook the papers again. "Where *is* that thing?"

I paused to let her jump in, but she was a hard case. I had the sudden urge to shove the papers into the mouthpiece of the telephone, thought briefly about where I'd really like to shove them.

"Ah, yes . . . yes, here it is . . . just as I thought . . . It wasn't Temple . . . It wasn't Philadelphia at all. It waass . . . it waaasss . . ."

"Harvard!" she barked. "For Christ's sake, Har—!"

"Harvard!" I shouted over the top of her. "Exactly right. Harvard Law School."

I leaned back, apologized twice more for the confusion, overthanked her, hung up, and ran a hand through my hair. Then I glanced at the money on my desk. Halfway there, I told the two Benjamins. More than halfway.

I picked up the phone again. Harvard would be a hell of a lot easier to deal with. Their law school was more interested in promoting the success of their graduates than hiding them from the police. And it was easier, I discovered when I got connected with the graduate school records office in Cambridge. A man answered this time, a man happy to tell me that Dalia Hernandez had completed law school and received her J.D. in 1975.

"Would you like to speak with the alumni office?" the man asked. "They probably have current information about her whereabouts, a phone number perhaps."

I told him I would, and he transferred my call. It was a woman this time, but her voice was strangely cold when I gave her the name I was looking for.

"You're not being very careful with my money, Agent Monk."

"I beg your pardon?"

"An agent from your Boston office called me already. Asked me the same questions about Jabalah Abahd. Don't you people talk to each other?"

"Abahd? No, that's not the name," I said. "Woman I'm looking for is Dalia Hernandez."

"Like I told your agent Bennett, they're one and the same. Dalia took a Muslim name about a year after she graduated from our law school. Jabalah Abahd does pro bono defense work out of her office in the District of Columbia."

She spelled the unusual name, furnished an address along with a phone number.

"The other agent," I said. "You sure he was one of ours?' "

"Talked like one of you people. I didn't see his credentials. Like I said, we spoke on the phone, but I had no reason to think he wasn't." Sounds of paper shuffling. "I made a note for the file," she said. "Bennett. Robert Bennett. Works out of Boston, he told me."

I stared at the wall opposite my desk. She was mistaken, of course. If she weren't, Special Agent Bennett's report would be in Lisa's paperwork already. But there was no use belaboring the point.

"You're right," I told her. "We should keep better track of one another."

I thanked her, hung up and sat quietly for a moment. *Robert Bennett.* I wrote the name on my notepad, along with the city, Boston. I picked up the phone, called Lisa, asked her to come to my office with the Thompson file, then went to the door and unlocked it. On the way back to my chair I reached out and snatched up the money on the desk. I pulled my briefcase up close and stuck the bills back into their hideaway. As I did so, I felt a throb of disappointment, and recognized the problem immediately.

I'd been looking forward to the gamble, but winning had been too easy, way too easy to get my blood pumping. Far too many agents could have done the same thing. It was a score, no doubt about it, but it didn't mean anything. Sure as hell didn't mean I was walking around lucky, not yet anyway. But I still couldn't help smiling when Lisa came through my door.

I told her what I'd just heard from the alumni woman at Harvard Law, and she smiled back. Despite her certainty that the Thompson file contained no reference to Jabalah Abahd *or* SA Robert Bennett, we double-checked anyway. Our smiles waned as we failed to find what we were looking for, and died altogether after my very short conversation with the FBI switchboard in Boston.

"She was mistaken," Lisa said, "your alumni woman. Had to be. She talked to someone named Robert Bennett, heard the words 'federal agent,' jumped to the wrong conclusion."

I nodded. It happens all the time, but there was still a problem. Why would another federal agency be looking for the same roommate? The coincidence was ridiculous. It was more likely that Robert Bennett was indeed an FBI agent, but not from the Boston office.

"Call Personnel at the Hoov," I told Lisa. "Bennett's out there somewhere. Let's get hold of him and see what's going on." I reached for the phone again. "I'll call Jabalah Abahd, set up a time for you to see her."

Lisa headed out the door. I glanced at my notepad for Abahd's office phone number, reached for the phone and punched the numbers. The lawyer answered the phone herself.

"May I ask why?" she wanted to know when I told her why I was calling. "I spent an hour with your Agent Bennett a couple of weeks ago. I didn't like talking to him in the first place. Frankly, I resent having to repeat that kind of story a second time."

I frowned at my reflection in the window to my right. Again with the Robert Bennett, but a new twist this time. "That kind of story? I'm sorry, Ms. Abahd, but I'm not sure what you mean."

"I take no joy in any of this, that's what I mean. Just seeing it in my old diary was bad enough. I told Bennett the same thing. What you need to do is find him and leave me out of it."

Hearing her words I felt a sudden buzz at the back of my

neck. *A diary . . . an old diary?* The buzz was replaced by a sense of anticipation I hadn't enjoyed nearly often enough since my days in criminal work. I had to see that diary for myself. I had to hear what Abahd had to say about it, why she'd kept such a record in the first place, and still had it with her all these years later. I thought about asking her right now, on the phone, but she was already reluctant enough as it was.

"Are you sure Bennett was an FBI agent?" I asked the lawyer instead. "That he wasn't a Senate investigator instead . . . or someone from the media? Sometimes people get confused."

"I don't get confused, Mr. Monk, not ever. I see FBI agents dozens of times a year. Robert Bennett was quite a bit larger than most of you, but he had the same credentials, the same dark blue suit, the same everything." She paused. "Is there anything else? I've got to be in court in ten minutes."

"Can I see you sometime this afternoon?"

"Not a chance. I'm in court till five."

"What about later this evening?"

"You're not going to go away, are you?"

"I can't force you to see me."

The silence on the other end grew long enough to make me wonder if we'd lost the connection. "Ms. Abahd?" I asked.

"I'm thinking," she said. "I'm thinking I have to see you, that I don't have any other choice." I heard the sound of shuffling papers. "My evening's free. If you really must, you can come to my home at seven."

She gave me her address, I told her I'd see her at seven. I hung up and stared at my reflection in the window to my right, then called Lisa.

"A diary?" she said, when I finished reporting my conversation with the lawyer. "Gotta see that, of course, but you don't have to do it . . . you don't have to drive out to Cheverly tonight. I'll get Jim Allen, we can catch a bite to eat, see her afterward."

Not a chance, I didn't bother to say. "You have plenty to do already. I don't want you to go home tonight until you've found this Robert Bennett. And I need a rundown on Jabalah

Abahd, a.k.a. Dalia Hernandez. Whatever you can wring out of the computer. By five o'clock. I want some time to go over it before I go to Cheverly."

I hung up and scheduled the rest of my day. A quarter to three, I saw by the clock over the door. I had a couple of administrative duties scheduled for today. I couldn't put them off, but they wouldn't take more than an hour at the most. I had an appointment with Dr. Chen at six, but that wasn't going to work anymore, not with the Abahd meeting at seven. Maybe he could squeeze me in earlier. I reached for the phone, called his office, spoke briefly to the doctor's receptionist, but no luck. Chen's book was completely filled. I canceled my appointment, then went to work on my chores.

As the newest of the supervisors, I was saddled with a number of jobs no one else wanted, the tedious but very necessary chores that somebody has to do to keep the place running. Today was code-changing day for the supervisors' bureau cars—bucars, we call them—and I was the one who had to change them. Our radios use specific electronic codes for the private channels we require to prevent the bad guys from listening to us, to keep the media from showing up when they shouldn't. The codes are changed on a regular basis for obvious reasons, and to change them I had to stop first at the tech room on the second floor. A few minutes later I punched the electronic keypad next to the tech room door and pushed through.

The room was huge, looked like a warehouse at Circuit City. Rows and rows of metal shelving lined the walls, filled with electronic gear of every size and description. Television sets, video cameras and recorders, FM radios—walkie-talkies as well as the heavy control units that were fitted into the trunk of every bucar in the basement garage—along with cellular telephones, computer terminals, and CRT monitors. A high-tech reliquary, a shrine to Our Lady of Silicon Valley. Looking at the shrine, I could only shake my head. I liked to think I could keep up with state of the art, but in here I knew better. In here I might as well be Amish.

But the techies themselves—the dozen men and women assigned to the technical squad—had to be out on the job somewhere. Only one appeared to be in residence this afternoon.

Gordon Shanklin—the most senior of the technical squad people, and an agent I'd spent years working with when I still did the kind of work that required his expertise—peered at me from his perch atop a stool at his workbench near the front of the room, then adjusted the baseball cap sitting backward on his shaggy head. His appearance no longer surprised me. In here the normal rules of dress and hairstyle didn't apply. Tech agents live in a different world, a quantum world of particles too small and too quick to measure, and the techies' interest in human beings was pretty much limited to eavesdropping. Shanklin and his buddies were not so much FBI agents as shamans, mystics best left alone to play with their incomprehensible toys. The official bureau more or less ignored their eccentricities.

"Dude," Gordon Shanklin said before I could speak. "Is it that time again?" He grinned. "Or are you slumming in your spare time?"

"You're right, Gordon, both ways. It is that time again, and I am most definitely slumming."

"Must be nice," he said, "upstairs with all the pretty people."

"Road to the top's a tough one, pal. Maybe you better start kissing my ass right now . . . before the rush."

He laughed in my face, then got off his stool and disappeared into the stacks for a moment, came back with my code-changer machine, a long thick black plastic device that looked like a TV clicker on steroids. He handed it to me, then climbed back onto his stool.

"Ever gonna see you more than once a month?" he wanted to know. "Ever gonna go back to working for a living?"

"Tell you what. Have your people get with my people, we'll do lunch."

"Fuck that," he said. "I can't afford lunch with you anymore, not unless I can figure out a way to beat you at liar's poker for the check." He laughed. "We do miss you down here, Puller. Come back when you can spend a few minutes."

I promised I would, then went downstairs to the garage.

The twenty or so supervisory staff cars, including my

own Chevy Caprice, were all parked in the same row near
the elevators, mine at the far end, Kevin Finnerty's only a
couple of steps from the elevator. I started with mine.
Opened the trunk to get at the radio unit bolted into place
back there. About the size of a big-city telephone book, the
control unit was a simple black steel box filled with electronic stuff I'd never bothered to study. All I cared about was
that the damn thing would work when I needed it.

I plugged my code-changer into the appropriate socket at
the rear of the box, pushed the correct sequence of buttons
on the hand-held unit, then waited for the high-pitched tone
that indicated the proper code had been entered. I unhooked
the code-changer, closed the trunk of the car, then started
down the line and repeated the process with the rest of the
cars, finishing with Kevin Finnerty's.

Twenty minutes it took me. I headed upstairs and returned
the unit to Gordon Shanklin, who was so deep into whatever
he was doing on his workbench he did little more than grunt
as I walked up, left the unit, and went back out the door.

My second chore took me to the switchboard on the first
floor.

Gerry Ann Walsh ran the switchboard better than anyone
I'd ever seen. A pretty woman of middle age, with short blond
hair and wire-rimmed eyeglasses, she smiled as I approached.

"The all-clear book?" she asked.

"You're way ahead of me, Gerry Ann. As usual."

She opened a small cabinet to her right, pulled out a spiral
notebook, and handed it to me, a book that contained the all-
clear codes for the various home-alarm systems connected to
our switchboard from the residences of agents and supervisors assigned to WMFO. Whenever a particular system got
triggered, the phone rang at the switchboard. Whoever was on
the switchboard would call the appropriate residence, and if it
was a false alarm—which was almost always the case—the
agent would give the operator an all-clear code, a four-digit
sequence that would stop the alarm and prove to the switchboard that there was no reason to send a response team.

There were lots of false alarms, I could tell just from the

wear and tear. The all-clear book's pages were wrinkled and
dog-eared from overuse, but there was no other way to make
the system work. All alarm companies operated the same way,
especially after the cops had begun refusing to send units until it was certain the alarm was valid and had begun charging
something like five hundred bucks for responding to mistakes.

My job was to make sure the book was still there, that no
one had stolen it, or had sold it for the obvious value it would
have to a burglar or a whole team of burglars.

I examined the pages for a moment, the lists of names
and corresponding all-clear codes, saw nothing amiss, then
handed the book back to Gerry Ann and went on my way.
Next stop, my last stop, the gun vault on the third floor.

The weapons vault was basically a gigantic safe, like the
main vault of a large bank. I had to consult the card in my
wallet for the combination before twirling it and swinging
open the heavy door.

About the size of a racquetball court, the vault's walls
were covered with weapons. On the wall to my left hung the
shotguns, several dozen big Remingtons hanging in rows.
Under the guns, behind substantial doors in the steel cabinets, was stored the ammunition, from birdshot to the rifled
slugs that could tear a grapefruit-size hole through human
flesh and bone.

To my right the automatic rifles, olive drab military shoulder arms capable of immense and lightning-quick destruction
when the need called for it. And handguns. Maybe thirty of
them, from tiny one-shotters that could be concealed in a belt
buckle, to hefty semiautomatic pistols—Smith ten-
millimeters and Sig Sauer nines. Every FBI agent is issued
his or her own weapon, a choice between the larger Smith-10
or the Sig Sauer, and agents are free to purchase and carry
other bureau-approved sidearms. But once in a while you
need a special gun, and this is where you come to get it.

My job was a general inspection to make sure everything
was clean and at least appeared organized. Also to check the
log near the single desk inside the vault to see how many
weapons were checked out, how long they'd been gone, and

whether or not they should have been returned by now.

I took about ten minutes in the vault, then locked it up and went back to my office at Squad 17.

I sat at my desk and ignored the paperwork. I couldn't make myself start so late in the afternoon, but I still had a chunk of time to kill before going out to see Jabalah Abahd in Cheverly. I felt a familiar and very pleasant flutter in my stomach as I decided what to do with it.

There was a brand-new card room across the Virginia line in Arlington. I'd be just another face nobody'd ever seen before. A couple of hours might go a long way toward replenishing my depleted briefcase. The fluttering rose up my body, a spreading warmth that made me want to bolt from my desk and head for my car. I grabbed my daybook from a pile of paperwork to my right, just to make sure I was indeed free. I opened it to today's page and saw that it was a good thing I'd checked. It had completely slipped my mind that Gerard Ziff had changed our regular Friday appointment to this afternoon at three.

I thought about the card room again, then decided to phone Gerard and put him off until later in the week. The French intelligence officer had information from Paris on several cases my squad was currently working, information we needed to make our deadlines. Despite that, the prospect of knocking over a fresh card room was too good to ignore. I could almost smell the felt on the tables, the invigorating aroma of fresh-won money. I could meet Gerard tomorrow morning for breakfast instead. I'd still get what I needed from him in plenty of time to make my deadlines.

I got as far as the telephone before an attack of good sense stopped me. In my business Gerard Ziff was an important contact, far too important to neglect.

So I locked my desk and headed for the tennis club.

FIVE

GERARD ZIFF WAS A SPY. HE WOULDN'T ADMIT IT AND I knew better than to ask, but that was the game we played. That and tennis.

As the French embassy's undersecretary for FBI liaison, it was his job—his nominal job—to broker the services of law enforcement in Paris and the rest of France to the FBI in Washington. My SPIN squad handled a number of investigations involving nominees who'd spent time in France and all over Europe, but that wasn't the only reason we used Gerard Ziff. His Gallic nose had been sniffing the Washington political air for years, and his sources inside the Beltway were often better than ours.

So we met once a week, the routine a pleasant mix of commerce and pleasure. First a set of tennis in the indoor club on K Street he belonged to, then down to business over a glass of something or other in the club's bar.

It was our habit as well to put a few dollars on the game, and in the locker room—royal blue carpet, mahogany lockers, musty odor of old money—he went into his ridiculous act, designed to equalize my ten-year age advantage and his flamboyantly mediocre ground strokes.

"I have the . . . how do you say it? . . . the *mal de tête* . . . the headache." He winced as he tied the laces of his tennis shoes, then groaned as he rose from the bench in front of his locker. "The Greeks," he continued, ". . . *mon Dieu*, the Greeks . . . a party at their embassy last night." He shook his head, his brown eyes sorrowful. "*Peut-être* . . . maybe . . . maybe we should just hit today. Maybe I should not risk the wager."

I laughed out loud. Gerard Ziff spoke immaculate and idiomatic English without a trace of an accent, except when he was running a game on me. The worse his English, the harder he was trying to screw me over. Today he sounded like a mixture of Pepé Le Peu and Maurice Chevalier. "You got the *mal de tête*, all right," I told him, "but if you're not on the court in two minutes you're gonna have the *mal de* everything."

He shrugged, then gave up the accent. "I'm not kidding this time, you asshole, not about the Greeks anyway, and their fucking *ouzo*. I gotta have alleys today. I gotta have *both* alleys."

"One alley." I couldn't beat my father if I let him use the full doubles court to chase me around in.

"Okay, damn you . . . but you only get one serve."

I shook my head. "Both serves."

"Four games then . . . I start four up, I get the serve."

"Two games, I serve."

He stared at me. "Right, like *that*'s gonna happen. Three games, I serve, I get one alley."

I turned the negotiation in a more important direction. "Hundred dollars?"

He winced. "I don't know." He spoke to himself for a moment. "Three games . . . I get the serve . . . I get one alley." He shook his head. "I don't like it."

"What *would* you like?"

His voice quickened, his tell that he was certain he had me now. "Two hundred for the set. You start four down. I serve first, but I take no alleys."

I kicked the carpet. I stared at the locker room ceiling, mumbled to myself, looked him in the eye. "Christ, Gerard, why don't you just stick me up with a gun, we wouldn't have to get all sweaty." Then I sighed. "Okay, okay. If you need money that badly . . ."

Startled by my sudden agreement, he tried to smile, but I had him and we both knew it.

Apparently he hadn't known it.

I'd never seen the spy play better.

Two of the best serves of his life in the first game, and I'm down oh-five before I've served a single point. I win the next three games, sweating like a pig to keep him pinned to his baseline. We go back and forth until he pulls a backhand out of his ass in the last game and at six-all we go to a tiebreaker. I serve first, ace him down the middle, he serves the next two, we split. He makes shot after shot until it's eight-all, his serve. All I've got to do is win the point, then handcuff him with a blistering serve into his body to finish him off.

It doesn't happen.

He serves a kicker to my backhand, comes to the net and stumbles into a volley that goes past me quicker than Kobe Bryant. Set point against me, my serve. I miss the ace down the middle by a whisker. Now it's hairy. I toss the ball for my second serve. It arcs through a distant light in the ceiling. I lose it for just a second, long enough to dog the serve into the top of the net. I stare across at him. He's got that huge Frog grin working as he comes forward, hand outstretched. I shake his hand, head for the showers to scrub away my disbelief.

Afterward we sat at an isolated table in the bar. From my pocket I pulled the same two hundred-dollar bills I'd wagered on my call to Berkeley and handed them over. So much for my return to the world of winning. Good thing I'd missed out on the card room. The damage could have been a hell of a lot worse.

"Maybe you should buy a Lotto ticket," I told him. "You ain't gonna get any luckier."

He shrugged. "Even a blind pig finds a truffle." He looked

around for a waiter. "Something to drink, Puller? Beer, perhaps, or a glass of wine?"

I was tempted. Gerard's idea of a glass of wine was a hundred-dollar bottle of wine, but my workday wasn't yet over. "Just a Coke," I told him. "Diet Coke."

His lips formed a straight line of disgust. He'd been in Washington almost twenty years, but still couldn't understand people who'd willingly drink such crap when there was wine available. The waiter took the order, came back a moment later with one Diet Coke, one cabernet. We drank a while, then got down to business.

"Bradley Long," he said, then reached for his briefcase and withdrew a single sheet of paper. He handed it across the table to me. A short memo bearing the letterhead of the French embassy. "Nothing ident on him, Puller. Sûreté, Paris Metro Police, Interpol's Paris Bureau. Nothing."

I took the memo, tucked it in the inside pocket of my suit coat, not surprised. Bradley Long was a former deputy ambassador to France and the current White House nominee for secretary of education. A family man, presumed to be squeaky clean, and so far he had turned out to be.

"The other matter," Gerard said, "Annette Hughes-Gardener. Paris found several references to her, so they'll need another week to assemble a report. I hope that doesn't jam you up on your deadline."

"Not at all." But it would, of course. Deadlines were deadlines. The Hoover Building didn't care whether the work was being done in Paris, France, or Paris, Texas. "Just give me what you can when you can."

I reached into a second pocket and brought out my own sheet of paper. "I have something new, Gerard." I handed it across. "Federal Judge Brenda Thompson. Supreme Court nominee." He nodded. "Thompson attended a month-long seminar on international law at the Sorbonne. Ten years ago, something like that. The exact dates are on the paper there."

Gerard studied the sheet. "Of course. I'll get something out today. Should have an answer by next Friday."

"Deadline's Thursday next week, and this is one I can't

delay. I know you don't like to do it, but can you use your STU-III phone or your computer net?"

He glanced at me. "We quit using the computer for stuff like this over a year ago. Too many people watching, you people with your Magic Lantern included." He stared at the sheet again. "Is there something else I should know here? Since when do you run checks on seminars at the Sorbonne?"

"You remember Josephine Grady?"

"Have you similar problems with Brenda Thompson?"

I shook my head. "Thompson has a housekeeper from Mexico, but you wouldn't believe the documentation. Green card, perfect IRS record, impeccable social security payments from the judge into her account. T's crossed, I's dotted. Gotta be the most perfectly credentialed domestic worker in the history of Washington."

"Why am I not surprised?" He sipped wine, put the glass back on the table. "And the White House. Still determined to add the first black woman to the Court?"

I smiled at Gerard's practiced naïveté, his pretense that he didn't already know the answer to such a question.

"Forgive me," he said, "but it still sounds like you've got another Grady in the works."

I lifted my glass of Diet Coke. Drops of condensation fell to the table. "I don't mean to give that impression at all. All we have is praise so far. Three hundred pages of it, not a word of derog."

"But there's *something*," he said, his tone persistent. "You know damn well we wouldn't be talking about her otherwise." He scowled at me. "The Sorbonne? Ten years ago? Gimme a break."

I shook my head. We go back a long way, Gerard and I. I trust him about as much as you can trust anyone in Washington, but Brenda Thompson wasn't just another case. Whatever she was up to, I was pretty sure it was no business of the French government.

"You wouldn't believe the lengths we're going to these days," I told him. "After Grady, the seventh floor rewrote the book." Paris has L'Elysée, and London Ten Downing. For the FBI, Mecca is the seventh floor of the Hoover Building.

He nodded. "I'll see what I can do."

"Thanks. It's important or I wouldn't ask. Kevin Finnerty is all over me on this one. Came down to my office personally, if you can believe that."

Gerard's hand with the wineglass stopped halfway to his mouth. He looked at me for a moment, then set it back on the table and checked his watch.

"Four-thirty," he said. "They might still be in the office in Paris. Maybe I can catch them."

He rose to his feet, grabbed his tennis bag, and hurried away.

I stared after him, puzzled by what he'd done, more importantly, what he'd failed to do. Gerard Ziff was a world-class handshaker, the instant he saw you, the moment he decided to leave. Every time, no exceptions. Until today. Until just now.

I got up to leave. Gerard's abrupt departure left me with time to kill. Maybe I could still get to the card room, do some damage there before I started for Jabalah Abahd's house in Cheverly. Unfortunately, the traffic would kill me. I wouldn't make it to Arlington till six, I'd have to leave half an hour later to get back over to Maryland, and that wasn't going to cut it. I didn't know how to walk away winners, and I wasn't about to fall behind early and abandon the money.

I could go back to the office, I told myself. Unless someone had come in and firebombed my desk, there were still two or three mountains of paperwork awaiting my attention.

Or I could eat.

There was an Italian place around here somewhere, I was sure. I would call Lisa from my table, have her e-mail the Bennett results and the stuff on Abahd to my laptop. I'd have plenty of time to go over it before my seven o'clock meeting with the lawyer.

I pulled out onto K Street, turned left. Guido's was on K Street. My head swiveled as I looked for it.

• • •

At Guido's Taste of Napoli I ordered a plate of gnocchi in the artery-clogging Alfredo sauce I was powerless to resist. The waiter hustled away and I called Lisa.

"Robert Bennett," she said before I could ask. "Personnel Division's never heard of him. I called the DOJ, nothing. Treasury the same thing. I even tried the Senate Judiciary Committee. *Nada*. If Bennett's a Fed, no one seems to know about him."

"What did you find on Abahd-Hernandez?"

"Still waiting for the computer clerks to get back to me. I'll call when they do."

I hung up and sat thinking until the waiter appeared with my meal. I was eating before he could even turn around, but two bites into it the phone rang again.

"Lisa," I said before she could speak. "You caught me with a mouthful of food."

"It's not Lisa, Agent Monk, and I'm glad one of us has time to eat. It's Jabalah Abahd. I was supposed to be in court all afternoon but my client pleaded guilty on me, so I can see you at six instead of seven."

I glanced at my plate of food, then told her I'd see her at six. I laid the phone on the table. Instead of two hours, I had half an hour. So much for an unhurried meal. I forked a couple of gnocchi and had them halfway to my mouth when the phone rang again. I held on to the fork as I answered it. Gerard Ziff this time.

He spoke as carefully as ever—a truncated code he insisted on using—as though Moscow itself were still listening. To give him his due, and from what we'd been hearing from our counterintelligence people, they probably still were.

"Nothing," he told me. "Civil and criminal, here and the other side. Nothing."

"What about the"—I fumbled for a euphemism—"your other friends?" I was referring to the intelligence files at the French embassy.

"Harder to access. Maybe sometime tomorrow."

Gerard couldn't get into those files without a written request, I knew, and the ambassador had put the clamps on such requests from the FBI following the discovery of Special Agent Robert Hanssen's criminal treachery. After Hanssen's fingers had been caught in the croissant jar, the French had decided the bureau could no longer be trusted with unconditional access to international secrets. Gerard would find a way, but he'd have to work on it a bit.

"Word of mouth?" I asked. French agents were just like FBI agents. Privy to lots of scuttlebutt that might or might not end up in an actual file.

"Nothing."

I thanked him, hung up, glanced at my watch. Traffic bad as it was, I better get going. I gobbled a few more bites of gnocchi, paid the bill, hustled out the door.

The rush hour was even worse than I'd anticipated, and the short drive to Cheverly took the better part of an hour. I phoned Lisa and told her about Abahd's call, then told her to quit waiting for the computer printouts and go home, that I didn't need them badly enough to keep her sitting around the office. She wanted to come out for the interview, but we agreed she'd never make it in time. She sounded reluctant to call it a day, and I had to smile. First office agents never want to go home. The day would come when she would no longer feel that way, or maybe in her case it wouldn't. Lisa was a determined young woman with a definite goal in mind. I wouldn't have her long, I knew, and I was surprised by a curious sense of regret about that. Easy, Puller, I told myself. You've got plenty on your spinning plate already. For once in your life, grab the pole and hold on for a while.

Abahd's street was lined with winter-bare poplars, and her jumbo two-story white house suggested she didn't defend the indigent because of any firsthand knowledge of poverty. I parked the Caprice out front, grabbed my briefcase and headed up the brick walkway to her bright-red front door. I pushed the doorbell and heard a two-tone chime, then the faint sound of what I decided was a door closing somewhere inside. I stepped back and waited for the front door to open, but it didn't.

I rang again. Nothing. I scowled at the door, then knocked on it, softly at first, then much harder. Still nothing. What the hell? Was the woman deaf? I'd had no sense of that during our brief conversations on the phone, but that really didn't mean much. Phones could be rigged to work as virtual hearing aides. Maybe she had a real one but didn't wear it at home.

I called out to her.

"Ms. Abahd! FBI! Agent Monk!"

I moved up close to the door, cocked my head and listened. Not a sound. I tried the door. It wasn't locked. I twisted the knob and cracked it open. Called out again, louder this time, repeated my name, listened hard, but still heard nothing. This wasn't going to cut it, I decided, then opened the door wide enough to stick my head in.

"Ms. Abahd!" I shouted. "It's Puller Monk!"

I gave her twenty seconds to respond, but she didn't, so I opened the door all the way and stepped into a wide, blue-slated entry. I could see into the formal living room—lots of dark furniture and embroidered upholstery—but I couldn't see any sign of life. She's got to be here, I told myself, no way she'd leave the front door open like this. Had to be in the back of the house somewhere, probably in a bathroom, or a distant bedroom. Somewhere she couldn't hear me.

I called out again, then moved a dozen steps into the living room and waited for her like a proper agent. Then I realized I was already too far inside for a proper anybody. Unwilling to be caught in her living room, I hurried back to the front door. "Ms. Abahd?" I called from the doorway. Again I waited, again she failed to show. And that did it for me. We had an appointment, I needed to talk with her today, and I no longer cared how I got it done. I went back in again, this time all the way to the far edge of the living room.

A long corridor extended from my right to the back of the

house. I poked my head into the hallway and called her
name again, said my name again. I cocked my head, thought
I heard her back there, some sort of movement, a wisp of
sound. She was back there, I could hear her, but I couldn't
very well walk straight into her bedroom. I had a better idea,
reached for my cell phone to call her, then realized I'd left
the phone in the car. I turned to go get it, but before I could
take a step I heard a different sound. A low moan. The distinct sound of someone in pain.

"Ms. Abahd!" I shouted as I hurried toward the sound.
"Are you back there? Are you all right?"

A louder moan.

I rushed down the corridor toward where it had come
from, turned into the first open doorway on my right, and
stopped dead, my attention riveted to the woman in the chair
in the center of the room. The woman duct-taped to that
chair. My eyes widened, an electric jolt of shock raced
through my shoulders and up the back of my neck.

Dear God!

I bolted to her side. She moaned again as I got there, but
it wasn't because she'd seen me coming.

Her eyes were duct-taped shut, but even if they hadn't
been they were now useless.

Her narrow face was a mangled bloody mess. Her nose
was flattened sideways against her cheek. Her jaw hung
loose, and the unnatural angle told me it was broken. Her
mouth was torn at the corners, and I could see punctures
where her teeth had penetrated the skin from the force of her
beating. There was blood all over her right hand. In her lap
was a single amputated finger.

I bent to her ear. "You're safe now," I told her, even
though I had no idea she could hear me. "Hold on. Help's on
the way."

I heard her try to speak. I put my ear against her mouth.

"FBI," she managed to whisper, her voice a spindly
croak. "Monk . . . *Agent Monk*."

"Yes," I told her. "I'm here. Just hold on a little longer."

Her thin body stiffened, then slumped, her head falling to

her chest. I reached to check the pulse at her neck, then realized I was wasting time. She needed a lot more help than I could give her. An ambulance, paramedics, the nearest trauma unit. I bolted around her and grabbed for the phone on the desk, jabbed 911, lifted the phone. "Police emergency," I heard, but before I could say anything a blow from behind sent me crashing against the nearest wall, from there to the floor. I scrambled to my feet, turned to fight.

A black-hooded giant stood facing me.

A growl came out of his throat as he hurried to finish the job.

SIX

HE HAD ME BY A COUPLE OF INCHES AND AT LEAST FIFTY pounds, but I managed to throw the first punch, a straight left directly at his Adam's apple. He flicked my fist away, his hand speed incredible for a man that size. I cocked my right leg and sidekicked at his knee. He twisted and my kick caught nothing but rock-hard thigh. Then he threw *his* first punch. I jerked away but too late. His right fist caught the tender flesh of my right ear and my head went numb. I slumped backward, then toppled to one knee. A high whistling started inside my head, and I knew what it meant, knew for sure I had to stay conscious as long as I could. I dragged myself to my feet, shook my head, and heard the whistling recede. I thought about the Smith-10 in my briefcase on the floor next to Abahd. I had to turn this fight in that direction.

The giant swung his right leg outward and upward in a short quick arc. I used my left arm to guard my head, but he fooled me. His black shoe exploded against my ribs instead. Again I went down. My vision turned gray, then black at the edges. The whistling turned to shrieking; the darkness began to close as I tried to focus on what I had to do to save my life.

Get up! I heard my mind shouting. *Get to your weapon!*

My feet scrabbled against the hardwood floor until I was on all fours. I pushed with my arms, made it halfway up before he kicked me again. This time the leg had less distance to travel before ripping into the same ribs. My head filled with colors—reds, purples, yellows. I gasped for breath, ignored the spike of pain that came with each attempt. Still on hands and knees, my head hanging, I knew he was coming. Convinced he had nothing to fear, he seemed eager to get it over with.

I was careful not to look at him, watched out of the corner of my eye for his black shoes. An instant later he was leaning over me. I arched my back as though I were going to vomit, then used the leverage to swing my left arm from the floor, to hurl the back of my fist directly into his nose. I heard a gravelly crunch as the cartilage gave way—and ignored the jolting pain in my hand as he stepped back. I lifted my head to see how badly I'd hurt him, but I shouldn't have bothered.

Jesus Christ, who is this guy?

Blood spurted from the middle of his face, but he made no sound. His nose lay crushed to one side, but the man showed no reaction. Nothing. Instead, he simply reached to his face, shoved the mess back into place. I winced at the sound of grinding cartilage, but an instant later he was coming back again.

I tried once more to get up, but got only as far as my knees. I lifted my hands to keep fighting, wondered how long it would take him to break my head wide open.

But suddenly he stopped, his head cocked. Despite the singing in my ears, I could hear the faint sound of sirens. He raced past me and out the door. I struggled to my feet, tried to go after him, tried to put one foot ahead of the other, but my body wasn't ready. I fell next to Jabalah Abahd, rose once more and managed to get out into the hallway. I stared toward the open front door. The giant was long gone.

I turned to Abahd. She showed no signs of life. This time I did check for a pulse, her neck first, then her arm, finally one ankle. Nothing. She was dead. Or so close to it, I could do nothing to save her.

I opened my briefcase, pulled the semiautomatic Smith-10 from it and went to the front door, stepped out onto the porch just in time to see the first of two Cheverly P.D. black-and-whites skidding to a stop in front of the house. The drivers leaped from their squad cars and crouched behind them, weapons drawn. In the next instant a spotlight blazed directly into my eyes. I started toward them, then froze as I realized what was happening, that I was an armed man coming from a house that had called 911. They were trained to shoot. They wouldn't hesitate to kill me. I could hardly blame them if they did.

I flipped my weapon toward the lawn to my right, but blinded by the light I couldn't see where it fell. I thrust my arms in the air, began to shout. *"FBI! FBI! I'm the one who called! There's a dead woman in the house! My weapon's on the lawn! My credentials and badge are in my pocket!"*

The response was immediate.

"Slowly," a deep voice ordered, "very slowly. Get your ID out of your pocket and throw it over here. Then turn around and lay on your stomach. Stay there until we tell you to get back up."

I did as I was told. Threw my black credentials case with the gold badge imbedded in the cover. Again I had no clue where it landed. I turned and lay on my stomach as ordered. A white-hot stab of pain from my ribs made me gasp. A violent throbbing in my right ear told me the numbness had worn away. I wanted to massage my ear, but knew better. I didn't dare move a muscle till they were satisfied I was no risk. And that wouldn't happen till they'd fetched my gun and ID, then called WMFO and verified my identity.

It took little more than a minute, thank God, before the spotlight went out and I heard more cars arriving. I was told to get up and come to the cars. I did so, my eyes slowly readjusting, enough so I could see a bright red ambulance, half a dozen more black-and-whites, and one unmarked unit from what had to be the Cheverly P.D., along with a gray sedan bearing the words Prince George's County Medical Examiner on the front door. Cops and medical personnel streamed past me into the house. From behind, a hand touched my shoulder. I turned to see a tall, thin man in a light-blue suit. He pulled back his jacket to show me the badge attached to his belt, introduced himself as Lieutenant Barra, Cheverly P.D. He didn't offer a first name, and I didn't ask.

"Christ," he said. "What *happened* in there?"

I took a very shallow breath, the pain in my ribs now fully awake, then told him.

He frowned at me. "But you had a gun."

"In my briefcase."

"You weren't carrying?"

"Just routine business. No reason to be."

"Jesus," he said, shaking his head. "You Feds."

I stared at him and felt the burn on the back of my neck. "Look, pal, you got questions about what happened, ask them. You got a complaint about me, take it to the Hoover Building."

"Yeah, yeah," he said. "In this business you gotta be ready, is all I'm saying." He glanced toward the front door, wide open now, police personnel coming and going as they worked the crime scene. "So what you're telling me, the lady walked in on some kind of madman burglar."

"What else could it be?"

He stared at the large house. "Nice house, but Jesus! you saw what the guy did to her . . . her *finger*, for shit's sake. What could she possibly have had in there she'd rather be tortured to death than give up?"

"Money," I said. "Maybe some kind of art collection." And I believed it. Despite the diary thing trying to claw its way out of my mouth, I wasn't about to say it out loud. Not yet. Not to this guy.

He glared, shook his head. "Don't start . . . don't even start with me. I know you guys far too well for that."

"I don't know what you're talking about."

"You tell me," the lieutenant said. "FBI comes calling, lady ends up dead. What are the odds?"

"Shit happens."

"It sure does." Sarcastic now. "You wouldn't believe the shit that happens." He looked back at Abahd's red front door. "Gonna need your statement. Let's do it inside."

I nodded, followed him up the walkway and into the house. We jostled our way through the homicide investigators and crime-scene specialists crowding the living room and up the hallway toward Abahd's home office and her dead body. So many people, I thought, but I knew why. The Cheverly P.D. was a big department, handled a lot of bad people and bad things, but a dead lawyer and a beat-up FBI agent in the same house had to get their blood pumping a whole lot faster than normal. I turned my head to avoid the blinding flashes from half a dozen cameras, then followed Lieutenant Barra to the formal dining room just beyond the living room. We sat at the long gleaming maple table. He pulled a small notebook from the inside pocket of his suit jacket. I told him what happened again, more slowly this time. When I finished, he asked the obvious question.

What had brought me to the house in the first place?

"Jabalah Abahd was the college roommate of a woman applying for a position in the government," I told him. "In my business it doesn't get any less exciting."

"Gonna need more than that, Monk, a whole lot more. Like a name, for starters. The government woman, I mean."

I shook my head. "It doesn't have anything to do with what happened here. Trust me, my being here was pure coincidence."

"Trust you?" He looked around at his people. It struck me he wanted to tell them what I'd said, wanted to share in the good laugh such a statement would bring. "Look, Monk, you're a witness to a murder, the only witness. Surely you know you're also a suspect. There's no trust for you here, and you can trust *me* on that."

"We've got rules," I told him. "I can't give you the name even if I wanted to."

"I don't care about your rules. This is a homicide investigation. My D.A. isn't going to let you stonewall us."

"Of course not. My bosses won't allow that either." A lie he didn't even bother showing a reaction to. "All I'm saying is I need to talk to them first."

"You better get moving then." He looked around the room. "These cases get awfully cold awfully quick. I don't have time to play politics. And I'll need elimination prints before you leave. One of the techs can do it."

"Get them from the bureau. Your lab will have them before you get back to your office."

He shook his head, opened his mouth to complain, then closed it again. Barra looked to be about fifty or so. He'd been around long enough to know when he couldn't win. It wouldn't stop him from trying, of course, but he had to know he'd heard all he was going to get out of me.

It was almost eleven o'clock before I got back to my father's ludicrous house. The unsellable geodesic dome Pastor Monk had bought as the final proof of his dementia, the act that had led to his relocation to Jack Quigley's nursing home, had left me with a house no one on earth was going to buy.

I was at a point several miles beyond exhaustion as I hurried through the door and up the spiral staircase to my bedroom. I went straight to the telephone on the nightstand, took the receiver off the hook and put the phone in the drawer, pulled off my clothes and let them lie where they landed, then uttered a groan of relief as I hoisted myself into bed for what was certain to be the night's sleep of my life.

But twenty minutes later I was still awake, sitting up in bed and groaning with frustration. My battered body wanted nothing more than sleep, but my mind was nowhere near ready to let it happen. My head began to bubble with activity, awash in thoughts, half-thoughts, and semiparanoid speculations that tumbled through my brain like damp laundry in a front-loading clothes dryer. Around and around they turned, until several things began to work their way to the surface. A number, to start with. A date actually—1972, the year 1972. Followed by my phone conversation with Jabalah Abahd, and the lawyer's reluctance to repeat to me what she'd already told the mysterious Robert Bennett. The same thing she'd found important enough to include in her diary at the time.

What had happened, I wondered, between Abahd and Brenda Thompson that made that particular year so troubling?

As I wrestled with the answer, I recalled Abahd's dying words.

FBI, she'd whispered. *Agent Monk*, she'd added.

What had she meant?

That whoever I was, I should call Agent Monk at the FBI?

That she knew it was me she was talking to?

The next question tightened my throat and made my ribs hurt all the more.

What if she were trying to name her torturer?

Christ.

Robert Bennett. Agent Bennett. Or—it could safely be assumed after Lisa's checks with the Personnel Division—*non*-agent Bennett. Maybe Abahd had seen his creds, just assumed he was me. I lay on my pillow and stared at the ceiling, looking for guidance—some kind of *deus ex geodesic dome* to bring me the truth—but nothing came. Nothing but yet another voice, this time one that sounded a whole lot like Matt Drudge.

"Quit stalling, Monk," the voice told me. *"You know damned well what happened. Judge Thompson realized she was about to be caught in a dreadful lie, sent a hit man to kill her old roommate to keep her from talking about what happened in '72."*

A quick stab of rib-pain kept me from laughing out loud.

Christ, Drudge, I answered, *Supreme Court nominees don't kill people. Federal judges don't do anything with hit men but send them to witness-protection programs. I may have been slapped upside the head, but I'm sure as hell not crazy.*

And even if I were, there was a far bigger problem with the Brenda Thompson using Robert Bennett to whack Jabalah Abahd scenario. Besides the lunacy of a federal judge's involvement in torture and murder, Judge Thompson had no idea we'd even *found* Abahd, or that we would *ever* find her. Nobody from my office had told her about our appointment in Cheverly this evening. No one knew about it but me . . . and Lisa, after I'd called her from the restaurant . . . and Jabalah Abahd, of course.

I checked the clock on my nightstand. Midnight. Shit. I had to sleep. I couldn't do anything without rest. TV was the answer, I decided. Better than a truckload of pills and booze for putting me under. I reached for the clicker but my hand stopped in midair as I heard a sound I shouldn't be hearing at midnight in my quiet little neighborhood.

A door closing. A car door closing. Or the trunk of a car closing, that's what it was.

I sat up, reached to open the hatch-type window in the sloping wall above the bed. The rain had stopped and the winter air was quiet enough to carry a lot of sound. I strained to listen, heard a new sound. The unmistakable sound of a foot crunching in gravel. Then a second crunch. And a third.

I stretched to get closer to the window, but the crunching disappeared. I formed a mental picture of the gravel pathway between the dome and the more conventional garage I used mostly for storage. Unless I was dreaming, someone was on or around that path. I got out of bed and slipped over to the window next to my dresser, slid it open and tilted my head in the direction of the garage. Nothing. Not a sound.

Until I heard another step in the same gravel. Just the one, this time, then quiet again.

I moved back to the bed, to the nightstand, opened the drawer, and pulled out my backup weapon, a Smith and Wesson .38 with a two-inch barrel, five rounds loaded and locked. I was overreacting, I told myself, but I didn't care.

My ribs still hurt enough to keep the giant in the black hood firmly in the front of my mind. I pictured him slipping through my back door, then glanced at my weapon. Five rounds might not be enough . . . might just make him mad.

Revolver in hand, I padded across the floor to the bedroom closet, snatched a pair of pants and a T-shirt, threw them on, and jammed my feet into a pair of tennis shoes, then crept down the spiral staircase into the living room. I held my weapon in both hands as I stepped across the back side of the living room, through the archway into the kitchen, to the back door.

I stopped short when I saw the knob turn, heard the scratching and scraping of someone trying to jimmy the lock.

I grabbed the knob, yanked the door open and leaped through it. From my right an arm grabbed at me. I pivoted hard, my finger all over the trigger when I heard the scream.

SEVEN

"Puller!" Annie Fisher shrieked. *"For Christ's sake, Puller, it's me!"*

"Annie!" I pulled her into my arms. "My God, Annie, what are you doing here? Why are you sneaking around like this?"

She clung to me as it began to rain again, hard at first, then even harder. I grabbed her hand and turned for the door, then stopped as I saw that it was closed and realized immediately what had happened. Bursting through it, I'd flung the door open, it had bounced back and closed behind me. I didn't even have to check to know that it was locked. And that I didn't have a key in my pocket. Shit. I turned to Annie for the key she'd been trying to use, but she shook her head.

"I dropped it, Puller . . . when you came at me like that." She looked down at the landing on which we stood. We both looked down, but the key wasn't there. The rain was a torrent now, and by the time I found the damned thing in the flower bed next to the steps, we were both drenched.

Back in the kitchen, rainwater streaming from our hair and clothing, I repeated my question.

"I wasn't sneaking," she said. "I was worried about you. I tried to call, a bunch of times, but your phone isn't working, so I came over." She reached for a dish towel lying on the counter, mopped her face with it, handed it to me. "I thought I'd . . ." She shook her head. "Hell, I don't know what I thought. I just wanted to see you, I guess. I still have your key, so I decided to use it. Slip in and surprise you."

She flipped the towel back to the counter, then moved toward me and opened her arms, put them around my neck. I kissed her forehead.

"I'm glad you did, Annie." I shook away the thought of what I'd been expecting, then held her at arm's length and inspected her trim body. "Did I hurt you?"

"Scared the crap out of me, especially when I realized you had no idea it was me." She stared at the revolver I'd set on the kitchen counter. "Mostly when I saw that thing in your hand . . . but I'm okay now."

I hugged her again, then kept my arm around her waist and aimed her toward the living room. "C'mon," I said. "I'll make you some decaf."

In the living room we stood together, dripping all over the Turkish carpet in front of the fireplace, until I turned and headed for the bathroom.

"Take your hat and coat off," I called over my shoulder, "shoes, too. I'll get us some towels." I winced as my aching bruises began to resurface, but it was surprising how much less painful they were already. I took a deep breath, very carefully, felt none of the sharp pain that would go along with broken ribs, and I was grateful for that. I had too much to do, and no time at all for bandages and recuperation.

From the bathroom I grabbed a stack of white bath towels, took them back to my off-again on-again special lady.

She sat waiting in the blue leather chair to the right of the Franklin fireplace in what I was forced to call a living room, although in the persistent circularity of a dome house it's hard to think in terms of rooms. Annie had removed more than her topcoat, I saw, and in her ivory-colored slip she looked like a friendly cat.

"You're soaked," she told me. "Get your clothes off before you ruin your carpet."

I started to, but stopped as I realized I couldn't. That she'd see my bruises and ask questions I couldn't answer without lying. She'd get mad, I'd get mad, and she'd go away for another couple of months. We were pathetic—we'd agreed on that for a long time now—but knowing didn't seem to help.

"I'll grab my bathrobe, Annie, and get the coffee started."

She nodded, then scrubbed at her hair with a dry towel. I left for the kitchen but stopped at the bathroom again, traded my wet clothes for a dry white bathrobe, zipped into the kitchen and got the coffee started.

Back with Annie, I built a fire to dry our clothes, then fell into the chair opposite her and watched the tongues of fire turn into a blaze.

"I've been thinking about you, too," I said a few moments later. "I wanted to call a couple of times, but . . ." The words seemed to die in the warming air.

Annie smiled. Her hazel eyes seemed sad to me, and that wasn't a good sign. There was an argument afoot, and I had no interest in another one. As infrequently as we managed to get together anymore, it seemed pointless not to enjoy it.

"I had the feeling you needed me," she said.

My stomach tightened as I interpreted her familiar words, another mantra from the latest of her twelve-step programs. I got up. "I'll get the coffee," I told her. "Why don't you grab the hall tree from the entry. Hang your clothes next to the fire."

In the kitchen I tried to think of a way to escape what I knew was coming. We had this particular dance down pat. She'd demand an accounting for something I'd done or hadn't done, I would get up on my hind legs, nostrils flaring as I began to shout. That I wasn't an addict, goddamnit . . . That I wasn't led around by inner demons telling me when to hit and when to stay. That the only reason I hid my gambling from the bureau was to keep my job. Period. End of story.

Then it would be her turn, for the familiar recitation of her own struggles.

Besides the D.V.M. after Dr. Annie's name, she was al-

most too proud of the A.A. that followed. I wasn't an alcoholic, but to her my gambling made me exactly the same,
just another junkie lying to feed his habit. I didn't lie to the
FBI—she claims—because I liked my job. I lied because I
was addicted to the job itself, to the action it provided, the
"juice" I couldn't live without. Most of all, I lied to avoid the
ordinariness I was terrified would sooner or later turn me
into just another loser.

Annie was wrong, of course, and a familiar heaviness
overtook me as I realized I wanted her to leave, to get out of
my house before it got ugly again. I'd heard it all before, and
far too often. I loved her, more or less, but I just couldn't listen to it anymore.

I poured coffee into a couple of red mugs, took them back
to Annie. She had already hung her clothes near the fire. We
sat and drank in silence until she broke it.

"I waited over an hour for you today," she told me.

"Today?" I looked at her. "You waited for me today?"

"Lunch. My birthday. Ring any bells?"

Shit. I leaned toward her. "Damn it, Annie, I forgot all
about it. We had a case come apart on us, and the day just got
away from me. I don't know what to say except I'm sorry."

"I tried to call you."

"Like I said, I was away from my desk. Did you leave a
message?"

She shook her head. I didn't say anything. There was no
point.

"I'm disappointed, Puller, that's all I'm saying." She
sipped coffee. "Tell me it's another woman. I can't believe
I'm saying this, but that's what I'd rather hear."

I scratched at the two-day stubble on my chin. To get out
of this I needed the truth for a change, and the truth was
clearly impossible. For once I had a valid reason, but one I
couldn't use. Dr. Ann Fisher was a good woman, would have
made a hell of an FBI agent, but she wasn't one. We both
worked with animals, but she didn't need a badge and gun
with hers. Annie knew the rules I had to live by, had known

them from day one, but that didn't stop her from using them against me.

"You're wrong this time," I told her. "You couldn't be more wrong, but I can't—"

"I know," she broke in. "I know you can't tell me what you were really up to." She sighed. "I should know by now not even to ask."

I breathed in and out a couple of times, then warned myself to calm down. Annie tried like hell to find a higher power she could trust, but despite her determination, she'd been up and down the twelve steps often enough to keep herself in top shape. And watching her struggle had only reinforced my contempt for the process. I'd had my fill of higher powers by the time I was ten years old. If I really were addicted to gambling, I'd find something a whole lot better than voodoo to help me kick it.

"I was working, Annie. It's not a nine-to-five job, never has been."

She smiled. "Let's not fight about it. You know what I want from you. Why don't we just leave it at that?"

But it was too late to stop the surge of resentment I didn't want to contain.

"Look," I told her, "it isn't what you think. It isn't anything like that."

Christ almighty, it was like listening to Pastor Monk all over again. Suddenly I was ten years old, trying to defend myself against his omnipotent claptrap.

"Damn it, Annie, I'm not about to explain anything to you. If you don't like it, you know where the door is."

To my amazement, she caved immediately. Just as I was ready to do some serious shouting, she was smiling broadly.

"Hold on, Puller. I'm not here to fight with you. I come in peace." Without warning, her grin turned wicked. "Actually, what I come in is lust."

My face got warm. Lust worked just fine for me, too, but not just now, not with the bruises already purpling my torso. I searched for an excuse she'd buy, but didn't even have to come up with one before the doorbell rang. I turned and stared at the front door. Annie showing up was one thing, but who else would be ringing my bell at this hour?

"Expecting company?" Annie said. "Am I interrupting something?"

"Don't be silly."

I rose and tightened the cinch around my bathrobe. I went to the door, looked through the peephole. Distorted by the fish-eye lens, Lisa Sands's nose was huge, her eyes slanting backward. Rain obscured her face, and water cascaded from the brim of her cowboy-style leather hat directly onto her shoulders, then down the front of her tan raincoat. I flung the door open and pulled her in.

"What the hell?" I said to her, then called to Annie in a louder voice, "It's Lisa Sands."

"It's who?"

"Lisa Sands," I said. "One of the agents on my squad."

Lisa stepped toward me without a word and threw her arms around me, squeezed me hard enough to make me groan. I could smell her hair, the wildflower shampoo. I hugged her back, and we held on to each other for a long moment before she pulled away.

"Thank God," she said. "Thank God, you're okay."

"How did you know? About Abahd, I mean, about what happened out in Cheverly."

"The office patched a call through to me at home about eight o'clock, from a Lieutenant Barra. He told me what happened and wanted to know why your phone has been busy all night. I've been calling here ever since."

"I took the phone off the hook. What did Barra want?"

Before she could answer, Annie called from the living room.

"Bring her in here, Puller. She has to be ready for coffee and a warm fire."

I glanced at Lisa, shook my head. "Probably not the best idea," I whispered, "not right now anyway."

Suddenly Annie was next to us. In her bare feet and rumpled slip, her shaggy blond hair, she looked like something out of a Tennessee Williams play.

"Ann Fisher," she said, her hand extended to Lisa. "Take off your raincoat and join us."

"Doctor Ann Fisher, Lisa," I said. "She's a veterinarian here in Fredericksburg . . . and an old friend."

Lisa glanced at Annie, then at my bathrobe. She smiled and I realized what I'd said hadn't really covered the situation. English is the world's most complete language, but even English doesn't provide a polite way of saying ex-lover, sometime lover, failed lover, unable-to-get-over-each-other lover. So I did the man thing, rubbed my hands together, cleared my throat, and let Annie take over.

"We're at the fireplace," she said.

She took Lisa's arm and guided her back into the semicircular living room, to the semicircular leather couch that matched the chairs and completed the grouping in front of the fireplace.

"Sit, please. You can add your raincoat to our clothes on the hall tree."

Lisa shrugged out of her raincoat, handed it to me to hang up by the fire. Her jeans accentuated the length of her legs and the gray turtleneck sweater was tight enough to remind me to quit staring.

"I'm sorry to intrude," Lisa said. "I tried to call."

"Didn't we all," Annie said, "but you're not intruding. I came unannounced myself." She pointed at her clothes next to the fire. "Got so wet on the way in, I thought I was going to drown." She smiled. "Actually, I'm the one who's imposing, I think. Surely you didn't come out to Fredericksburg at this time of night just for a cup of coffee."

"No, I guess I didn't, but I still should have called."

"Must be an important case." Annie glanced at me. "Puller's squad does background investigations, he tells me. I wouldn't think you'd have such things as emergencies."

"Normally we wouldn't," Lisa told her, "but it's different with SPIN cases."

Annie looked at me for a translation.

"Special Inquiries," I told her. "S–P–I–N. For the White House."

"Secrets," she said, drawing the word out. "Where the bodies are buried, which closets hold the skeletons."

Lisa chuckled. "Not many, I'm sorry to say . . . bodies *or* skeletons. Mostly routine, I'm afraid." She sat forward. "I'm a lot more interested in what you do. Like every little girl, I was sure I would grow up and take care of animals. Then I did grow up and discovered two things. Men, for one, and the impossibility of getting into vet school. Law school was easier, I'm sure."

"Oh, I was careful to leave some time for men as well, but thanks for the compliment." She picked up her coffee, sipped, set the mug down. "Come on, you two," she said. "Lighten up a little. One secret, that's all I'm asking. Invent one if you have to, I'll never know."

"Make a note, Lisa," I said. "Next skeleton we uncover goes straight to the doc."

Annie held up her hand. "Okay, okay, I get the picture." She glanced at her watch. "I better get going anyway. Got a horse on the operating table first thing in the morning. You can't believe how hard it is to lift one that high."

We laughed as Annie gathered her clothes, took them to the bathroom and came out a minute later ready to go. I walked her to the door, gave her a hug, a kiss on the forehead. She whispered into my ear.

"Hang on to her, Puller. Lisa's a good one."

She pulled away, leaving me to translate, then opened the door and disappeared into the misty gloom. I closed the door, stared at it for a moment, then rejoined Lisa at the fireplace.

"I'm sorry," she told me again when I got there. "I really didn't mean to interrupt, but I had no choice. Lieutenant Barra told me about Abahd, that you'd been in a hell of a fight, but I got the feeling he was more interested in what I could tell him than the other way around. He said you seemed okay when you left, but I had visions of your car crumpled up against a bridge abutment." She shook her head. "What the hell happened? I want to hear it from you."

I told her. Her eyes widened before she came to the same conclusion as Lieutenant Barra and the ghostly voice of Matt Drudge.

"Can't be a coincidence," she said. "The night you show up to see her diary, she gets killed?"

"Doesn't sound right to me either, but consider the alternative. Even in the world of probabilities there's a hierarchy. It might be improbable as hell—walking in on a burglary like that—but Judge Thompson having something to do with it takes us right off the chart." I shook my head. "In this job you've got to go with the odds first, look into the long shots only after there's no place else to go."

"So where *do* we go, boss? Regardless how or why she died, Abahd had something bad to say about Thompson. There's got to be a way to find out what it was."

I glanced at the grandfather clock near the foot of my spiral staircase. Almost two A.M. I turned back to Lisa.

"Go away so we can both get some sleep," I told her. "I have a couple of errands to run in the morning. There'll be too many cops at Abahd's house to start there, so meet me at her office at noon."

EIGHT

ACTUALLY, I HAD ONLY ONE ERRAND TO RUN THE NEXT morning, one I'd come to hate over the past year, but could put off no longer. A chore that would take three hours, no matter how much I wished it to be less. An hour to visit the man I was expected to love, two more to make me forget him again.

According to Jack Quigley, my father's condition had gotten worse, but I had to see for myself, so at nine o'clock I headed out of my dome and across I-95 to Pinewood Manor in Chancellorsville. On the way I called Karen Kilbride and told her I wouldn't be coming into the office until after lunch.

Twenty minutes later I walked down a nondescript hallway, through an open door into an equally austere bedroom, and stared at Pastor Jonathon Monk. Just the sight of him made my brain heavy, a sensation like someone stuffing my head with wet cardboard, mashing it tighter and tighter to stop me from thinking.

I crossed the distance between us, to the unadorned wooden chair by the window nook in which my father sat. An equally uninviting chair sat opposite the man. I pulled it away a few inches to put a little more distance between us, then settled into it. My head grew even more impenetrable as I forced myself to begin.

"How are you feeling, Dad?"

The question had two purposes, neither of which had anything to do with how Pastor Monk was feeling. The first was to get the conversation started with some semblance of normalcy. The second was to remind him who I was.

Jonathon Monk said nothing, began to blink over and over, faster and faster. Worse today, the blinking, even worse than last week. I would talk to the doctor about it afterward, although I wondered why. We could talk about it for days, but it wasn't going to change anything. The old man was history. Nobody was getting out of this room alive, including me.

"I can't see anyone today," he said at last, his voice wispy as smoke. "I'm working on my sermon for tomorrow." He raised a bony arm and pointed toward the door. "Come back tomorrow afternoon, after services." Then he shook his narrow head, the dried-out skin of his face jiggling as though it were no longer firmly attached to the bones underneath. "No, not then, not tomorrow, either. Sundays my wife and I listen to the radio."

I held my tongue. I'd read as much as I could stand about this cruelest of killers, the disease that wouldn't let the old bastard go until it had returned him to infancy. I'd been living through it with him for almost two years now. This was where I should remind him that today was Tuesday, that his wife and my mother had killed herself a quarter of a century ago. This was where I wanted to remind him that she'd longed for death just to be rid of him, that I'd been ready to arrest him myself for the torture that had driven her mad.

That's what I should be doing, but I was too tired for self-indulgence, and that brought up the question of who was really the sick one here. Was it my father, with his few remaining gray cells still rooted in the Church of the Faithful Brethren, the church *his* father had founded? Or was it me—allegedly still *compos mentis*—but less and less *compos* as I beheld the man who'd taken away both my childhood and my mother, and had now reentered my life to take whatever was left?

I knew better than to reduce the situation to such simple terms, but my gut didn't. Wouldn't it be nice, I found myself wondering more and more often these days, to have a *real* father to help figure it out? To ever have had a real father for that kind of help?

"I brought you a milkshake," I told him. I held out a white Dairy Queen sack with red lettering. "Vanilla. The nurse says you keep asking for vanilla milkshakes."

He grabbed the bag, but glanced over his shoulder toward the door. "Don't tell my father. I'm not allowed to eat in my good clothes. He'll beat me if he finds out."

He tugged at the perfect knot in his necktie, and I shook my head. His mind was like an infected hard drive, filled with valid information, but so randomly accessed it had become useless. Pastor Jonathon Monk, son of Pastor Puller Monk and his wife, Sarah, could no longer keep track of the chronology of his life, but he kept his one good suit and shirt and tie immaculate, and wore them every moment they weren't at the cleaners.

Now he tore at the Dairy Queen sack, threw it aside, and peeled away the paper enclosing the plastic straw. He tried to poke the straw through the plastic lid, but I had to do it for him. He smiled briefly before he lifted the milkshake toward his mouth and began to suck. I saw with relief that it had melted enough to make using the straw possible. Fastfood milkshakes could be a problem that way. Dairy Queen was about the only one that seemed to get it right.

The Pastor eyed me. "How's school?" he demanded.

I pondered the question. This was the tricky part. The old man could be asking about anything connected to any kind of school. Kindergarten all the way to my new-agents class at Quantico.

"Mormons," he said before I could answer. "Lots of Mormons."

I nodded. We'd been down this road a number of times, and for the moment at least we could share the same page.

"Quite a few in the bureau," I told him, "going back to the Hoover days."

In the senility of his own last years, J. Edgar had formed the idea that Mormons were congenitally incapable of corruption. Luckily for him, he'd died before finding out otherwise.

"Good people," Pastor Monk said. "Not Christian, of course, but . . ."

He seemed to lose his train of thought, and I had to smile despite the stuffy feeling between my ears. Alzheimer's had given my father the unique freedom to come out with the god-damndest nonsense, and nobody could do anything about it. Suddenly his head slumped to his chest, stayed there for a few moments. When it came back up he was weeping, his eyes watery blue puddles, his withered cheeks running with tears.

"Couldn't save them," he said, his voice choked. "Only ones I couldn't save."

The Mormons—I expected he was talking about—and in a normal conversation there would have been no question. I reached for him despite myself, unable to stand the sight. I tried to pat his heaving shoulder, to make him stop, but a moment later he was perfectly composed, then quivering with anger.

"*Blasphemers!*" he raged. "False prophets! *Deceivers!*"

He bowed his head and I could see his thin lips moving. Praying, no doubt, for the lost tribe of Latter-Day Saints. That they be spared God's righteous wrath for their heresy. I didn't have to hear the words themselves to know what they were. I'd heard them all before, and a whole lot more, many of which had been aimed directly at me. I said a short and silent prayer myself, a prayer from my past, but one I'd been using more and more of late. An accusation—to be honest—more than a petition. *Dear God, if you really exist, why didn't you come down and rescue my mother and me when it still mattered?*

The Pastor began to blink again, over and over and over. His head began to nod. The milkshake cup slipped out of his fingers and bounced against his leg on the way to the carpet. I reached across and picked it up. The plastic top had kept the shake from spilling. I stood and walked to the cheap ve-neer chest of drawers opposite where we sat, set the milk-shake on it, in case the Pastor wanted it later. Then I turned and left the room.

Back in the reception area, a voice stopped me.

"Mr. Monk?"

Shit. Quigley. I turned to see him approaching.

"Look," I said, trying to keep my voice level, "I told you the money's coming. Now if you'll excuse me." I turned to leave, but he scurried around to block me.

"It's not the money, Mr. Monk, although as I think about it, I guess that's what it will turn out to be."

"Just tell me what you need. I don't have time to chat."

"His condition is worse, I told you that on the phone the other day. You may have noticed the perseverative blinking, the increasing inability to maintain present-day reality."

I felt my fingers clenching as I listened to him, disgusted at his choice of words. Not *his* blinking—my father's—not *his* memory damage. I couldn't remember ever loving the old bastard, but he wasn't gone yet. The Pastor still deserved the simple respect of a pronoun.

"He's going to need more watching," Quigley continued. "Around the clock soon, at least that's the way it normally goes."

This time I nodded. "Just give me the bottom line."

And some way to come up with it.

I didn't need a psychiatrist to tell me why I did it, why every time I saw my father I had to go straight to a card room. And the new one in Arlington was just the ticket. I thought for an instant about the irresponsibility of playing poker when the Brenda Thompson case was spiraling into the toilet, but only for an instant before I pointed the Caprice toward Arlington and stepped on the gas.

It was a typical card room, I saw when I got there. A dozen or so round tables with green felt tops, about half of them filled with gamblers. Straightforward fluorescent lighting from the ceiling, too bright, but what the hell. Cashier's cage against the far wall, lots of smokers in the room, a blue haze hanging like swamp gas above the players. Muted voices, not a lot of talking. Nobody here for the conversation.

I twisted my gold pinky ring for luck, went to the cashier's cage and traded three one-hundred dollar bills for a tray of chips, chose a table at the back of the room—always at the back, where I could see the whole room as well as the front door—and got the nod to join the three men already seated. We exchanged names all around. I pulled my chair up close and arranged my chips. The hand already in progress ended, and I threw in a five-dollar chip to ante up for the next one.

"Straight poker," the man to my right said, a portly fellow with a shaved head who'd introduced himself as Jim. "Five card draw, no frills."

We began to play. Four or five hands went by before I realized I'd made a mistake by coming, by thinking there'd be anything for me in a place like this.

Jim had described the game as no-frills, but that wasn't the word for it. It was no anything at all, and certainly not what I needed after a visit with the Pastor. The problem wasn't losing, it was just the opposite. I couldn't possibly lose to these bozos. Talk about your tells, the three of them might as well have given me a printout of their hands.

"Man oh man," Jim said after each and every deal, "man oh man oh man," except when he drew the cards he needed, when he added yet another "oh man."

To Jim's right, Alan loosened his old-fashioned skinny necktie just before he bet, unless he was going to bluff, when he tightened it. Like cinching up your saddle, he must have thought, before heading out after the Indians.

But the third guy—Joey, he called himself—took the prize. Joey'd read once that a good poker player never changed expression, had obviously decided to go one better, to have no expression at all. None. His face was placid as new snow, but unfortunately for him only when he had the hand he wanted. The rest of the time he did exactly what the rest of us did. Grinned, grimaced, pouted, just like a real human being. *What could you possibly be thinking?* I wanted to ask him, as I raked in the pots he gave away when he wasn't stone-faced.

I stood it as long as I could, until the hand that finally sent me packing.

Joey deals. I come up *bupkes*, a couple of fours, nothing

with a face on it. I take three cards, no help. Alan takes one card. Examines his hand, lays his cards on the table face down, loosens his skinny tie, shrugs, takes it all the way off, stares at it as though he'd never before removed it completely. Four of a kind, I'm guessing . . . at least.

"Oh man oh man oh man oh man oh man," from Jim. Holy shit, five oh mans this time. *Can he possibly have a royal flush?*

I glance at Joey, wonder for a moment if he'd died. His face might as well be carved from granite. I can't even tell if he's breathing.

I check my own hand again. Maybe I missed something, but I haven't. My fours are still slumped in solitude, surrounded by numbers that don't add up to a nickel. What the fuck, I say to myself. You're not having any fun anyway.

"To you," Joey tells me, his voice impatient.

I throw in two black chips, the table limit. Two hundred dollars, just to see what they'll do. I don't have to wait long.

"Oh man," Jim says, checking his cards again, shaking his head. He chucks his cards into the pot face down. "Man," he says, not even the "oh" this time. Alan's cards follow immediately, he grabs his tie, puts it back around his neck, doesn't know whether to cinch it or leave it alone. I turn to Joey, his face distorting with pain as he adds his cards to the pile. I drop mine on top of the rest of them, face down, then reach to scoop in the pot. Jim's hand starts toward my cards, but I look into his eyes and he backs away.

Outside in the Caprice I opened my briefcase and replaced my pinky ring, added four-hundred-eighty dollars to the secret stash.

I could almost hear Gerard Ziff's voice in my ear.

"*You what?*" he was saying. "*You quit winners? Jesus God, what's the matter with you?*"

But he'd know better even as he said it.

We were gamblers, the Frenchman and I, part of the brotherhood. He wouldn't need me to explain to him why I'd quit . . . why I'd walked away without every cent of their money. It wasn't about money, we both knew that. It wasn't even about winning and losing. It was about playing the game. About the risk. Without the risk of loss, there's no gambling. What I had going in the card room was little more than stealing.

I checked my watch. I had an hour to get over to Cheverly, to meet Lisa at Jabalah Abahd's office. Despite my aches and pains, I was aware of my impatience to get there. The game was afoot, as Sherlock Holmes liked to say. I didn't smoke a pipe or play the violin, and the only doctor I'd ever shared rooms with was Annie Fisher, but the detecting game itself was exactly the same, and suddenly I couldn't wait to get started.

Before I could, my cell phone rang.

"The ADIC wants you again, Puller," Karen Kilbride told me when I answered. "Wants to see you. Now."

I grimaced at the phone. Lieutenant Barra hadn't wasted a whole lot of time going over my head to Kevin Finnerty.

"What should I tell his secretary?" Karen wanted to know.

"To quit bothering me, that I don't have time for Finnerty's nonsense today." Silence from the other end, Karen's shock so vivid I could almost feel it through the phone in my hand. "Or," I continued, "that I'll be there as fast as I can. Whichever you think is best."

I took the time to call Lisa, tell her to stand by until she heard from me, and twenty minutes later I was sitting in Kevin Finnerty's office. His big jaw was tight, his lips turned down at the corners, but that was pretty much how he always looked. I checked for his tell, but his normal stack of paperwork was off to one side. Maybe I'd been wrong to expect trouble from him. Maybe he was just checking on my progress in finding the missing roommate.

"Could it be, Mr. Monk," he began, "that you've forgotten how our system works?"

I sat up straighter, began again to watch his paperwork as I played my first card, the classic "dumb-ass agent" card.

"I'm not sure I understand, Mr. Finnerty."

"I got a call from the chief of police in Cheverly. He was very upset. What happened out there?"

I told him. Told him what Lieutenant Barra wanted, that he wanted Brenda Thompson's name, that he wanted to know specifically why I was at Jabalah Abahd's house in Cheverly.

"Abahd?" Finnerty said. "Is that name supposed to mean anything to me?"

"The missing college roommate. She changed her name."

"She was dead when you showed up to interview her?" He scowled. "And you let the killer get away?"

"Didn't exactly let him, no. We fought, but he got by me and out the door."

"Where was your sidearm?"

"In my briefcase. It's a SPIN case. I had no reason to wear it."

"How long has it been since you've read the manual of rules and regulations?"

The question was not meant to be answered.

"What about the A.F.O. case?" he continued. "You were assaulted, were you not? You are a federal officer, are you not?"

"He's already a murderer. Seems a little silly to add kicking an FBI agent into the mix."

"It's not your decision to make. Your job is to present the facts to the United States Attorney's office, let them decide."

"Of course. When we arrest him. Adding a technical violation to the charges isn't going to make catching him any easier."

He sat back, his eyes closed for a moment, then swung forward again.

"I spoke to the legal division a few minutes before you got here. They agree we do not want to introduce Judge Thompson's name into this. Legal will contact the chief of police in Cheverly, tell him to subpoena you if they must. We can challenge the subpoena until they give up and go away." He stared at me, those gray eyes of his especially chilly this morning. "Unless, of course, you have something that might help them solve the homicide. We can't be in a position of withholding evidence."

"Nothing. Outside of a dead body and the presence of the man who'd murdered her, I couldn't testify to anything else."

What I did have—the diary thing—wasn't anything except a highly theoretical motive, didn't come close to the standard for evidence. Not yet anyway, and I wasn't about to spread the theory around the Hoover Building until I had some facts to back it up.

"And the problem with the Thompson case," Finnerty said. "What did the judge say when you went back to her?"

I told him her explanation—that she'd forgotten the missing three weeks, that she had not in fact told Lisa Sands the sick aunt had died, only that auntie had been expected to die but hadn't.

"SA Sands insists the judge is wrong," I told him. "Showed me her interview notes. The notes support her claim."

"Agent Sands is a first office agent, a woman first office agent. She made a mistake. Add your own notes to the file, make it clear Judge Thompson cleared up the misunderstanding. With the roommate dead, your investigation is complete. I know the deadline is more than a week away, but you don't need that much time anymore. I'd like to see the report before the weekend."

He pulled a file from a stack to his left, opened the cover, then looked up at me.

"Is there something else, Mr. Monk?"

I thought about his question for a moment. Now was the time to object, but I couldn't make myself do it. Not until I had something better to say.

NINE

I STOPPED BY MY DESK TO CHECK MY MESSAGES AND SIGN out some of the mail that was beginning to pile up. One thing led to another and it was an hour before I broke away, summoned Lisa, and told her we would drive over to Abahd's office together.

By the time we got there it was pouring rain, freezing rain. The office was one of many in a converted industrial building near Dupont Circle. There were no police around when we arrived, and Abahd's secretary, her eyes heavy with the shock of what had happened to her boss the day before, told us why.

"They were here most of the morning," the heavyset young woman told us. "Two detectives and a crime-scene specialist."

"They take anything?"

The woman shook her head. "Made some copies, but this is a business office. We still have clients. We can't give away our files and records."

"We're sorry to intrude," Lisa said, "but we need to look through her desk as well."

"Help yourselves," she said. "Just don't take anything without telling me."

Inside Abahd's office it was too cold to work. I walked

around the desk and closed the factory-type windows that had been left open. Raindrops splattered against the glass, and the dull gray light that came through added to the bleakness of our task.

Abahd's desk was stacked with files. Her criminal clients' files, I saw, when I looked through a few of them, along with notes about her strategy for trial, records of phone calls made and received, the usual stuff you'd find in a trial lawyer's office. I pushed them around but saw nothing to interest me. The desk itself was what you call double-pedestal, a center drawer with two large drawers on either side.

"Why don't you take the left side," I told Lisa. "Regardless who Robert Bennett turns out to be, Abahd might have made notes of their conversation, and what she told him about Brenda Thompson."

She nodded and I bent to examine the center drawer myself.

Desk supplies, mostly. Pens and pencils, a ruler, paper clips and a stapler, scissors, a half-empty pack of gum, and a fresh tube of lipstick.

The two drawers on the right side were filled with the same type of files as those on the desk, their little plastic tabs sticking up in an orderly row, even smaller names typed on the tabs. I concentrated on the top drawer first, bent lower to scan the names, saw nothing that meant anything to me. I closed the drawer and went on to the bottom one. Exactly the same thing: files, tabs, little names, no Brenda Thompson, no Robert Bennett.

I considered taking the time to go through the files one by one, but decided it would be counterproductive. The Cheverly P.D. would do that, probably had already done so. Besides, it was unlikely that notes pertaining to Thompson or Bennett would be stuck into a file that didn't bear either one of their names. I closed the drawer, turned to help Lisa.

"Whattya got?" I asked her.

"No Bennett, no Thompson, lots of other stuff."

I bent over her shoulder. My chin touched her hair and I backed off a little, not far enough, however, to avoid the wildflower scent. I ignored it, mostly, then got back in close again. She was still examining the top drawer on her side.

"Personal files," Lisa said, "looks like to me. Household accounts, receipts and warranties, bank records, stuff like that." She turned her head suddenly enough that our noses almost collided. This time I couldn't make myself retreat. "Want me to copy some of this?" she asked.

"If you see something we can use."

She nodded, began to open folders and examine contents. I took another whiff of her hair, then straightened up and stared out the window at the rain. The reflection of my face didn't look happy. Searching for something is always tough, but it's even more frustrating when you're basing the search on guesswork.

Abahd had been pretty clear—at least in my mind—that she had bad news about Brenda Thompson, but it was possible I'd read too much into her words. That I'd wanted to read too much into them. That in my need to elevate the suspense I was trying too hard to make this special, something to get my juices flowing again.

"Hey," Lisa said, right in the middle of my soliloquy.

I looked at her. "Hey what?"

"No home phone bills."

"And?"

"And phone bills are all that's missing." She pointed at the drawer. "Like I said, these are household files, and everything else is here. Gas and electric, newspaper, water bill, cable TV, car lease, Visa and Mastercard, stuff like that, all here. Including her Verizon cell phone account. Everything but the bills for her home phone."

I turned and walked out the door, went over and spoke to the secretary for a moment before going back to Lisa.

"The only phone bills the secretary keeps at her own desk," I told her, "are the ones for the telephones here in the office. Abahd's home phone bills should be with the rest of the personal stuff in her desk in here." I nodded toward the file drawer. "You can't find any phone bills at all? Not even old ones?"

"Haven't looked yet, not for the old stuff."

She bent over the drawer, rifled through the other folders, plucked one out and straightened up with it. She opened the folder and glanced through the contents, turned to me.

"End of mystery. Here they are." She rifled through them. "Except for this month's. But Abahd might have misplaced it . . . or hadn't gotten around to filing it yet."

"The rest of the bills, had she filed them already?"

"All there, neat as a pin. The old phone bills all show the pay-by date as the fifth of the month. If Abahd didn't lose it, it should be here with the rest of them." She paused. "We can get it from the phone company, if you think it's important."

"Might not be important at all, but there's no way to know without looking at it." I stared out the window at the rain. "What about long-distance carriers? Sprint or IDT . . . one of the others."

She checked the folder again. "Sprint mostly, but a couple others, too. Looks like she uses whatever's handy at the time. She gets the bills separately from the regular phone bill." Lisa paused to flip through a dozen or more pages, then shook her head. "Nope. No current bills from either of them." She looked at me. "We can get the same subpoena for their records."

"We could if we had the luxury of unlimited time, but we don't, so we've got to go to plan B."

To Quantico rules, in other words, although this wasn't the time or place to go into the details of those rules with my newest partner. I pointed at her purse on the desk.

"Got your cell phone in there?"

She did, and a moment later it was in my hands. I punched numbers.

"Go through the latest of the bills," I told Lisa, while I waited for Gerard Ziff to answer. "You know the number we're looking for."

When Gerard answered, I dispensed with our usual pleasantries. "Telserve," I told him. "I need a quick favor."

"From me? You people have the same contacts I do . . . or perhaps your typing fingers are broken. If that's the case, I'm dreadfully sorry."

"I don't want to use the bureau computers for this," I said. "It's a long story. Can you or can't you, I need to know right now."

"I can do it, you know I can. But we try not to, unless there's no other choice."

"There's no other choice."

"Give me the phone number."

"I've got three of them. Four, actually, now that I think about it."

"You're pushing it, my friend."

"Just think how grateful I'll be. What you can twist out of me next time we play tennis."

"I can't wait." He paused and I heard sounds of papers rustling. "Give me the numbers."

I picked up one of the old phone bills, read Jabalah Abahd's home number to him, then grabbed a cell phone bill and gave him that number, too. I had to pull my notebook from my briefcase, check the notes of my interview with Judge Thompson to get the third and fourth ones, the judge's home number, along with the number of the phone in her chambers.

"The last two," Gerard said. "Double-check them, will you?"

I read them again, slowly.

"Give me a minute," he said. "You want to hold the line?"

"E-mail them to my bureau laptop," I told him. "You have the address."

"Can't do that, not to that address. Got your Palm Pilot with you? The one with your personal e-mail account? I've got that address as well."

"Yeah, I do, but—"

"We'll use that one instead."

"The screen's too small. I'll go blind look—"

I stared at the phone in my hand. He'd hung up. Spies, I thought, nothing was ever simple with a spy. I saw Lisa looking at me, and it was easy to anticipate her question.

"Telserve," I said. "Ever run across them when you were a D.A.?"

"Telserve . . . One word?" I nodded. "If I did," she said, "I don't remember."

I wasn't surprised. I'd been an agent a long time before I knew about them either.

"It's a high-tech company in the Middle East. Business to business. A service company for the telecommunications industry."

"Middle East? You're going to get American phone records from the Middle East?"

"American, European, Asian . . . anywhere there's a telephone."

She frowned. "I feel like I'm in a television commercial, but I have to ask anyway. How can they possibly do that?"

"Pretty simple, really. If you have seven or eight thousand high-tech pros involved, and contracts with most of the world's telephone and Internet service providers."

"They work for the phone companies?"

"Customer care, order management, but most of all billing. Every time you make a call, a computer sends the data—not the voices, of course, but the phone numbers involved and the duration of the call—to Telserve's mainframe. The supercomputer does the rest. Makes sure each call is billed properly, each of their client companies gets the correct amount of money."

"You mean there's a record of every call I make? Every call *everybody* makes? All in *one place?*"

"There are exceptions. Top-level government phones in this country are excluded, same in the rest of the world." I looked at her. "But it sounds worse than it is. With or without Telserve, every call is computerized anyway. You can see that just by looking at your bill. It's the fact that almost all of them are in one database that makes some people queasy."

"I can see how it would. Especially when it's so easy to access."

"It's almost impossible to access, that's the only reason it's allowed to exist."

"But I just heard you do it. Heard you tell your friend that you didn't want to use a bureau computer to do it. I gather he has his own computer, and doesn't mind at all."

"Oh, he minds, but we go back a long ways. Besides, no one's harmed. We could get subpoenas—duces tecum subpoenas from the U.S. Attorney's office—but there're two problems. Kevin Finnerty would find out about it, and we don't want to bother him with details. Secondly, we don't know exactly which service providers are involved, especially for Brenda Thompson."

"This Gerard. Who is he?"

"A friend, I told you. I shouldn't have let you hear his name."

"I've forgotten it already."

"Be sure you tell the inspectors that. Or the Senate subcommittee." Her eyes widened before I grinned. "A joke, Lisa, an old bureau joke." I stopped grinning. "I'm not about to do anything to get you into trouble. Trust me, I'm neurotic about that. You might not know all the details, but as long as I'm in charge you're going to be protected."

She cocked one eyebrow at me, but my cell phone rang to break the moment. Gerard Ziff on the other end.

"I'm forwarding your information now," he said. "See you Friday?"

"Friday, yeah, at the club. And bring the two-hundred bucks you're holding for me."

He laughed and hung up. Hadn't even asked what my request was all about. Must be awfully busy, I thought. Nosy bastard never forgot to ask.

I pulled my Palm Pilot from my briefcase, opened my e-mail, then downloaded the attachment Gerard had forwarded. I shook my head as I scrolled through the pages of tiny numbers. I knew what I was looking for, but nothing jumped out at me to indicate contact between Jabalah Abahd and the judge who claimed to have lost track of her. Which meant nothing, of course. Not until each of the numbers was analyzed far more closely than we were prepared to do here in Abahd's office.

I closed up the Palm Pilot and put it away. When we got back to the office I'd give the data from Gerard to our computer analysts, let the whiz kids see what they could come up with.

I told Lisa as much.

"Isn't that a lot of work," she said, "when we could just go to Thompson and ask her?"

"Bad idea. Never ask a question that important until you already know the answer."

She stared at me for a moment. "But . . . but how . . . ?" She shook her head. "That doesn't make any sense, Puller. With the roommate dead, how can we possibly *know* the answer?"

"We can't. Not if we keep looking in the wrong place for it. Not if we keep looking here in Washington."

TEN

I DROVE US BACK TO WMFO, TOLD LISA TO GO HOME AND pack for a two-day trip to Virginia, down to Brookston. I let Karen Kilbride know where we'd be, that we expected to be back sometime Friday, then returned a few phone calls and ran through a pile of fresh mail on my desk while I waited for Lisa. I considered calling Kevin Finnerty to let him know where we were going and why, but decided to wait until we got back, until we'd done what we could to tie up the loose ends and present him with a done deal.

An hour later Lisa was in my office with a small blue overnight case in her hand and a purse slung over one shoulder, ready to go.

"One second," I told her, then scribbled a note for Ted Blassingame, my principal relief supervisor, reminding Ted to run the ticklers tomorrow, to double-check the progress of several cases with short deadlines. I grabbed my raincoat.

"Let's go," I said.

We walked together through the deserted bullpen. There was a mandatory legal-training seminar down the hall and the agents on my squad wouldn't be back for at least an hour. We were almost out the door at the other end before Karen called out to me.

"Puller," she said, "wait a second." She held up the phone in her hand. "You better take this. Says her name's Annie. Sounds like she might need some help."

I laid my raincoat over the edge of the nearest desk. "Give me a minute, Lisa." I walked back to my office and grabbed the phone. I didn't bother to use my chair.

"What is it, Annie? I'm just on my way out the door."

"I need a man," she said, then giggled. "I need a man real bad." Another giggle, this one louder and longer. "You know where I can find one?" Laughter this time, a slightly manic sound that I recognized and could hardly stand to hear.

"Annie," I said over her laughter. *"Annie!"* She stopped, then giggled again, then did nothing. "Where are you?" I asked her. "Damn it, Annie, where *are* you?"

"Your house, silly." Giggle. "Where else would I come when I need to get laid?" Same semihysterical laughter. "How shoon—soon, how *soon*—can you get here?"

Shit. I looked around, saw Lisa through my glass wall, watching me. I sighed, then spoke into the phone again. "Half an hour. Promise me you won't leave."

She was giggling again as I hung up. I turned toward the door again just as Lisa came back through.

"Sorry," I told her, "but I've got a problem. We'll have to leave tomorrow morning."

Lisa's dark eyes flickered. "Annie? Nothing serious, I hope."

I shook my head, but I was lying. To someone like Ann Fisher booze was as deadly as a loaded shotgun, but I was right to lie about it. Annie's problem was hers, hers and mine. Lisa had no need to know about it.

"I have to help her with something is all," I said. "Enjoy your evening. My house is on the way to Brookston. Pick me up at seven in the morning."

She looked at me. "If there's anything I can do . . ."

"Nothing. You really want to help, go home and figure out a way to find the truth in Brookston." I smiled. "And bring some doughnuts and coffee when you come."

• • •

I set a land-speed record getting to my dome in Fredericksburg, one eye on the traffic, the other in the rearview mirror
for flashing red lights, but it was still thirty-five minutes before I walked through my front door. Too long, I saw when I
got to the semicircular kitchen.

Annie was sitting at the table, her head in her hands, my
bottle of Glenfiddich on the table next to her, a nearly empty
glass next to it.

She turned as I approached, then lifted her head. Shit.
Her watery eyes were dull and red, her blond hair spiking in
all directions. She'd been giddy on the phone but now she'd
gone past happy, past horny, straight on to outrage. A whole
day in less than one hour.

"God damn you, Puller," she muttered. "You and the
fucking white horse you rode in on."

I touched her shoulder but she jerked away.

"I'm sick of you," she said. "Just because you show up
when I call doesn't make you *better* than me . . . not a goddamned *bit* better. Only difference is you won't admit it."

I glanced at the bottle, couldn't remember how much had
been in it last time I'd seen it. "What's the damage?" I asked.
"How much have you had?"

She shrugged. "Here, at your place?" She glanced at the
bottle. "Don't worry, I didn't drink all your fucking Scotch."

"Where did you start?"

"My house . . . my office . . . how the hell do I know?"

"Did you call your sponsor?"

"Fuck my sponsor. She's just like you. Powerless, she
keeps telling me . . . We're all powerless. I'll help you, she
says, we'll all help you. Bullshit. I don't need her . . . I don't
need you. Go find somebody else to take care of your guilt."
She dropped her head into her hands again, her shoulders
quivering as she wept.

My guilt. I shook my head. That's the problem with
sleeping with drunks. So charming most of the time, so eager to hear the story of your life, so quick to use it against
you later. Used to make me mad, Annie's claim that I

wouldn't have anything to do with her if I didn't feel so guilty about ignoring her twelve-step ideas, but I knew better now. Knew she was right, mostly. That regardless which of us was right, it was a waste of time to talk about it.

I picked up the Glenfiddich and her glass from the table, took them to the counter, put the glass in the sink, the bottle in a cupboard to my left. Then I moved a step to my right to start a pot of coffee. Not for her, for me. It was going to be a long night.

Drowned out by the pounding water of my morning shower, the insistent sound of Lisa's car horn on Thursday morning took a few moments to penetrate. I turned off the shower and toweled off before tiptoeing past the still-sleeping Annie Fisher, barefooting my way down the spiral staircase and cracking open the front door to peek past it. There sat Lisa, behind the wheel of her bucar, a two-year-old Pontiac something or other.

"One second!" I shouted, sticking my wet head past the door jamb, but careful not to let her see the rest of me. "Just got to slip on my shoes!"

I could see her frowning at my breach of protocol. Under the rules of bureau carpooling, "one second" means the agent being picked up is at least half dressed and reasonably ready to go, while a wet head and hidden body indicates no such thing. She beeped twice more, stiletto-sharp blasts, but grinned as she did so, to let me know she was kidding, that she realized despite my churlish behavior I was still her supervisor. I couldn't help grinning back. I was beginning to like the woman.

Eight minutes later I was in the passenger seat next to her, ready for the hour-long drive south to Brookston. She nodded toward the two styrofoam cups in the holder behind the shift lever. "One of those is yours," she said, "and there are doughnuts in the sack."

I sipped coffee as Lisa eased through the winding streets of my neighborhood, then headed east through downtown Fredericksburg and out into the countryside toward the little town in Cobb County that Judge Thompson had identified as the place where her aunt, Sarah Kendall, had died.

Lisa turned to me. "Anything I should know before we get there?"

"Enjoy the drive. You know what we're looking for. No point wearing ourselves out on it before we get there."

Through the Virginia pines, their branches sagging with rainwater from last night's storm, we passed the villages of Sealston and King George, then hooked up to a meandering two-lane state highway east toward Westmoreland County.

"Gorgeous out here, isn't it?" Lisa said. "The trees, I mean, and the pastureland. Hard to imagine it filled with soldiers killing each other."

I'd been thinking the same thing. It's part of living in the middle of all this history, but especially vivid in the open spaces, the few remaining acres that continue to resist the advancing real estate developers. The Confederates had held at Fredericksburg—despite the thousands of blue hats who died trying to clamber up Marye's Hill to get at them—but a hundred and fifty years later not a shot is fired at the builders who seem determined to cover the battleground with "affordable housing." Life is for the living, I know, but still. There's plenty of room for everyone in this magnificent countryside. Why build tract houses on ground so recently bloodied?

"You haven't been here in spring yet," I said, "or for the change, the leaves turning just before they drop in the fall. Every shade of crimson and scarlet, twenty kinds of yellow, traffic on the Interstate stopping dead to watch." I was quiet for a moment just thinking about it. "Almost makes the mud season tolerable."

"Didn't see much of that in El Paso, either mud or leaves changing. Two seasons is all we had. Colder than hell, hotter than hell."

"Southern California for me, a little town outside San Diego. We didn't even have two seasons. What we had ranged from 'real nice' to 'totally awesome, dude,' depending how close you got to the beach."

I opened the doughnut sack, took a full breath of deep-fried lard, then plucked one out and held the bag out to Lisa. She made a face and I bit into the doughy sweetness and moaned with satisfaction. Lisa grunted, reached to turn up the windshield wipers, indicated her disapproval of my nutritional ignorance by stepping a little harder on the gas. A mile or so later she turned to me and ignored my suggestion we avoid guessing about the Thompson case until we got to Brookston.

"The judge told me," she began, "that she left Cal before the commencement ceremony. That seems strange to me, considering her background, to miss such a significant day in her young life."

"It does to me, too, but I don't want to develop a theory before we even get to Brookston. It's an easy way to shut off your mind to other possibilities. A bad way to do business, our kind of business anyway."

"What's the fun if you can't take a wild guess?"

"It's not supposed to be fun." But it is, I didn't tell her, if you do it right.

"I vote for pregnancy," she said, ignoring me completely. "The old standby, I know, but that doesn't mean it's not still valid."

"Nothing at the University of California showed her as pregnant, and she wasn't when she got to Yale. The case agent in New Haven would have seen some evidence of it in the university medical-center records, or heard about it from former classmates."

"And there'd be a child somewhere, obviously. On Brenda Thompson's personal security questionnaire for sure." She turned the wiper speed up, the heater down a bit. "Unless she left the baby in Brookston."

I nodded. Abortion had been my first thought as well, but like I'd told her, I wanted to let it come out of our investigation, not go down there just to prove it. I told her that, but she continued to press her case.

"Let's say she was six weeks pregnant at Cal, found out from an off-campus doctor, that way there'd be no university medical record to check. She makes a quick stop in Brookston to have an abortion, takes a couple of weeks to get her head straight again, then moves on to New Haven."

"She'd know in six weeks? That she was pregnant, I mean?"

"If she had a reason to worry, yeah. Things happen. Sometimes a girl starts checking awfully quick."

"Nineteen seventy-two," I said, thinking out loud. "July. *Roe v. Wade* . . . Seventy-two or seventy-three, wasn't it?"

"Seventy-one for the first arguments, reargued at the end of seventy-two, I think, then decided in January seventy-three."

"But everyone knew how it would be decided."

"Doesn't matter, it was still illegal. If that's what happened to Thompson, she'd have missed being legal by a couple of months."

"You know what they say about close."

She was quiet for a minute.

"Got to be it, though," she said. "Abortion's still a pretty hot item for a Supreme Court nominee . . . so hot that David Souter wouldn't even admit to talking about it." She shook her head. "Had the nerve to tell the Senate Judiciary Committee he'd never even *discussed* the issue. Hard to imagine Thompson getting away with actually having one, an illegal one to boot."

I nodded. It was hard to forget about Justice Souter's ludicrous assertion, and how willing the senators had been to believe it, to do anything rather than face up to an issue that still topped the list of litmus tests for new nominees to the high court. Even with a legal abortion on her sheet, Brenda's nomination would be dead before it got started.

I stared past Lisa and out the driver's window. Rain slanted past us, from clouds low enough to touch the treetops.

"And that brings us straight back to motive," I said. "With stakes that high—the Supreme Court—you can throw out the rule book. The Greeks launched a thousand ships for one face. Compared to that, Thompson lying about her past to save her one chance at immortality seems downright reasonable."

Lisa slowed as we approached a logging truck, stacked high with telephone-pole-size logs. She edged into the oncoming lane, looking for an opening to pass, then slid back into line.

"Miscarriage," she said. "There's miscarriage to consider as well. Or a stillbirth. Maybe even sudden infant death after a normal birth. If Thompson had a baby who died within minutes or hours, she might have chosen to leave it out of her personal history altogether. Might have been too painful to take with her into a new life."

"That's why I don't like to guess. Her time in Brookston might just as easily be unrelated to any kind of pregnancy. She might have been an alcoholic, or a pothead. She was sure as hell at the right college for that, at the right time as well." I paused. "Maybe she stopped in Brookston to dry out, to get her head together for law school."

She nodded. "You're right, that could be exactly what we're looking at. I suppose she could even have gotten herself arrested in Brookston. Stopped for speeding maybe, with an ounce of grass in her car. Cops took that stuff pretty seriously back then."

"I like the idea, but if that happened she'd have a rap sheet. Our NCIC check would have picked it up."

"A 1972 arrest? There was no National Crime Information Center back then. Gotta be a bunch of records never got transferred over to the new system . . . especially from rural departments like Brookston."

"Can't eliminate the possibility, that's for sure."

"So what's the plan?" she asked. "Down there in Mayberry, I mean."

I reached for the last doughnut, took a moment to eat a bite. "Let's start with the sheriff's department. Hit the county clerk's office, then maybe the hospital. That should give us some idea what we're up against."

She nodded and we fell silent, stayed that way until we crossed the line into Cobb County. The Pontiac's digital clock read eight-ten when we left the highway and drove down Main Street, a solid stretch of classic small-town one-story buildings that could have been lifted directly from the back lot of a movie studio.

The Cobb County Courthouse was a mile or so down Main, and carried out the same nostalgic motif. Green lawns, white brick construction, red-shingled roof. Parking was out back. The lot was empty except for three green-and-white patrol cars along with a couple of unmarked units, the stripped-down Fords and Chevys that fool no crooks anywhere. Lisa parked our bucar next to one of them and we grabbed our briefcases.

It continued to rain as we hiked up the long flight of steps, swung the twelve-foot high oak door out of the way and entered the sheriff's office. Inside it was all wood and fresh varnish. The smell reminded me of the front pew I'd grown up in back in California, and I tried not to inhale any more of it than I had to. Behind a chest-high counter, a uniformed woman smiled at us.

"What can I do for y'all?" she asked.

I showed my credentials. "The sheriff around?"

She lifted a phone, spoke into it briefly, then turned back to us. "Sheriff Brodsky should be with you in a few minutes." She waved toward a couple of plain wood armchairs against the nearest wall. "Y'all can sit right over there until he comes."

We retreated to the chairs. Above them, on the beige-colored wall, hung the green-and-gold official seal of the sheriff's department.

Ten minutes later we were still sitting there. Four more minutes passed before I coughed politely and made a show of looking at my watch. The officer at the counter smiled.

"Shouldn't be but another minute or two."

I nodded, then told myself to relax. We'd come without an appointment. Not many people kept us waiting like this, but sheriffs were among the few who did.

A door behind the counter opened suddenly, and a powerfully built man wearing the same uniform as the receptionist emerged from it. He moved to a small gate to the right of the counter, opened it, and approached us. We stood to meet him.

"Edward Brodsky," he said, his voice blunt, his brown eyes reflecting the wariness FBI agents become accustomed to seeing from the locals.

I showed him my creds, introduced Lisa, then gave him the opportunity to extend his hand. He didn't.

"My office is just down the hall," he said, then turned and strode back through the same gate and doorway from which he'd just come. Lisa and I had to hurry to keep up.

I inspected the lawman's back as we walked down the long corridor. Brodsky was as much a descriptor as a name. The sheriff was wide enough across the shoulders to show home movies on, his brown hair short and sprinkled with gray. A perfect stereotype, I decided. Life imitating art. A man whose friends probably called him Bull.

Inside his office I saw that I was wrong.

ELEVEN

The sheriff was no stereotype, that was for damned sure.

From the upscale furnishings in his office to the pipe rack on his desk, the David Hockney reproductions on his walls to the soft classical music—Haydn, I was pretty sure—Edward Brodsky was anything but what he looked. A bull of a man he might be, but I was willing to bet nobody'd ever stuck him with the name.

His big desk was a nice grade of dark maple and the dove-gray carpet looked like wool. Behind the desk was his "glory wall," the framed documents and photographs he'd accumulated through the years. The one that caught my eye went a long way toward explaining his abrupt demeanor. Wood-framed, it featured a dark-blue background on which were mounted the distinctive gold badge of the L.A.P.D. and a chrome-plated pair of handcuffs. On a gold plate fastened to the bottom of the frame were the dates, 1966–1996.

I thought for a moment about the years of conflict between FBI–LA, and the Los Angeles Police Department. All the way back to Hoover himself. From the Black Dahlia case to the 1984 Olympics, the Rodney King beating to corruption in the infamous Ramparts Division. Cases the bureau didn't want any more than Parker Center did, but had no choice about investigating. Christ, no wonder Brodsky didn't like us.

The sheriff circled the desk to a high-back leather chair, sat, gestured toward the matching black leather armchairs down front. We sat. He stared at us for a moment.

"What brings you to Brookston?"

I almost mentioned the badge and cuffs on the wall behind him, but decided not to. Sleeping dogs and all that. No point making it any worse than it appeared to be.

"We're working on the president's latest nominee for the Supreme Court. Judge Brenda Thompson. She told us she lived here in Brookston for a few months in 1972. I'd like to run her name through your records department."

"You could have done that on the phone. Surely you didn't drive all the way down here for a records check."

I looked at him, then argued with myself. Old habits are hard to break—his attitude was proof of that particular bromide—but I could probably afford to take the high road. Probably had to, as a matter of fact. Whatever Brenda Thompson had been up to in Brookston, we had little chance of finding out without Sheriff Brodsky's help.

"Actually," I told him, "there is something else."

"Thought there might be."

"Adoption records, Sheriff. Any way to see them?" Not a real lead, but a good way to test our new relationship.

"Got a court order?"

"No court order, but a release form. From Judge Thompson herself."

"She'd be the mother?"

Shit. Not a great way to start. Now I had to say the words I'd been trying to avoid.

"I'm afraid I can't say anything more, Sheriff. I mean no disrespect, but it's just not possible to tell you that."

He grinned without a trace of warmth. "The more things change . . ."

He didn't bother finishing. Didn't need to.

"No court order," he continued, then leaned forward with his big forearms on the desk. "That's the problem. Adoption records are more protected than anything we deal with. Nothing but a court order will even get you in the door."

He looked away for a moment, then back at us.

"You'd want to look for abortion records, too, I imagine."

I shook my head. "We're talking 1972 . . . a year before *Roe*. Not likely there'd be any records before that."

"Hard to know for sure until you look."

I nodded but didn't say anything. I looked at my watch, then at the sheriff.

"Can you point us toward the county clerk's office?"

He pointed upward. "Next floor. Right above our heads."

We started to get up, but his voice stopped us.

"How long you plan to be around?"

"Hard to say. We've got some other routine stuff to do, but we'll touch base with you before the end of the day."

He shrugged. "Suit yourselves. Call me if you need any help."

It was one of those things you say, I realized, but it was the friendliest he'd been since we'd come through the door.

"We'll do that, Sheriff. Thanks."

We rose and left his office. He didn't bother to show us back to the reception counter but we didn't need the help. In the stairwell to the second floor, Lisa turned to me.

"What the hell was that all about? The attitude, I mean."

"Retired cop, Lisa. L.A.P.D."

"Of course. I saw the badge and cuffs, too. But Jesus . . ."

"Get used to it, partner." I started up the stairs. "After a while you'll stop caring."

Upstairs, the customer service counter at the Cobb County Clerk's office had been recently varnished, the smell even stronger than in the sheriff's department. A young man wearing a white shirt and black string tie stepped up to help us. I flipped my creds open and he nodded.

"We need to verify a death record," I told him. "The name is Sarah Kendall. Died in 1972. June 1972."

He scribbled on a pad at his elbow. "Just give me a

minute," he said, then grabbed the pad and hustled away to an oak filing cabinet, slid out a narrow drawer and removed a small white card, brought it back to the counter.

"Sarah Kendall, yes, right here." He glanced at the card and frowned, then at his pad. "Wait a second, though," he said. "Did you say 1972?"

"June 1972 . . . probably late in June."

He held out the card. I took it from him, examined the fading typescript, then nodded at the 1991 date, satisfied at having confirmed what Lisa had been told over the phone. It's never a good idea to trust information you get over the phone. Now it could go into our report.

"I'll need a copy of this," I told him. "Certified and ex-emplified."

"Of course." He started away, then came back. "It'll take a few minutes. Is there something else you'd like to see while I do it?"

I nodded. "Marriage records. For 1971 and 1972, please."

The clerk moved to another oak file cabinet, this one closer to his desk, opened the middle drawer, pulled out a spool of microfilm, and brought it to us.

"You'll need the reader for this stuff," he said. He pointed at a battered machine in the corner, then led us to it and strung the spool into the machine. "Just turn this crank," he began, but I cut him off.

"I'm an old hand," I told him. "We'll call if we need you."

I waited until he was gone, then began to crank.

I felt Lisa move up close and watch over my shoulder. Her hair smelled even better than it had the other day, the wildflower scent even more inviting out here in the country. Her shoulder felt warm where it was touching the back of my left arm, and I had to force myself to concentrate on the task at hand.

I started with marriage records from June to December 1971, but saw almost immediately there was no point. Twenty names before the middle of July alone, twenty young black women who had married in Cobb County. At that rate we would have at least a hundred names, and there was no way to work with that many. Not at this stage anyway.

"Not a chance," Lisa said, her mind as close to me as her body.

I went back to where the clerk was working on the death record. He looked up at my approach. Lisa stayed behind but I knew she was listening.

"Sarah Kendall," I said, "have you got anything else on her? Who she was, who she was married to? Maybe what she did for a living?"

He chewed his lower lip for a moment. "She'd be in fictitious names registration if she ran any kind of business here."

"Would you mind checking?"

The clerk went to a second file cabinet, came back empty-handed.

"Nothing," he said.

I glanced at Lisa and she came over to us. "What about churches?" she asked. "If she were a regular churchgoer, where would we start looking?"

"Our records wouldn't have that . . . church stuff, I mean." He paused. "Come to think of it, we *could* have that. Her marriage certificate would show a church, if she was married in one." He went away and came back, showed us the certificate. "Baptist," he said, his voice proud. "Same as me. She was married at my church, the one I just started going to. Emmanuel Baptist, out on Falls Lane."

I studied the certificate. Copied the data into my notebook. "How do we get to the church?" I asked.

"I can save y'all a trip by calling Brother Johnson, if you want."

It would save time as well, I thought, but once again the telephone was not the way to go. The kinds of questions we would be asking had to involve eye contact and body language, so I asked for directions instead, got them, and headed with Lisa back to the parking lot.

Halfway to the church my brain began to turn heavy again.

I'd never seen Brother Johnson's Emmanuel Baptist Church, but I'd spent the first third of my life there nonetheless. I knew what it would look like, smell like, sound like, and I didn't want any part of it. Besides, Lisa didn't need me along just to ask a few routine questions. She could drop me off by the side of the road, go ahead on her own to interview the reverend, come back and pick me up. It sounded like a good plan until I realized what would happen. That Lisa would stare at me in surprise, demand to know what the hell I thought I was doing. That I didn't know her at all well enough yet to tell her.

Fifteen minutes later we were there.

The church building lay at the end of a wooded lane about two miles from the courthouse and turned out pretty much as I'd pictured. Not much larger than a single-family home. White shingles, faded blue trim, same color blue on the double doors leading inside. What it didn't have that I'd expected to see was a steeple. The only thing that distinguished Emmanuel Baptist Church from the grange hall we'd just passed was the plain wooden cross above the front doors.

Lisa parked the car out front and we went up the walk to those doors. I turned to her. "You do the talking this time. I want to watch the preacher."

Which wasn't the whole truth. I did want to watch him, but I needed to watch myself as well. My track record with preachers wasn't good, my fuse far too short with the clergy. A lot safer to keep myself out of it.

"Sure," Lisa said, as she grabbed the brass handle on the right-hand door and pulled it open.

An eighty-something black man looked back at us from the front of the church. A tall man with a short ring of curly white hair around his mostly bald head. His eyebrows were white as well, but as we approached him I saw something I couldn't remember seeing before. His eyes were dark brown, but the lashes were just as white as the rest of his hair, and the effect was startling. He straightened up from the work he was doing on the church's old-fashioned organ, smiled with a full set of perfect teeth as he walked up the aisle to greet us.

I began my routine search for his tell as Lisa did the credential thing and introduced the two of us to him. Reverend Johnson's smile stayed in place—no mean feat considering what his memories of earlier American justice and the FBI must have been—but I wasn't surprised. Preachers learn to smile early in the game, to keep on smiling even though they know better. His voice was thin but still had plenty of strength.

"How may I help you folks?"

"We're trying to run down some information on Sarah Kendall," Lisa told him. "The young man at the county clerk's office told us she'd been married in this church. That you yourself had performed the ceremony."

His smile disappeared for an instant before coming back even stronger, but he was too slow to keep me from noticing. One more time and I'd own him. He fiddled with the hearing aid in his right ear.

"That's better," he said. "Now what was that again?"

Lisa repeated it.

"Sarah Kendall," he said, his words slow. "Yes. Yes, I believe I did marry her and her husband. Sarah was a member of my church for more than forty years, God bless her, right up to the day the Lord took her home." He smiled again. "Why don't you folks come into my office? We'll be more comfortable there."

I glanced over his shoulder at the raised pulpit, then back up the rows of plain wooden pews to the open front doors, and through them to the bucar outside. Talking to the preacher out there in Lisa's Pontiac would have been just fine with me, but wherever his office turned out to be it was better than where we were at the moment. Standing next to that pulpit that I couldn't even stand to look at.

"That's very kind of you," Lisa said. "Perhaps you could lead the way."

He did so, Lisa right behind, me hanging back. The varnish smell was just as strong as it had been at the courthouse, but more authentically churchy here. We passed the pulpit and I tried to ignore it, but it was too late. My stomach clenched hard enough to stop me in my tracks. A series of images flashed through my mind before I could stop them. Images I'd never been able to forget . . . or forgive.

Sally Ann Hampton had been every bit as precocious as I was, another teenager filled with raging hormones and just as much curiosity, but Pastor Monk hadn't seen it that way at all. In his book the wages of sin were death, and that's what he tried to do to me when he caught the two of us behind the pulpit. Until the janitor showed up and pulled him off, long after Sally Ann had buckled up her bra and beat it out of there.

Now just the sight of a pulpit was enough to bring it all back, and most especially what had happened at services the very same night. The hideous humiliation of Pastor Monk's public condemnation, the vilification that had banished Sally Ann and her family from the congregation, followed by his scathing denunciation of his own wife and my mother as the Jezebel who'd allowed her son to become a fornicator. Finally, horribly, his order to the congregation to shun my mother for her sin, the order that took from her the only thing in the world she cared about, that reduced her life to misery and inevitably to the suicide that Good Old Dad took as the ultimate sign of her unworthiness.

Rage has no sense of time and space, I've been told by one shrink or another since that night, and looking at Reverend Johnson's pulpit almost thirty years later, the feelings were still strong enough to make me sweat. I shook my head in an effort to dislodge the pain, then hurried to catch up with Lisa and Reverend Johnson.

"Like I said," the preacher began, once we were seated before the unadorned wooden desk inside his tiny office, "I knew Sarah very well." He glanced out the door in the direction of the organ. "Matter of fact, she played that very organ until she was too sick to come to church anymore." He shook his head. "I work on it every week, but it's never sounded the same since she passed."

"How about her niece?" Lisa asked. "Brenda Thompson. You must have known her, too."

His smile went out completely. He turned from Lisa, stared at the ceiling. "Brenda Thompson," he mumbled. "Sarah's niece, you say."

He looked back down but still not directly at either of us. Fiddled with his hearing aid again, cleared his throat, then massaged the entire front of his neck and spoke quietly into the top of his desk.

"I thought I knew all of Sarah's people, but I never met any Brenda Thompson." Now he did look at Lisa. "Should I have?"

"Not at all, sir," she said. "But what about church records? Would you have something to refresh your memory?"

A soft chuckle. "Records? Lord, no. Everybody knows everybody down here. Don't spend a whole lotta time on records."

I stared at him. *No records?* Good thing Pastor Monk wasn't here. Wouldn't he have something to say about that?

Lisa glanced at me and I nodded that I'd heard enough, seen enough. Lisa thanked him for his time. We shook hands, and he showed us out to the front doors, closed them behind us. Before we could get to the car I could hear the insistent hammering of a single note from the organ. In the car Lisa started the engine, but turned to me before putting it into gear.

"Well? What do you think? He telling the truth?"

"You tell me."

"He's lying about not knowing Brenda Thompson. Kept his body angled away from us, his eyes anywhere but on mine. Then the throat rubbing. Like he was trying to squeeze the words up his neck to get them out of his mouth."

I nodded. Good girl, I would have said in a less-militant era. Maybe it was time to start taking her to the card rooms with me.

"Where now, boss?" she wanted to know. "Where do we go to find out *why* he's lying?"

"The hospital. Got to be one around here someplace."

"What about release forms? The only release we've got is signed Brenda Thompson. If the reverend doesn't even admit knowing her, why would we think Thompson would use her own name if she ended up at the hospital?"

"Never hurts to ask."

"May not hurt to eat half a dozen doughnuts either, but that doesn't mean it's a good way to use your time."

"I have a cunning plan."

She stared at me. "It sure as hell better be."

TWELVE

I'D LIED.

I didn't have a cunning plan for storming the hospital. I didn't even have a mediocre one, so I went with what I did have. FBI credentials, and a brilliant and gorgeous partner. I kept Lisa in reserve, held out my credentials as the records nurse at Cobb County General Hospital approached from her side of the high counter.

A beautiful young woman, her cinnamon skin glowed against the starched white of her uniform. Her thick black hair was pinned dancer's style on the top of her head, and her effortless posture suggested the same formal training. She smiled and I found myself wishing I'd worn a nicer suit. A tag on her lapel identified her as Helena Evans.

She examined my identification. "What can I do for you?" she asked.

"We're looking for anything you might have on a Brenda Thompson." I gave her the judge's date of birth, her social security number. "Any record to indicate she's been a patient here at the hospital."

"You have a release form, of course."

I produced it from my briefcase, handed it over. "You can keep it if you need to. I have plenty."

She examined the release form, looked up at me. "Brenda Thompson? *Judge* Brenda Thompson?" She pointed to the current issue of *Time* next to the computer on her desk, to the judge's picture on the cover. "That Brenda Thompson?"

I nodded. "We're just finishing up the background investigation. You're one of our last stops."

"Is she from around here? I don't remember reading—"

"Just passed through, back in the early seventies."

Helena Evans stared at us. "My God, you people are thorough."

I gestured toward the computer on the desk behind her. "Would you mind checking?"

She smiled, then turned away and typed on her keyboard. She looked at the screen and typed again, then looked at us and shook her head.

"Sorry, I don't get anything on her." She returned the release form. "Is there something else I can do?"

"There is, actually, but this is a bit unusual." I smiled again but she was a bit less radiant all of a sudden. "If I wanted a printout of hospital admissions for a certain month in a certain year, would your database be able to provide one?"

She glanced at the computer, then turned back to me.

"I could do that, yes . . . but if you're talking about thirty-some years ago, it wouldn't be in the computer. I'd have to do some manual searching." She paused. "I hope there's no problem with Brenda Thompson, I really do. We've been waiting a long time for . . ." She smiled again. "But I won't bore you with all that. What I'm trying to say is I wish her the best."

"Just tying up loose ends. Touching all the bases."

"I'll be proud to do my part if it means she makes it through. All you have to do is clear it with our administrator, Mr. Faydeux. As soon as he gives me the okay, I'll get right on it."

She reached for her phone, spoke into it, hung up. Thirty seconds later the administrator showed up. A short heavy man, sixtyish, wearing a cheap suit and a cigarette-burned necktie. Spider veins in his thickened nose had burst to form a reddish-purple thatch that made it the star attraction on an otherwise nondescript face. He brushed a hand across skimpy hair the flat black color of a cheap barbecue, then stepped forward to offer a handful of yellow fingers. Lisa shook them first, had to tug a little to get her own back from him.

"Priestley Faydeux," he said, in an accent with more bayou in it than Brookston. "What can ah do for you folks?"

I decided to use Lisa on him, nudged her with my arm to get her started.

"We need something from your records," she said. "I'm hoping you can help us."

He smiled with teeth only slightly less yellow than his fingers. "Of course, ma'am, anything you want just ask."

She repeated what I'd asked Helena Evans in the records room.

His smile turned false. "Would you want to see the records themselves?"

"If we could."

"But you don't have any release forms."

"I'm afraid we don't."

"What about a court order, then? We can work with a court order just as well."

"No court order either."

"Can't help you, then. Our legal people have been very specific about releasing information without proper authority."

I noticed his good-old-boy accent had disappeared.

"I can understand that in a criminal case," Lisa said, "but this isn't a criminal matter. The only thing we're here for is to help Brenda Thompson get on the Supreme Court."

"I'm sure you think that's a very good reason to overlook our rules, but Brenda what's-her-name will just have to make it on her own like everybody else."

Helena Evans interrupted, her voice sharp. "Look, Priestley, surely we can make an exception this time. We wouldn't be hurting anybody. All we'd be doing is helping a deserving woman, a deserving black wo—"

"That's enough, Ms. Evans," Faydeux told her. "Your job is to file these records, not decide who does or doesn't get to look at them."

"But you're being unreasonable," Evans said. "Nobody's ever going to know. What possible reason would you have to—"

Faydeux stepped toward her. "Not another word! You're on thin ice around here as it is. Don't make me go to the board with another complaint."

Helena Evans grew taller, appeared so ready to go after her boss I found myself leaning forward to stop her. But she turned away, rage evident in the hard set of her shoulders as she strode back to her desk and sat down. She refused to look in our direction, but I was sure she was still listening.

"I wish you could be a little more flexible," I told Faydeux, "but I can't order you to break the law. Agent Sands and I will be around for a while. If we come up with a court order we'll call you."

The administrator harruumphed, clearly ready for us to get the hell out of his kingdom. We didn't bother shaking hands this time, but on the way past Helena Evans's desk, I paused.

"Thank you so much, Ms. Evans," I told her. "We understand your good wishes for Judge Thompson. Be assured we will pass them on to her personally." I paused. "We can only hope this won't delay the process long enough to harm her chances."

Outside, I opened the driver's side door for Lisa, then went around and climbed into the passenger seat. She turned to me before starting the engine.

"You really think that worked . . . that she'll call us?"

"Depends how much she hates Priestley Faydeux."

"Then get ready to answer the phone. I couldn't even stand to shake his hand. She's gotta despise him."

"She wouldn't be the first woman to bite her tongue just to keep her job."

"Or the first man," Lisa was quick to say, although she didn't have to. I can name dozens of us who do that every day. As a matter of fact, the bureau's filled with bitten tongues.

"I'll bet you dinner she calls," Lisa said.

"And drinks?"

"Dessert even, if you're man enough to eat it."

I grinned, then accepted the wager before she could change her mind about it. Helena Evans might or might not call, but either way I couldn't lose. Either way Lisa was mine for the evening.

She fired up the engine, started to back out of the parking space, then stopped and looked at me for instructions. I checked the dashboard clock. A few minutes past eleven. Maybe what I wanted was food, a good solid cheeseburger to jump-start my brain. I remembered passing what looked like a decent place to eat when we'd driven into town.

"There's a place on Main, Lisa, back on the way out of town. Looked like a decent motel, got to have a café. Take us there. We'll talk about it over lunch."

She pulled the shift lever into reverse, backed out and headed for the street. "We spending the night?"

"Might as well. We need to figure out where we're going with this." I grinned. "When Nurse Evans calls, who knows where it'll lead?"

She rolled her eyes, then swung the bucar left out of the parking lot.

We hit six consecutive stoplights before coming to the Brookston Inn, an Old-South design with two white columns flanking the entrance to the lobby, wide-canopied pines towering over the café next door. A dysfunctional neon sign next to the street blinked "acancy . . . acancy . . . acancy." Lisa pulled into the parking lot and I went into the lobby.

"Two rooms for tonight," I told the teenager behind the desk. "Something quiet."

"This is Brookston, Mister. It's all quiet."

I signed and paid. He gave me a pair of keys.

"There's a double door between them," he said, "but you can lock your side, okay?"

Good thing, I thought. You never could tell what Lisa

might get up to, so far from home. I was still smiling at the idea when I got back to the car. Lisa wanted to know why.

"Just daydreaming." I pointed toward the rear of the building. "Second floor, last two on the left."

She parked near the stairs leading to the second deck. We walked upstairs, then along the outside passageway to her room. I handed her the key.

"I'll be next door," I told her, then glanced at my watch. "Lunch in ten minutes?"

She frowned. "A lady needs twenty. I'll tap on your door."

I left her as she was turning her door key, used mine on the room next door, then swung the door open and recoiled from an assault of Pine-Sol that pushed me half a step backward. I forged ahead, through the door and across the nylon carpet toward the single bed against the far wall, surveyed the skinny furniture, the dime-store Civil War print above the bed. I shook my head. My career had taken me to a lot of small towns over the years, to any number of Motel 6's, but this was most definitely my first Motel 3.

I used the bathroom, splashed water on my face, ran a hand through my hair, then did what everyone does in a motel room, turned on the television and clicked my way to CNN. The Dow was up, I saw, and the Nasdaq down, but I didn't much care. I had no bet on either one. Another school shooting filled the screen, this one in Switzerland, of all places. I turned away from the TV and reached for the phone. I'd left Annie asleep back at the dome, but it was a good idea to check in with her again, just to make sure she wasn't in even worse trouble this time. I called my home number, no answer. I called her veterinary office in Fredericksburg. She was there, her nurse told me, but busy with an animal. Did I want to hold? I didn't, I told her, but I was relieved to hear that my doctor was once again on the wagon.

I hung up and turned back to the TV, aimed the clicker to jab the off button, but stopped when I caught the letters FBI

superimposed below the serious network news face of Wolf
Blitzer. His voice rolled somberly through the story.

"*. . . came as a complete surprise to Capitol Hill*," he was
saying. "*Senator Randall's opposition to the bureau's con-
troversial DCS1000 program—formerly known as Carnivore—has been consistently vehement, and the FBI's plans
for enlarging the program with the addition of Magic
Lantern has drawn her specific condemnation. Senator Randall's Intelligence Oversight Committee has supported her
position that the bureau's latest update to the e-mail monitoring program represents nothing more than a death blow to
the Fourth Amendment, and her astonishing change of heart
this morning has Washington insiders buzzing. Our Catherine Crier has more.*"

The picture changed to the familiar blond reporter, standing in front of the Hart Senate Office Building, but I'd seen
and heard my fill of the ruckus surrounding the e-mail interception program, and this time I hit the clicker for good.

Most FBI agents are ambivalent about the DCS1000 program, and I'm no exception. As an agent, I agree that the
ability to monitor criminal e-mail is critical to the bureau's
mission, but as a citizen I share some of the current leeriness
about the potential for abuse. Senator Jeannette Randall's
oversight committee was charged with making sure such
abuse was headed off before it even got started. And the senator had been adamant—until this morning, if CNN was
right—about what she called the terrible risk of Magic
Lantern, and the slippery slope it represented. "*Star Wars*
meets *1984*," Randall had labeled the new technology, but
that was a bit hysterical for me. No matter what kind of program the bureau came up with, it would depend entirely on
legitimate federal warrants before being utilized. Her argument badly underestimated the lengths to which America's
federal judges would go to make sure nothing Orwellian
came to pass. No judge would allow the government to
eavesdrop on computer keystrokes without one hell of a lot
of probable cause.

Still, Randall's opposition had been remarkable—which made her apparent change of heart even more baffling—but I knew better than to waste time puzzling over it. Fifteen years inside and around the Beltway had taught me nothing if not cynicism. Something had changed hands, that much was clear. Money, sex, power, or a combination of all three, and it was simply useless to wonder which of them or why.

Lisa's rap on the door broke my train of thought, and I joined her in the passageway. We descended the stairs and a minute later walked through the lobby and into the attached café.

We chose a Chinese-red vinyl booth at the very back of the half-full room. The café buzzed with dozens of conversations. A veteran waitress shuffled up to us, pad in hand, pencil at the ready. Her short brown hair was mussed, her face and the front of her light-blue smock sagged with wrinkles. She handed over the menus, gave us a full twenty seconds to make a choice.

"What can I get you folks?" she demanded in a tone heavy with the suggestion that she'd been watching the clock for at least an hour already, that it would be just fine with her if we had nothing at all, that it was a long damned way for her to walk just so we could eat.

I looked at the menu, a photomontage of greasy piles of meat and potatoes, then picked the least objectionable, a double cheeseburger with a side of fries. Lisa grimaced, then ordered a chicken salad for herself. There wasn't any picture of it, I noticed. Probably didn't sell three a year.

But when the food came I realized I'd made another of my hasty judgments. The cheeseburger was among the best I'd ever eaten, not overdone, a smoky flavor I found irresistible. The fries were crisp and greaseless, the coffee an exceptional blend of vanilla and some kind of nut. For her part, Lisa dispatched her salad with a speed that made it unnecessary to ask how she liked it.

We ate without a lot of conversation, but afterward, coffee cups filled with that wonderfully aromatic blend, we got back to business. Or tried to, anyway. The morning had been pretty much a washout. With the chilly reception from the sheriff and nothing at all out of Reverend Johnson and the hospital, there wasn't much to talk about.

"You want to go back to the sheriff?" Lisa asked after awhile.

"Why not interview the trees?"

She got my point. "The reverend, then. Maybe he's had time to repent."

"We're not through with him, trust me, but I'm not going back there empty-handed."

She grinned. "We could try door-to-door." She impersonated my much deeper voice. "Anybody here," she growled, "know what Brenda Thompson did, and why she did it?" Lisa laughed out loud, then reached across the table to touch the back of my hand.

"Did you bring the Thompson PSQ?" I asked.

She lifted her briefcase, put it on the table, and opened it. Pulled out a document of about two dozen typed pages, the personal security questionnaire the judge had filled out to get us started on her background investigation. She handed it to me and reached into the briefcase for a second document.

"I made a second copy," she said, "just in case."

We sat—she with her copy, me with mine—turning the pages, looking for something the month-old investigation might have missed.

"Hey," Lisa said, pointing at the questionnaire, "Brenda Thompson has a grandmother around here . . . not exactly around here, but not all that far away. We could drive there in an hour."

I shook my head. "We don't do grandmothers." Immediate family only is the rule in background investigations and it's one of the few Hoover-era rules that still makes sense. "You ever heard of the Grandma Principle?"

"Let me guess. Grandma might know, but she'll never tell."

"Hitler's grandmother would have described him as impulsive, a little trouble getting along with others, but all in all a very good boy."

"Funny . . . but a bit facile, don't you think? My grandma wouldn't bad-mouth me either, but she's too religious to lie if the FBI asks her a direct question."

"You got one? A question for Thompson's granny, I mean?"

"I sure do. What happened to make Brenda go to Brookston, then lie about it the rest of her life? How's that for starters?"

"Too subtle. But your point about your own grandmother isn't a bad one. A woman Thompson's grandma's age is probably just as religious. Probably more devoted than ever to keeping her soul in good shape." I took another sip of coffee. "Where does she live?"

"Williamsburg. Southeast of here, seventy miles, maybe a bit farther. If we leave right now we can see grandma today and still get back here in time for a late dinner."

I slid toward the end of the booth. "Little Red Riding Hood probably said the same thing," I told her, "but if you do the driving, I'll watch for the wolves."

THIRTEEN

BEFORE WE LEFT THE BROOKSTON INN, I STOPPED AT THE front desk to check for messages. Nothing, the desk clerk told me. I told him to forward any calls to my cell phone. I thought about the records nurse at the hospital, but didn't mention her. Despite my bet with Lisa, it was unlikely she'd call. Helena Evans might hate her boss's guts, but she knew better than to blindside him.

She fooled me.

My cell phone rang before Lisa and I were halfway to Williamsburg. We were crossing the Mattaponi River on State Highway 33 near the town of West Point when I had Nurse Evans on the line.

"I can't talk long, Agent Monk," she said. "Faydeux took the afternoon off after you left, and I got to thinking about what you'd said about Judge Thompson. About how she might not get the job if you can't complete your investigation."

"I was hoping you might."

"I can't give you records, not without copying them, and I can't risk that. What I can do is read you a short list of names. You wanted the names of black women admitted to the hospital in the month of June 1972. At least that's what you told me."

"If you give them to me, I can get a subpoena."

"Would my name come up?" For the first time there was fear in her voice.

"Absolutely not."

"Okay," she said, "you got a pen? There are five people on the list."

I told her to go ahead. She gave me the names, I wrote them down.

"Gotta go," she said. "Hope this helps."

I laid the phone aside. Behind the wheel, Lisa glanced across at me, grinning. "Where you gonna take me to dinner?"

"Anywhere you want . . . as much as you can get on your tray."

She grunted. "Read me the names."

"What's the point? You feeling clairvoyant all of a sudden?"

"Humor me."

"Irene Cavanaugh's the first one—by date of admission—and the second is Lynette Williamson. Then Jasmine Granger, Glen Ellyn Tate, and Samantha Brown." I looked at her. "Anything come to mind?"

"Samantha Brown, maybe. Has a made-up sound to me, like a stage name or something."

"I want to be there when you use that to get a subpoena."

"How much farther to grandma's house?"

I checked the map. "We'll hit I-64 in a few miles. Head south. About twenty miles to Williamsburg, looks like." I folded the map, tucked it into the pocket built into the car door.

Lisa flipped on the wipers to counter the latest shower. We continued along the two-lane road until we got to I-64, then took the Interstate to Williamsburg, looked for an exit that would take us to the banks of the James River. A few minutes later we were there.

Waterside House, the luxury nursing home in which Brenda Thompson's grandmother now lived, stood on a low rise not much more than a hundred yards from the river. Lisa parked in the paved lot on the west end of a five-story brick building that looked more like a colonial mansion than a place people came to die. We stood together on the brick walkway bisecting an elegant sweep of front lawn. The judge had to be paying a fortune for this kind of luxury, I decided. A pile of money to have Grandma Williams wheeled out once a day into the exclusive southern breezes. I couldn't help wondering about that. Brenda Thompson made a very good salary, but she did not come from money, and her financial disclosure statements didn't show any unusual wealth either.

Lisa stared at the main building. "What a dump," she said.

"More like a honeymoon hotel than a nursing home, isn't it?"

"What I've heard, a lot of the same stuff goes on."

It was just as nice inside.

We peeked into a large room just off the lobby, where a number of residents napped in front of a humongous television screen. The Home Shopping Network, I saw, a screen filled with immense styrofoam fingers bearing gargantuan faux-diamond rings, an even bigger person extolling their affordability. I glanced out the nearest window at a flock of river birds above the water, some motionless in an updraft, others diving like missiles into the food-filled water. Growing old might not be so awful done this way, I thought, then looked back at the listless gathering in the TV room and shook my head. Dying is dying, no matter where you do it.

At the front desk the receptionist called for someone to take us to Prudence Williams. A few moments later a large man in a snow-white uniform came around the corner and escorted us to a room on the fourth floor. Inside the room, fresh-cut flowers stood on the dark-wood nightstand by the bed, along with a silver water pitcher and crystal glass. The orderly told her who we were, then left us alone.

Prudence Williams lay on the bed, her tiny body half-covered by a white comforter, her miniature face rumpled as a used bath towel. She wore a stunning red satin jacket and a tan hearing aid rode the right temple piece of her frameless glasses. Perfume hovered, an expensive scent that I recognized but couldn't name. Unfortunately, her expression did not match the bright conviviality of her jacket.

Grandmother Williams wasn't pleased to have a visitor, I guessed from the sour look on her face, but maybe that wasn't it at all. Maybe it wasn't visitors she objected to, but the FBI in particular. As had been the case with Reverend Johnson, she'd lived through a dreadful time without much help from her local FBI agents. She waved a bony hand at the upholstered chairs next to the bed. We sat.

"Who did you say you are?" she asked before we could even get settled. Her voice was even skinnier than she was.

I glanced at Lisa. I told you we'd be wasting our time, I wanted to say.

"FBI, ma'am. I'm Special Agent Puller Monk." I hoisted my credentials so she could see them. "And this is Special Agent Lisa Sands. We came to talk about your granddaughter, Brenda. About her nomination for the Supreme Court."

"The Supreme Court? What about the Supreme Court, Mr. . . . Mr. . . . *who*?"

"Monk, Mrs. Williams, Puller Monk. I need to ask you a few questions about Brenda. What kind of person she is, what she was like as a child." The lady tipped her head toward me, and I raised my voice. "About her days as a college student out in California."

"She doesn't live in California, Mr. Bunk."

"Monk, ma'am, with an 'm.'" I spoke a little louder. "No, she doesn't live there, but she did study at Berkeley."

Grandma frowned, leaned even closer toward me and cocked her head. I slid my chair a bit closer. "What kind of a student was she?" I hollered.

She shrank backward. "Sweet Jesus!" she yelled, "what you tryin' to do, Chuck, blow my hearing aid into the goddamn river?"

I pulled back, then glanced at Lisa before trying again. "I'm very sorry, ma'am. I just have a few questions, if you don't mind."

Good God, I thought, it was the Grandma Principle to the tenth power, and even worse. The woman was not only deaf, but meaner than hell at the same time. I reached for my briefcase, ready to close up shop, until I caught Prudence Williams shaking her head.

"Please forgive me," she said. "I know I shouldn't yell, but it's so frustrating sometimes. Either I can't hear, or I hear so well it drives me nuts. I can't remember what happened two minutes ago, but I can't forget terrible things that happened eighty years ago. Hell, I'm not even sure it's my own life I'm remembering!" Her head quivered with the force of her words. "Take my advice, Mr. Dump, don't get old. Old sucks."

Before I could stop myself, I burst out laughing. "I'm sorry. It's just that I don't hear someone your age use that expression every day. And it's Monk, ma'am, with an—"

"Of course it is," she said.

So she wasn't crazy, I decided. She wasn't a crotchety old bitch, and she could call me anything she wanted to.

She waggled her stubbly chin toward the table to the right of her bed. "Pour me some water, will you?"

I poured water from the pitcher on the nightstand into the glass next to it, leaned close to hand it over. As I did so, I took a moment to study the woman's eyes. There was something wrong here, I realized. In that desiccated face, her eyes were wrong.

I recalled a famous picture of Robert Frost during the Kennedy inauguration ceremony. The poet's face had been ancient, a landscape of craters and crevasses more like the surface of the moon than a human face, but his eyes were completely different. Young. Clear. Ageless. Prudence Williams's eyes were exactly the same. They should have been bloodshot, the pupils hidden in red and yellow murk, but they weren't. They were as clear as Frost's had been. She might not be a poet laureate, but she sure as hell wasn't senile either.

"What was Brenda's childhood like?" I asked.

"Her father was a no-good bastard who took off the second she was born. My daughter wasn't a whole lot better. I reared Elizabeth after the court sent her to me. And I'm glad I did."

"Her father's name was Willie Thompson?"

"No-good *bastard*!"

"Her three brothers all have different last names."

She stared at me. "Where you been livin'? That ain't no thing."

I managed not to laugh this time, but I could sense Lisa starting to shake. It was just too bizarre, to hear street talk come out of that mouth. I found myself looking forward to hearing what she'd say next.

"So Brenda used the name Thompson even after she married."

"That's right, Mr. Punk. Somethin' wrong with that?"

I shook my head. "When Brenda was in college, she had a roommate, Dalia Hernandez."

"Never heard of her."

I left Dalia for later. "Brenda told us she spent a few weeks in a town near here, a place called Brookston, just after she finished at Berkeley, just before she went on to Yale. Do you recall that?"

Prudence Williams's face screwed itself into concentration. "*What*-ston? Around *here* someplace? Why the hell would she do that?"

"She told us her aunt, Sarah Kendall, was dying and she came back to Virginia to help out."

"Sarah *who*?" She shook her head. "She never had no aunt named Sarah."

She blinked several times, then yawned before closing her eyes. She stayed that way, motionless, until I wondered if she'd gone to sleep. Or worse. I turned to Lisa, then leaned over the bed, ready to listen for some sign of breathing. Suddenly her eyes snapped open, and I sank back into my chair.

"But that don't mean much either," she continued, "that this Sarah what's-her-face wasn't an actual family member. Hell, where I come from *everyone* is aunt somebody or other."

Her head sagged against her pillow, her eyes closed. This time she spoke without opening them.

"But I don't remember no Brookston. Brenda would have written to me about it, I'm sure, but I just don't remember."

"Did you save her letters, ma'am? Would you have any from her college days?"

"Lord, no! There were hundreds of them!" She looked around the room, seemed to consider expending a gesture before giving up the notion. "Where the hell would I keep them? Why you want to see a pile of old letters anyway?"

"I need to verify what your granddaughter told me, about Brookston I mean. I thought you might have one she mailed from there."

Prudence Williams surveyed the room, then smiled, her teeth a gleaming tribute to the artisan who'd made them. "Pays for all this, my little Brenda."

I felt my shoulders beginning to slump. As a non sequitur her answer was just as perfect as her teeth. While the old girl wasn't completely daffy, she wasn't entirely there either. I didn't bother checking with Lisa before I started to put away my notebook. Suddenly Prudence Williams held up her hand.

"Wait. Don't go. Please don't go yet. I just might have a letter." She pointed at an antique chest of drawers under the window across from the foot of the bed. "Might be in the drawer over there." She motioned me toward the chest. "What else have you got to do, Special Agent Monk?"

I smiled. *Now* the lady knew not only my name but my title.

Lisa walked to the chest of drawers, followed Grandma Williams's instructions to the proper drawer, recovered a small bundle of age-yellowed envelopes encircled by a brittle rubber band, brought the bundle back to the bedside and handed it to her. Prudence Williams slipped off the rubber band, selected half a dozen letters from the packet and held them out in a hand that trembled enough to make the envelopes shake. I took them, examined the postmarks, and shook my head.

"No, not these," I said, unable to hide my frustration. "It's 1972 we're interested in. These letters are from the fifties." I started to hand them back, but Lisa took them from me instead.

"Of course, we'll look at them," she told Grandma. *Don't be such a prick,* I was pretty sure she was saying to me.

Lisa pulled the letters out of the envelopes and began to go through them, nodding and smiling like just another family member enjoying the memories. I cleared my throat softly, then harder, until she glared at me. I turned to walk away but her voice stopped me.

"Maybe you'd like to take a look at this, Puller."

I took the letter from her hand. A note on plain tablet paper, I saw, the kind schoolchildren use, written in neat but childish handwriting. Something about school, I read, skimming quickly until I got to the end, until my eyes stuck fast to the printed signature. I held the letter up to Prudence Williams.

"This isn't from your granddaughter, ma'am. Not Brenda, anyway. See the signature? That isn't her name at the bottom."

She took the letter, squinted at it, moved it away slightly, adjusted it into focus. Then she laughed, a sudden yelp that straightened me up in my chair.

"That child!" she said. "I bought lots of storybooks for her in those days. One of them had that story about Aladdin." She peered over the top of the letter at me. "The boy and his magic lamp?" I nodded. "There was a princess in the story, too . . . Princess Jasmine. The boy fell in love with her and so did my little Brenda. '*I'm* going to be just like Princess Jasmine someday,' she used to tell me. 'You just wait and see if I don't.'" Prudence Williams stared again at the signature, then at me. "And she is, don't you know? She damn well is."

FOURTEEN

PRINCESS JASMINE. JASMINE GRANGER.

Outside in the bucar, we didn't waste time talking about the connection before going to work on it.

Assistant United States Attorney Jim Franklin and I had done a lot of good work together in the days before my promotion to supervisor took me away from the criminal side of the house, and we still got together for lunch often enough to keep our friendship up to date. I reached for my cell phone, punched the number for his private line at the United States Attorney's office in D.C. He answered the first ring.

I told him what I needed, a subpoena duces tecum for all Cobb County Hospital records under the name Jasmine Granger.

"Shouldn't be a problem," Jim said, "but verbal authorization doesn't work too well outside D.C. You got your laptop?" I told him I did. "Send me an e-mail," he continued, "along with a brief outline of your probable cause, and what you hope to find in the records. I'll send an electronic duces tecum to your e-mail address. Show it to the hospital administrator. Any problems, call me back here at the office. I'll be here most of the evening."

I told Lisa what he'd said. She looked at the dashboard clock. "After five already, Puller. We're running out of day."

"Hospitals never close."

"But Faydeux isn't there. He took the day off, remember?"

"He'll be there. Our subpoena will order him to produce his records. He'll have a choice. Give them to us in Brookston tonight, or haul them to federal court in Washington tomorrow. Take a wild guess which one he chooses. I'll call his office right now; they'll call him. My guess is he'll get there before we do."

I grinned at the prospect. It was beneath me to gloat, but what the hell. I'd eaten enough crow over the years to rejoice when the feathers were in somebody else's mouth.

"Grab my laptop," I told Lisa. "Type up the subpoena and e-mail it. You'll find Jim Franklin in my address book."

She got to work. Thirty-five minutes later we had our subpoena, and not long after that we were handing it to Priestley Faydeux in his office. He was every bit as mad as I'd hoped he'd be.

"I was on my way to dinner with my wife," he said when he read it. "Can't this wait until tomorrow?"

"Of course," I told him. "If it's inconvenient, we'll go back to Washington. You can bring the records up there tomorrow." I shook my head regretfully. "Court's awful busy these days. No way to know exactly when the judge would be able to see you, but you'd be back in less than a week for sure."

Lisa and I turned together toward the door leading out of the administrator's office, but he didn't let us get that far.

"Oh, for Christ's sake! Let's just do it now." He jumped up from his desk and stormed toward the door into the hallway. "You people are all alike," he muttered on his way by us.

We followed Faydeux out the door and down to where the records were kept.

"Ms. Evans has gone home," he said when we got there. "I'll have to look for the damned things myself."

He sat at Helena Evans's desk and whacked at the keyboard on her computer, stared at the screen and scribbled something on a pad of paper near his elbow, took the pad with him back into the stacks. Two minutes later he came back out with a single yellow folder, removed three loose pages from it, then stepped over to the copy machine and made copies for us. I took them, nodded at Lisa, and we turned to leave. I could still hear the administrator muttering halfway down the corridor to the front door.

We returned to the café at the Brookston Inn, but this time decided to take the food with us back to my room. We had business to discuss, and didn't want to have to be careful about who might be listening. Inside the room, we stared for a moment at the bed before Lisa grabbed a chair from next to the window and pulled it up close to the bed.

"You take the bed," she told me. "Sit back and make yourself comfortable."

She went to the window and drew the drapes to give us more privacy. I fumbled for the switch at the base of the lamp on the nightstand, turned it on. The soft glow made Lisa all the more beautiful, and it didn't do me any harm either. I set our sack of food on the nightstand, shrugged out of my suit coat and tossed it across the foot of the bed, loosened my tie and kicked off my shoes, then reached for the bedspread and pulled it far enough away to prop up the pillows to use as a backrest. Lisa sat in her chair and we ate our hamburgers in silence. When we finished, she looked at me.

"I'm sick of Diet Coke," she said. "Did you bring any serious drink with you? Other than gin, I mean. Gin keeps me up all night."

Didn't sound all that bad to me, but I didn't say so, and there *was* a bottle of Scotch in my overnight bag, of course. No veteran FBI agent goes on the road without a bottle of something, especially to a town small enough to risk having to go without.

"Glenfiddich," I told her. "In my overnight bag. Closet next to the bathroom. Glasses in the bathroom, still wrapped in plastic."

I heard her rummaging in the closet, then in the bathroom unwrapping glasses.

"No ice for me," I called, "but if you bring the plastic bucket, I'll go get you some."

"Ice? And ruin good Scotch?" She came out of the bathroom with two glasses, an inch or so of whisky in each one. "Water in yours?" she asked. I shook my head and she grinned. "You're a pretty cheap date, aren't you, boss?"

"The cheapest."

She came over and sat in her chair again, handed me a glass, took a good long pull at her own. I did the same, then sighed. Single malt was hideously expensive, but it only costs a hundred percent more to go first class. I looked at Lisa. Obviously she felt the same way. Her head was back, her eyes closed. She brought her glass up a second time to finish it off.

"Okay," she said. "All better now." She waggled her fingers for my glass, rose out of the chair. "Freshen yours while I'm at it?"

"Why don't you just bring the bottle."

I watched her hips as she headed back to the bathroom. Her straight skirt had bunched up a little when she sat, and the hem had ascended to midthigh. Now it sank slowly as she walked. I watched it closely in case it rode back up, even more closely when she came back with the bottle. She set it on the table just as I reached for it. Our fingers touched and I felt a very pleasant jolt. Relax, I warned myself. Do not get started down that road.

She kicked her shoes off, sat in her chair, and tucked her legs beneath her. She sipped her whisky for a moment, then rose to her feet. A moment later she'd come around the bed and joined me on top of the spread.

"God," she said with a sigh. "This is so much better than that chair."

She fluffed up her pillow, sat back and sipped her Scotch. We stayed like that for a while, like old army buddies, the Scotch doing what Scotch was supposed to do. I started feeling manly and noticed her body language turning feline.

Graceful, languid ... eyes even softer now ... thick dark hair just tousled enough to make me want to touch it.

I took a hefty slug of single malt, forced myself to think twice about what seemed to be going on here. Then I closed my eyes and decided to lighten up. Lisa Sands might work for me, but there wasn't a reason in hell we couldn't be friends tonight, just another pair of tired employees enjoying a drink at the end of the day.

"D and C's don't have to be related to pregnancy," she said, pretty much destroying the mood I was starting to feel. "Matter of fact, they ordinarily don't."

"For some reason I've always put the two of them together."

"Pelvic bleeding, that's all it takes to get one."

I reached over the edge of the bed for my briefcase, retrieved the three-page medical record we'd just brought back from the hospital. A skimpy record: one procedure and a couple of administrative pages. I pulled it close and read aloud from the surgeon's typewritten notes.

" 'Jasmine Granger admitted July 2, 1972. Presented with pelvic bleeding following spontaneous abortion. Dilatation and curettage indicated. Procedure removed fetal and placental tissue. Patient cleared for release July 3, 1972.' " I looked at Lisa. "Miscarriage, right? That's what spontaneous abortion means?"

She nodded. "But I have my doubts about how spontaneous it might have been. Nobody gets murdered for a thirty-year-old miscarriage."

"I wouldn't think so, either, but there's the record."

"Doesn't mean much. Pre–*Roe v. Wade*, a lot of hospitals preferred to go along with the fantasy that botched back-alley abortions were nothing more than simple miscarriages. They didn't want any records the cops might see, didn't want to do anything to bring the law down on mostly poor girls with nowhere else to go."

We sipped whisky in silence for a while.

"One thing I really don't understand," Lisa said a few moments later. "Brenda Thompson was and is a brilliant woman. Why would she make up a name at the hospital, then use her true date and place of birth?"

"What first-year law student would foresee a nomination to the Supreme Court? She couldn't possibly have known in 1972 that she'd be in the position she's in today." I swallowed what was left in my glass, reached for the bottle. "She knew better than to use her real name, but just didn't see any point in lying about the rest of it."

"Still leaves Aunt Sarah. Why tell me a story about the real Sarah Kendall, knowing how easy it would be to disprove? Why not just make up a name? After thirty years we wouldn't have come up with a damned thing."

"Think about it. When you found the gap in her residence history, the missing three weeks, what did you do?"

"Called her up, asked for an explanation."

"In your official FBI voice?"

She grinned. "I guess I *can* sound pretty official at times."

"More like scary, but we all do that. It's the heart and soul of the myth, and lose the myth, we got nothing." I readjusted my pillows, sank against them once again. "My point is you surprised Thompson. Didn't make an appointment to see her, didn't give her time to prepare. Standard operating procedure when you suspect that lying might be involved."

"But she's still a federal judge. You're telling me I intimidated her right out of her senses?"

"*Because* she's a federal judge, you did. She might be bent, but she's not a professional liar. You do the same thing to a con man—walk in on him like that—and he'll come back with the most perfect story you ever heard. Not a word of truth, not a word you can prove is a lie."

She poured another half inch into her glass, settled back. "The preacher's lying, too. Now that we've got the Jasmine Granger name and the medical record to go with it, we've got some leverage."

"Except that we're here to get information, not give it. He may very well know that a woman called Jasmine Granger had an abortion, but not that Granger was actually Brenda Thompson. If we go to him he'll make the connection—after we already asked him about Thompson—and we can't have that. Not with something this volatile about a nominee for the Supreme Court." I shook my head. "Best to leave him out of this, at least for now."

We fell silent. I found myself peeking at my partner. Again at her hair, but now at her breasts and her legs as well. I tried to tell myself that the tension in my thighs, the thickening in my groin, were the direct result of her equally tantalizing brain, but who was I kidding. I could enjoy her brain anytime I wanted to, but it shouldn't make me want to paw the carpet.

Lisa turned toward me just as I was leaning toward her, then swung her legs off the bed and got to her feet.

"I'm tired, boss," she said, "and a little too cocktailed to stay here any longer."

I watched her gather her clothing and start for the door. Suddenly I didn't want her to go. Wanted to hear her say she was already where she wanted to be, that my bed would work just fine for the both of us. But she didn't, and in the next moment she was gone.

FIFTEEN

BACK IN ASSISTANT DIRECTOR KEVIN FINNERTY'S OFFICE AT WMFO the next morning—closer to noon, actually—Lisa and I sat together on his big couch as the ADIC expressed his satisfaction with our work.

"What you came up with down in Brookston doesn't look good for Judge Thompson," he told us from behind his desk, "but that's not our concern. The White House isn't going to like what you've discovered, but the president will understand. After what happened with Josephine Grady, he'll especially grateful for what we've done on this case."

He smiled briefly and I realized this was the part where we were supposed to thank him and return to our hut at the edge of the universe, but I just couldn't make myself do that.

"We're not finished, boss," I said. "The Jasmine Granger connection is compelling, but it's not enough, nowhere near the standard we'd need for evidence. It's not likely Brenda and Jasmine are two different people, but I think we better find out for sure."

"Can you produce something evidentiary? Good enough for a court of law?"

"No way to know until we try."

I told him about Reverend Johnson, but he hit me with my own argument about reinterviewing the preacher.

"You'd have to tell him why you're asking," the ADIC said, "and you know better than that."

Finnerty turned his head to the side. I followed his gaze to the mandatory portrait of J. Edgar Hoover, the black-and-white version showing the old bulldog in his heyday. Hoover's eyes seemed to follow both of us as the assistant director turned back to me.

"You did your job," he said. "We've done our job. The White House doesn't care about proof. The president will call Thompson into the Oval Office and ask her. If she had an abortion she's history, but either way we're out of it."

"What about the Abahd killing?" I decided it was time to bring up Robert Bennett and the diary, but before I could, Finnerty cut me off.

"We're on that already. Legal just got a Prince George's County subpoena for your testimony. We'll work it out with them, let you know when you'll be needed."

"Work it out with them? I don't think—"

"Relax, Monk. There's a bigger picture here, a whole lot bigger than the death of another defense lawyer. Prepare your report, include everything up to and including the point where you went back to see the judge. Attach an administrative section detailing what happened at Jabalah Abahd's home, along with what you discovered in Brookston and Williamsburg. Have it on my desk by tomorrow morning."

I sent Lisa back to her desk to assemble the Thompson report, then called Gerard Ziff to confirm our regular afternoon meeting at the tennis club.

"I was just about to call you," he said. "I can't play tennis today. I've got to drop my embassy car off for new tires, but I've got a better deal for you than tennis. You pick me up at the gas station, I buy you lunch at La Maison."

I smiled. A meal at the *très* expensive French restaurant on Wisconsin Avenue in Georgetown was more than a good deal, it was a great deal.

"You got it, Gerard. Tell me where and when."

"Twelve-fifteen. The 4200 block of Connecticut Avenue. Best Price, the place is called. I'll be waiting out by the curb."

"I'll be the hungry man picking you up."

"*A bientôt*," he said, or that's what it sounded like.

But he wasn't at the curb when I got there an hour later. Gerard was still inside, I could see him through the plate glass window.

I pulled into the lot, past the huge inflatable display out front, a smiling ten-foot-tall balloon man with a tire under one arm and a sign on his cap that read "Best Price—Everything for Less!"

A minute later Gerard was in the car with me.

"You people get your tires here?" I asked him. "Surely you can do better than a gas station. And it can't be for convenience, either. There's got to be *something* closer to your embassy."

"Tell me about it. Some empty suit in Paris cut a deal with Best Price for tires and batteries. The gas station chain buys the tires directly from Michelin in France, charges us for putting them on the cars."

"You need special tires?"

"They're not special at all. That's the part I've never been able to understand. The only difference I can see is that they have a white code stenciled on them, to make sure they're not resold to any other tire dealer in this country."

I grinned. "So much for hiding your secret identity."

"So much for empty suits in Paris."

"Bureau did the same thing to us a few years ago, only it was gasoline, and the post office. We had to gas up at post office fuel depots or write a memo explaining why we didn't. Moronic. Lasted six months. Saved about a hundred dollars."

"You hungry?"

"La Maison's on Wisconsin, right?"

He nodded and we were off.

At the restaurant, the maître d' seated us in a dark-green leather booth toward the rear. I looked around the room and recognized more than one politician. It wasn't surprising. La Maison was a favorite for all types of congressional members and the civil-service chiefs who served them.

We traded small talk until the waiter brought our food and left again. Gerard took a bite of his poached salmon, followed it with a spear of asparagus.

"The Brenda Thompson thing," he said. "Her confirmation hearings start a week from Monday, I see in the papers. Your investigation went well, I presume."

He was back at work already, I realized. The casual question, the almost bored disinterest in the answer. Washington political chat, nothing more.

"Without a hitch," I lied. "Smooth as silk."

"But didn't you tell me you had a problem with her early on? The day you asked me to call Paris about her?"

I'd told him no such thing and he knew it. "Not really. Just touching all the bases. You know the bureau." I gave it a full beat before I asked a real question, careful to keep my voice just as bored as his. "Why do you ask?"

"No reason. Just keeping the conversation going."

He ate more salmon, I continued with my *poulet en croûte*. Despite his nosiness I was determined to enjoy my lunch.

"And the phone records," he said after a while. "Was the Telserve information useful?"

"Very useful. Thanks again for doing it so quickly."

"So what's next for her? Thompson, I mean."

"Just the Senate confirmation hearings. Then on to glory."

He glanced at me, and I couldn't help thinking he knew better already, that he was just trying to get me to confirm what he'd already been told. He lifted his wineglass. I held up my glass of water.

"To glory for Brenda Thompson," he said. "Nothing would please me more."

As usual Lisa had outdone herself, I saw when I got back to my office and examined the Thompson report she'd assembled and put on my desk for my signature. Once again, I saw that I'd been justified in assigning the case to her despite her lack of seniority, and in going to Finnerty to get authorization for doing so.

A report of the size required for a Supreme Court nominee is a massive undertaking. No one agent could write the whole thing in the few weeks we get to finish the investigation. Hundreds of already written pages come in from agents all over the country, sometimes all over the world as well. The case agent in the field office where the nominee lives—Lisa Sands in the Thompson case—must assemble the pages and prepare the administrative cover pages, the index, and a synopsis of the important findings of the investigation.

What Lisa had provided me was a 392-page document in praise of Judge Brenda Thompson, along with the four skinny administrative pages Finnerty had ordered to summarize what had happened in Abahd's house in Cheverly and what we'd discovered in Brookston. Four pages designed to go no further than the director's office at the Hoover Building, where it would be detached before the report went on to the Oval Office, its contents relayed by mouth and in person to the president himself.

It was standard operating procedure—the administrative section—a way for the field agents to explain to the Hoover Building why this or that had or hadn't been done, why questions had been brought up in the report's body then left unanswered. But that wasn't the only reason for its existence. It also kept certain information deep inside the bureau's files, where it couldn't be seen by outsiders without a Freedom of Information request—a request the bureau could stall until the seeker gave up and went away.

After the president heard about Brookston, he would call Brenda Thompson into the West Wing, demand an explanation for embarrassing him, then throw her out the back door and into the real savagery that would follow. Washington being Washington, the details would get leaked to the media and that's when things would turn really ugly. The press would rip her to shreds. After they finished she wouldn't even be able to go back to the job she had before, would disappear into the vast pantheon of American losers, would resurface only as the answer to an obscure question on future college tests.

I thought about that for a moment, about justice and the often peculiar ways it could be found. Thompson had lied, at the very least, and the murder of Jabalah Abahd still had to be accounted for. It was distinctly possible that the judge's public humiliation would be the least of her problems.

I grabbed a pen and initialed the cover page of the report, authorizing it to go upstairs to the ADIC. Then I called Lisa's desk in the bullpen.

"I owe you a dinner," I told her. "A real one, I mean. Somewhere without pictures on the menu. We can leave from here after work, go someplace close."

"God, Puller, I don't think I can stand another meal in a restaurant this week." I felt a distinct sag of disappointment, but before I could argue, she continued. "Tell you what. You buy the groceries, I'll do the cooking. How's that sound?"

"Are you sure?" I crossed my fingers. "Are you sure you'd rather do that?"

"I'd love to stay in and cook. And after the week we've had, I don't care about healthy. Bring me red wine and some kind of dead animal, something that had parents until very recently. Maybe a couple of potatoes I can bake."

"Dessert?"

"On top of steak and potatoes?" She hesitated. "Oh, hell, can we have cherry pie?" She paused again. "What are you trying to do to me?"

It was on the tip of my tongue to tell her, but thank God she interrupted before I could.

"I need some time, though," she said. "A couple of hours to turn into something you won't mind dining with."

"How about seven?"

"Great. My address in Alexandria is on the office roster. You're a pretty good agent. You shouldn't have any trouble finding me."

SIXTEEN

"I HAVEN'T REALLY HAD A CHANCE TO SETTLE IN YET," LISA told me, after she'd poured us a couple of vodka martinis and started the tour of her condominium in the heart of Alexandria.

"I still need to ship some things from El Paso," she went on. "Artwork, mostly, but a couple of pieces of furniture, too. Stuff I wanted to pack myself that I didn't want to trust to the movers."

"Looks pretty good to me the way it is."

I stopped at a grouping of three eye-catching prints, hanging in the living room where no one could miss them. Goya, I thought, as I examined the first of them—a windswept scene featuring a circle of seventeenth-century aristocrats dancing under a mostly leafless tree on the banks of a river—but the other two were mysteries.

I told Lisa what I'd been thinking.

"You're right," she said, "the first one *is* Goya. 'Dancing on the Banks of the Mazanare.'"

She moved to the next one, a very dark room this time, a young boy seated next to an open window, staring at his bruised and bloody feet.

"Bartolome Murillo," she said. "Earlier than Goya. 'Young Beggar,' he called it. The original has been in the

Louvre for over three hundred years." Her voice dropped a bit. "Lots of beggars around at the time, plenty of children like this to choose from. I've always wondered where Murillo got the courage to actually show one of them to the people who paid him to paint." She nodded toward the Goya. "People like that, I mean. The people dancing while the child tries not to starve."

I stepped to the last picture in the trio. Larger than the other two, almost three feet across, and abstract as hell. Large black letter A, along with a short algebraic equation and some formless scribbles, surrounded by a rough brown border against a plain background of pale violet. Definitely not seventeenth century, or the next one either. I looked at Lisa.

"This one finishes the story," she said. "Twentieth century. Antoni Tapies. It's called 'Lettre à 1976.'"

"Dare I ask what it means?" I waved my hand toward all three of the prints. "You say there's a story here."

"For my father there was. For me, too, although I didn't live it like he did." She shook her head, said something in Spanish.

I looked at her. "Sorry, I'm afraid I don't—"

"Always the rich, always the poor. *Siempre los ricos, siempre los pobres.*"

"What about this one? What's the big A mean?"

"A fresh start, a new beginning."

She reached for my arm. "Come on. Let's freshen our drinks."

To get to the kitchen we went through the dining room. The table had to be eight feet long, dark and massive, the chairs as well. On the wall behind the table hung a framed tapestry, a hunting scene in the Middle Ages. The room reminded me of a refectory in a Castilian monastery. I could almost see the monks gathered to dine, almost hear their mumbled prayers before the meal.

The only thing that didn't jibe was the setting Lisa had laid for us. Crystal wine goblets, heavy silver utensils, oversized plates rimmed in gold leaf. Silver candleholders, green tapers already lit. No Spanish monk, I'd have been willing to bet, had ever seen such luxury. The abbot, maybe, but none of the working stiffs.

"Wow" was the only thing I could think to say.

She laughed, her eyes somehow even more magical in the candlelight. She'd dressed to match the decor, I realized. A white blouse buttoned to the neck, frilly, relieved by a topaz brooch hanging close to her throat. Dark-blue skirt, tight around her hips, then flaring away in pleats to fall an inch above her black boots. Formal and casual, all at the same time. Her thick dark hair brushed her shoulders, and the effect stunned me into silence. We stood that way for an awkward moment before she spoke.

"Let's go back to the living room, Puller. I'll bring some munchies. We can sit for a while, enjoy our drinks before cooking."

In the living room—after she'd fetched a silver platter covered with tapas—we sat across from each other in matching upholstered chairs, dark chairs with swirls of red, green and yellow in a sort of Oriental pattern.

"Close," she told me when I said as much, "but it's Moorish. Almost the same thing, when you think about it."

"I'm confused," I said after dispatching two of the tapas, baked dough wrapped around some kind of spicy meat. "You speak Spanish with what sounds like native fluency, but your English doesn't have a trace of accent, and your last name is nowhere near Hispanic."

She laughed, took a sip of her martini and set the glass on the coffee table between us. "You haven't read my personnel file, have you?"

"Not closely enough, obviously, but I was seriously thinking about looking at it again before coming over here tonight."

"Looking for . . ."

"An advantage, of course, although I wouldn't say that to anyone but another FBI agent. An edge. Something to know about you that you wouldn't know I knew."

"Am I as threatening as all that?"

"I don't know yet. I guess what I really want to ask is who *are* you? I know the basics, but the way you handle yourself, the way you respond to me as your supervisor . . . Nothing about you makes sense for an FBI agent less than a year out of Quantico."

"Wonder Woman, that what you're saying? By day a mild-mannered new agent, by night . . ." She laughed. "You can fill in the blank tomorrow morning."

I stared at her, not sure I'd heard her correctly. She leaned forward, stretched her arm across the table to touch mine.

"Okay, Puller, I'll behave." She stood suddenly. "Give me your glass. If we're going to start telling the truth, we'd better have another drink."

I handed her my glass, she took both of them away. I could hear her in the kitchen. Refrigerator opening and closing, clink of ice, her voice humming a ballad that sounded familiar. I thought about what she'd said, about telling the truth. I shook my head. Not a bad idea, one day, but probably not tonight.

Then she was back, sitting in her chair, one leg crossed over the other.

"I'll go first," she said. "My father's name before he came from Spain—before the Spanish Civil War made being an outspoken intellectual a very dangerous thing to be—was Luis Saenz, but when he got to El Paso he found himself treated as just another Mexican, even though he had light skin and blue eyes. His first impulse was to leave, to leave Texas altogether, but his cousin lived in El Paso and his cousin was the only person in the United States he knew. So he worked his tail off to learn English without an accent, and became Lewis Sands. He'd been a certified public accountant in Barcelona, a respected professional, but until he became fluent enough in English he had to work as a bookkeeper." She smiled. "He married an Anglo, I wasn't born until he was sixty. After he'd become successful enough to fill our home with the things he'd given up by changing his name. The things that were all around him the day he died."

"And your mother?"

"Mom's much younger. Dad might have given up some Spanish things, but he never gave up their ways. He married a woman twenty-five years younger, and I never heard her complain about it."

"UTEP first. I do remember that from your file. Then law school, and the D.A.'s office back in El Paso."

"I moved up to Austin for law school, but I really loved El Paso, and my father was getting pretty old by the time I got out into the real world. The district attorney in El Paso was hiring, so I went back and became a prosecutor."

"Must have been a tough job to leave. Prosecutors and judges run the world you and I live in. Why switch to our level?"

"The boredom. As the new kid, all I got were misdemeanors, by the truckload. A pipeline filled with petty criminals from both sides of the border. I felt more like a garbage collector than a prosecuting attorney. A monkey could have done my job. One day I had a real case for a change, got involved with a couple of FBI agents, realized I wanted to be them instead of me."

"Happened that way for me, too, except I was a C.P.A. sick to death of sitting behind a desk and waiting for the clock to get to five." I shook my head. "Now look at me. Sitting behind a desk all day. I'm not watching the same clock, but other than that, it's pretty much the same."

"You call the last few days sitting behind a desk?"

"Of course not, but I don't get enough weeks like this one, out on the street where I belong. Makes it all the harder to go back to the tedium."

"So why were you out among the rabble this time? You could have assigned somebody else to go to Brookston with me. You didn't have to work with me yourself."

I glanced into those eyes. Was she having fun with me? The vodka was running higher in my brain now, and I almost slipped up and told her the truth.

"I did have to work with you," I told her instead. "Supreme Court nominee, really bad downside potential for the supervisor. No way I sit back and let somebody else determine my fate."

"A control freak. Do you keep such tight rein on everything, or is it just SPIN cases?"

"Part of the job, I guess. Hard to survive if you let go of the wheel for long." Boy, was it ever, but this wasn't the night to get into that. I glanced toward the kitchen. "I'm starving. Why don't we take a crack at those groceries?"

It had started to rain again as Lisa mixed a couple of salads and warmed the French bread I'd brought with the groceries. I laid the filets on the preheated broiling grill, and the kitchen began to fill with good smells. I opened a bottle of Pepper Lane cabernet. Ten minutes later we were ready to sit down.

Back in the dining room, the candles were an inch lower, but the light was just as mellow. Lisa disappeared for a moment, and when she came back there was music playing. Ella Fitzgerald and Louis Armstrong. We sat across the big Spanish table, nothing between us to block our view of each other. We sipped cabernet, listened to Ella and Louis. I lifted my glass.

"*Amor y pesetas,*" I said, repeating a Spanish toast I'd memorized in the days when it was important to be California cool.

"*Y tiempo para gustarlos,*" she responded. The language sounded so much better coming out of that beautiful mouth.

We ate in a comfortable mixture of small talk and silence, the wine gone far too quickly. I thought about the second bottle I'd brought, mentioned it to Lisa, but she shook her head, and it was a good thing. A couple of martinis, two and a half glasses of cabernet, and I was brimming with good fellowship and so—I was certain—was she. We continued to chat as we finished the steaks, and by the time we'd worked through the cherry pie we were pretty good friends. Afterward I rose and picked up my plate, came around the table and reached for hers, but she took the one I was holding and set it aside.

"Forget about the dishes," she said. "Where I come from, the night's for dancing."

She came around the table, grabbed my hand, and led me into the living room.

"Take off your shoes, for God's sake," she ordered. "You're too damned tall as it is."

I did so as Ella and Louis came to the end of their set. We waited for the next CD to start. Linda Ronstadt, I heard a moment later, with the Nelson Riddle orchestra, Linda's voice so pure it gave me shivers.

Lisa slid into my arms and we began to dance. I looked at her, at her hair and her eyes, at the look in those eyes as she put her head on my shoulder. Relax, Puller, I told myself. She works for you. This isn't what you came here for. There isn't a single good reason for holding her like this and smelling her hair. No possible good can come of it.

And other lies.

I went on like that through the first song, but the second one was even tougher.

Lover man, oh, where can you be?

The words wobbled around in my brain, then finished me off.

I lifted my arm from Lisa's back and used my hand to pull her face up to mine. I kissed her mouth and she kissed mine. Our arms tightened around each other, our steps no longer keeping time with the music. Suddenly we were leaving the living room, pausing just long enough for her to pick up the second wine bottle and the corkscrew, me the glasses. Moments later we were in her bedroom. She left the door open after we got there. What little light there was from the hallway was more than enough as she led me to the bed.

"Sit," she whispered.

I sat on the edge of the bed.

She put the wine bottle on the nightstand, grabbed the glasses from me and did the same thing with them, then stood in front of me and unsnapped the fastener on her right hip. Her long skirt slipped to the floor. I looked at her legs, all the way up to her white bikini panties, then down again. I could hear my breathing grow ragged over the music. She reached behind her back and unbuttoned her blouse, shrugged her shoulders until it fell away. Her bra was so white it made the tops of her breasts look tan, even in the middle of winter.

"Now you," she said, her voice husky as she pulled me to my feet.

She undid my belt, unzipped me, and eased my pants down. I stepped out of them and reached for my polo shirt, pulled it off and flipped it into the corner. I reached for my shorts, but she whispered, "Not yet."

We lay together on the bed for an instant before I kissed her again, then slid down her neck and kissed the tops of her breasts. I brought my hand up and undid the fastener on her bra. It fell aside. Her breasts were perfectly round, small enough never to sag, big enough to fall in love with. I kissed each of them, all around the nipples, then the nipples themselves. She arched her back, her breathing suddenly faster. I slid down her belly, tugged at her panties with my teeth. She reached down and pulled them aside. I could smell her, and in the next moment I was tasting her. Then I was rising to my knees and pulling her panties down. She lifted her legs and I slid them past her feet.

"You want to make love to me?" she whispered.

I'm not sure I said anything intelligible as I tugged my shorts off and did just that.

We moved together, faster and faster. She came first, a warmth spreading through her body that I couldn't get enough of, then a single long gasp, a shudder, and a sudden tightening of her arms around my neck. I groaned in the warmth of her breasts, the smell of her body, the taste of her skin.

Afterward we lay together, our legs entwined, our breathing gradually coming back to normal.

"Yum," she said.

"Indeed," I said.

And that was about it for conversation.

After a while, she looked down my body and smiled. "Goodness, Puller. Is that a dagger I see before me?"

I looked down, and damned if it wasn't.

She slid down my body this time, used her mouth to turn the dagger into a broadsword—a bigger dagger, anyway—and we did it all again.

This time we did talk afterward.

She propped pillows against the headboard and we sat together. In an old movie we'd have been smoking cigarettes, but we did just fine with the bottle of wine we'd brought along. I poured cabernet into her glass, then in mine.

"Do I still have to call you boss?" she asked me.

"When have you ever?"

"I was pretty bold. You could charge me with sexual harassment, I suppose."

"You could plead insanity."

She laughed, kissed my neck. "You think I didn't intend to get you in here? That you just walked in and swept poor little me off my feet?"

"Well, I better read you your rights, then."

"I demand an attorney."

"I'm an accountant."

"Close enough."

I rose on one elbow. "You have the right to think about me when I'm gone. You have the right to call me up and make me come over here and do this again. You have the right to come to my house and do the same thing. If you cannot afford to get to my house, I will provide transportation both ways." I leaned closer. "Do you understand your rights?"

"I do."

"Do you waive your rights?"

She reached down and gripped my diminishing manhood. "I've got your waiver right here, counselor." She gave it a little tug to show she meant business. "And I'm not afraid to use it."

"Not the briar patch," I said. "Please don't throw me in the briar patch."

We laughed hard enough to make us careful with the red wine on the pale yellow sheets.

Then we tried again, but it was too late and we were too drunk. We gave it our best shot but fell asleep in the attempt.

The next morning, Saturday morning, we were not quite as giddy.

I joined her at the kitchen table for coffee. Her eyes were a little slower this morning, too. She'd been thinking, I discovered when she began to talk.

"Dr. Annie," she said. "Your veterinarian. Am I getting myself into a problem here?"

"We lived together for a while. Up to about six months ago."

"I'd have to object to that answer as nonresponsive. What happened? That's what I really want to know."

"I'm not sure, Lisa. We just used it up, I guess, whatever we had."

Lisa shook her head. "You, maybe. Maybe *you* used it up, but I saw her the other day when I showed up." She reached out and touched my hand. "By the way, I'm glad I did show up. The two of you weren't wearing much clothing. I didn't like the looks of where that was going."

"What about you?" I asked. "You can't possibly be unattached."

"Not unattached, just divorced." She took a sip of coffee. "Carl's a Texan. The very idea of moving to Washington sent him scurrying."

"Kids?"

"I had a feeling we shouldn't have any, not until we'd been married a few years. One of my better decisions, as it turned out."

"And what about this decision? What about last night?"

She smiled. "Not something you'd find in the new agents' guidelines, but I can live with it if you can." She picked up her cup, drank from it. "Can you?"

I thought about what Annie had told me about my spinning plate, about leaving the security of the post in the center. Right now I could feel my momentum sliding toward the outside of that plate, and it was all I could do to keep from throwing myself to the very edge. Annie was right, of course. For me, life had reduced itself to two stages: on the edge, or waiting to get back to the edge. I looked at Lisa. It was going to be fun out there on the edge with her.

"I don't think the office will be an issue, if that's what you're asking. You won't be on my squad much longer, not after the work you did on Brenda Thompson. You're on the fast track for the Hoover Building, lady. It won't be long before I'm reporting to you. Before you'll be the boss sleeping with her tootsie."

She grinned. "But I'll never forget the backs I climbed over to get there, will I?" She touched my hand again, squeezed my fingers. "Trust me, I'll never forget the little people."

"Little person by day, maybe, but by night . . ."

She threw her napkin at me. "That's it. Time for you to go. I know it's Saturday and I don't have Brenda Thompson anymore, but I'm still an FBI agent with a boatload of cases. All the Thompson case did is put me further behind. Weekend or not, I've got to get to getting."

The old joke is true, the one about the guy fucking himself to death and the mortician needing an hour to get the smile off his face. I sat behind the wheel of my Caprice, leering at the drivers around me as I cruised on down to the office, feeling for the first time in a while like a whole man again.

I was still grinning when I turned on the Chevy's AM radio, punched the button for WDC—"All Talk, All the Time"— and listened to the usual morning roundup of murder and mayhem that passed for news. Still grinning when the announcer turned to news from the White House. Stopped grinning when I heard the name Brenda Thompson. Forgot all about grinning when I heard what he said about her.

SEVENTEEN

My cell phone rang before the announcer got all the way to the end of the story. Lisa's voice was a perfect reflection of my own incredulity.

"Did you *hear* that, Puller? Did you hear them say we *cleared* her?" Her voice rose even higher. "What the hell are they *talking* about?"

"Got to be a mistake. Finnerty is always in his office on Saturday. I'll go see him as soon as I get there, find out what happened."

"Not without me, you're not. My name's on that report. I'm the one who'll take the hit when Thompson's abortion comes out, and you know it will."

I didn't even have to think about it to know how right she was, on both counts. Only ten months into her probationary first year, she could be fired for almost anything, much less a major screwup on a Supreme Court nominee. With her name on the Thompson case ticket, she'd be out on the street in minutes when the judge's abortion went public. And it didn't help much to know that I'd be the one standing out there right next to her.

But that didn't mean she was going in to see the ADIC with me.

Kevin Finnerty did not like women, especially women

FBI agents. His loyalty to Hoover's decades-long refusal to admit women was legendary; his disappointment when the Department of Justice finally mandated their inclusion continued to this day. I'd been surprised when he allowed Lisa to take the Thompson case in the first place, I wasn't about to make it even worse for her by confronting the ADIC in her presence. Finnerty wouldn't allow it, would use it to sidetrack her career.

"You can't come," I told her. "Don't bother arguing. I'll get back to you in an hour."

"Damn it, Puller . . ." She stopped, then sighed. "Okay, okay. I'm leaving the house in a few minutes. You can find me in the squad room."

The meeting with Finnerty was a short one.

"I can't imagine what you think you're doing," he told me when I asked the question. "I told you yesterday how this works, and I don't intend to go through it again."

"It's my job," I said. "It's up to me to—"

"It's not up to you to do anything, Monk. I made you a supervisor, but that doesn't mean what you apparently think it does. Your job is to handle the agents, to make sure they're doing their jobs, to keep them from screwing up and embarrassing the bureau. That's all I want out of you. The rest of it is up to those of us who run the place."

I stared at him, the back of my neck burning, my breathing turning shallow and rapid. I had the ridiculous urge to leap across his desk and punch him in the nose, but I settled for more words instead.

"All I'm saying is that this is wrong . . . that the questions about Thompson, about Brookston and the judge's roommate's murder can't possibly be overlooked." Suddenly I realized I should never have let it get this far without telling him the rest. "There's something else, boss. A diary. Jabalah Abahd kept a diary. And there's a phony FBI agent . . . a monster. Calls himself Robert—"

He picked up a pile of papers, hurled it to the desktop.

"Enough!" he roared. "Don't say another word!" His rage was so sudden, so complete, I could only stare. "If you'd found something provable you might be right! *But you didn't!*" He took a breath and I could see him fighting for control. "What you have is nothing but circumstantial guess-work. Even you can't be stupid enough to think the White House cares about your speculations."

I was on very thin ice now, but I'd stopped caring.

"That's what I'm trying to *tell* you! We *can't* stop now! If nothing else, we've got to go back to the preacher. The man was lying. All I have to do is lean on him." I lowered my voice. "And that will lead us to the killer . . . the phony agent . . . the real story here."

"God damn it, Monk!" He reached for the paperwork, shouting again. "It's a very simple concept! I tell you when to start, I tell you when to stop! What part of that don't you understand?"

"That's ridiculous!" I yelled. "We're not children you can order around like—"

His fist crashed down on the desktop, the sound like a rifle shot.

"Shut up!" he roared. "If you want to keep your job, don't say another word!" He rose to his feet. "Get out! Get out of my office and do what I pay you to do!"

I jumped to my feet as well, felt myself starting toward him before I realized what I was doing. I turned instead, strode to the door, yanked it open, and left him alone.

On the other side, Barbara Perkins was staring at me with wide eyes.

I advanced on her, ready to open my mouth and yell at someone who wouldn't be able to throw me out, but I didn't.

"That man is a lunatic!" I told her instead, but I didn't wait for her to respond before I was out the door and on my way down to Lisa.

"It's *over*?" she said after I'd summarized the disaster upstairs. "We just *stop*?"

I had to get my breathing under control before I could make myself repeat what Finnerty had told me about that.

"If we want to work here," I told her, "we stop. I don't know about you, but I need this job."

"I do, too. We all do, for Christ's sake! You're telling me we just forget about it?" Her voice rose. "If we'd known this was going to happen, we could have stayed in Brookston until we broke the preacher and came up with the paperwork. I never would have come back here without it."

She stared over my head for a moment, breathing even harder than I was now, then swung her eyes back down and glared at me.

"Damn it, Puller, we can't just quit! At least let me go back and talk to Reverend Johnson. Let me go down there and beat it out of him."

I couldn't miss the rage flashing in her dark eyes. It was lucky I was a cardplayer. Now I had to say words that made my stomach burn just to think about saying them, but my face would reflect none of the disgust that went along with them. She'd put into her own words my feelings exactly. If there was ever a time to go to Quantico rules, it was now, but Lisa couldn't be allowed to know that. Her future was bright with promise. To get where she wanted to go, she had to learn to accept these kinds of decisions, this kind of failure. Like it or not, fair or not, the Thompson case was over. She had to let it go. We both had to let it go.

But before I could even begin, she was on her feet and out the door. I waited for her to turn back to me, to tell me she understood, to tell me I wasn't the bureaucratic prick I sounded like. She didn't, of course—I'd been a fool to expect her to—and a moment later she was gone.

I went where I always did when the rage refused to go away.

Finnerty's words burned in my head all the way to Pinewood Manor, and I knew why. I'd paid a lot of money to the best shrink in town to tell me. I could almost hear Dr. Suskind's voice as I drove out to Chancellorsville. It's not the Thompson case, he would be telling me, it's not that at all. You knew what Finnerty was going to say before you went in there, don't pretend you didn't. You also knew he'd treat you like a child, and you're behaving like one now. To act like you're outraged at the way he treats you is a lot worse than childish . . . it's just plain stupid.

Well, fuck you! I wanted to tell my old shrink as I pulled into the parking lot of the nursing home. Fuck you and the Freud you rode in on. I didn't need his help to know what I had to do to keep myself from getting even more destructive.

My father lay asleep when I got to his room. The overhead fixture was off as I slipped through the door, but there was plenty of light coming through the lone window for what I was there to do. I strode to the computer I'd installed on the desk against the far wall, the desk where Pastor Monk spent his days polishing the sermon no one would hear.

The NFL divisional playoffs had started today, but it was too late to get down on the Saturday games, so I concentrated on tomorrow's instead. One game in particular, the San Diego Chargers and the Seattle Seahawks. The Seahawks were six-point favorites in Las Vegas, but the Chargers had been my team since childhood, and there was no doubt in my mind they'd cover the spread.

I hit the power switch and the low-end Compaq whirred to life. It hadn't cost a lot, the entire setup, but it was only meant to do one thing, get me connected to the Internet, to Sportsman.com, the site I used almost exclusively for betting on sports. They would ask for money, of course, and my latest brand-new Visa card still had a few thousand dollars I hadn't yet lost.

I glanced at my father in the bed. Even asleep his face was accusatory. Well, fuck you, too, I muttered, and your own silly rules. I grabbed the Compaq mouse and clicked my way to the link for tomorrow's Chargers game, then threw a thousand dollars at the game.

I logged off, shut down the computer, and left the room.

Halfway back to my Caprice, I realized it hadn't worked.

I'd done everything I always did when it was important to prove I hadn't turned into a nutless wonder. More than I always did. A thousand dollars was the biggest single bet I'd ever made on a football game, but the feelings of self-loathing were still there. For the first time it was going to take something more than the sports book to get rid of them.

I thought about what it *was* going to take. About Quantico rules.

About what I had to do to make the ache go away.

A mile from the Baptist Church in Brookston, I called Sheriff Brodsky to let him know I was back at work in his town.

"They put you back on the case?" he wanted to know.

"Back on the case? I'm still on the case if that's what you mean."

"So it was you who sent the other man?"

"I don't know what you're talking about. What man?"

"Bennett. Agent Bennett."

The hair on my arms started to buzz.

"Big guy," Brodsky continued. "Broken nose. He was just in here. Left about twenty minutes ago."

"What did he want?"

"Same thing you and Agent Sands asked me about. Brenda Thompson. And the preacher, too. Reverend Johnson."

My body stiffened. I mashed the accelerator to the floor. The car leapt toward Brookston.

"Where did he go, Sheriff? Where was he going when he left your place?"

"To the preacher, to the church out on Falls Road. I gave him directions."

My hands tightened on the steering wheel, the knuckles white. I felt my face turn to ice.

"The church, Brodsky . . . get to the church. *Now!* And bring a shoulder weapon!"

"Damn it, Monk, what the hell's going on? What are you—?"

"Do it!" I hollered. "*Just for Christ's sake do it!*"

I cut him off, punched numbers for Lisa. She'd still be at her desk, she didn't do anything but work. But she wasn't there. I let her phone ring a dozen times, then called the switchboard.

"Puller," Gerry Ann Walsh said. "I was just talking about you."

"I'm looking for Lisa Sands. She's in the office, but I can't reach her at her desk. Can you page her for me?"

"That's what I'm telling you. She left three hours ago. Told me you might call."

"Where did she go?"

"Hold on a second, let me check her three-card." A pause, then, "Brookston, Puller. A church down there. She told me you'd know what it means."

I hurled the phone aside, floored the gas, skidded around the next corner and up Falls Road. Seconds later I slid to a stop in front of the church. I saw Lisa's Pontiac as I threw open the door and raced up the walk. The church door was ajar as I smashed through it and felt my heart stop.

Their bodies lay a dozen feet inside the church.

Squarely in the center of the aisle, Lisa and Reverend Johnson shared the same sticky pool of thick, dark blood.

EIGHTEEN

MY VISION TURNED GRAY. I SLUMPED IN THE DOORWAY, THEN fought an attack of lightheadedness and nausea that left me gasping. I turned away, unable to look, then back at the bodies, wanting them to disappear, hoping they would no longer be there, that I'd somehow . . .

I raced to Lisa's side, then stopped, jerked the Smith-10 from my belt holster. The son of a bitch might still be here! Then I looked at the bodies again and realized he wouldn't be here anymore. Blood changes very quickly in the open air. It was already beginning to mat. Bennett was long gone. I holstered my weapon and bent to Lisa, forced myself to examine her corpse.

Her body lay crumpled against the preacher, her chrome-plated Sig Sauer in the fingers of her right hand. Reverend Johnson's face was gone, most of the back of his head gone. Bone and blood stretched away up the aisle.

I fell to my knees next to my partner. The front of her suit jacket was frazzled by the shots that had ripped through her body. Her head was intact, but her hair was matted with blood. I rocked back and forth on my knees.

"Oh, Christ, Lisa. Oh, Christ . . . oh, Christ . . . oh, Christ."

I realized what had happened.

She and the preacher had heard their killer at the door, had come to see who it was. He'd burst through and shot them. Lisa had drawn her weapon but she'd been too late. She'd been hit squarely in the chest, had gone down immediately. The taller preacher had taken a round directly in the face.

Ears singing with shock—unable to accept her death—I willed myself to go through the motions of checking for a pulse. Felt nothing at her neck, or her right wrist. I pulled at her clothing to get at her chest, but my fingers struck something hard.

My head seemed to explode as I realized what it was.

I ripped her clothing away, tugged the armored vest aside.

I crouched over her, yanked at her bra, jerked at the clasp in front until it came loose and the cups fell away. Her chest was already purple from one side of her rib cage to the other, but I could see no blood on her breasts, no penetrating wounds anywhere on her torso.

The Kevlar had stopped them.

The bullets were still in the vest, but they hadn't reached her body.

They were imbedded so deeply in the flexible armor I couldn't have pried them out with a crowbar, but they hadn't even punctured her skin.

I laid my head on her chest. Now—my ear directly over her heart—I could feel a heartbeat, thready but regular.

Yes! Oh, dear God, yes!

I raised my head and began to shout.

"*She's alive!*" I screamed at the top of my lungs. "*You didn't get her, you son of a bitch! She's still alive!*"

I grabbed my cell phone to call for an ambulance, but before I could dial 911 Sheriff Brodsky burst through the door. The shotgun he carried looked small in his meaty hands.

"She's *alive!*" I yelled. "Get the paramedics!"

He grabbed for the radio on his belt, barked commands into it, then sprinted back out the door. Had to have some emergency medical equipment in the patrol car.

I tilted Lisa's chin up, parted her lips, and started mouth-to-mouth. Three breaths . . . gentle chest massage . . . three more breaths, more chest massage.

As I pushed gingerly against her damaged ribs, I examined Lisa's head and felt a heaviness in my throat. Her hair was soaked with blood. So much of it she had to have been hit in the head as well. Probably when the killer turned his weapon on the preacher.

I used one hand to rub the worst of it away, not sure I wanted to see the damage underneath. As I rubbed, fresh blood welled from an area above her right ear. But the wound wasn't deep, I discovered. Like all scalp lacerations, even minor ones, it had bled like hell, but it hadn't killed her.

I looked back at the door, listening for sirens, for an ambulance to give Lisa what I couldn't. I stared at her bloody face, shouted at Brodsky again. My throat tightened, my hands clenching and unclenching. *C'mon, people!* I wanted to scream out, but there was a better way to use the time.

I bent to Lisa again, held her head in my hands, and spoke quietly to her. There was no sign she could hear me, but I kept talking anyway. As much for me as for her, I realized, but it didn't matter.

I thought about the man who'd done this to her. *Bennett. Robert Bennett.* A rage strong enough to blur my vision rose through my body and into my brain. I didn't know who he was, or *why* he was, but when I found out—when I did know—I would finish him.

I would hurt him first, but when I was through, he would be dead.

At the Brookston Community Hospital, Sheriff Brodsky was waiting when I climbed down out of the ambulance, as the paramedics lowered the gurney with Lisa on it and raced away through the double doors to the emergency room.

"Agent Monk," he began, but I pushed him aside.

"Not yet," I shouted as I ran after Lisa.

I could hear his feet pounding as he came after me.

But I needn't have hurried. In the emergency room they wouldn't let me stay with her while they worked.

It would be better for everyone, the ER nurse told me, if I returned to the waiting room. She went back inside and pulled a white drape around the team as they struggled to get Lisa stabilized. I turned around and looked for Brodsky, who signaled for me to follow. He led me through a short corridor into an empty waiting room. Linoleum floor, cheap chairs and couches, fluorescent fixtures overhead. We stood facing each other just inside the door. The harsh light rebounding from the pale yellow walls gave the sheriff's heavy face a ghastly hue that only added to the horror of the last hour.

"I'm sorry about your partner," he said, "but you do realize this changes things between you and me."

I nodded, but he continued before I could speak.

"This isn't Washington," he said. "We do not have murders here. We do not have shootings in churches. We don't have FBI agents gunned down, and I have no more time for games." He pointed to a pair of upholstered armchairs facing each other in the far corner. "We're going to sit down. We're going to start over. You're going to tell me the truth. What you're really doing in Brookston." He paused. "And what it has to do with Judge Thompson."

I stared at him. It was pretty clear he wasn't going to be stonewalled, not when a murder had been committed in his town, one of his citizens blown away in a church, of all places, but still I had to be careful. At least for a while longer. In the end—just like with Lieutenant Barra and the Cheverly P.D.—I'd have to come clean, but for now it was going to be business as usual.

So I told him nothing.

Nothing but the bureau mantra about national security and his lack of need to know.

His eyes narrowed. "Who's Robert Bennett? And where was he when you got to the church?"

I just shook my head.

"I saw his credentials, Monk. I've seen enough of you people to know he's an FBI agent. Unless you tell me differently, I also know he killed Reverend Johnson, tried to kill your partner."

I said nothing.

He rose to his feet. "I'll be at the district attorney's office, in case you change your mind. And at the Hoover Building with a warrant for obstruction of justice as soon as I can get there." He paused. "Unless we go up to D.C. together. Unless we can work this thing together."

"There's no *we*, Sheriff. Assault on an FBI agent is federal. My bosses will never let you get involved. You know the drill."

He slid forward in his chair, his voice hardening.

"Look, Monk, I knew the drill before you were an FBI agent. I knew the drill when I was working homicide in L.A., getting fucked over by you people out there." His tone got even sharper. "I could write you a book about the drill!" He paused and took a breath, trying to regain his poise, but it didn't work. "And I know something else," he said. "Reverend Johnson doesn't have *anything* to do with the federal government. He's one of *my* people. An FBI agent killing him *gets* me involved, has *already* got me involved. And nothing you say makes a goddamned differ—"

"It isn't my decision, Brodsky. From here on, this is way out of my hands. I can't do anything on my . . ."

My voice died as I saw a doctor come through the door.

I rushed to him. Bloodstains matted his green scrubs. His mask hung around his neck. He peeled his gloves off and held them in one hand.

"Your partner's stable," he said, and I began to breathe again. "The body armor saved her life, but her ribs are bruised, and the gunshot wound above her ear is more serious than it looks. Had to be a .45 caliber or even bigger. The shock of even a glancing blow has caused some swelling inside her brain."

My throat tightened. Brain damage. Christ. I felt myself shrink from the words. I couldn't even imagine Lisa like that. "Is she conscious? Can I see her?"

He shook his head. "We gave her something for the pain. She's sleeping."

"Can she be moved? Please don't misunderstand me, but wouldn't she be better off in a trauma center?"

"I'm not offended. We don't see these kinds of things here. It would be better for her in Washington."

"The swelling in her brain. Should we wait till it goes down?"

"In a perfect world we would, but you've got to weigh the risks either way. Trauma to the brain can turn very dangerous very fast. The helicopter they send will have better equipment than we do to deal with a sudden emergency. And they'll be computer-linked with ER docs on the other end who see hundreds of gunshot cases." He rubbed his hand across his eyes, pulled his surgical mask up over the top of his head. "If she were my partner, I'd get her up to D.C. as soon as possible."

The hospital's helipad was crude by big-city standards, nothing more than an addition to the parking lot out back. I was standing with the sheriff in the rain at the edge of the tarmac, my eyes shut against the blast of wind-driven rainwater when the medevac chopper landed.

The first two people out of the aircraft were clad in white. They ran toward us in a crouch as the massive blades continued to whip the surroundings into a frenzy. I pointed toward the emergency room doors as they jogged past. The next two were FBI agents, had to be. Blue suits, red ties. I didn't know them, couldn't remember ever having seen them. They came forward in the same crouch, motioned in the shriek of noise for us to follow them back into the hospital.

Inside the ER waiting room, the taller of the two showed me his credentials. "Tom Jeffreys," he said. "Office of professional responsibility. I'm assuming you're SA Monk."

I nodded, introduced Sheriff Brodsky. Nobody shook hands.

"We need to speak with SA Monk in private, Sheriff," Jeffreys said. "I'm sure you understand."

Brodsky glared at them, then at me. He looked like a man

who wanted to hit someone, but a moment later he turned and walked away. I could hear the pounding of his footsteps down the hallway.

"OPR?" I said to Jeffreys after the sheriff was gone. "So Robert Bennett really is an FBI agent."

Jeffreys said nothing. Doing to me exactly what I'd just done to Brodsky. Clearly I was in the middle of something far above my need to know.

"I'm not here to answer questions, Monk," he said. "What I really want to know is what you're doing here."

Which was exactly what Kevin Finnerty demanded to know when I got back to him an hour and a half later at WMFO. It was pushing nine o'clock on Saturday night when I sat down on the couch in front of his big desk. I didn't bother watching for his tell this time. He was already manhandling his paperwork before he lit into me.

"I warned you," he said, "you *and* Agent Sands. I told you the Thompson case was over. I made it clear that her report was the last thing she was expected to do. She ignored me. You supervise her. I can only assume you authorized her to continue."

"I *ordered* her to continue," I lied. "I know what you said, but I know how the system works, too. I couldn't close Thompson without reinterviewing the preacher. I understand your anger, but don't take it out on Special Agent Sands. She was doing nothing more than following my orders."

"Am I supposed to be impressed? Am I supposed to admire your attempt to cover for one of your people?" He sat forward in his chair. "If I had my way—if Mr. Hoover were still alive—I would fire you on the spot. But I can't . . . not yet anyway. Sands is a different story, she's still in her first year. The moment she gets out of the hospital, she's history. In the meantime, both of you are suspended. Neither of you will set foot in this or any other FBI office until I say so."

"What about Robert Bennett?" I said, with nothing much to lose at this point. "Who the hell—?"

"Damn it, Monk, there is no Robert Bennett. No FBI agent Robert Bennett, at any rate. I have no idea what happened down there in Brookston. My OPR people will sort it out and get back to me. Whatever they find, it's no longer your concern." He stared at me. "Do you understand what I'm telling you? That I will not tell you again?"

I rose without a word and left the room.

NINETEEN

THIRTY MINUTES LATER I WAS AT QUEEN OF ANGELS HOSPI-
tal near L'Enfant Plaza, the D.C. trauma center to which
they'd airlifted Lisa. They'd transferred her to ICU, I was
told, and I couldn't get in to see her. I wasn't about to leave,
however, so at half an hour before midnight I settled into a
chair in the ICU waiting area and began to fret.

Just before three o'clock Sunday morning, a nurse came
to find me. I bolted from the chair and she answered my
question before I could even ask it. "Ms. Sands is stable,"
she said. "She's conscious, but we're keeping her in IC until
the swelling in her brain is completely reduced. You can
have a few minutes with her, but I'm afraid that's all."

She led the way. I had a hard time slowing down enough
to keep from walking right up her back. Along the way I
glanced at some of the other patients, old people mostly, really old people. Desiccated faces attached to withered bodies, empty eyes staring at nothing as they waited for the end.
The sight did nothing to make me feel better.

Lisa was in room 24, a large room divided into separate
enclosures by light-blue draperies on metal runners around
each bed. Her eyes were closed. I glanced around the cubi-
cle. She was hooked up like an astronaut to a six-foot stack

of electronic monitors, every function of her body under continuous observation.

The nurse left me alone with her.

Lisa was sleeping, I decided, although under the garish fluorescent lighting her skin had a greenish pallor that startled me. I touched her arm. Her eyes opened, then widened.

"Puller," she said, her voice raspy and weak. She held her hand out to me. "I was hoping you'd show up."

I squeezed her fingers, then turned and grabbed the single metal chair shoved against the drapes around her bed. I pulled it up close.

"I don't know what to say, Lisa. I'm so goddamned glad you wore your vest." I looked at the floor, then back at her. "I'm sorry I wasn't there to help you."

"It was the same guy . . . huge . . . smashed nose. The guy who beat you up."

"They're looking for him now. We've got people down in Brookston already."

"What about Finnerty? What's he have to say about all this?" She closed her eyes as she winced from the pain she still had to be feeling despite her meds. "I guess what I'm really asking is am I fired?"

I looked at her, at the bandages covering her head and half her face. She would need to know the truth sooner or later, but not while she was still like this.

"He's pissed off, but it'll pass." I reached out and touched her hand. "After all, you were down in Brookston trying to protect him from another mess like Grady." I forced a smile. "He might even give you a bonus."

I turned away to avoid the look of relief in her eyes.

I spent the rest of the night in a chair by the foot of her bed, but left her sleeping in the morning to try to get my own head back in some kind of order.

Lost in thoughts as malignant as cancer, I almost missed the Quantico exit off I-95, had to swerve across three lanes to make it. I drove much too fast through the piney woods and red Virginia clay, tires squealing against the two-lane road that took me the mile or so to the FBI academy, past a dozen brick buildings to the immense gymnasium out back. Inside, I hurried to the locker room, to one of many head-high stacks of wire baskets, unlocked the one assigned to me, changed my clothes for shorts, sweatshirt, and high-top Nike Air Jordans, then headed for the weight room.

Row after row of Lifecycles stretched out before me, step-machines, rowing machines, and treadmills. Tons of free weights and Nautilus equipment.

I grabbed a pair of twenty-five-pound dumbbells, sat on the end of a nearby bench and did curls—three sets of ten—first with my weaker left arm, then my right, until I was gasping for breath, until the floor was soggy with sweat. Then bench presses. Ten quick reps with a hundred and fifty pounds, then five at two-hundred, and a warmdown with ten more at an even hundred.

It began to work. The pain in my gut dissipated. The terrible images of Lisa in the church, in the hospital, began to fade. The questions about Robert Bennett only got worse, however.

He wasn't an FBI agent. I didn't waste a second dismissing the possibility. FBI agents don't exist outside the official rolls. That Bennett was impersonating an agent was another thing altogether. Such a thing happened a lot, the benefits too obvious to enumerate.

But what did the criminal calling himself Bennett hope to gain by what he was doing? What was there about Brenda Thompson's secret abortion that Bennett could turn into personal gain? What could be important enough to him about her secret that he was willing to kill a real FBI agent to keep it hidden?

A familiar voice interrupted.

"Hey, Puller, you gonna play b-ball this morning?"

I glanced toward the doorway, toward the gangly figure of Glen Rogers, like me another Quantico gym rat. I shook my head. Our regular Sunday morning game was going to have to do without me this time.

"Too much to do," I told him. "Gonna run the lines and call it a day."

Glen disappeared. I grabbed a towel and headed for the main gymnasium.

Like everything else at Quantico, it was oversized. In addition to the central basketball court, there were four baskets along each side for the smaller courts that ran across the main court. Retractable bleachers were drawn back against the side walls, making the place look even bigger.

At the far end, Glen Rogers and the rest of the guys were already hard at their four-on-four half-court game. For a moment I thought about changing my mind and joining them, but decided not to. I needed more pain than that, so I ran the lines instead.

I jogged to the main court baseline, opposite the game at the other end, bent at the waist and raced fifteen feet to the near foul line, dug to a stop—shoes squealing against the varnished maple—and sprinted back to the baseline. Without a moment's hesitation to the top of the key and back. Then to the three-point line and back. Finally to midcourt, all the way to the ten-second line and back.

Then again. And again.

Five times altogether.

Finally, chest heaving, my eyes sweat-burned, I stopped, stood with my hands on my knees, my head down. Jesus Christ, I thought, but it had worked even better than the weights. For a few moments at least I'd forgotten all about Thompson and Bennett. My breathing returned to normal as I straightened up and started for the showers, and my second decision about the Brenda Thompson case in as many days.

Eyes closed against the pounding water, hair filled with shampoo, I knew what I had to do. Even more importantly, what I would never be able to convince myself not to do.

And I knew something else as well. That there's a big difference between quitting and stopping. Just because Finnerty had demanded I stop didn't mean I was about to quit. I turned off the water and left the shower room.

I glanced at the clock at the far end of my row of lockers.

Glen Rogers's game would not wind up for an hour. I would have plenty of time to think of a way to attack him.

I started by badgering Glen into holding off his shower until I finished with him, then followed him out of the gymnasium to a squat building next door, another brick building that matched the rest of the campus, but this one without windows and a roof buried under a forest of antennas.

At the front door he pushed a button set into the jamb, stared directly into the video camera mounted above the door. I heard a loud click, Glen twisted the knob and pulled the door open. We went through and headed for his office, down a bare concrete hallway to a room even smaller than mine back at WMFO.

Glen moved to his desk and sat. I took a plain metal chair from the corner and sat across from him. He was hard to see behind three computer-monitors and several other electronic gadgets I didn't even try to identify. His mustache and goatee made him look like central casting's idea of a psychotherapist, and come to think of it we'd played that role with each other more than a handful of times through the years.

"What's going on?" he asked. "Looked like you were trying to kill yourself back there."

"I won't waste your time trying to con you. I need a bird."

Rogers's smile disappeared. I talked faster.

"I've got a problem, Glen. A big problem. Can't solve it any other way."

He stared at me, then got up and went around his desk to the door, closed it carefully, went back and sat down. His volume dropped.

"What the hell are you talking about, a satellite? Where did you get the idea I could *do* something like that, even if I wanted to?"

"You *can* do it. Don't even start up with me about that."

"You're wrong, my friend, but let's say you're not, just for grins. Let's say I have the power to divert a bird from one of a hundred national security matters that use a hundred percent of their allotments. You run a SPIN squad. What kind of case could you possibly have to justify it?"

I could have told him. Maybe I'd still have to, but not yet.

"All I need is a cell phone locate. Don't tell me you aren't set up for that, that you're not doing the same thing all day."

"Not for background checks we aren't."

I glanced back at the closed door, dismissed an urge to get up and lock it. I pulled my chair a shade closer to the desk.

"It's not national security," I said, "not yet at least, but there's no telling what it could turn out to be."

"So what? You still can't walk in here and—"

I held up my hand. "I wouldn't ask if I didn't have to." I stared into his dark eyes. "We go back, Glen, and not just basketball either. Lots of nights and weekends in the same car before you got transferred out here. We saved each others' asses more than once. I owe you, but you owe me, too."

"Damn it, that was different." The grimace on his face suggested it was horseshit to bring that stuff up, to use it on him for extortion. "A whole lot different."

"You owe me," I repeated, ready to say it as many times as it took.

"The old days are gone. What we did on the street has nothing to do with the kind of thing you're asking."

"You owe me."

"This isn't about *us* anymore. This is about the rules, the manual of rules and regulations. The manual specifies who uses these birds and why. I can't just pass out satellite time like tickets to a Redskin's game."

"Fuck the manual. We're talking about Quantico rules."

"Sure we are, but still. I like this job. You're talking about get-your-ass-fired time."

I looked around his bunker. "What's the worst they can do? Make you sit in a little concrete room with no windows?"

Glen Rogers opened his mouth, looked like he wanted to argue some more, then closed it again and shook his head. He glanced toward the closed door, then leaned toward me.

"Tell me what you need, you son of a bitch. Do it quick, then get the hell out of here before someone sees me with you."

TWENTY

BACK AT THE HOSPITAL I WAS RELIEVED TO DISCOVER THAT Lisa had been moved to a nursing floor. I stopped in the doorway of her room, a single room this time, and gave a soft wolf whistle.

"Hey!" I told her. "A little makeup, you clean up pretty well."

"If you say so . . . but I've decided one thing." Her voice was much stronger this afternoon. "I've had all of this place I can stand."

I moved to her, leaned over, and kissed her mouth. She kissed me back, not at all the kiss of an invalid. Her hair was brushed, her eyes lightly made up. I could smell the wildflowers in her hair, taste her lipstick on my mouth.

"No more bandages," I said.

"Light covering on my head wound, but you have to pull my hair aside to see it." She patted her chest. "The bruises are hidden, too. To see them, you'd have to pull aside my—"

"Enough," I told her. "It's all I can do to keep from jumping you right there in your sickbed. Don't make it any harder." I glanced down at the front of my pants. "More difficult, I mean."

"Stop," she said. "I'm feeling better, but it still hurts my chest to laugh."

But it didn't hurt her at all to get back to the Thompson case.

"We're not letting go of this, Puller, not now . . . for sure not now."

"I couldn't agree more."

Her eyes widened. "Wait a minute. I was ready for an argument. What happened?"

I touched her hand. "You happened, Lisa. The bastard who tried to kill you happened."

"We can get started the second I get out of here."

I chewed the inside of my cheek. Lately, all I seemed to be doing was lying to her.

"Of course," I said. "The moment you're ready to go."

Back in my car, I reached for my cell phone. With a murder investigation going full blast, Brodsky had to be in his office. He was. I told him what I needed, that he was now officially part of my team. He grunted, then promised to call as soon as he had something. Maybe I imagined it, but he sounded less angry. Almost like he meant it.

The Chargers game started at four o'clock Sunday afternoon and sitting in my semicircular living room at the dome, I was grateful to have something to do while I waited for the sheriff to come up with the telephone number I had to have to get a lock on Robert Bennett.

But I wasn't nearly so grateful after the first quarter, after two San Diego fumbles and an unforced interception gave the Seahawks a twelve-point lead. Even less grateful when Seattle built its lead to fifteen.

I knew better than to expect my Chargers to actually win a big game for a change, but they had to get it together enough to lose by fewer than six points or my thousand bucks were down the sewer with the rest of the money I'd lost over the past year.

As the game wore on, my hopes continued to descend.

With a minute and a half left in the game, San Diego kicked a field goal to close the margin to eight. Then they stopped Seattle three-and-out, but my stomach began to hurt as I realized what was going to happen.

Thirty seconds left, the Chargers are in easy field goal range, but what difference did it make? All I needed was a field goal, but San Diego had no choice but to go for the touchdown and the two-point conversion. A long shot, the touchdown improbable enough, the extra points twice as tough.

Two failed hail-Mary passes into the end zone later, I was even flatter broke than ever. I stared at the screen. Shit. I reached for the clicker, but the ringing phone interrupted.

"Nothing," Sheriff Brodsky told me. "Not yet anyway, but I've got deputies all over the county working on it."

I thanked him and hung up. I watched the post-game show for a moment before turning the TV off. This was getting ridiculous, I told myself. First the Chargers, now the sheriff.

How can a man lose every single fucking time?

Brodsky called back at a quarter to four the next morning.

Half asleep, it took me a few seconds to understand what he was saying.

"That's what I'm telling you," he said. "One of my deputies just called. He's canvassing motels out on I-95. Finally talked to the night manager at a place called Trucker's Rest. Gas, food, lodging. Open all night. Manager looked through his cards for the name Robert Bennett, found nothing. Deputy described the broken nose, still nothing. Manager went outside and brought back the kid who pumps gas at night. My officer went through the routine with the young man. 'Hell, yes,' the boy tells him. 'Hell, yes, I remember the guy with the busted nose. Used the self-serve, then wanted me to wash his windows. I told him it was against the rules and he told me he'd shove the gasoline hose up my ass if I didn't do it.' "

I felt my eyebrows rising as Brodsky continued.

" 'Those goddamned eyes,' the kid tells my guy, 'empty and staring at me . . . and I couldn't stop looking at his nose.' "

I blinked. "Kid get a name?"

"Guy paid cash."

"What about the car? An ID on the vehicle?"

"A big gray van, he's certain about that much, but nothing else."

"Damn it."

"I'm not finished, Monk."

"Please, Sheriff, it's too early in the morning to play games. Why don't you just tell me what you came up with?"

"Video. The truck stop has digital cameras mounted out at the gas pumps. To nail the people who don't pay."

"What did you see?"

"I saw the man who was in my office calling himself Special Agent Robert Bennett. I saw the gray van . . . and the tag number."

Suddenly I was wide-awake, a familiar surge of energy running through my body.

"Who's it come back to?" I asked.

He read the printout from the Department of Motor Vehicles.

I scribbled hard to keep up.

TWENTY-ONE

I READ MY NOTES BACK TO HIM.

"2002 Ford E-150 commercial van. Registered owner Southeast Fitters Warehouse. No individual listed on the registration."

I repeated the address, a street I was pretty sure was a bit south of Union Station, but even as I looked at the numbers I knew better than to believe them. Satan would need a Zamboni before a professional killer would offer such an easy trail to follow. I told Brodsky as much.

"I've got a bigger problem," he said. "Your people down here—the agents working the assault on Lisa Sands—they need this, too."

"It's not ready for them yet. Not till I check it out myself."

"Why not use the locals? M.P.D. can handle this without leaving their desks."

"That's what I'm afraid of. I need to see the place myself. Get some handle on where to go with it."

"You're asking me to sit on something I can't sit on."

"Couple of hours, that's all. Soon as it gets light outside."

"I'll be waiting."

• • •

The address in southeast Washington was half a dozen blocks south of Union Station, not far from the grandeur of Capitol Hill but more distant than that from the congressional lifestyle. The area was one of those trying to come back from generations of poverty and crime, but there was a long way to go. It was a few minutes past seven o'clock when I steered the Caprice around the last corner and started up the street Brodsky had identified. Old houses, medium-size apartment complexes, nothing industrial.

I scanned left and right when I hit the block where Southeast Fitters Warehouse was supposed to be, but there were still nothing but apartment buildings. I slowed down and read every number on both sides of the street, but the one I wanted wasn't there. Not at all surprised, I grabbed my cell phone to set up my next lead. Probably another waste of time, but if you have a lead you cover it. You want to do the job right, you cover every last one of them.

A quick phone call to the Postal Inspector's Office gave me a physical location for the post office box listed by DMV records as the address for Southeast Fitters Warehouse. The F Street South Post Office was some distance from the phony address, and the postmaster himself was already waiting for me by the time I got there.

"Southeast Fitters Warehouse?" he said, after I displayed my creds and told him what I needed. "I can show you the index card for that box, but you might not find that name on it."

"Maybe I'll see something else that helps me."

The postmaster was both plump and close to retirement, wearing a white dress shirt but no tie. He led me to a series of dark wood file cabinets, opened one of the drawers and flipped through the contents, stopped to pull out a three-by-five card. He handed it to me.

"I was right," he said. "No company name. We don't accept them, you know, not unless we get a person's name along with them." He smiled, his lips twisting at the corners. "We have to have somebody to contact for late payment, to kick out if there's any other trouble."

I examined the card. The name wasn't Robert Bennett, of course. *Benjamin Allard*, the box holder had printed, and provided as his home address the same numbers Brodsky had given me for Southeast Fitters. I scribbled the name in my notebook, gave the card back, and thanked him for the quick service.

"Always glad to help the bureau, Agent Monk. I used to see Mr. Hoover once in a while. With that other fella . . . that Clyde what's-his-face."

"The director was a man with many friends," I told him, the mandatory bureau response. "Could have been anybody."

"Don't make 'em like that anymore, that Hoover."

"They don't, sir." I shook his hand. "They surely don't." Our sudden rapport emboldened me. "Can you show me the box itself? What's in it?"

He squinted at me. "Need a subpoena to see the mail."

"Just the box then, without the mail."

His head started to shake again, so I used my trump card. "One time," I told him. "One more time for Mr. Hoover."

He stared at me, then turned and walked away. Well, I'll be damned, I thought, not even for dear old Jedgar. I turned and headed back toward the front door, but two steps later his voice stopped me.

"Where you going, Agent Monk? Didn't you say you wanted to see it?"

I hustled after him. He led me around a corner to a long row of the open back ends of post office boxes, then along the row itself until he reached the one I wanted. He turned to me and bless his heart didn't say a word. Didn't point at it. Didn't even glance at it. What he did do was walk away.

I struck like a reptile, my hand grabbing and coming back out with seven pieces of mail. I flipped through them. Bills, credit card solicitations, an offering to the box holder from Jiffy Lube to change his oil for next to nothing, finally a

real-estate flyer. Each addressed to Southeast Fitters Warehouse, care of this very box. I examined the envelopes more
closely, everything in the little windows, looking for another
name. Attention somebody or other, something like that, but
I saw nothing until I got to the last one.

The real-estate pitch was addressed, I saw, to the attention of Jerry Crown. I copied the name into my notebook,
thanked the postmaster one more time before heading out
the door.

Out in the Caprice, I called Henry Valenzuela, the computer analyst at WMFO to whom I'd given the telephone
data from Telserve on Wednesday, the long list of telephone
calls to and from the numbers assigned to Jabalah Abahd
and Brenda Thompson. I told Henry what I was looking for,
and he promised to call as soon as he had something for me.

Then I called Lisa at the hospital. She was as happy to
hear from me as she was sick of staying in bed.

"I'm busting out of here," she told me, and when I didn't
say anything, she hastened to add, "The doctors can't find
any reason to keep me, and they want the bed for someone
who really needs it."

"When? I'll come get you. How soon can you be ready?"

"How soon can you get here?"

At the hospital, she was packed and eager to leave.

I looked around the room. "Where are all the flowers?"

"They were too nice to throw away, especially your roses,
Puller, so I distributed them up and down the hall."

She stood. I grabbed her suitcase. We started out the door,
but a nurse stopped us.

"What do you think *you're* doing, Lisa?" she scolded.
"Nobody walks out of here on their own two feet." She
grinned. "Give me a second to call an orderly with a wheelchair."

Lisa shook her head. "I've been walking up and down the
hall for two hours. I don't need a ride to get myself to the

front door." She nodded her head toward me. "And I've got this hunk to catch me if I fall."

The nurse checked me out, then stepped closer. "Be quick, then," she whispered, "and if my supervisor catches you, tell her you slugged me and took off on your own."

Downstairs, I left Lisa long enough to get the car and bring it back. I got her safely belted in, then pulled away from the curb and jabbed the brakes to avoid a white-coated orderly pushing an empty wheelchair. I reached over and grabbed Lisa's arm to keep her from jolting back and forth.

"I want to ask you something," I said. "Just say no if you don't want to."

She looked at me, raised her eyebrows.

"Let me take you to my house," I continued. "Let me take care of you for a couple of days."

She shook her head. "You're welcome to take care of me, but not at your house. Don't ask me to explain, but I need to see my apartment again. A woman thing, most likely, but that's what I want right now."

I pulled up to the parking booth, gave the attendant my ticket and a dollar, then edged the Caprice into traffic and looked for Twenty-fifth Street. I could take it south to the Rock Creek and Potomac Parkway, hook up with the Arlington Bridge, and be at Lisa's place in Alexandria in twenty minutes.

At her house I carried her suitcase into the bedroom, got her settled into bed.

"Hungry?" I asked her. "Shall I get you something to eat? Or fix something for you maybe?"

But her eyes were already beginning to droop. "Nothing, Puller. Thanks so much, but all I want to do is go to sleep."

I left her to do just that, careful to make sure her front door had locked behind me before I went to my Caprice and headed home.

Henry Valenzuela called before I could get there.

"Benjamin Allard," he said, "the first name you gave me? I get nothing by that name."

"What about the other one? Crown. Jerry Crown."

"One call. Six days ago."

The hair on my arms began to vibrate. Before I could ask, Henry continued.

"One call from Crown to the second number you gave me for Brenda Thompson, her work phone, I presume, from the downtown area code. Ninety-seven seconds. Tuesday, the seventh of January."

"Thirty minutes? That's all you can give me?" My fingers tightened on the telephone back in the dome. "Jesus, Glen, I've got a cell phone number for you, but I can't do anything with half an hour."

Rogers snorted. "Count your blessings. There are three Iraqi intelligence officers clearing dead drops in Chicago, a Russian I.O. in Philadelphia, and another one in Los Angeles. I'm risking every last centimeter of my ass to give you even a single second."

"Russians? We're still working intelligence officers out of Moscow?"

"You know better than to ask me that."

I hung up, then punched numbers for Brodsky. I told him what I'd come up with: the new name, Jerry Crown, and the cell phone number from Telserve.

"Gotta be our guy," I said. "Or somebody awfully close to him."

"Still have to find him. It's not like we can call him up and ask him where he is."

"Don't have to ask him." I told Brodsky about Glen Rogers's satellite. "The second he answers we've got him."

"Where do I meet you? Where'll you be?"

"Head for D.C. as fast as you can. Call me when you get close."

"I'm on my way."

I'd barely set the phone down when Glen Rogers called me back. His voice was urgent. The counterterrorism squad in Chicago was screaming for the satellite.

"Got to do your thing right now, Puller, or forget about it for today."

Shit, I thought. I should have stayed downtown, but it was too late for that. "Stand by, Glen. You should get a signal from Crown's cell phone in a few seconds."

I hung up, retrieved the phone number from my notebook, picked up the phone again and punched the keypad.

"This is Citibank," I told the gruff male voice that answered. "I'm calling to make sure you don't miss our one-time offer of zero percent for the first thirty days. If you act now, I can guarantee quick approv—"

The line went dead without a word. Obviously Mr. Crown was already a customer. The phone rang.

"We have signal on your target," Glen Rogers told me. "In the District . . . Fourteenth and K . . . west edge of Franklin Park. I can keep the bird on him for another twenty-seven minutes but you're on your own after that."

I tossed the phone back in the cradle, raced for my car. I'd never make it to Franklin Park in twenty-seven minutes, but maybe Crown had put down for the day. Maybe my luck with the video from the truck stop would hold long enough for me to get a fix on him.

TWENTY-TWO

"PACKAGE MOVING," GLEN ROGERS TOLD ME BEFORE I WAS halfway to the D.C. line. "Heading northwest. Just came out of Scott Circle into Massachusetts Avenue."

"How long can you stay on him?"

"How close are you?"

"Twenty minutes at least, probably more. I can't do this without you."

"Step on it then . . . I'll do the best I can."

I mashed the pedal, but the traffic got worse and worse.

"Target's at Sheridan Circle, Puller. Still northwest on Mass Ave."

Glen paused and I could hear another voice in the background before he came back on.

"Sorry, pal, but I'm outta here."

"No!" I shouted. "One more min—"

But the line was dead.

I banged the steering wheel with the heel of my hand. Crown was too far ahead. Or Robert Bennett, or whatever else he was calling himself today.

I thought about chasing him anyway, checking out the Sheridan Circle area, and Mass Ave. Looking for the Ford van from Brodsky's video. But I didn't think about it long before I started laughing at the idea. Only in a very bad movie would I find it, and once I did the problem would only get worse. I'd still have to follow him by myself, and it would take the same lousy scriptwriter to make that work, too. On my own there'd be no way to stay with him without being made in the first ten minutes. Out here in the real world, it takes at least three vehicles to do the job right.

I picked up my cell phone and called Brodsky, told him what happened.

"I still have to come to town," he told me. "I've got a murderer to catch." He paused. "And I've got to tell the agents in Brookston."

I stared through the windshield as raindrops began to fall.

"They'll overreact, Sheriff. We're too close to this guy to let a mob of FBI agents scare him off."

"That's not our call to make."

"Let's talk first, is all I'm saying. We'll meet in the morning, figure out where we are. I want this guy even worse than you do. Trust me, I'm not going to do anything to hurt our chances."

"Trust you? Where've I heard that before?"

"This isn't Los Angeles. I need you too much to lie to you. Give me tomorrow morning. Just a few more hours." I paused. "Besides, can you get any closer to him without me?"

I heard him take a breath and blow it out through his lips.

"We're going to your office tomorrow, Monk. We can talk first, but we're definitely going to your office."

"Sorry," Glen Rogers told me by phone after I got back to the dome. "I didn't have any choice."

"I knew that could happen. You told me going in."

"But you were so close."

"We'll do better tomorrow."

"*Tomorrow?*" His contrition evaporated. "Jesus Christ, there *is* no tomorrow! You told me yesterday this was just a—"

"All you have to say is no."

"Damn it, you know I can't do that. You're really taking

advantage here, Puller. A real friend wouldn't even have asked in the first place."

He had me there, but the only thing I could do was sweat him. I started by closing my mouth. After a while the silence loomed like a third person on the line.

"That's it?" he said at last. "You're not even going to try to bullshit me?"

"What you're seeing is the turning over of a new leaf."

He slammed the phone in my ear, but I knew he didn't mean it.

"Just Brodsky," the sheriff told me Tuesday morning over Denver omelettes at the Okay Eats, a chain of diners that, despite the name, continued to flourish around D.C. We'd chosen the one about a block off Massachusetts Avenue near Dupont Circle, and the food wasn't bad.

"Monk will do for me, too. Brodsky and Monk."

"Sounds like a men's store."

I looked at him. The man had actually made a joke.

"We'll probably need a clothing shop," I told him, "with just the two of us out here."

He nodded. "I brought some gear. Hats and caps, three pairs of sunglasses, couple of jackets, and a reversible raincoat." He sipped his coffee. "And some fake whiskers to hide my face."

"Same here. A couple of mustaches and a goatee, from my days on the surveillance squad. Plus a woman's wig, if it comes to that."

"Keep the wig in your car, Monk, unless we're trying to pass me off as a Bulgarian shot-putter." He actually grinned. "We want to follow the man, not scare him to death."

Another joke. Christ, the guy was almost human.

"He might like Bulgarian women," I told him.

"That could be even worse."

"They say if you've never tried it . . ."

He grunted, attacked his omelette with manly vigor, then took a sip of coffee, spoke with the cup in his big hand. "It was around here you lost him, isn't that what you told me last night?"

"Almost exactly here."

"And you first spotted him on K Street?"

"Franklin Park. I told you about the P.O. box in Southeast, so that gives us a third option."

He frowned. "You can sit a long time waiting for a professional to check his mail drop."

"Agreed, but how does that explain finding his name on the envelope in his box? A pro would never let that happen, either."

"Computers. Half the mail is computer generated these days. You don't have much control over the names in your mailbox anymore."

I leaned toward him. "Look, Brodsky, about going into the office . . ."

"Forget it. I thought about that last night. Way I see it, I'm working my own case out here. You're an FBI agent. I've told you. From here on it's your problem."

I nodded, but wasn't about to say anything that might make him change his mind. We finished our omelettes before he spoke again.

"Where do you want to start this morning?"

I gave him the post office address on F Street, and directions for getting there. "The box was full yesterday, so he just might show up today to clear it. Why don't you give it a shot while I cruise up and down Mass Avenue and wait for Glen Rogers to call."

"Save it, Puller. You knew damned well I'd do it."

Glen's weary tone indicated our little spat wasn't over yet, but I could mend that fence later. My grip on the cell phone loosened as I asked him to confirm what he'd just told me.

"Northwest," he repeated, "that's where we've got him right now. Not far from where you lost him last night."

"How far north? I'm at Dupont Circle."

"A few blocks. Short street called Riggs Place, heading east toward New Hampshire Avenue."

"I'll take New Hampshire out of the Circle. How far's Riggs Place?"

"Four or five blocks, looks like. He's getting close to the avenue."

"Call his turn into New Hampshire."

"Roger." Then, half a minute later, "Left turn . . . heading north again."

"Washington Heights. Stay by the phone, Glen. I'll get right back to you."

I punched the speed dialer for the number I'd entered an hour ago.

"Brodsky," the sheriff said instantly.

"Package north. Get to Sixteenth Street, take it all the way up to where New Hampshire comes in. Call me when you get there."

The line went dead. Good man, the sheriff. Professionals don't waste time on pleasantries. Even a few words use up way too much of it. I speed-dialed Glen.

"New Hampshire," he told me. "Crossing S Street."

I hit the accelerator. I was closing, but Crown was still a couple minutes away.

"Left turn, Puller. Straight north on Seventeenth."

I crossed S, swung north on Seventeenth, slowed down. Best not rear-end him. Until I had to.

"Approaching Florida," Glen said. His voice quickened. "Check that . . . quick left into . . . into Seaton Place, looks like. Small street. Heads up, it's a dead end."

I spurred the Caprice toward the intersection, stopped short, and pulled into the curb, grateful for Glen's warning. More than one surveillance had been burned when seven bureau cars piled into a cul-de-sac together.

"Package stopped on Seaton Place," Glen said. "And I'm gone."

The line went dead. I called Brodsky to direct him to my location, then made a quick drive-by down Seaton Place.

The gray Ford E-150 with the same tag number from the video sat half a block down the street on the left side, in front of a small and very attractive apartment building. Used brick, brilliant white woodwork, bright red shutters outlining the leaded glass windows, a bronze eagle over the front doors.

Several things occurred to me as I stared at the building. If he lived here, our gorilla was doing it in style. If he didn't, we just may have been lucky enough to find his keeper.

TWENTY-THREE

BRODSKY SHOWED UP TWENTY MINUTES LATER, DROVE PAST the van, then came back to my car and agreed with me that we had a problem, that the problem was Seaton Place itself. The street wasn't actually a cul-de-sac, as it turned out, but a very short street that was just as bad for our purposes. Crowded with upscale apartment buildings, each of them featuring dozens of windows looking directly down on the street, Seaton Place was a lousy place to work a surveillance.

There were too few other cars on the street, for starters, and far too many members of the dreaded Neighborhood Watch Program, scourge of surveillance teams from Oregon to Maine. Even if Jerry Crown himself wasn't looking out his front window, one or another of his neighbors would be. Sitting in our parked cars like burglars casing their next job, Brodsky and I would be spotted immediately. Police would be summoned. Surrounded by M.P.D. cruisers, we'd stand out like brown shoes at an opera.

"We've got to bookend him," I told Brodsky.

"I'll move to the other end of Seaton, where it runs into Florida. With you around the corner on Seventeenth, he won't be able to get out without one of us seeing him."

"Not until tonight anyway. After dark it won't be so simple."

"For him either. When it gets dark we can move in closer."

Brodsky drove west toward where Seaton emptied into Florida Avenue. I set up where Seaton hit Seventeenth. We were in good position, as good as we were going to manage with only two men and two cars. Jerry Crown could drive up and down Seaton all day long, but he wasn't going anywhere else without us tagging along.

Day turned to evening, evening to night, and beyond.

"Blue Cadillac heading your way," Brodsky said over his cell phone at three o'clock Wednesday morning, the sheriff's voice still strong despite the hour. He described the sedan turning onto Seaton Place. "Single occupant. Woman. Let me know if she doesn't come past you. I'll do a drive-by to see where she stopped."

I did see her, a few seconds later, as the Cadillac slid past me and turned south on Seventeenth. I told Brodsky, then asked him for the drive-by anyway, just to make sure the van hadn't somehow slipped past us. A couple minutes later he called to report that nothing had changed, but this time he added something new.

"Just a feeling, but this is beginning to concern me."

I had to smile at his better and better manners. Another FBI agent would have put it a little differently. *You've got to be fucking kidding! Just because the van's still there doesn't mean shit! We're just gonna sit here and pretend he hasn't already left it behind?*

No matter how kindly he'd said it, Brodsky had a good point.

With only two of us out here, we couldn't follow any of the dozens of vehicles that had passed. Jerry Crown might have walked out the door and caught a ride with a friend fifteen hours ago. We could sit for days without ever seeing him again. It happens.

"I'm thinking IAFIS," I told him, referring to the bureau's Integrated Automated Fingerprint Identification System. "And I have a latent kit in my glove compartment."

"Tricky," Brodsky said, "especially in the middle of the night. Worth the trouble, though. Gotta be more effective than just sitting here. At least we'd get his real name."

The sheriff was right about that, too. Technology had at long last made it feasible. IAFIS had changed a system that once took weeks to identify a set of latent fingerprints into a process now measured in minutes. Even better, it didn't give a damn about phony names. Jerry Crown, Benjamin Allard, Robert Bennett—the killer had chosen the names for his own purposes—but to the bureau's supercomputer his identity was just another string of 0's and 1's. All I had to do was lift a readable fingerprint from the van, send it to IAFIS, and let the tiny world of quantum physics do the rest.

"Problem's the streetlight," Brodsky said. "Can't very well shoot it out. It'll be tough to dust the van for prints right underneath it."

"Prints'll be greasy, especially on window glass. My special tape might work without dust."

"Still gotta have a reason to be out there."

"Maybe I'm just looking for my dog."

"Got a leash?"

"Has to be an all-night Rite Aid around here someplace."

"Gotta be."

"Pick up a couple of plastic bags while you're at it, and a scooper. Give me a second to get into place before you take off."

I kept our phone line open while I drove into Seaton Place and got myself positioned as far from any streetlight as possible to watch the van.

"Okay, go," I told Brodsky. "I've got the eye."

He hung up without responding, and I slouched in the driver's seat, head low in the darkness, all but invisible as I waited for him to return. The back of my neck began to tingle and I welcomed the sensation as a sign not only of readiness but of a gambler's awareness as well. I loved this—I'd known that forever—and despite the cold and the rain and the fatigue and the bottle of piss in the backseat, I couldn't imagine a better place to be.

And the proximity to our prey made me feel even better. Just the thought of getting another crack at him warmed me enough to turn down the heater. I'd already crushed his nose, but that was nowhere near enough punishment for the bastard who'd tried to kill the woman I might love. The son of a bitch who now lay cozy in his bed, warm and comfortable while I sat out here in the freezing rain. My hands ached with the urge to attack him. To race up his stairs, crash through into his apartment, and settle the score. To feel the crunch of reshaping his nose again. To smell his blood and taste my satisfaction.

Brodsky was back.

I started the car and drove to him, pulled the Caprice up to his Buick sedan, the front of my car toward the rear of his, driver-side windows only inches apart. A position cops call "sixty-nining." I zipped my window down and he handed me what he'd bought. A six-foot leather leash with a big fat collar on one end. A handful of plastic grocery bags. A bright green plastic gardening scoop. Then something I hadn't ordered.

"I didn't mention it before," he whispered, "but I brought something else from my office."

I looked at the stuff he'd passed through my window, recognized the black metal object he'd included with the dog gear. A magnetized transmitter not much larger than a pack of cigarettes, but more than powerful enough to grip the Ford van through hell or high water. Not state of the art, but plenty good enough for our needs.

"Might not get a better opportunity to put it on," Brodsky added.

"Where's the other half?" A transmitter wasn't much good without a receiver.

"Don't need a receiver. Just tune your commercial radio

to AM 638, you'll hear the sound. Single sharp beeps, but intermittent. Staccato when the target's stationary, slower when he moves, real slow when he approaches the edge of transmitting range."

I nodded. We parted to return to our original stations, but I couldn't help glancing in my rearview mirror at the sheriff's car and the man sitting behind the wheel. He was a pro, no question about it, but why wouldn't he be? Despite the history of rancor between us and them, the L.A.P.D. was world-class in every respect. Far better than we were in keeping the street scum from taking over. As a homicide dick, Brodsky represented the cream of the crop. He was a hard-ass but I was damned lucky to have him along.

Moments later I was back under the darkness of a score of overhanging evergreens. I reached into the back seat, selected a Redskin's cap and a mustache, glanced at myself in the rearview mirror, then took the cap off and brushed my hair down toward my eyes, put the cap on again, this time pulled the bill even further downward. Jerry Crown had seen me only once and he'd been too busy kicking my ass to study my face. This time he wouldn't even see that much.

I grabbed the bags and scooper, leash and transmitter, tied the plastic bags around the handle of the scooper, dropped the heavy little radio beacon into one of them, then reached into the glove compartment for my latent fingerprint tape. I tore off several six-inch strips of the special tape that I hoped would work without dusting, put them in the same bag, then left the car and locked it up before hitting the street.

TWENTY-FOUR

ON THE SIDEWALK I DECIDED TO ADD ONE MORE ELEMENT
to my disguise.

I looked around under the trees, found a small piece of
bark, then removed my left shoe and laid the bark inside. I
put the shoe back on and took a couple of uncomfortable
practice steps. The limp was perfect. Made me look shorter
and a lot less threatening, but even more importantly it suggested I was handicapped, and people are taught from childhood to turn away.

I clutched my bag, leash, and pooper-scooper, then
headed for the van. Limped toward it in a soft zigzag pattern,
pantomiming "here boy, here boy" gestures, like Marcel
Marceau in a Redskins cap as I drew closer and closer. At
the driver's window, I bent to look under the van for the dog
that by now even I was beginning to think might actually exist. I reached into the bag for the transmitter, stretched my
arm under the van and used the transmitter to probe for solid
steel. A moment later I heard a solid *clunk* as the magnet
grabbed hold. I tugged at it but the radio beacon held fast.

Still crouched underneath, I grabbed my strips of fingerprint tape, straightened up slowly and used one of them on
the driver's side window frame, one on the area around the
keyhole in the door, the last one on the window itself. There

wasn't enough light to see what I'd come away with, but unless Jerry Crown had wiped down the car I should have
something. Unfortunately—my luck running the way it
was—the only thing it might turn out to be was dirt.

I limped away from the van, shaking my head with the
exasperation of a man who'd left his bed for another one of
Fido's goddamned nocturnal prowls. I shuffled over to the
other side of the street, peering, staring, whistling softly,
moving my mouth as though yelling but trying not to wake
up the neighborhood at the same time.

Fido, you son of a bitch, where are you?

I gritted my teeth against the pain in my shoe, limped a
little faster as Brodsky's car came into view at the other end
of the street.

"Haven't got a scanner in that car of yours?" I asked
when I got there. "And a fax machine?"

"Not in this car. We put them in the cruisers last year, but
I don't have either one."

"Kinko's, then," I said. "Do you need a transmittal
form?"

"Got a couple in my briefcase." He stared at me. "Get in
the car, Monk. I can't stand watching you limp around like
that. I'll drop you off at your car on my way."

The sheriff was back even quicker this time. He sixty-nined
me again, spoke in a voice barely above a whisper.

"Take the bureau a couple of hours, they told me. I gave
them your cell phone number for callback."

I looked down the street toward the van. "I think we can
back off a while. Why don't you go grab a bite to eat?"

Which was surveillance code for the opportunity of using
a real bathroom for a change, for emptying one's storage bottle without resorting to pouring it in the gutter, an act guar-
anteed to get somebody's attention at a time when you can't
allow that to happen. He nodded. I glanced at my own bottle
in the back seat, but there was no question of asking him to
take it along. A fisur man—physical surveillance man—

holds his own water, one way or the other. What a fisur man never does is ask somebody else to schlepp it for him.

"Nothing?"

I stared out into the darkness as I tried to make sense of what the Identification Division was telling me ninety minutes later. "Nothing at *all*? Not even in the *civil* files?"

I listened as the woman on the other end of the phone at the bureau's fingerprint center in Clarksburg, West Virginia, told me again that the latent fingerprints Brodsky had submitted by fax from Kinko's matched nothing in her records. I thanked her and hung up, then called the sheriff.

"Doesn't make sense to me, either," he said. "I've never had anything come back from Clarksburg 'no record.' "

"Sure as hell not for this kind of maniac."

"Nothing wrong with your lifts, I know that for sure. Four perfect fingers, didn't even need a glass to read them. Three ulnar loops, a tented-arch on the little finger."

"Gotta be a mistake. Crown can't possibly be clean."

I checked the clock on my dash panel. Nearly six in the morning, not yet dawn this time of year. The rapid beeps from radio station 638 continued to indicate the van hadn't moved. The rain on my roof joined in to make a sort of syncopation that was almost musical. *Drum-beep-drum-beep-drum-beep* . . . something like that.

"What've we got here for range?" I asked Brodsky. "How far away can we get and still be sure of catching him moving?"

"A mile at least, out where I come from, but in the city with all the traffic and electronics maybe four or five blocks. Far enough he'll never spot us."

"What if we were up off the ground, up in a building maybe?" I had a very specific building in mind.

"It's a line-of-sight process, but we can lay significantly farther back the higher the elevation. Any chance you can get a plane up?"

"If we had a week maybe, to get my request okayed." A

request that as a suspended agent I couldn't even make, although I didn't bother to tell Brodsky that. "I was thinking of something a bit lower. The Hilton is just down the way at T Street. Won't be higher than thirteen stories"—by statute no building in Washington could be—"but we should be able to use it as a command post."

"What kind of budget have you got? I'm working a murder case, but the county will never pay for the Hilton."

"I'll put it on my credit card." What was left of it. "We can work it out later."

"I'll hold my position here until you get us settled in. You better get something to eat while you have the chance."

I hung up and started for the hotel. The odometer clicked off seven-tenths of a mile before I pulled into the parking lot and nodded. This was a good break. A room at the Hilton would give us the one thing we couldn't possibly go without. Rest, proper rest, not the hunched-over-the-steering-wheel catnaps that pass for sleep in surveillance work. In the kind of work that often turns real violent real fast, rest is a weapon as valuable as a gun. Without it you can end up dead.

In the lobby, I signed a Visa chit for the cheapest single room on the top floor of the tower facing north. A mere four hundred dollars a night, the clerk told me over the top of his nose as he grabbed the card and slammed it through his machine. I hustled upstairs and straight to the portable radio/alarm clock on the nightstand, tuned it to 638 on the AM dial, heard the quick and steady beat from our transmitter and nodded again. We were still a long way from pulling this off—the two of us by ourselves—but the playing field was for the first time starting to level.

We did it in shifts.

Two hours on, two off.

The sheriff and I watching the bastard stay in his apartment, both of us hoping the killer hadn't decided to take early retirement. That his big gray van wouldn't just sit there until the wheels rusted. It wasn't likely, but in fisur work nothing is impossible. Just because he refused to move didn't mean we could take our eyes off him. Doing so would violate the first rule of the game, and the consequences were pretty damned predictable.

The protocol is a simple one.

The target does absolutely nothing for days and days, sometimes months and years. The watchers—always under-manned, underrested, underfed, and overwhelmed—watch without blinking for all that time, then turn away for ten seconds to work the cramps out of their shoulders, at which point the target disappears. It's happened to me, it happens to everybody at least once, from energetic young agents to burned-out old bastards who spend their shifts endlessly scribbling on long yellow pads, recalculating to the last penny their retirement pay.

But not this time, Brodsky and I agreed.

This time we had the advantage. This time we had the Hilton on our side. After a two-hour shift, we could come back to a soft bed and a real toilet. We didn't have to get our rest in the back seat of the same car we hadn't left for twelve hours, legs drawn up, trying to sleep, trying to ignore the monstrous odor of rotting fast-food, old newspapers, and our own dreadful gas.

It's hard to explain to outsiders why FBI agents put up with it, allow ourselves to be treated worse than the Taliban infantry, and I don't have an answer, either. Maybe it's like the guy who shovels elephant poop at the circus. Maybe we just plain like the smell.

"Stand by, Monk. He's on the move."

Brodsky's call came just after twelve o'clock noon on Thursday, just as I was leaving the hotel parking lot to relieve him.

"Out the front door," he continued, "toward his van. I have the eye, but you better hurry."

"Three minutes," I told him. "Call him out and I'll join up with you."

I turned up the commercial radio in my dashboard. AM 638 was loud and clear, the beeping from the transmitter slowing as the van began to move away from my position.

"South on Florida," Brodsky told me. "I think we've got ourselves a pro here. He's looking around, checking his mirrors. I can't hold him much longer."

I hung a U and shot south on Seventeenth, made a quick left on T Street, and caught the van just as it turned north on Connecticut. I fell into the traffic out of his sight line, listened to the steady beeping of the tracking device from my car speakers.

"Got him," I told Brodsky. "North on Connecticut. I'll call the streets."

I called out the streets, one after another, all the way up Connecticut to Rock Creek Park, over the park to the Duke Ellington Bridge. "Right turn," I said. "East on Calvert . . . the Ellington Bridge. Come ahead, I'm going by."

"Got him."

In the rearview mirror I saw Crown swing right onto the bridge, then Brodsky's dark green Buick sedan make the same turn two cars later. I took a quick right, another right, and was once again ready.

"East on Calvert," Brodsky said. "Left turn signal blinking . . . first street is . . . first street is Adams Mill Road . . . looks like a left into Adams Mill Road." He paused. "That's it. Left turn Adams Mill. I'm going straight on Calvert."

"I've got him," I said. "Get back in line."

I followed Crown for thirty seconds—conscious of the steady beeps from the radio—until he signaled for another left turn.

"Left signal again," I told Brodsky. "Turning left, but it's still Adams Mill Road. I'll go right on Quarry."

I watched in my mirror as Brodsky slid into place and I made the right turn, then did another U and got back to the sheriff in time to see Crown slow along Adams Mill before swinging left into the parking lot at the National Zoo. He stopped at the booth and paid the fee. Brodsky and I did the same thing—flashing badges would have saved us the money, but you never know who's watching at a time like that—then followed Crown past the long parking lot at the north end and along the narrow road skirting the park until we got to the southernmost end, where Crown turned in.

Brodsky continued past the lot. I pulled into it but stayed as far away from Crown as possible while the killer found a place and put the van into it. He opened the door, got out and stood for a moment, looking around the half-empty lot as though searching for someone.

I grabbed my binoculars from the passenger seat, swung them up in time to get a good look at his face. His nose was healing, I saw, but still pretty ugly. I hoped it hadn't stopped hurting, as he began to walk toward the zoo entrance.

"I've got an eye on the van," Brodsky told me from somewhere beyond our position, "if you want to take him inside."

I grabbed a straw hat from my surveillance bag, slapped a quick brown goatee on my chin.

"I'm on my way. I'll call you if I lose him."

I mingled the best I could in the straggly pedestrian flow, past the series of small ponds on our left on the way to the nearby south entrance, but made sure to keep Crown in view. Except on TV or in the movies, losing sight of the package is almost always the end of the surveillance, and people can do the damndest things when you aren't watching.

This time the problem was speed.

Crown's long legs were gobbling up the pavement much faster than the meandering bunch I was using as a shield. I had to pick up my pace as well, even if it meant risking him noticing. Fortunately the walkway stretching into the park was a wide and straight one, and I could see Crown easily from thirty yards behind him. He'd hurried past the information booth on the right without a glance, which was no great surprise. He knew where he was going, of course, and I was pretty sure he hadn't come to see the animals.

We passed the big restaurant on our left and made straight for the monkey island about two hundred yards dead ahead. I hung back a little farther, careful not to jam up with him if the monkey exhibit was his destination.

It wasn't, I saw a moment later.

Crown made a right turn toward the Think Tank—the animal-cognition center—at the east edge of the zoo. I had to hustle to catch sight of him as he veered right again and strode to the great cats exhibit on Lion-Tiger Hill. This time he did stop, and so did I, a couple dozen yards away and safely screened from his view by a thicket of bamboo and a small grove of Himalayan pines.

Thank God for the evergreens, I thought. At this time of year the skyscraper oak trees were completely bare, offered me no protection at all. Crown stood directly in front of the low wall dividing the lions from those the big cats wouldn't mind eating. He was joined by scores of tourists attracted to the power and beauty of the beasts as they lounged beyond their pondlike safety moat.

I watched as one of the cats—a male huge through the shoulders—strolled along the other side of the moat, swinging his eyes from side to side as though counting the house for this afternoon's performance. His golden-brown head stopped as he seemed to recognize Jerry Crown, one predator to another.

Crown turned and walked to the small plaza directly across from the lions, an area filled with tables and chairs. Every table was occupied. He moved to the nearest one, stood like the lion as he stared at the family seated there. The father looked up, then gathered his wife and two small children and hurried away. Jerry Crown took the father's chair, sat and stared at the lions. Waiting, I hoped, for the someone who pulled his strings.

I wedged myself into the three-deep crowd still gawking at the lions, out of Jerry Crown's sight line. The blue-black sky began to drizzle. Around me umbrellas popped open, a few at first, then a forest of them. Another break for me. Even someone searching for me would have no chance to get a look at my face. I peeked past a red, yellow, and blue golf umbrella. Jerry Crown was still alone.

I raised the collar of my rain jacket, glanced at the same lions Crown was looking at. Unlike his fascination with

Crown, the big male showed absolutely no interest in me. I moved a step or two closer to Crown's table and waited for something to happen.

Three and a half minutes later it did.

A second man walked past Jerry Crown's table, paused for an instant to pull his gray fedora closer to his eyes against the suddenly slanting rain, before moving on. As he walked away, Crown rose and followed him. I couldn't see the other man's face, but there was something about his rigid posture and the way he walked that I recognized. A moment later the back of my neck began to tingle as I realized why it was so familiar.

It *couldn't* be, I told myself. It can't *possibly* be.

I stepped back a few feet, ready to hurry to a position the two of them would have to pass to get wherever they were going.

I saw Crown following the second man, neither of them in an apparent hurry, just a couple of guys enjoying a day at the zoo. A dozen steps farther on, the second man stopped and turned back in the direction of Crown without actually looking at him. In that moment I had a perfect view of the newcomer's face, directly into his eyes. I flinched away from the unexpected contact, but Kevin Finnerty did not appear to notice.

TWENTY-FIVE

MY MIND WENT BLANK. IT COULD NOT BE KEVIN FINNERTY, but it was.

No matter how impossibly absurd, the assistant director in charge of the bureau's flagship field office was meeting with a professional killer. A red-hot flash of rage climbed up the back of my neck and exploded in the center of my brain. Before I could stop myself I went after them.

But two steps later the cell phone in my pocket began to vibrate.

Brodsky. Had to be. I wanted to keep going but I couldn't.

The sheriff was there to watch my back, I couldn't possibly ignore him. I sidestepped behind a huge yellow umbrella and retreated to the bamboo thicket, where Finnerty and his goon wouldn't be able to see or hear me. I pulled the phone from my pocket, hit the call button.

"Get out of there," Brodsky snapped. "We've got counter."

"Two units," the sheriff told me when we got back to his Buick in the parking lot. "Brown van to our right, light blue Ford sedan in the row ahead of us. Next to the black Range Rover."

I saw the Ford sedan immediately, but it took me a moment to locate the van near the end of the row we were in. A drab brown commercial van with a magnetized sign sticking to the passenger door.

"Yankee Drain Cleaning?" I said. "That the one?"

He nodded.

"How'd you spot them?" FBI agents are trained to spot countersurveillance, but it takes a lot of practice. Even for an ex-L.A. cop, Brodsky had done well to pick them up. "Besides the sign on the door, I mean. We use the same thing on our own vans. Drain cleaners one day, roofers the next. You must've used them in the P.D."

"Everybody does."

He looked out the window, spoke without turning back to me.

"Two men left the Ford just after you followed Crown toward the gate. They didn't look like tourists to me, so I checked around the lot for their mother ship. The drain-cleaning van caught my eye right away."

"Except for the sign it looks pretty ordinary to me."

"See the ladder? Strapped to the top?"

"Lots of trucks carry ladders."

"Wired with antenna cable? Running from the rear of the ladder to a through-hole just above the back door?" He looked at me. "Not a lot of people would notice, but not a lot of people have rigged the same setup."

"The ladder's an antenna. Should have caught that myself." I looked at the truck. "So who are they?"

"I guess that depends on who you saw inside with Jerry Crown."

I told him. He raised his eyebrows but said nothing.

"That's all I get? Did you understand what I just said?"

"I'm stunned. Is that what you'd like to hear?" Brodsky shook his head. "I've been on the job too long for that. Takes a lot more to surprise me these days." He paused, looked at the truck, then at the Ford from which the two men had left to follow me inside. "You don't recognize the vehicles."

"No, but that doesn't mean a whole lot. I haven't been to

our surveillance off-site for a year and a half, not since Finnerty made me a supervisor. I have no idea what the special operations group is driving these days."

"How about the bureau radio in your car? Maybe you can catch them talking to each other."

"Could have done that a few years ago, but it's a lot different now. The SOG people use secure frequencies to keep away from crooks with scanners. They've got too many channels for me to sort through, and they're very careful to stay off the air unless they absolutely have to communicate."

"Maybe Finnerty's out here working a case."

"Jerry Crown's a murderer, a torturer. The only business the bureau would have with him is taking him off the street." I stared through the windshield at the rain that had suddenly gotten worse. "I didn't get the feeling they were in there to arrange a surrender."

Again we fell silent, and I used the pause to begin doubting myself. Already wondering if I could possibly have seen what I did. And detecting the countersurveillance didn't help, either.

"Let's give them a test," I said. "I'll go for a little drive and you can watch what happens."

"The van's an electronics base unit. It won't follow you. And the Ford's still empty."

"Could be another unit out here, though, or more than one. At least a hundred vehicles in this lot. No telling who they might be." I reached for the door handle. "Call me on your cell when I get to my car. We'll keep the line open till we finish."

He nodded. I got out of his Buick, walked back to my Caprice, climbed in, and started the engine. My cell phone vibrated before I could back out.

"Ready?" I asked him.

"Go."

I backed out of my space, headed toward the exit out of the parking lot, paused when I got to the frontage road to give a watcher time to catch up, then turned left with the flow of traffic back out toward the zoo's main entrance.

I watched my rearview mirror, saw three cars and a pickup truck make the same turn behind me. No help. Too many vehicles. Nobody'd send four units after one car in an enclosed situation like this. I checked for oncoming traffic, saw a gap, and flipped a sudden U-turn, started back toward Brodsky as I watched the drivers who'd been behind me as they passed. No professional would duplicate my change of direction, I didn't even bother looking for that, but radios would be used. It wasn't likely, but microphones might flash into view before disappearing just as quickly.

I caught nothing as I went by. If it happened, I didn't see it. I wanted to be reassured, but knew better. Most FBI surveillance agents use microphones built into the visor above the windshield, and the ones who don't are careful to keep their mikes below window level.

"I didn't see anything," Brodsky told me over our open phone connection.

"What about brake lights?" No matter how well-trained you are, it's easy to hit the brakes when your package does something sudden or unusual. A sure way to get yourself burned.

"Nothing."

"You make a note of the cars?" In case the same ones came back to the parking lot while we were still there.

"Of course."

"One more try, then. This time I'll take the bridge back to Adams Mill Road, do another U-turn."

"Roger."

I slowed down to cover the few hundred yards to the small bridge across Rock Creek, then hit the gas and sped across the bridge. On the other side I slowed again. One car appeared behind me, then two. I let them catch up before accelerating. Just before I got to Adams Mill, I cut another U-turn, right in front of an oncoming red SUV. I heard the driver's angry honk, saw in the mirror his uplifted finger. I noted the two cars that had been behind me across the bridge, a white Lexus coupe, a dark blue something-or-other sedan. Again I looked for microphones, again I saw nothing.

I watched the cars until they disappeared from view on their way to Adams Mill Road. Then I went back to Brodsky, stayed in my car, and used the phone to talk to him.

"I'm not sure," I told him, "but I didn't see anything obvious."

"I didn't either."

"Got any ideas?"

"Do you know what Finnerty drives?"

"Black Mercury Marquis, if he's using his bucar. Big four-door. I don't know about his POA, his personally owned car." But I realized what Brodsky was suggesting. "I'll cruise the lot to see if I can find the Marquis. We might as well sit on both of them, Crown *and* Finnerty. Follow the one the drain-cleaning van takes out of here."

We kept the line open while I looked for Finnerty's black Mercury. It didn't take long to find it. The big sedan was only fifty yards away, in the very back row. I told Brodsky, then pulled my Caprice into a parking space where I could see the ADIC's car in my rearview mirror. I turned the engine off and slouched in the seat. The rain had stopped for a change, but the temperature had dropped, cold enough now to snow. I reached up and adjusted the mirror to give me the best view of Finnerty's car, then settled back to wait. It was my first chance to reflect on what I'd seen.

There had to be an explanation, one that made more sense than what it looked like: that Kevin Finnerty was out here working with a killer for hire. That the ADIC was seriously off the rails, sanctioning murder, like a real-life "M" in a James Bond movie.

But Brodsky's suggestion that Finnerty might be legitimately working with Crown was a tempting one to entertain anyway, given the alternatives. Could it be their meeting had nothing whatsoever to do with Judge Brenda Thompson? I was shaking my head even before the question had time to register.

For starters, Kevin Finnerty didn't work cases, hadn't been on the street for thirty-five years. Not since the late sixties, at least, when J. Edgar Hoover singled him out of a herd of young fireballs and elevated him directly to headquarters, to direct important bureau programs at first, then back to the field to head up the most important field offices, and finally back to Washington to become an assistant director by the time he was thirty. In the years since then, Finnerty had made himself the second most powerful FBI man in history. The president may have appointed our director, but even the director understands who really runs the show.

I tried another scenario, just for size.

Say Brenda Thompson had gone on her own to the president. Say she told him about Crown, about some kind of dreadful problem she was having with Jerry Crown. Say the president had ordered Finnerty to take care of it secretly. That would make the two guys from the blue Ford the ADIC's bodyguards, here to protect him in a dangerous mission. That would make the brown drain-cleaning van a bureau listening station, here for the sole purpose of recording the meeting.

Pretty damned improbable, I admitted, but certainly not impossible. Brodsky and I were here to catch Crown. Could it be possible that Finnerty was trying to do the same thing?

"Crown's out," the sheriff said over our open phone connection. "On the way to his car." He paused. "Unlocking it. Behind the wheel. Backing out of his space."

"The blue Ford?"

"Nothing. Nobody there yet."

I swiveled my head to look at the brown van as Brodsky's voice continued. "Crown's leaving the lot. Want me to follow?"

"Only if the drain cleaners do."

"Roger."

But the brown van didn't move. I watched Jerry Crown's gray van turn left and follow the frontage road north toward the main entrance. Neither the blue Ford sedan nor the brown surveillance van made any effort to follow. It wasn't Crown they were here for. Suddenly I saw Kevin Finnerty striding toward his car.

"There he is now," I told Brodsky. "Eleven o'clock. Coming this way."

I slouched deeper in my seat as the ADIC made his way to his Mercury Marquis, unlocked it, and climbed in.

"Brown van's backing out," Brodsky said. "Blue Ford, too."

The blue Ford left the lot first, followed several cars later by Finnerty's Marquis, then, two cars after that, by the drain cleaners. I had to admire the way they were doing it, whoever the hell they were. The ahead-and-behind technique is a good one, especially when you have a pretty good idea where the target's going. A lot less likely for a watcher to get burned that way.

Brodsky trailed me out of the same lot, and the whole bunch of us rolled north on the frontage road, back toward the main entrance. The brown van followed Finnerty's Marquis out of the zoo property and turned left on Adams Mill Road. We did the same thing. Suddenly I couldn't see the blue Ford anymore.

"Ford must have turned right," I told Brodsky. "You can catch it if you hurry."

"Roger."

On my own now, I concentrated on Finnerty and the drain cleaners.

Up ahead, the ADIC swung right onto Porter Street and followed it west toward Connecticut Avenue. The brown van dropped way back as it made the same move, in no obvious hurry to bumper-lock the ADIC. I pictured the intersection at Connecticut Avenue. The brown van had to know where Finnerty was going. If not, they were way too far back. This time of day the traffic on Connecticut was fierce. Miss the light, the van would never catch the ADIC again.

Maybe that's where the blue Ford had gone, I told myself. The other way around on Adams Mill, to get in position to catch Finnerty if the van got stuck at the light. Again I had to admire the tradecraft. In a slipshod world, it was an unusual thing to see.

A few minutes later we were at the intersection of Porter and Connecticut. The light was red. Finnerty would turn left, of course, back toward WMFO, or toward his house in Kalorama Heights. Both were south of the intersection, and the brown van would follow.

The light changed to green. Finnerty's Marquis was the third car through, turning left just as he should have. The van edged left to make the turn behind Finnerty but at the last moment veered to the right and whipped around the corner on Connecticut heading north. Directly away from Finnerty's Marquis. I felt my stomach tighten as I recognized the most basic of antisurveillance techniques. They were dry-cleaning—in spook speak—and that meant they suspected someone to be following. Watching for someone to duplicate their reckless lane change. Leaving me no choice but to continue my turn in the wrong direction.

I did so, then took the first street to my right and stomped on the gas. Another right and I was paralleling the van, then a third right and a quick left back onto Connecticut. I searched the street ahead of me, but they were gone. Shit. I glanced in the rearview mirror and saw the van half a block behind me. I'd outrun them, encircled them too fast to stay behind the van. I swung into the curb lane and dawdled along until they went by. Now we would see how good they were.

The van continued up Connecticut for a mile or so until we approached the stoplight at Nebraska. The light was green as we got close, but the van slowed as if the driver were lost. Horns began to honk and I knew what was about to happen. I'd done the same sort of thing so often I might as well have been driving the van myself. The light turned yellow—the van at a complete stop now—but when the light turned red it shot through the intersection. More horns honked, a couple of angry shouts rang out. In the next instant the van was back in motion up Connecticut and I was stuck at the red light, with the same problem as before. If I blew through it I'd cause a commotion the van would see, would recognize me for what I was. Only this time it was worse. If I let them go this time, I wouldn't ever catch them again.

I looked both ways to make sure I wouldn't kill or be killed, then raced through the intersection. They'd probably made me already, when I showed up the second time on Connecticut. Now there was nothing left to do but bumper-lock them.

Half a minute later I was right on their tail.

If they'd made me, they would follow the book, take me all over hell, anywhere but back to their base. I glanced at my gas gauge, even though I knew it was full. No surveillance agent starts an operation without a full tank.

I settled in for the long haul.

Just before we got to the D.C. line at Chevy Chase, Maryland, the van turned right at Northhampton Street into the surrounding residential area. We passed a small library on our right before the van turned left on Chevy Chase drive and accelerated into all-out escape mode. By the time I made the same turn it was almost out of sight in the winding neighborhood. I floored the Caprice, relieved at least to know that at this time of day there was almost no one on the narrow streets.

Up ahead the van made a left. I shot after it, kept on its tail through a series of quick turns and squealing tires. I saw a school zone looming and to my relief the van turned down another street to keep away from it. By doing so they'd come closer to identifying themselves for me. Really bad guys don't give a damn who they run over. Whoever these people were, they weren't prepared to endanger little kids.

I'd lost track of street names by now, but at the next intersection I ran out of luck.

The van went through, but before I could get through behind them a red SUV blew the stop sign to my right. Suddenly it was right in front of me. I could see the wide-eyed driver trying to outrace me before I hit him. He almost made it but inexplicably skidded to a stop. I stomped the brake halfway through the firewall, but couldn't stop before I hit him in the rear quarter-panel.

My airbag exploded in my face, then sagged away. I slumped against my seat. The damage from the collision was insignificant—I'd almost been stopped when I struck the SUV—but the drain-cleaning van was gone, and I'd be here at least an hour with the other driver.

The man was out of the car when I came around to talk to him. Dark hair, not very clean dark hair, long over his collar. Suit and tie, European cut with the thin shoulder line, narrow waist, and tighter-than-American trousers. A diplomat, maybe. This part of town was filled with them.

"Are you hurt?" he wanted to know.

I changed my mind about the diplomat part. He didn't have any trace of an accent.

"Thank God you're a good driver," he continued. "I didn't even see the stop sign." He lifted the cell phone in his hand, showing me the reason he hadn't.

"I'm okay," I said, then looked at him, surprised at the flatness of his affect. I spent a lot of time with people under stress, and he didn't look all that shook up.

"Guess we better trade info," he said. "Get us both on our way."

Together we examined the damage. My plastic bumper had flexed and retracted the way it was designed to do, and with the exception of a couple of insignificant scratches there was no damage to my Caprice. His Toyota Four-Runner wasn't quite so lucky. The dent in his rear quarter-panel would have to be pounded back into shape and repainted.

"Look," he said, "I don't want to get my insurance company involved here." He glanced back at the stop sign. "It was my fault. My car is the only one damaged." He looked at my bumper. "Would a hundred bucks be enough to buff out those scratches?"

I shook my head. "I don't need any money, but I do need your ID, your driver's license and registration."

The bureau was pretty strict about that. People have a way of coming back later with claims impossible to deny if you just walk away from these things.

"Of course," he said. "Registration's in my glove compartment."

I followed him around to his car. He'd left the door open. He climbed in and reached across to the glove compartment. I glanced at the edge of his door, then looked closer at the maintenance sticker glued there. The sticker featured a drawing of a big goony service-station attendant holding a tire and smiling. I bent closer. "Best Price Service", the sticker said. "Tires and Batteries a Specialty." I felt myself frowning. I'd seen that guy before. As a matter of fact, I'd been at that very service station.

I backed away and bent to examine the front tire. A Michelin tire, but that wasn't what started the tightening in my gut. Lots of people buy Michelin tires. I bent even closer, until I could read the imprinted code numbers stenciled in white above the small numbers designating the size of the tire. Stenciled white numbers I'd been told not long ago would appear on only a few very special Michelin tires in this country.

I straightened up, leaned into the car, right up into the driver's face.

"Good job," I told him. "I've got to give you that much." I glanced up the street where I'd last seen the brown van before it disappeared. "You think they made it back to the barn yet?"

He stared at me. "What are you talking about? What the hell is that supposed to mean?"

"It means it's time for you to shut up. It's time for you to call Gerard Ziff and tell him we're on our way."

TWENTY-SIX

WHILE THE DRIVER OF THE SUV CALLED GERARD, I PHONED Brodsky to bring him up to date. This was the point where I was supposed to tell him he couldn't come along, couldn't be allowed to join us to wherever Gerard had in mind to take me. That he had no need to know. That I would brief him when I got back. It was what the rule book called for. What the Hoover Building would demand. But that didn't mean I was going to do it.

First of all, he'd throw a fit. Secondly, he had as much need to know as I did, and every right to know. Besides, Gerard Ziff had started it, and I didn't give a damn what Ziff thought anymore.

Both the sheriff and the spy showed up at the same time, Gerard driving the drain-cleaning van I'd been chasing. Ziff pulled up to the intersection from which his man and I had moved our cars, then lowered his window.

"Get in the back," he told us. "The door's open."

Brodsky glanced at me. I nodded, then followed him to the rear of the van. On the way I heard Gerard order the SUV driver to return to the embassy.

The slender dark-haired man who opened the back door nodded curtly as we climbed aboard, then returned to the swivel chair in front of his gadgets. And what gadgets they were. The van's interior looked like the control room at NASA.

On the wall to my left, half a dozen television monitors sat in a rack six feet high, an equal number of videotape recorders in the rack next to it. Fifteen or twenty radio-frequency scanners occupied another rack on the same wall. On the opposite wall were the cameras. Shelves of them, each camera secured by straps to keep it from falling. Nikons to Hasselblads, Polaroids to Sony digital cam-corders, a sixteen-millimeter motion picture camera, and several built-in baskets of lenses—tiny document lenses all the way up to the two-thousand-millimeter leviathan clipped like a fire extinguisher to the bulkhead behind the driver's seat. Then the listening gear. Wee microphones in their own baskets, a parabolic unit the size and shape of a satellite dish held against the ceiling of the van by bright chromium fas-teners. Finally, enough audiotape recorders to start up a new radio station.

I looked at Brodsky for his reaction, but his face showed no expression at all. I stepped toward the driver's compart-ment, past a black curtain that divided the working space from the driver.

Gerard turned at the touch of my hand. "Something to see, isn't it?" he said.

"I didn't come up here to congratulate you. All I want to know is what's going on? And where we're going."

"Give me ten minutes. You can ask all the questions you want to when we get there."

I went back to Brodsky, already sitting in one of the three captain's chairs that rotated to face any direction. I didn't have to tell him what Gerard had said—he had to have been listening—so I sat in the second chair and tried to turn off my brain until there was some reason to use it. The van started to move. The driver made a hard right turn and I braced my legs to keep from falling to the floor. Brodsky glanced at me, I stared back at him. The quiet Frenchman in the third chair did nothing at all.

• • •

"Forgive the melodrama," Gerard told us after we'd reached our destination, as he held the rear door open for us to leave the van, "but no one can be allowed to see you near this building."

We stood for a moment in the semidarkness of what I decided was a subterranean garage. I could smell the oil that no amount of cleaning ever gets out of a concrete floor. I could hear water dripping somewhere beyond the forest of support columns thick as redwoods. As my eyes adjusted to the lighting, I realized we were surrounded by cars and trucks.

"Come this way please," Gerard said. "And welcome to you, Sheriff Brodsky. Please forgive my lack of manners before, but time is important at the moment."

Brodsky nodded but said nothing.

Gerard led us through the gloom, hit a buzzer next to a tall metal door. The door opened and we passed through. On the other side we stood quietly. The high-ceilinged room stretched away like an oversized entrance hall, a number of corridors running from it toward wherever and whatever lay beyond. Gerard bent to speak to a young woman sitting at a small desk close by, then straightened up and turned back toward us.

"Follow me. The ambassador is most anxious to see you."

We trailed him to the second corridor on the left, then down the hallway to a conference room done in wine-colored carpet and mahogany paneling. Indirect lighting made the immense cherry conference table in the center of the room gleam like polished leather. Beyond the head of the table stood a big-screen TV. Two standing flags dominated the front corners of the room. The French tricolor and Old Glory. The American flag looked to be the newer of the two, and I couldn't help wondering if it had been brought in especially for us.

Gerard led us to the head of the table, motioned for us to sit, but remained standing himself.

"Welcome to France," he said. "Once again I'm sorry for the cloak and dagger, but I think you'll agree it was necessary in this case." He touched a button built into the tabletop. "The ambassador will be here in a moment."

"Damn it, Gerard," I started, but stopped when a door off to our right swung open and a movie star came through.

At least that's what the man looked like.

A tall man with an impressive sweep of thick gray hair and a silver mustache, immaculate European-cut dark suit draping his muscular body, he strode to us and stood next to Gerard.

"Monsieur L'Ambassadeur," Gerard said, "permit me to present my friend from the FBI, Special Agent Puller Monk, and his associate, Sheriff Edward Brodsky." He turned to us. "Gentlemen, I have the honor of introducing his excellency the French ambassador to the United States, Jean-Louis Marchand."

I stood to shake the hand he'd extended, but said nothing. Ambassador or not, this was bullshit. Marchand turned to Brodsky, shook the sheriff's hand as well.

"Sit, please," he told us. "Since our man called with Agent Monk's demand to know what was going on at the zoo, we have been talking nonstop with the Quai d'Orsay. Our president himself has been consulted. He has given me his orders. I am here to carry them out."

I nodded but continued to say nothing. I wanted to think it was because I was in control of the situation, but the truth was I couldn't think of a single thing *to* say.

"It's a matter of diplomatic immunity, Agent Monk," Marchand continued. "Your demand of Mr. Ziff is noted, but—with respect—we have no legal or moral obligation to include you in the business of the government of France."

I stared at him for a moment, then glanced at the sheriff and rose to my feet.

"Come on, Brodsky. We've got too much work to do to listen to this garbage."

The ambassador shrugged. "*Je regrette* . . . I'm sorry you feel that way, but surely you understand."

"I hear what you're saying, Mr. Ambassador, but that has nothing to do with my own obligations in this matter. The moment I leave here, I'm going to the Hoover Building, to the director of the FBI, most likely with him to the Oval Office." I smiled. "I, too, regret the inconvenience it may cause you, but surely you understand."

Marchand turned to Brodsky. "Perhaps you can help me here, Sheriff. Perhaps you can prevail upon Agent Monk to—"

Brodsky held up his big hand. "I don't care about your diplomatic immunity either, Mr. Ambassador. I'm here on my own homicide investigation, a murder in Cobb County. You were following my killer. I want to know why."

Marchand sighed, glanced at Gerard Ziff, then turned back to me.

"I will have to call my president again."

"No, you won't. You know damn well he gave you a fallback if you couldn't bully me out of here."

He smiled. "You're an interesting man. As a matter of fact, we do have authority to handle this particular contingency, if need be."

"I thought you might."

"Please sit down again."

We did so. He addressed his words directly to me.

"I can't help recalling a famous story about your President Lyndon Johnson and J. Edgar Hoover. Johnson's advisors begged him to fire Hoover, who was by then a senile despot. President Johnson refused. 'I'd rather,' he told his people, 'have the old bastard inside the tent pissing out than outside pissing in.'"

Ambassador Jean-Louis Marchand smiled.

"I don't like the way you've extorted your way inside our tent either, Agent Monk, but you're here now, and we will just have to make the best of it."

Then he nodded at Gerard, and the spy began to speak.

TWENTY-SEVEN

I REACHED FOR MY NOTEBOOK, BUT GERARD SHOOK HIS head. "No, Puller," he said, "not on paper. None of this goes on paper. Not ever. Trust me, you won't have any trouble remembering."

So I sat back and listened.

"Forgive me if I bore you with history you undoubtedly know better than I do, but this all started with Hoover and his COINTELPRO assault on the Fourth Amendment, back in the sixties."

I nodded. Hoover's counterintelligence program, COINTELPRO, was before my time, but I'd heard all the stories. Especially the infamous Library Awareness Program, a benign name for a hideous policy that targeted the nation's public libraries, that forced FBI agents to recruit librarians into informing on anyone reading or checking out leftist literature. Jesus. Talk about the Taliban.

"But COINTELPRO didn't originate with Hoover," Gerard said. "The man who actually designed and built it was Kevin Finnerty."

I stared at him. That was something I definitely didn't know. I checked Brodsky for a reaction. Nothing.

"But I'm getting ahead of myself. Prior to Finnerty's entry into the bureau, Hoover was fighting a losing battle to keep himself relevant. Clinging to remnants of the glory he'd won from his fight against the Communist Party in the United States. By the mid-sixties their political arm, the CPUSA, was for all practical purposes dead. His agents told him that without the attendance of FBI informants there wouldn't be any meetings at all, but Hoover had no intention of giving up the communist enemies who'd made him a national treasure. He forced the bureau to keep up the fight until Attorney General Bobby Kennedy finally shut the program down for good."

Again I'd heard the stories.

"The loss of his beloved enemy devastated Hoover, until he came up with a new one. The civil rights movement was flaring up everywhere, and it didn't take ten minutes for Hoover to brand Dr. Martin Luther King a Communist puppet working directly for the Kremlin."

I nodded. Hoover's blatant racism had so disgusted the Kennedy administration, both JFK and his attorney-general brother vowed to get rid of the old bastard, to restore the FBI to the control of the Department of Justice. But before they could do it, Hoover lucked out again. The antiwar movement's increasingly violent protests made it impossible to topple the director, a man ordinary Americans considered their last hope against anarchy.

"Hoover recognized that to keep his iconic stature he had to cripple the rioting students. In a time of national fear, a program like COINTELPRO looked pretty good to everyone." Gerard smiled. "A bit like today's Carnivore program, I might add."

He stopped smiling.

"Hoover was now free to attack with a vengeance, and his victims included not only library users but any American who dared question the wisdom of a war nobody believed in anymore. Men who looked up from the graves of their sons to ask why. Women working for equality in the workplace. Women Hoover forced his agents to classify in their reports as 'known female liberationists.' "

But knowing all this, I still wondered about the point Gerard was trying to make.

Finnerty's involvement with COINTELPRO was news to me, but not exactly earthshaking. There'd been plenty of public support for Hoover's program at the time, and condemnation had come mostly after the fact, when the academics finally figured out what was really going on. But COINTELPRO was long dead now, every bit as dead as Hoover himself. The idea that Kevin Finnerty was trying to dig the old tyrant back up, along with his preposterous ideas, was ludicrous.

"How long have you been watching him?" I asked. "Finnerty, I mean."

"He was twenty-four when Hoover brought him to headquarters to develop COINTELPRO. He's sixty-one this year."

"Thirty-seven *years*?" I swung around to Ambassador Marchand. "The French government has been spying on Kevin Finnerty for four *decades*?"

The ambassador looked at Gerard, and I knew why. Gerard was like me, expendable. It was his job to say the words. Should the *merde* hit the fan, the splatter would be kept far away from Marchand.

"Not at all," Gerard said. "Not at the current level, anyway. But we have kept ourselves aware of Finnerty's career since Hoover's death in 1972." He paused. "Much more so since the World Trade Center attack and the war against terrorism . . . with Carnivore and it's newest spinoff, Magic Lantern . . . finally, with the growing American acceptance of government snooping in order to keep the country safe." He shook his head. "What we've discovered isn't good. We dare not ignore it any longer."

I sat forward in my chair. "We? You're including me?"

"That wasn't our plan, not until you intruded."

"Intruded? I still don't even know . . ."

My voice died as I recalled our afternoon at the tennis club again, Gerard's bizarre reaction to Finnerty's name.

"The other day at the club," I said. "You weren't in a hurry to call the Paris police, not about Brenda Thompson, anyway. You were rushing back to the ambassador so he could make a different call altogether. So he could call your government directly."

"I made a mistake to let you see my reaction, a stupid mistake. Now we have to let you in, to keep you from destroying the progress we've made toward getting rid of Finnerty once and for all."

"Again with the 'we.' Who the hell are you talking about?"

"Us, Puller. The small community who live on this planet. Without an unbreakable democracy in your country we're all endangered. We might not like you, but we can't allow you to collapse." He glanced at Brodsky. "So we watch. We watch you, we watch everybody. We all of us watch each other."

"Maybe so, but by watching *me* you mean the FBI. By 'me' you mean Kevin Finnerty. What you're telling me is you think the *FBI* is attacking our Bill of Rights. That an assistant director of the FBI is *heading* the attack. You can't mean that. Even if you do, you can't possibly expect me to take your *word* for it."

Ambassador Marchand broke in.

"Of course we don't, Agent Monk. Our president has also authorized us to show you something no American has ever seen. But first you must listen a while longer. Our evidence will mean nothing without perspective."

I looked at him, shook my head, then nodded for Gerard to continue.

"Carnivore," he began. "Its nominal purpose is to monitor criminal activity that uses e-mail. With court authority, it enables the bureau to read e-mail messages between criminals. It's a powerful weapon against both criminals and terrorists, and the strict need for federal court oversight makes it simply an extension of the telephone wiretapping that has existed for years."

"I know all that already."

"Magic Lantern is another story altogether. This program enables the FBI to monitor individual keystrokes on a suspected computer. Every single character the keyboard sends both to RAM and to the hard disk, including e-mail sent throughout the country and the world. Virtually, the entire record of activity for a computer and the person using it. It still requires a court order, but the opportunity for abuse is hundreds of times worse. An unscrupulous FBI agent can see much more than e-mail, can monitor every Web site a computer visits, every word posted to a message board, every book or magazine either bought over the Internet or researched via the World Wide Web. In the hands of a renegade agent, Magic Lantern is personal liberty's worst nightmare. If that renegade is the assistant director in charge of the Washington Metropolitan Field Office—privy to the most sordid secrets of the capital's highest leaders—the entire American government can be compromised."

I wanted to argue, but Gerard was right.

Carnivore was a slippery slope, and the French government wasn't the only one who thought so. On the heels of 9/11, Magic Lantern had barely squeaked through the House, but its passage had drawn a renewed wave of protest, and there was no way the Senate would concur. I told Gerard as much, that to me the issue seemed moot.

"We thought so, too, until Senator Randall changed her mind."

I stared at him as I remembered my own reaction in my motel room down in Brookston when I'd seen the CNN story of the senator's abrupt about-face on the issue.

"I don't know how that happened, either," I said, "but Jeanette Randall's subcommittee is not the entire Senate. All her people can do is recommend passage of the new bill, or deny it."

"And when is the last time the Senate turned down anything her committee wanted?"

"Not often," I had to admit.

"Try never."

"Never, then, but Senator Randall must have had her reasons. She must have discovered something important to make her come so far around in the other direction."

Gerard moved to the big-screen TV behind him, pushed some buttons, then stepped aside as the screen grew bright. He held the remote controller in his hand as he spoke.

"She did, indeed," he said. "I think you'll agree she certainly did."

He aimed the clicker and the screen came to life. The picture quality was perfect, so was the sound. The videotape was as professional as anything done in a studio.

On the tape, Kevin Finnerty and Senator Jeannette Randall were seated at a restaurant table. A tuxedoed waiter with a heavy French accent brought coffee, then asked if they wanted menus, bowed and left when they waved him away. In the bottom right-hand corner of the screen was the time, 9:52 A.M., and the date. The same day, I realized, that I'd seen that CNN story.

I turned to Gerard. "What the hell is this? How . . . ? Where did you . . . ?"

"Later," Gerard said. "Just watch first. Just watch and listen."

TWENTY-EIGHT

ON THE SCREEN, KEVIN FINNERTY SET DOWN HIS COFFEE CUP.

"I know, Senator," he said to Jeannette Randall across the table, the camera's wide-angle lens providing a perfect view of both of them. "I know you have an important committee meeting in an hour. I wouldn't have asked for these few minutes were it not absolutely necessary."

"You should be a politician, Mr. Finnerty. You're here for one reason only. Because I'm turning you people down. Because you're hoping for an eleventh-hour reprieve."

"Magic Lantern is too important for politics. I just want you to do the right thing."

"To give you carte blanche, you mean. To let you and your people have whatever you think you can get away with."

Finnerty leaned toward her, his voice ice-cold now.

"You're making a big mistake, a huge mistake. We need Magic Lantern. To have any chance at all against the kind of people we're fighting, we must have it."

She shook her head. "Half my committee agrees with you, but they don't have the votes to make it happen. Thank God there are still a few of us who care about the Bill of Rights."

"We're alone here, Senator. Don't bother to make a

speech. We all care about the Bill of Rights, but if you think innovative law enforcement will bring down the Constitution, you're simply wrong."

"You call dismantling the Fourth Amendment innovative? Have you read it lately?"

"I read a lot of things. Mostly about the animals who hide behind it to keep themselves out of prison."

"Better that some go free, wouldn't you say? Better that than an innocent man in prison."

"Spend a day inside, Senator. See how many innocent ones *you* can find."

"That isn't the point and you know it."

"We don't want to do *away* with the Fourth Amendment—I shouldn't even have to tell you that—but the world has changed. The Framers didn't have telephones, couldn't possibly have foreseen the anonymity of cyberspace. Sure as hell they wouldn't agree that computers come with an inherent right to privacy. Or that the government has no right to treat electronic criminality differently than any other kind."

"Magic Lantern goes much further than that."

"Not one bit further. Same rules, same safeguards. Our program doesn't change any of the basics."

"It doesn't have to change the rules, not when it's impossible to tell when you're breaking them." She appeared to stare over his head for a moment, then straight into his eyes. "It's the fox and the henhouse, Mr. Assistant Director. The bureau has always walked a fine line with the Fourth Amendment. The Magic Lantern program—batteries of supercomputers monitoring the keystrokes of millions of home computers—puts you way over that line." She shook her head. "You're not going to do it on *my* watch. *Never* on my watch."

"We're in a war, and you talk about fine lines, about breaking rules . . . the *possibility* of breaking rules. Well, what about the bad guys? How many rules do you think they might break?" His voice got louder. "You don't give us this, we *can't* win!"

"Win what? Your version of the Land of the Free? A country where the FBI decides who's free and who isn't?"

"That's uncalled for, Senator, and I resent it. An even playing field is all I want for this country, for what's left of this country, thanks to people like you. What we've got now is anarchy. Drugs and violence. Metal detectors in our schools, for Christ's sake!" He leaned toward her. "The Bill of Rights protects the people from their government, but who's supposed to protect the people from themselves?"

"My God, I hear you talk like that and I'm all the more convinced I'm right." She was almost out of her chair now. "You might want to overthrow the Constitution, but don't expect me to help. If you're trying to form a police state, you'll have to climb over my dead body to do it."

"I guess that's up to you. But it doesn't need to happen that way."

She sat back again. "What's that supposed to mean? Are you actually *threatening* me?"

"Quite the opposite. I very much want to help you."

Finnerty reached for the black leather briefcase on the floor next to his chair, lifted it to his lap and withdrew a manila envelope, closed the briefcase, and returned it to the floor. He slid the envelope across the table. Senator Randall stared at it for a moment, then at him.

"What's this?"

"You have family in California, Senator."

"Get to the point."

"There are twenty photographs in that envelope, along with a summary report. I'll start with the first picture."

She pulled the documents from the envelope, examined the top photograph.

"My daughter, Sarah," she said. "Sarah Hansen and her husband, Jack. My grandchildren." I could see her touch the picture and smile, but the smile disappeared as she looked back at Finnerty. "There better be a damned good reason for this."

"There's never been a better reason." He pointed at the

top photo. "Whole family here, looks like, on the deck of their house in La Jolla, the blue Pacific behind them. Couple of million dollars worth of house, easy."

"Jack's a lawyer, a Boalt Hall lawyer. Trust me, he can afford it."

"He's a member of the bar, I'll give you that, but I don't think he goes to his office much."

"What are you getting at?"

"Exhibit 2, Senator, the second picture. Sarah and Jack at a nightclub in Tijuana. See the man sitting to Jack's right? Lots of hair, lots of teeth?"

"God damn it, Finnerty, Jack's an international lawyer. He's got clients everywhere! Not only Mexico but all through the Caribbean and South America. A certain amount of socializing goes with the territory."

"Of course, it does. In this case it's a few miles south of Tijuana . . . the Rosarito Beach Hotel. The man in the picture is Nogales-Rios. Juan Pablo Nogales-Rios."

Senator Randall grabbed the photo and stared at it, then flipped the photo back to the table. "So Jack and Sarah had dinner with a suspected drug dealer. In a foreign country. So what?"

But her voice gave away the truth. I could see it in the language of her body, as well. She was a professional politician. Had to know what was coming.

"Suspected drug dealer, you call him," Finnerty said, "the DEA's number one target worldwide." He cleared his throat. "You're a bright lady, Senator. I'm neither fooled nor impressed with your act."

She shrugged. "Last I heard it isn't against the law for a lawyer to have a thief as a client. As a matter of fact, it takes us right back to the Bill of Rights, doesn't it?"

Finnerty pointed at the stack of photos. "The next eighteen pictures show Jack and Nogales-Rios together in seven different Latin American countries. No Sarah, thank God, but plenty of young Jack."

Her voice became a monotone. "Same objection,

Finnerty. Habeas corpus. Show me something other than your travelogue."

"That's why I'm here. The summary report I've included goes way beyond the pictures. And it doesn't look any better for him, either."

"I'd like to see it."

He shook his head, but now his voice fairly dripped with concern.

"The bureau shares your distress. We're worried more than anything about what might be ahead for Jack. The possibility that your son-in-law could be set up even if, as you suggest, he's completely innocent."

Senator Randall said nothing. Finnerty shook his head again, for all the world an old and trusted family friend, filled with compassion for a woman on the verge of disaster.

"What can happen down there in Latin America," he said, "what we've seen happen in Mexico, in Central and South America, is almost too terrible to describe. Especially with the kinds of enemies Nogales-Rios has made."

Again he shook his head.

"No one wants your son-in-law to suffer in the kind of prison we see only in movies, in the kind of country where they've never even heard of habeas corpus. With a wife and family horrified they'll never see him again. Afraid he's dead, but even more that he might be wishing he were."

Finnerty's voice slid to a lower register.

"And you. Mother and grandmother. Your family shattered by events even a United States senator has no power to control."

She stared at him, her hands drumming the table. She looked down at the photos again, and the report, then back at him. He spoke before she could say anything.

"DEA's made Jack a target. They want to sweat his family—your family—to make their case, and believe me they can do it. I think it's political this time. I think DEA is targeting Jack because of you, and I want to put a stop to it."

Her shoulders sagged. I thought for a moment she might

collapse, but slowly her head came back up. The blow had
staggered her, but she struggled to maintain her composure
as the ADIC continued.

"I'd like to work this out at headquarters level. With the
DEA director himself. Suggest to him that Jack's been working with us, that he's put himself in considerable danger to
neutralize Nogales-Rios."

She said nothing, but he answered the only question she
could possibly have had.

"I don't know, Senator. I don't know if it will work, but
I'll do the best I can."

She appeared to draw a deep breath and blow it out
slowly. She turned away from the camera. Her shoulders
rose and fell, trying, I could see, to come to grips with his
odious quid pro quo. When Senator Jeannette Randall turned
around again her face was blank with despair, then contorted
by tears she could no longer control.

TWENTY-NINE

I CONTINUED TO STARE AT THE TV SCREEN LONG AFTER THE images had disappeared.

"Where *were* they?" I asked Gerard. "A restaurant, of course, but that isn't really my question. Kevin Finnerty's as close as you can get to the top of the FBI. *Runs* the FBI, people have been saying for years. How did you *get* something like this?"

"You didn't recognize La Maison? We were just there for lunch."

I glanced at the screen again. "I was more interested in what Finnerty was doing than where he was doing it."

"Have you ever met the owners?"

I shook my head.

"I beg your pardon, but you have. As a matter of fact, you're sitting with them right now."

"La Maison? The French government *owns* . . ."

He simply nodded.

"But an entire restaurant?" I said. "Wired like a sound-stage?" I shook my head. "Just the logistics . . . running a restaurant . . . people to hire and fire. And the *chefs*, for Christ's sake! La Maison is a great restaurant. How do you come up with the chefs?"

"My country is up to its ass in them. And no Frenchman minds firing somebody once in a while."

I looked around for a window, despite knowing a room like this wouldn't have one. Suddenly I needed to see the real world, rain and all, warts and all. To check that there was still a world out there.

"The king is dead," I said. "Long live the king! That's what your videotape looks like to me. There's nothing left of Hoover but bones in a dress, but he's still alive." I stared at Gerard. "As long as Kevin Finnerty is around, the old bastard's still alive."

"Paris agrees with every word you say."

"And Brenda Thompson's going to be his next victim, the next Jeannette Randall."

"What else could it be?"

"Christ."

Then I realized what was wrong. Why he had to be wrong.

"The Randall stuff's new, relatively new. But what about Thompson? Whatever Finnerty's going to use on her has to be more than thirty years old. Where would he get something like . . ."

My voice died as I knew where.

"You can't be serious, Gerard. You can't be telling me those files actually *exist*." I turned to Brodsky, then back to Ziff. "That Hoover's secret files are still out there."

"I don't think there can be any doubt."

"But how did you . . . How long have you . . ."

"We don't know for sure, for absolute certain, that's what Finnerty is using, but we can't deny the possibility. My government was looking for them the day Hoover died back in '72. I can't speak for the rest of the world, but I suspect we were not alone."

I just looked at him. At this point I would have believed anything.

"We thought we had them early on," Gerard continued, "a few hours after his death, but they disappeared. Vanished without a trace. I think we're right, but we'll never know until we actually see them."

"So you've got more video. More of what we just saw."

"Enough to satisfy our suspicions. Added to what I've inferred from your unusual inquiries this past week about Brenda Thompson, we know we're right about what he's planning for the judge."

"Hoover died thirty years ago. How could anything he dredged up hurt anyone now?" The instant I heard my question, I knew the answer. "Of course, Gerard. You call them Hoover's files, but they're not, not anymore. Now they're Finnerty's. The ADIC is using Hoover's *system*, not necessarily the same information. Or maybe a combination of the two. Gathering intelligence any way he can, using it to rebuild the bureau back to the days when Hoover ran the government."

"And not just Finnerty, I'm afraid."

I stared at him. How much worse was this going to get?

"At least two others," Gerard continued. "Bureau people as well, from the sound of them, but we haven't yet been able to make an ID on either one."

"From the *sound* of them?"

"From context, yes. From Finnerty's end of the phone calls we've intercepted."

"A wire? You're running a wire on him?"

Gerard glanced at the ambassador. "Something like that."

"And the restaurant. How long have you been watching him at La Maison?"

"Only since we bought it and sent him an invitation to the grand reopening. Invited him to enjoy privileges reserved for Washington's most important people. He showed up, of course—few bureaucrats can resist such an invitation—and we made sure our people put him at a special table. A very special table. When he began to come back regularly we made it even easier for him. No matter the line outside, no matter the day or time of day, Kevin Finnerty always gets that same table. Fact is, nobody else is *ever* seated there. And he's such an egomaniac we've never overheard him even wondering how it could possibly happen that way."

"Hoover and Clyde Tolson never did either, from what I've heard. Not La Maison, of course, but the same table at Harvey's out on Connecticut Avenue every night of the week."

I looked at Gerard as a second thought crossed my mind, but he shook his head.

"No, we didn't own Harvey's. And we didn't have to, in those days. Hoover was so powerful, had so much public support, he didn't bother to hide what he was doing."

"But you still didn't answer my question, not really. Are you tapping Finnerty's phones now? Right now, every day?"

He shook his head. "The firewalls on his phone system at his office and his home are unbeatable. We didn't even bother to try his office, and his home phone calls—both incoming and outgoing—hit four or five satellites at the same time. Half a dozen cities around the world showed up on our pen register."

"So how . . ."

"Microphones."

"Bugs? If you can't tap his phone, how could you penetrate his house?"

"We didn't. The bureau sweeps his house too regularly to make in-house microphones an option." He paused. "But they didn't sweep the house across the street."

"You bought a *house*?"

"Of course not."

"Don't try to tell me you rented one, I know better than that. Nobody ever *sells* a house in Kalorama Heights, much less rents one out."

"You wouldn't believe what happened. The newly retired couple across from Finnerty's house won an all-expenses paid vacation on the Côte d'Azur. You should have seen the looks on their faces. We paid for the first month, but they liked it so much they stayed another thirty days on their own money before coming back home. Enough time for us to get what we needed. To know for sure what your assistant director is up to."

Of course. The bureau uses the same ploy, although not quite as grand as the French Riviera. Four free nights in Cancún is more our speed. Fun in the sun. All you have to do is listen to a one-hour sales presentation, from an undercover FBI agent with a flair for smarm.

"So you don't have it anymore," I said, "the lookout."

"Unfortunately not."

"I'm confused about something else. What Finnerty did with Senator Randall is awful, but we have laws against that sort of thing. He's nothing more than a criminal. You have the evidence. Why not just take him down?"

"How would you suggest we go about it?"

"You and your ambassador take what you know to the president of France. Let your president deal directly with the White House. Believe me, the Oval Office will do the rest."

Ambassador Marchand interrupted.

"You are suggesting we tell the White House that the Republic of France has been running intelligence operations in his country for decades, that we still have one going right under his nose. That we have infiltrated his FBI, devoted an entire restaurant to doing so. That we run covert and entirely illegal surveillance in and around the three branches of his government. That we . . . I think you get my point."

I nodded. I'd been wasting time even bringing it up. So I turned back to Gerard and changed the subject to what had brought me here in the first place.

"What about today, then? At the zoo. What was Finnerty doing out there with a thug like Jerry Crown? If that's his real name."

"It isn't," Gerard said, but didn't elaborate. "The fact is we don't know what they were talking about out there today, not yet anyway. Our tech people are downloading the raw data now, turning it into something we can listen to. They'll bring it in here when they finish."

"If Crown's not his name, what is it?" I summarized my

Tuesday telephone conversation with Harvard Law School, and the one with Jabalah Abahd. "I came up with the name Robert Bennett early on. It's either the same guy, or you're right about Finnerty running an entire network."

"Jerry Crown and Robert Bennett are indeed the same man. But his true name is Vincent Wax."

I glanced at Brodsky, but he shook his head to indicate the new name meant nothing to him either.

"Who is he?" I asked Gerard. "Vincent Wax."

"He's got FBI credentials and badge, the same weapons, the same access to FBI files and records. Nobody can find him on the official rolls, but he looks like an agent to me."

"Except that he's a killer." I paused as I realized what else that might mean. "Christ, Gerard, did you know? Did you have information before Wax killed—"

Gerard interrupted with a firm shake of his head.

"Absolutely not. As I said, Finnerty and Wax meet very infrequently. We have an extremely covert operation going on here, but it doesn't include letting people be murdered just to keep it secret."

"So why didn't you tell me about him after what happened to the lawyer in Cheverly? Why haven't you—"

I stopped talking as I heard a knock on the conference room door behind us.

The door opened and a thin young man with glasses too big for his face came in with what looked like a digital receiver-tuner under his arm. He walked up to where we were sitting at the front of the room, set the electronic box on the table. Gerard didn't bother to introduce the technician as he unfurled some wires from the box and plugged them into electrical outlets built into the top of the conference table.

"How did we do?" Gerard asked him.

"Not as well as I'd hoped."

The man's voice was dry and uninflected, the tone of a technician more interested in his equipment than what it was being used for. The same tone I was used to hearing from our own techs at WMFO.

"To keep out of the intermittent rain," he began, in English just as good as Gerard's, "the targets chose a partially protected bench directly in front of a large signboard. The board was dirty from the rain of the past few days and provided a less than acceptable surface for an interferometric laser intercept."

He looked at me and I nodded. Laser snooping had become old hat. The bureau—as well as every other secretive agency—had learned long ago to draw the curtains whenever there was important business to discuss.

"The laser," he continued, "bounces a continuous signal at the dirty surface—the dirt itself, actually—which is vibrating with the sound waves produced by the targets themselves as they talk. The reflected beam interferes with the outgoing beam and the computer digitizes the resulting disturbance and converts it to audible speech." The technician cleared his throat. "Unfortunately the rain eroded our signal quality badly, but we used a second computer and a fuzzy logic program to make the intercept at least recognizable."

"What about pictures?" I had to ask. "Get any video?"

Gerard took the question. "We don't need pictures. We know who they are. Only thing that matters is what they talk about and what they're planning."

The technician touched a switch on the box. A sort of hissing—"white noise" it's called in the trade—filled the room, the box obviously plugged into the conference room speaker system. The voices were metallic, Finnerty's pretty much unrecognizable, but the context made it unimportant. Clearly the ADIC was in charge.

"We've got sixty seconds," the voice that had to be Finnerty's said. *"I'm not pleased with what happened in Brookston. You were told to make sure they were both dead."*

"I was sure. The preacher's head was gone, for Christ's sake. The Sands woman was covered with blood. I still can't believe she's alive."

I stared at Gerard, opened my mouth to talk, but he held a finger against his lips and glanced toward the technician.

Not with him in the room, Gerard was telling me, so I shut up and continued to listen.

"*Well, she is alive,*" Finnerty said. "*That's why I'm here today. She and her supervisor can no longer be . . .*"

A second hiss of white noise covered his words. I glared at the technician.

"The rain," he said. "Must have been a sudden squall against the signboard. There is not much to be done about that."

We continued to listen. The voices kept fading in and out.

"*. . . Monk, too,*" Finnerty said, "*most of all Monk . . . He and the woman are . . . This time you have to be god damned . . .*"

The voices died in another blizzard of interference.

I turned to Gerard. "Damn it, what good is—"

Before I could finish the question, Finnerty's voice crashed into the room with a clarity I felt all the way down my backbone.

"*You've got forty-eight hours to make sure they're dead!*"

The recording disintegrated into nothing but static. The technician turned off his machine.

"That's it," he said. "I presume that was the end of the conversation, but even if it wasn't, we didn't pick up anything else."

I stared at the electronic box as Finnerty's order to Vincent Wax continued to reverberate through my head. The ADIC's plan to extort Brenda Thompson—to "own" America's next Supreme Court Justice—was a clear threat to national security, maybe to the well-being of the whole world, but all of a sudden it had become much more personal as well. A secure planet was a good thing, hard to argue against that, but it wouldn't do Lisa and me much good if we were too dead to enjoy it.

The moment her name passed through my mind I used my cell phone to call Lisa at home. The pressure of my grip on the phone increased as I waited for her to answer. I waited through the first six rings, then heard her answer ing machine. I let go of the breath I hadn't even been aware of holding as I listened to her ask if I would leave a message.

"Damn it, Lisa," I said after the beep. "Where the hell are you?" I paused. "Pick up if you're there."

Nothing.

"Look," I said. "Get out of your apartment the second you hear—"

Her voice burst in.

"Puller. I was in the shower."

"Don't say another word. Just get out of your apartment. Hang this phone up and get out. Now!"

"But . . . What are you talking—"

"Call me back from your car. And don't use your bucar. You can reach me on my cell."

"I don't understand. What's going—"

"Now, goddammit! Right now!"

She hung up and we waited in silence until my phone rang forty-five seconds later.

"I'm at the French Embassy on Reservoir Road," I told her. "Look it up if you don't know where it is. I'll wait for you here."

I broke the connection, then turned to Gerard and tried to assure myself Lisa would be okay until I could get her back inside my corral.

"When will he do it?" I asked him. "When will Finnerty go after the judge?"

"Too soon, and that's our biggest problem. Her Judiciary Subcommittee hearings should end tomorrow afternoon, and her name will probably go to the full Senate for confirmation on Friday." He shook his head. "It's too quick. We'd counted on a couple of weeks at least, her being the first black woman on the Court, but now we're down to forty-eight hours. There's no way we can get set up that soon."

"Then why are we wasting time? Why aren't we out on the street already?"

Ambassador Marchand answered. "We can't do anything

about what he'll do to Brenda Thompson. The only thing we *can* do is wait for Finnerty's next victim to appear. Continue gathering intelligence for next time."

"Next time? Were you listening, Mr. Ambassador? What more do you people need than the corruption of our Supreme Court? A death threat against two FBI agents?"

"I didn't say nothing *should* be done, Agent Monk, only that *we* can't do anything."

"That's bullshit. I need you. You think I can just walk into the FBI director's office and tell him what I saw today? What I heard Finnerty order Vincent Wax to do? And expect him to believe me?"

I wheeled on Gerard, but he said nothing. Clearly he knew better than to take my side. I spun back toward the ambassador.

"So what the hell *do* you people do? I understand you can't take Finnerty to court, I know you can't compromise your government, but we're talking about murder here. Two murders already, another two on order. What does it take, for God's sake?"

Marchand shook his head. "I wish we could help you, but in this country all we *can* do is watch, until the time comes when we have no choice but to act."

"And what's that supposed to mean? What are you talking about, act?"

"That you will never know, Agent Monk. No American has ever known about that."

I paused for a moment to compose myself.

"Well, this time is different," I told him. "This time an American does know. This time an American is taking over. I have no intention of waiting for Finnerty to try again. I don't intend to die to keep your government out of this, and I sure as hell won't sit back and watch him take over the Supreme Court either."

"All I'm telling you is that we won't help."

"You will help. As a matter of fact, you will work right next to me until I don't need you anymore."

"Be reasonable," Marchand said. "Even if Paris authorized such a thing, there's still the time problem. What can we possibly do in forty-eight hours?"

"Nothing . . . not if we don't get off our asses and get started."

There was a long silence. I could hear Marchand breathing, before he turned to Gerard, but Gerard just shrugged.

"I told you," he said to his ambassador. "I told you about this man. I told you what would happen if he caught us."

Silence again, a long pause. I leaned toward Marchand, making myself bigger, so big he couldn't refuse me. But he did.

"It's out of the question, Monk. I'm sorry, but—"

I talked right over the top of him.

"I'll give you an hour to talk to Paris, Mr. Ambassador." I turned to leave, then turned back to him. "If you want me after that, I'll be at the Hoover Building with my director."

He didn't have a chance to respond before Brodsky and I walked out the door.

We waited for Lisa at the embassy front gate. She showed up twenty minutes later and we went back inside. After a full hour of threatening, bribing, and shouting, the French finally surrendered, and the three of us returned to Lisa's Toyota Corolla for the drive to the sheriff's car, still parked where he'd left it at the scene of my crash. The rain had stopped while we'd been at the embassy, but it started again as we got back to his Buick. It was pouring when I turned around to the backseat.

"You don't have to do this, Brodsky. We're going to color outside the lines here. You'll still get Vincent Wax. I'll deliver him personally, but this might be a good time for you to—"

His scowl stopped me.

"Do I really have to respond to that?" he demanded.

I stared directly into his gray eyes. I turned away and looked out the window to my left. A family ran past as they tried to escape the downpour, but the two little boys went out of their way to stomp every puddle, their parents laughing too hard to scold them. Such simple lives, I thought. No Kevin Finnerty for them to worry about. No matter if I stopped the ADIC or died in the attempt, these people would never know the difference.

"It could be a few days," I said to the sheriff. "Maybe longer before we get the whole mess cleaned up."

"We still using the Hilton?"

"It's only money."

"Where do I meet you in the morning?"

"I don't know yet. Lisa and I have to talk to Brenda Thompson first. We need to clear up one or two things before we're ready to start."

THIRTY

IT WAS ALMOST FIVE O'CLOCK WHEN LISA AND I FLASHED our creds at the armed courthouse guards and went into Judge Thompson's chambers. We strode past Thompson's clerk before he had a chance to react, tapped on the judge's chamber door, and walked in on her. She looked up from her desk, her eyes wide.

"Agent Monk," she said. "Did we have an appointment?"

We didn't, I told her, then introduced Lisa. "You spoke with Agent Sands the other day on the phone."

The judge nodded, but I could see she wasn't pleased to see my partner up close and personal. We sat in the matching leather chairs in front of her desk. I gave her a moment to relax, then went straight to the point.

"You've been lying, Judge. To the president, and to the bureau in the form of your personal security questionnaire. To Special Agent Sands when she called you on it. To me when I came to see you."

Her mouth opened to interrupt, but I held up my hand.

"Sarah Kendall wasn't your aunt. She wasn't terminally ill in 1972. She didn't die until twenty years after you said she did."

"I didn't say she was my—"

"Please, Judge. Stop embarrassing yourself."

She swallowed hard. It was likely she'd seldom been spoken to like this, certainly never in these chambers, and never in her life by an FBI agent.

"You were pregnant," I said. "You went to Brookston to have an abortion." I had nothing to lose by pretending I had admissible evidence of that. "You got butchered by someone in a back alley, had to go to the hospital. You used the name Jasmine Granger to get yourself patched up." I paused. "And you've been lying about it ever since."

The judge began to rise from her chair, her eyes furious, but in the next instant she slumped backward. She exhaled, the sound like air coming out of a balloon, then stared at me with nothing left in her eyes but failure. She tried to look away, but I locked onto her eyes and wouldn't let go.

"You can't imagine how much it shames me to admit this," she said after a long moment, "but everything you say is true. I've been lying for a long time. I hoped to keep on getting away with it forever."

She stopped talking to stare at me.

"How did you find out?" she continued. "How did you ever come up with the name?"

"You wrote letters to your grandmother. You signed one of them 'Princess Jasmine.' "

"Princess Jasmine." She shook her head. "I had a big imagination back then, but that was when I was a girl. Believe me, I was no princess down in Brookston. Just a terrified young woman who'd run out of choices."

"Jasmine Granger. Where'd the Granger part come from?"

"From the church where I found Sarah Kendall and the work she was doing for girls like me. From a flyer on Reverend Johnson's desk, announcing a monthly supper at the grange hall next door."

"Reverend Johnson and Sarah Kendall, that's how you found the doctor."

Her shoulders lifted, her voice suddenly stronger. "I didn't know what else to do." She paused. "What else *could* I have done?" The question wasn't meant to be answered.

"I shouldn't have had to find out this way, your honor."

"I wish you'd stop calling me that. I don't feel very honorable just now."

"It's time for the truth now."

Her eyes darted over my shoulder, as though she were hoping to get past me somehow and away from what I was digging for. Then the most famous district court judge in America exhaled slowly and sank back into her chair. She fiddled with her hair, at the scarf around her throat, and finally leaned forward and began to speak.

"It happened," she said, "a week before the end of my senior year at Berkeley."

She stared at a spot over my head and her voice leveled into a monotone.

"It was a fund-raising party in San Francisco, at the Mark Hopkins Hotel. I'd worked as a political volunteer for two years, ringing doorbells, stuffing envelopes. My reward was an invitation to the party."

She closed her eyes, looked like a woman watching an old film in her brain. A movie she'd seen a million times.

"Halfway into the evening I was introduced to a congressman, a great-looking man who acted like I was the most important woman he'd ever met. We had a couple of glasses of wine together, and the next thing I knew he had invited me upstairs to his room. I should have known better than to go. I was young, but not that young. I'd grown up with guys hitting on me, but it never entered my mind he would be like that."

Suddenly her eyes were wet, as she continued in a lower voice.

"There was nobody else in his room, of course. They'd be along soon, the congressman told me, but I knew better. We had another drink, then another. After the second one he wanted a kiss. He came to my chair, pulled me up into his arms. I know how stupid it sounds now, but I kissed him back. I wanted to kiss him, and I did, over and over. My head was reeling with booze and lust, but I knew damned well I didn't want what happened next."

The judge's body appeared to shrink as she wiped at the tears on her cheeks.

"He wrestled me toward the bed. I sobered up in a hurry, then yelled at him to stop, but he was much too strong. I started to scream but he clamped a hand over my mouth and nose, a hand so big I could no longer breathe. He used his other hand to tear my dress off, then used both hands on my underwear. He was crazy, in a trance almost, and I was afraid he might kill me."

Her words began to stumble, as though she couldn't make herself say them.

"He started behind me . . . my face in the pillow. . . . I never felt pain like that before. . . . I screamed with relief when he finally rolled me over, but he wasn't through with me yet. . . ."

Her breathing was ragged now, as though she were right back in that room with him.

"I have no idea how long he took, but he did whatever he wanted to me for what seemed like hours, then got up and pulled his pants back on. Tightened his belt. Left the room without a single word.

"I sat there on the bed for God knows how long, so stunned with shock I couldn't even cry. I raged at myself for letting it happen, shouted into the mirror that I'd encouraged it to happen. I went home and showered until my skin burned, but I could still smell the son of a bitch on me three days later."

"What did the cops say?"

She looked at me like I was crazy.

"This was 1972, Agent Monk, thirty years before any semblance of equal justice. I was a college student, a *black* girl"—there was no mistaking the fire in that word—"and he was a member of the House of Representatives. I knew how it would go. His denials, the press conference that would focus on his good works and my obvious motive for extorting him."

Her voice was hoarse now.

"I wouldn't have had a chance! He'd go on to his next victim, I'd be labeled for life. He'd already raped me once, no way was he going to destroy the rest of my life as well." She glared at me. "But he has, hasn't he? He has ruined me. And you're here to make sure of it!"

"You got pregnant?" I didn't bother to hide the skepticism in my face. "He raped you and you got pregnant?"

"I couldn't believe it either, wouldn't have known so quickly if I hadn't been consumed by the possibility. But there was no denying what the doctor told me a month or so later. I fell apart, couldn't stand the thought of waiting for commencement day, so I went home to Washington.

"I went to my church here in D.C., the same one I'd been going to since I was a kid. I told Reverend Lewis—he died fifteen years ago—that I'd been raped, that I was carrying the rapist's baby and I couldn't live with that. He told me about Brookston, about the black church down there, and the unlicensed doctor who would help me. During the procedure I began to hemorrhage. Sarah Kendall took me straight to the local hospital." Brenda Thompson looked at me. "And you know the rest."

Fresh tears rolled down her cheeks.

"There isn't a day goes by I don't mourn what happened. That I don't want to cry out at the injustice . . . my impotence in the face of that miserable bastard's power. At his absolute certainty I'd never do a thing about it." She glanced around her chambers. "And I keep fighting every day . . . doing what I can to make sure the same thing doesn't happen to somebody else."

"You said he was a congressman, Judge Thompson, but not who he was . . . who he is."

Her features hardened. "No, Agent Monk, not now, not ever. You people can no longer keep secrets . . . and you know what will happen when it comes out. I have no proof, nothing to hold up as evidence."

Now her words were as defiant as the look in her eyes.

"I want to be on the Supreme Court more than you can imagine, but if the cost is ripping those wounds wide open for the public to gawk at, I won't pay it. What happened to me has nothing to do with my qualifications. I'd rather keep the job I have than give that monster another shot at me."

"I can't force you."

She stared over my head. Her shoulders sagged, and

when she continued, her voice was barely louder than a whisper.

"But it's still the end, isn't it? No matter what I tell you or don't tell you, your report is going to end my nomination."

"The president already has our report of what we found in Brookston, not including what you just told me, of course. But you claim he's said nothing to you about it. And your confirmation hearings couldn't be going better. Unless something happens in the next two days, you could be home free."

"Home maybe, but not free. I'll never be free."

"Another question. Why did you make it so easy for us? Why did you tell Agent Sands a story she could check out so quickly, discover your lie so easily? Why not make up something we could never uncover?"

"Because you're the FBI, that's why." She turned to Lisa. "For all I knew you already had what you needed to destroy my nomination. For all I knew, you were trying to trap me in a lie. End my nomination that way."

Still talking to Lisa, she said, "I was stunned to hear about what happened to you in Brookston, to you and Reverend Johnson. There hasn't been a black church shooting in years. It makes me sick to think of it happening again."

Lisa nodded. I searched Brenda Thompson's face for duplicity, for a sign of the same hopeless lying she'd done throughout our first interview, but saw nothing to indicate as much.

"Even after what happened to your old roommate?" I asked her.

"I'm not following you. Dalia Hernandez? You found Dalia after all?"

She didn't know. I could see it in her eyes. So I told her what had happened in Cheverly.

"Dear God," she said. "Dalia was murdered, too? How could I have missed that? How could I not have seen it somewhere?"

I told her why she hadn't. The name Jabalah Abahd wouldn't have meant anything to her. She sat back, her eyes closed, then opened them and leaned toward me.

"I know what you're thinking. I agree the coincidence is clearly unlikely. But your conclusion is preposterous. You can't be saying people are getting murdered because of me." She sat straight up. Her eyes widened as she made the next leap. "Dear God, you're thinking *I* did it . . . that I *hired* the killer!"

I described Vincent Wax, the man in black who'd killed Abahd and Reverend Johnson. Who'd tried to murder Lisa as well.

She sat back, shaking her head.

"You know my record. How can you suggest I'd commit murder for a seat on the Supreme Court?"

"Kevin Finnerty, our assistant director at WMFO. Do you know him?"

"Of course. He runs your office, for God's sake. How could I not know him?"

"When's the last time you saw him, or spoke to him?"

"I don't know . . . a few months ago, I think, maybe longer. Why? What's Kevin Finnerty got to do with this?"

I looked at her. She knew better than to think I was here to answer questions.

"Other bureau officials, then. How much contact do you have with the Hoover Building?"

"I have friends over there. The director called personally to congratulate me on my nomination."

"What about Robert Bennett? Rob Bennett."

"Never heard of him."

"Vincent Wax?"

She shook her head.

"What about Jerry Crown?"

"Same answer. The name means nothing to me."

"You're lying again, Judge. You do know Jerry Crown. He called you here at your chambers a week ago."

"Lots of people call my chambers, but I'm not the only one here, you know. I don't speak to everyone who calls."

"You talked for nearly two minutes."

"I did not speak to anyone who identified himself as Jerry Crown."

Again I searched her face, her eyes. Again I saw no indication she was lying.

"Maybe," she said, "this would be easier if you just tell me what's going on."

"Who else knows about what happened to you with the congressman? What you did down in Brookston."

"Nobody. Sarah Kendall, of course, before she died. My minister here in Washington, Reverend Johnson in Brookston, but they're both dead, too. And the church doctor who did the abortion. I guess you'd have to include the doctor and nurses at the hospital who patched me up afterward."

"Your husband?"

"What would have been the point of that?" She closed her eyes for a long moment, opened them again to look at me. "So what now? What am I supposed to do while you decide my future?"

"I wouldn't presume to say, your honor. All I do is report what I find. Whatever it means for you we'll just have to see."

Back out in the Caprice and on our way over to WMFO, neither of us said a word until we were halfway there. Lisa was the first to break the silence.

"I want you to promise me something, Puller. That we'll find that congressman, the bastard who raped her. Not now, of course, but when this is all over."

I nodded. It would be interesting to see how macho he was with a pair of Vice-Grips around his nuts. My face flushed with anger as I thought about what the congressman had done, when I considered what Kevin Finnerty had in mind for continuing Brenda Thompson's ordeal.

I would need a second pair of Vice-Grips, I decided. There should be a few pairs of them in our tech room at WMFO. We could pick them up right now, when we stopped at the field office for the rest of what we'd need in the morning.

THIRTY-ONE

I MADE LISA WAIT IN THE UNDERGROUND GARAGE AT WMFO while I went upstairs. I couldn't allow her to be seen with me, and she'd be just as safe in the car. Even Kevin Finnerty knew better than to have Vincent Wax kill her in the FBI's basement.

Upstairs, I considered my first problem. I had a shopping list to fill, but it was only a quarter after six. Like every other field office in the FBI the place was still humming. Word of our suspension had to be the talk of the building, and Finnerty's order for us to stay away would have been made just as clear to our fellow agents as it had been to us. I didn't have to go to my office on the third floor, which took some of the pressure off, but it still wasn't going to be easy.

I started at the tech room on the second floor. Not much danger getting busted down there where the techies lived. They never got the word about anything. Gordon Shanklin grinned as I came through the door.

"Puller? What is this? A second visit so soon?"

I went past him without a word, to a shelf against the nearest wall. I grabbed my radio code-changing unit and hurried toward another shelf farther down the way, where I selected a handful of miniature TV camera/radio transmitter assemblies and a single tiny microphone attached to a ten-foot length of black electrical cable. I selected a leather satchel from a collection of them on another shelf close by, stuffed the gear into it, and headed back out the door.

"Sorry to be rude," I told Gordon on my way by. "But you know how it is at the top."

I heard him snort as I started for my next stop.

There was no doubt in my mind that Finnerty's Mercury Marquis would be in the garage in the basement. The ADIC never went home before nine o'clock. And the car was there, I discovered when I stepped out of the elevator and into the garage. I didn't bother to check on Lisa, sitting in my Caprice down the row. She couldn't be anywhere safer.

Code-changer in hand, I went through the motions of opening the trunks of three supervisors' cars and pretending to test their codes, then moved to the ADIC's Mercury next to the elevator. I went around to the driver's door, opened it to get the keys to the trunk, but saw they weren't hanging in the ignition. I scanned the seat, looked behind the visor, went through the glove compartment and the console between the front seats. Finally, I searched the floor of the car itself, but they were gone.

I walked down the length of the garage to the car maintenance area, a large space that looked like a gas station without the pumps. Freddy Vitek was the night man this week. He crawled out from under a Ford convertible when I called his name, wiped his hand on a red shop rag as I told him what I needed. He stepped inside his tiny office, opened a wall-mounted case, and plucked a set of keys from the hundreds hanging on the hooks inside, then handed them to me without a word and went back to his Ford.

Back at Finnerty's car I opened the trunk and bent inside to inspect his radio unit. From my pocket I pulled the microphone/transmitter unit and long cable I'd removed from Gordon Shanklin's collection upstairs. I bent closer to the radio unit, located the auxiliary power supply socket at the rear, plugged the end of the cable into it, then ran the black cable through the pass-through at the rear of the trunk and up behind the back seats of the car. I crawled back out of the trunk, walked around the car and peered inside to check my work. I nodded. Couldn't see a damn thing. Finnerty wouldn't either, not unless he made a point of looking for it.

I walked the ADIC's spare keys back to Freddy Vitek. He didn't even bother to acknowledge me as I passed by on the way to the cabinet in his office. I replaced the keys and headed back upstairs.

At the main switchboard on the second floor, Gerry Ann Walsh was busy handling calls. She looked at me with questioning eyebrows.

"Don't bother," I mouthed. "I know where it is."

I walked around behind her and grabbed the all-clear book from the top drawer of the gray metal file cabinet at the back of her space, opened it, and made a mental note of the code I needed, then replaced the book.

"Thanks," I mouthed again as I left Gerry Ann to her callers.

Next it was the gun vault on the third floor, the same floor as my own office in Squad 17. Now I had to be more careful.

I spotted a couple of agents from my squad talking in the hallway ahead, so I ducked into a doorway until they moved on. I double-checked to make sure the coast was clear, then hustled to the gun vault, twirled the combination, and was in and out in less than a minute. I tucked a Sig Sauer nine-millimeter semiautomatic into my briefcase with the electronic gear, along with the four-inch silencer I would attach to the pistol later.

Back in the garage, I climbed into the Caprice and smiled at Lisa. She smiled back as we headed back up to the street and on our way to Brodsky at the Hilton. Before we got there, I called my father's nursing home and caught Jack Quigley in his office.

"Cutting it close, aren't you?" he told me. "We were getting ready to box up his stuff and have it ready for you to pick up when you come to get him."

I told him why I was calling, that I was ready to use my Visa card to settle the account, to keep my father right where he was.

"You're going to pay?" he said. "You're actually going to give me some money?"

"I'm in a hurry, Jack."

"How much? How much you want to put on the Visa card?"

"All of it."

"Ninety-five hundred dollars? You're kidding, right?"

"You want it or not?"

He shut up and ran it through.

That night at the Hilton we rehearsed. Lisa, Brodsky, and I, along with Gerard Ziff, who came over to get his instructions for the next morning. I practiced for a couple of hours on a few of the skills I hadn't used for a while, performing them over and over as I worked to get ready. Brodsky gave me a few tips from his detective days, a couple of things I'd never thought about.

"Look," he told me around eleven-thirty, as we were finishing up for the night, "just think of a lock as a woman."

His smile showed he wasn't accustomed to using it.

"Get in there and feel around. Hit the right place, it'll open up for you."

I stared at him. "Another joke? Jesus, Brodsky, don't tell me you're finally letting go."

He quit smiling. "Just took awhile, Monk, that's all. A lotta bad history, lotta bad blood. For you people, too . . . Don't think I haven't noticed." He glanced at Lisa. "But you two . . ."

He let the words die, then started again.

"We're both here to get what we need, that's all I'm telling you. And you're not doing the feeb thing . . . not running a game on me." He paused. "What I'm trying to say is that you don't suck."

I grinned at him. Lisa touched his beefy shoulder.

Gerard Ziff went home. The rest of us went to bed.

THIRTY-TWO

WE WERE IN PLACE AT SEVEN-FIFTY-EIGHT THE NEXT MORN-
ing. From here on in, the exact time of day would begin to
mean something.

Lisa was using my Caprice, parked around the corner in
Kevin Finnerty's neighborhood, waiting for her first assignment. Brodsky was at Vincent Wax's apartment on Seaton
Place. Gerard was at the French embassy to coordinate
whatever we came up with, to provide whatever technical or
manpower needs we might have if their drain-cleaning van
turned out not to be enough.

I was by myself in that van, just around the corner from
Finnerty's three-story brick house on Belmont Road in
Kalorama Heights. At eight-fourteen I picked up my cell
phone and called the ADIC at his office.

"Puller Monk," I told his secretary. "Is Mr. Finnerty in
yet?"

"Of course he is," Barbara Perkins growled, "but he's out
at Quantico already. At the SAC conference. You can call
him if it's an emergency." Her tone suggested it better be an
emergency if I planned to bother her boss.

I told her it wasn't important, then hung up and punched
Brodsky's number.

"Wax's van is still here," he told me, "but the battery on our locator transmitter is just about gone."

"Finnerty's tied up," I said, "but the wife's car is still in the driveway. Lisa will take her when she leaves. With the transmitter gone, you better tighten up on the van. Forget about discretion from here on in. Just make sure Wax doesn't come over here until I'm finished inside." I paused. "And Brodsky?—"

"Quit worrying," he told me. "He won't get anywhere near Lisa either."

Next I called Lisa.

"You ready?" I asked her.

"I was ready yesterday. Finnerty made sure of that."

"Look, Lisa"—I tried to think of a way to say it—"I need you for this. But I need you even more *after* this, know what I'm saying?"

"I'll be careful, boss."

But she wouldn't be, I knew, and I wouldn't expect her to be. We were both FBI agents. She would do whatever it took to keep Finnerty's wife off me. Anything less would be an insult to both of us.

Finally I called Gerard at the embassy.

"It's a go," I told him. "Just as soon as the wife leaves."

I broke the connection, then started the van and pulled around the corner and into Finnerty's street. Close enough to his big brick house to see his wife's dark blue BMW sedan in the driveway, far enough way to keep her from spotting me if she cared to look. The street was quiet. In a neighborhood this nice it was probably always that way.

I glanced at the clock in the dashboard. Eight-thirty-two. I refused to think the worst, that Finnerty's wife would choose today as stay-at-home Thursday, or that she wouldn't leave until the maid showed up at two o'clock for what Gerard had described as her regular afternoon cleaning session. That I'd have to come up with some kind of ruse to get both of them out of the way long enough to accomplish what I needed to do. Going into the house without proper backup and preparation was risky enough. I sure as hell didn't need another complication.

All I could do was move my seat back, settle in, and wait.

An hour and a half later the ADIC's wife came out her front door.

Dressed to the teeth, she strode to the BMW sedan in the circular driveway and got in. Lunch, most likely, or some heavy-duty shopping. She'd be gone at least an hour, I was certain, and the maid wouldn't show up until long after I was gone.

I punched Lisa's speed-dial number. "Blue Beemer's out. I'll call the direction when she starts to move."

I watched the lady start the car and pull out of the driveway, turn west toward the first intersection, sweep past me and around the first corner toward Lisa.

"Got her," Lisa said before I could report. "I'll put her down and get back to you."

Twenty minutes later my cell phone rang.

"She's down," Lisa said. "Looks like lunch with friends."

"Stay tight on her. I'll need an hour."

"Count on it."

I put the phone back in my pocket. Despite the situation, the potential for disaster, I found myself smiling at the team I'd assembled. My homicide-dick sheriff, my ex-prosecutor, my tennis-playing French spy. And their leader. A gambling-addicted father-hating dome-owning son of a bitch who knew better than to tilt at windmills but couldn't make himself stop.

I started the engine, drove halfway up the block, right in front of Finnerty's house now, parked at the curb, and shut down the engine. I opened the door, got out, adjusted my white coveralls, then turned back and reached for my leather satchel with the gear I'd lifted from Gordon Shanklin's tech room. I pulled it out of the van, then closed and locked the door. The Neighborhood Watch probably had a fix on me already, but all they were seeing was a hardworking drain repairman, eager to start his day's work.

I strode up Finnerty's circular driveway. At the forest-green front door I examined the lock and realized that Gerard Ziff's people had done their homework. The Baldwin lock system was exactly as the French technicians had described, exactly the same as the one I'd spent an hour practicing on last night. The polished brass pull and the keyed deadbolt gleamed with quality, but they'd never been designed to baffle any sort of lock man at all. I took a quick look up and down the street, then dropped to my knees.

From my overalls pocket I pulled a tan leather pouch, opened the drawstring, and withdrew the two picks it would take to turn the lock. A tension wrench and a hook, black-steel tools that except for the color reminded me of the tray next to a dental chair. I bent closer to the lock, then reached into the same pocket for a tiny cylinder of spray lubricant, spritzed the misty oil directly into the lock.

I inserted the tension wrench into the keyway, twisted it slightly to the right until I felt it trying to turn the mechanism that would slide the bolt out of the door jamb. I pushed the steel hook into the lock right alongside the tension wrench, then used the technique I'd worked like a dog to perfect back in training school, had used more than a few times since.

I jiggled the hook to lift the teeth, the tension wrench to keep them from slipping back down. One after another, five in a row, before I twisted both tools to the right and turned the lock. I felt my eyes widen. Under twenty seconds? Amazing what could happen when you mixed adrenaline and WD-40. I realized my hands were shaking. Couldn't be fear, I told myself, but I was lying and didn't mind admitting it. An agent who feels no fear is either crazy or awfully damn new.

I stood for a moment to gather my wits, then opened the door.

A shrill whistling tone greeted my entrance, the warning signal that started the forty-five-second countdown before the system would send a silent alarm to the switchboard at

WMFO. I moved to the nearest telephone, on an antique table in the living room, picked it up, and dialed the office switchboard.

"It's Kevin Finnerty," I said to a voice I didn't recognize, a young man who couldn't possibly have recognized mine. "You're going to get a silent alarm from my house. I tripped it by mistake. I need you to reset the system."

"Yes, sir," the kid said. I could hear him turning to reach for the all-clear book behind him. "Just give me your clear code and I'll reset it."

I did so. He thanked me and hung up. A moment later the shrill tone disappeared and I went to work.

Kevin Finnerty's home was even bigger inside than it looked from the outside. Complete coverage was out of the question. I would have to make some choices. I looked for a place to start.

On the hardwood flooring in the living room, Persian carpets separated three distinct groupings of furniture. Nice stuff—traditional, with lots of flowery fabrics—but I wasn't interested in the furnishings. The floor-to-ceiling gray stone fireplace at the far end was what caught my eye. And the bookshelves flanking it, almost completely filled with leather-bound books, the various gaps filled with a variety of small bronze sculptures.

I set my satchel down on the floor next to the shelves, opened it, and grabbed a very special leather-bound book to add to the collection. Two inches thick, a pseudo-volume containing not a word of text. I laid it open to check the real contents, the L-12 assembly I'd swiped from Shanklin. A miniature video camera, microphone, and transmitter, along with a half-dollar-size battery. A smaller, smarter version of the bureau's old WQM60 I'd used in the past.

I lifted the book to the shelf on the left side of the fireplace, shoved it between two others, then stepped back to check it out. The leather binding matched the rest of the books, and the decorative tooling on the spine hid the minuscule lens peering out into the room. I trusted that these bookshelves served the same purpose in this house as in most homes, more decorative than functional. Wouldn't do to have either of the Finnertys reach directly into the lens for a late-night read.

I closed the satchel and continued down the long hallway toward the back of the house.

The next left was the TV room, the sixty-inch Matsushita console dominating the front wall. Top of the line, I saw. Theater-quality surround-sound speakers, DVD and VCR included. Two matching green leather recliners facing the screen. In addition to the floor speakers running off the digital amplifier/receiver, the TV set had its own built-in speakers in the front. I pulled the woven-fabric cover from the right-side speaker, installed another L-12 assembly, not built into a book this time, of course. I backed up to inspect the installation.

The speaker fabric was perfect, loosely enough woven to allow the lens an unobstructed picture, but far too dense for anyone in the room to notice the camera behind it. Now the Matsushita was a TV with two functions. Kevin Finnerty might not be watching it, but it would sure as hell be watching him.

I stepped out of the room and continued up the hallway until I found Finnerty's home office. The door was closed. I opened it and went through, closed it behind me and looked around.

Walnut shelves lined the wall to my right, but there were few books. The shelves were covered with framed photographs of Kevin Finnerty with famous people. Jimmy Carter, Ronald Reagan, the Bushes, father and son. But most of all, J. Edgar Hoover. Half a dozen pictures of Finnerty with the bureau's first director. In them Finnerty looked like a kid, but the old man's complexion already resembled the bronze statue in the Hoover Building's interior courtyard. The only nongovernmental people I spotted were Billy Graham and Pat Robertson. Just the sight of them made me queasy.

There were no women, no blacks. No Mrs. Finnerty, no children.

The books were memoirs, I saw, authored by some of the same people in the pictures. The most prominently displayed was Hoover's *Masters of Deceit*, his 1958 diatribe against domestic Communists, a book containing little more than jingoistic phrases designed to entertain the Joe McCarthy lovers who constituted its readership.

I moved across the red-and-blue Tabriz carpet that covered much of the maple flooring. Matching blue-leather armchairs faced an antique walnut desk in front of the ceiling-high window that dominated the room. Another Hoover picture sat on the desk, facing the room. I recognized the old man's last official portrait, taken about 1960, freezing him in combat position against the Kennedy brothers' latest onslaught. The first director's unmistakable blocky handwriting covered the lower third of the portrait. I stepped closer to examine the inscription. "To one of the chosen," I read out loud. And it was signed simply *Edgar*. I felt my eyebrows lift. Hoover's use of the name only a handful of people on the planet dared utter told me a hell of a lot more about his relationship with Kevin Finnerty than a hundred rumors.

Two telephones stood side by side on the desktop, one standard, the other a STU-III phone—a secure transmission line we called the batphone—that sat atop an electronic box. When connected to a similar phone anywhere in the world, the batphone's signal could not be intercepted. Finding it here didn't surprise me. Bureau regulations require using the STU-III phone for anything even remotely resembling a classified matter, and there are no exceptions. As the assistant director heading the Washington Metropolitan Field Office, Finnerty had to maintain a STU-III phone here at the house. Seeing it, I now understood something else.

Gerard had mentioned the problem of tapping Finnerty's conversations—chasing the signal from satellite to satellite, country to country—and the batphone was the reason why.

Finnerty's office was the most logical choice for any sort of meeting with Judge Thompson, but I couldn't use another L-12 book on these bookshelves. There were too few books, for one, and unlike those in the living room the ADIC probably read these. Every night, maybe.

I checked the blue-velvet drapes drawn tight across the massive windows. I couldn't use the drapes themselves—God knew what would happen if Finnerty decided to open them; I pictured the bug bouncing on top of his desk—then noticed the matching valance above the drapes. No matter what Finnerty did to the drapes, the padded and velvet-covered valance was screwed solidly to the wall behind it. A bug planted there was going nowhere.

I stepped behind the desk, laid my satchel on the gleaming desktop, opened it, and grabbed another mini-assembly, this time attached to a needle-sharp chromium hook. I used Finnerty's chair, pulled it next to the window, and stood on it to inspect the valance. Across the top, all the way across, blue pleating had been stitched into place.

I reached behind one of the pleats near the center of the span, hooked the L-12 securely into place. With a tiny knife blade from my pocket I cut an all-but-invisible slit, pulled the fiber optic lens just far enough into the slit to allow the lens to see. I fluffed the material back into shape, climbed down and looked at my handiwork. Perfect, I would have had to climb back up on the chair to find it again.

I closed the satchel once more, pulled the chair back into place, then policed the area to make sure I'd left no trace of my presence. Satisfied, I headed for the door, but froze in place when I heard a soft knock.

"Señor Finnerty," a woman's voice called, followed by a second knock, this one slightly louder. *"Tengo correo, señor. ¿Está aqui?"* Then in heavily accented English, "You are home, Mr. Finnerty? I have mail, sir."

I stared at the door. Damn it, Gerard. *What the fuck was she doing here already?*

The knob began to turn.

I looked for a place to hide.

THIRTY-THREE

BOLTED FOR THE DESK, BUT STOPPED AS I REALIZED I'D never get there in time.

I fell to my knees instead, sorting through my satchel like a real drain-cleaning guy looking for the electronic instrument he needed to find the problem. The maid would never buy it, of course, but it was the best I could do. I waited for the door to open, for the questions she'd want answered.

But it didn't open.

I stared at the knob. It was no longer turning. I heard the maid's footsteps retreating down the hall.

My chest rose and fell as I reminded myself not to celebrate too early, that the maid was still out there someplace. Might even be calling the police for all I knew. Certainly might be listening for me from some other part of the house.

I turned to inspect the windows behind the desk. No help. They were sealed tight, the leaded-glass panes designed never to be opened. I slipped over to the door and put my ear against it, but couldn't hear a sound. I turned the knob and opened it a sliver. Now I could hear music—salsa—a radio playing, or a television set. The sound was distant, so I opened the door a little wider. The music was coming from the other end of the house, far in the back. The maid was most likely closer to the music than she was to me. It was now or never.

I pulled the door open and ran on my toes to the front entry, out the door and back to the van. I sat for a moment while my breathing returned to normal. Damn it, that had been far too close, and that wasn't even the worst of it.

The maid had obviously come in after I was already there, but I'd heard nothing from the alarm system. It hadn't been reset properly by the kid back at the office switchboard. The maid was bound to have noticed. She would have been ordered to call Finnerty or his wife any time there was a problem with the alarm. Bureau tech people could be on their way right now.

I started the van and drove slowly up the street, then called Lisa and told her to come back to me, that there wasn't any reason for her to stay on the wife anymore. I directed her toward where she could find me, a couple of blocks away from the Finnerty residence.

"Did you have time?" she wanted to know, after she'd joined me in the French van, after I'd told her what had happened with the maid, and what I feared might happen when she discovered the alarm malfunction.

"The bugs are in there all right," I said, "but we've still got work to do with the feed."

I crawled past the black curtain into the back of the van to inspect the monitors. The pictures from the house were clear as a digital camcorder's, but the transmission quality was only part of the equation.

"Great pictures," I called to Lisa, "but we're still too close to the house. If the cops or the bureau show up we can't take the chance of being anywhere near the place."

"So what do we do?"

"Get behind the wheel and drive. I'll tell you when to stop."

I watched the monitors as she drove us farther away from the house. She stopped half a minute later. "How are they now?" she called back to me.

"Just as good. Where are we?"

"Still too close, I think. But I see a grove of sycamores down the way. Big trees."

She drove more quickly now. The pictures began to degrade, then turn unusable. A minute or so later she stopped again, asked again.

"No good," I told her. "We're out of range now. All we've got is white noise . . . nothing but snow . . . no picture at all." I looked around the inside of the van, saw what we needed. "Find me a tree," I told her. "A nice fat tree."

"I can do better than that. I can give you a choice from a hundred of them."

I went up to the driving compartment and looked over her shoulder. She'd delivered us into the middle of a sycamore grove, a forest of trees that would do just fine, although they were a little too winter-bare to be perfect.

The grove was at the edge of a forest that stretched off toward Rock Creek Park. I could still see Finnerty's street in the distance, so line of sight for the transmitter would be adequate, and hiding the van back here couldn't be better.

"Pull as far into the trees as you can," I told Lisa, then went back and grabbed the relay transmitter that would make the whole setup work for us. Shaped like a boomerang but smaller, the transmitter came with its own battery pack and heavy-duty cabling.

A moment later the van stopped. Lisa walked around and opened the back door. I carried the relay transmitter to the door and hopped to the ground.

We worked quickly.

Lisa stood lookout as I used wood screws to fasten the boomerang to the back side of the broad trunk of a sycamore that was ten feet deep into the forest and had a clear line of sight to the house. The boomerang was omnidirectional, would accept the signals from the bugs I'd put in the house and shoot them out in every direction at once. With a range exceeding one mile, we could sit axle-deep in the waters of Rock Creek and still enjoy both picture and sound.

Back in the van, I drove this time while Lisa watched the

monitors. Down toward Rock Creek, up a wide dirt path, into a clearing between heavy bushes. I pulled to a stop.

"Well?" I asked over my shoulder.

"Couldn't be better."

I parked the van and climbed back to join her. The pictures were not quite as good as they'd been at the curb outside the house itself, but I could fix that. I twisted and tweaked the switches and knobs, dials and LCD displays, until the picture was perfect. Finnerty's living room, TV room, and office lay perfectly centered, each room crystal clear on its own monitor screen.

I fine-tuned the volume on the sound board next to the monitors. The maid's salsa music was still there, louder toward the living room but indistinct in the office. I nodded at Lisa. However this thing ended up playing out, we were as ready as we'd ever be to getting it started.

THIRTY-FOUR

FINNERTY'S WIFE CAME HOME AT TWO-THIRTY-FOUR THAT afternoon. From our captain's chairs in the van in Rock Creek Park, Lisa and I watched her move in and out of view as our cameras recorded her routine.

I found myself staring at my partner's profile as she watched the monitors. In the tight space, the citrus-flower combination of her perfume and shampoo was intoxicating. I watched her breasts rising and falling with the rhythm of her breathing, then caught her glancing at me. She smiled a quick smile and turned away even faster.

Our behavior made me smile.

Ever since we'd become lovers we were going to absurd lengths to keep our new relationship from intruding into the workplace. Like a pair of animals circling a suspiciously dangerous watering hole, we waited for only the safest moments to drink. Needing the water to stay alive, needing to stay alive to drink the water.

Kevin Finnerty came home at five-seventeen, and I was happy to see it. According to Gerard, the ADIC never came home before nine o'clock. It was a good sign, especially on the evening before Brenda Thompson's Senate hearings were expected to conclude.

An hour later the Finnertys sat down to eat dinner in front

of the television. CNN, I realized, as I recognized the voice of Aaron Brown. Again I was impressed by the quality of the devices I'd hidden inside the house. Not only were the pictures of Finnerty and his wife sharp and clear, but the sound was even more perfect.

We listened as Aaron Brown delivered the latest news about the centuries-old battle in the Middle East. We continued to listen as he changed the subject to the mounting concern over flooding in San Antonio. But we really listened when the topic turned to Judge Brenda Thompson's amazingly rapid progress through the confirmation process, and we were riveted to our headsets when the anchorman threw the story to Catherine Crier on Capitol Hill.

"... *all the veteran Senate-watchers are agreeing, for once,*" Crier was saying. "*After the Clarence Thomas fiasco, the Judiciary Committee will do anything to avoid another spectacle of a black nominee for the Supreme Court being roasted alive by the senators. It appears certain that her hearings will end by noon tomorrow, that confirmation by the full Senate will follow immediately after lunch . . .*"

I turned to Lisa.

"You were right, Puller. It is going to happen tonight."

On the TV-room screen, Kevin Finnerty showed no reaction to the CNN story we'd just heard. He continued eating without a pause. On his plate was a real dinner, but his wife had only a salad. A bottle of wine sat on a small table between them. She was drinking from a large wineglass. There was no glass on his side of the table. She drank deeply, emptied the glass and reached for the bottle, poured out the few ounces left in it.

"Sweetheart," she said to her husband. "Would you be kind enough to open me another bottle?"

"Why don't we wait awhile, dear. Maybe a nice port after we finish eating."

"I don't want any port . . . just another bottle of the merlot."

"No more wine, Margaret. You know what Doctor Abra—"

"Don't *bother* then. I'll get it myself!"

Lisa and I looked at each other. The sudden change in her tone carried a lot of backstory.

His wife started to get up, but Finnerty reached out and stopped her with his hand. "Sit down!" he snapped. "You will have no more wine! Don't make me tell you again!"

Lisa spoke without looking at me. "Consistent son of a bitch, isn't he? No better with her than he is with the rest of us."

We fell silent as we continued to watch and listen, but Lisa turned away after a few minutes. I knew why.

Most people would argue that marital intimacy was exclusive to the bedroom, but they'd be wrong. I'd watched enough scenes like this one to know when people were really naked, and seeing it made both Lisa and I feel a little like perverts. And it didn't help to know how few FBI agents would think we were crazy to feel that way.

Peeping is the lifeblood of a professional watcher, and the FBI is filled with people who relish the job. Just the prospect of catching sight of a naked woman can energize a team of watchers for hours, but the real brass-ring is actual copulation. The shrinks have a name for the disorder. *Reaction formation*, they call it. The phenomenon by which respectable people choose laudable careers that allow them to perform the same acts they would otherwise be sent to prison for.

Surgeons get rich by dismembering people, commodity brokers even richer for gambling on everything from orange juice to pork bellies. Priests gain heaven through extraordinary attention to the boys choir, fundamentalist pastors are free to beat their sons till they bleed. And FBI surveillance teams get overtime pay for watching people fuck.

Movement on the screen caught my eye.

"Looks like dinner's over, Lisa. For Finnerty anyway. And wifey's toasted enough to take her all the way through till morning."

Mary Margaret was already nodding off, wineglass dangling from the tips of her fingers, a smallish puddle of purple merlot forming on the carpet near her feet. Finnerty walked out of the picture. I glanced at the office monitors, hoping to see him open the door and come through.

And he did.

He closed the door behind him, moved straight to the desk, around it to the high-backed leather chair. He sat with his back to the camera. His right hand reached out to the pewter-framed photograph at the head of the green blotter, to the picture of J. Edgar Hoover I'd seen earlier, the one with the intimate inscription. He straightened it, but his fingers lingered for a long moment before he let it go and went to work.

We heard drawers opening and closing, watched him open one or another file on his desktop, jot some notes, rearrange some pages, then go to another one. Fifteen or twenty minutes later he rose from his chair and walked across the carpet to the bookshelves against the wall to the camera's right. He stretched on his toes to remove a single volume, then reached into the empty space. There was a loud click and the bookcase appeared to move. He grasped a lower shelf and pulled gently until the bookcase pivoted away from the wall. He stepped toward what had to be a recessed door. I met Lisa's glance.

"Has to be a wall safe," I told her. "Probably bureau-installed."

She nodded. We turned back to the picture.

Finnerty appeared to be working a lock, until he stepped back and pulled open a grey metallic-looking door. Six feet high, I judged, much taller than a standard wall safe. In the next instant Finnerty stepped past it and disappeared into the wall.

Moments later he came back out with two files, one slender, one almost three inches thick. The thick one was dog-eared, the other pristine, but both covers were the same nondescript tan color the official bureau had long-ago abandoned in favor of the white and brown in current use.

The ADIC left the vault door open, returned to his desk, and chose the thick file first, opened it, and appeared to read. He made some notes, then opened the skinnier file and did the same thing, read a few pages, made more notes. Then he rose again and took the files back to his vault and disappeared into it once more. When he came out this time, his hands were empty.

Back at the desk, he gathered his notes, opened his briefcase, and laid them inside. Then he got up and walked out of the room, reappeared in the TV room, where he took one look at his passed-out wife and shook his head. He walked over to her, touched her shoulder, then shook it. After a long moment, she came to life, stared at him with wide eyes.

"Go to bed," he told her. "I've got to work late, and I don't want you sleeping in this chair all night again."

She nodded, grunted as she got out of her chair and shuffled out of the room. Finnerty shook his head again, then followed her. My microphones followed the sound of his footsteps down the hardwood floor of the hallway toward the front of the house. A moment later we could hear the front door open, then close again. Finally, faintly, we heard the sound of his car starting.

"Shit," Lisa said as she jumped toward the driving compartment.

"Drive," I said as I crawled up to join her.

THIRTY-FIVE

HE TOOK US TO THE SUPREME COURT.

Lisa and I didn't say much as we tried to keep up with Finnerty's Marquis through the streets on the way to Capitol Hill, to keep up with the much faster car without being spotted. We spent the time listening instead for some sound from the microphone I'd planted in the ADIC's car, but we heard nothing more than car sounds. Tires against the road, engine accelerating and backing off, the tiny squeal of disc brakes. At least the bug was working.

Before we got to the Supreme Court building, just off Capitol Plaza on First Street, I'd already called Gerard at the embassy. It was time to bring him and his people into play.

My microphone in Finnerty's car was a necessary hedge against the chance that the ADIC would choose somewhere other than his own home to attack Brenda Thompson, but it wasn't good enough anymore. It hung the entire operation on the premise that he'd use his bureau Marquis instead, and that was nowhere near a certainty. Or that he'd use any car at all for that matter.

Gerard and his laser technician—the same guy from yesterday at the embassy—had been standing by for just such an emergency. They were on the street moments after I called, had joined Lisa and me in the drain-cleaning van not five minutes after we'd stopped on Capitol Hill, far enough away from Finnerty's car to keep him from spotting us in the darkness.

I could see his black Marquis perfectly, however, parked under the pallid streetlights along the circular driveway that ran through Capitol Plaza, the grass and tree-covered area outside the less-photographed back side of the Capitol. It was eight-fifty-three now, and the plaza was pretty much empty of pedestrians or vehicles. It had turned colder during the day, and it wasn't raining for a change.

"Hope the weather holds," the laser tech said as he went through the process of aiming his machine at Finnerty's car, our only option now that we had no clue where the Thompson meeting would occur. "Conditions are absolutely perfect," he continued, "as long as it doesn't rain, and this thing goes down inside one of the two cars."

I took a moment to call Brodsky.

"Still here," he told me when I asked. "Wax's van is parked out front. He hasn't come out all day."

I told him what we were doing, that I'd get back to him the moment we finished. He told me he'd call if Vincent Wax made a move.

At nine-o-seven, a second car pulled into the parking space behind Finnerty's. A tan Volvo sedan, couple of years old, not the sleeker body style of the new ones. A moment later, Judge Brenda Thompson got out of the car and walked toward the black Marquis.

"Finnerty's car," I told the laser tech. "With what I put in his trunk, we won't need you after all."

But Finnerty fooled us.

"Goddamnit!" I growled, as the ADIC got out of his car and joined Brenda Thompson halfway between the two automobiles. They weren't going to use either car. Now we had to scramble.

I turned to Gerard, but he and his tech guy were already reaching for other equipment, something to eavesdrop on a conversation in the open air. Most likely a parabolic mike, but even that wouldn't be any good if Finnerty took her for a walk instead, which was exactly what I would do in his place. I had a sudden picture of them walking along, our van rolling next to them, then shook my head to chase it away.

I watched through my binoculars as the two of them stood outside his car and talked. A moment later he turned and pointed at the magnificent Supreme Court building across First Street. In the crisp clear air the building was lighted from top to bottom and shone like a lighthouse beacon. Through my binoculars I could see clearly the famous words on the pediment above the massive collection of marble columns out front. Equal justice under law. The promise to those who came to petition the Court. Reading them again tonight I shook my head. Not if Kevin Finnerty had his way.

My cell phone rang.

Brodsky's voice was urgent, but remained flatly professional.

"We've got a problem," he said. "Wax just came outside, got into the van, and drove it into the parking garage under his building. It's got a security gate. I can't get in there, I can't see him anymore. I don't know if there's a back way out, and if I check he could disappear on me."

He hung up but his words lingered.

Wax was out of pocket.

The man with orders to kill was out there on his own.

I watched as Finnerty clapped his arms around himself and stomped his feet, suffering from the cold. He pointed at the judge's Volvo, and they walked to it together. Brenda Thompson opened the door and slipped into the driver's seat. Finnerty went around and got in the other side.

Now what?

Do they drive? Again what I'd do. Or do they stay?

As though reading my mind, Lisa started the van's engine and we waited for the judge's car to move out.

It didn't.

I could hear through the supersensitive mike in Finnerty's backseat the sound of the Volvo's engine starting, but a moment later it died again.

I turned to the laser tech. He had his gadget trained on the

Volvo's driver's-side window. He put his fingers to his lips, then reached to turn up the volume. Suddenly the voices in the Volvo were not only clear but immediately recognizable. I glanced at the tape machine next to the interferometer console and nodded to the tech as I saw that he'd already turned the recorder on.

"*No, I won't!*" Judge Thompson was saying. "*I won't move this car one inch until you tell me what this is all about!*"

"*Suit yourself,*" Finnerty said, his own voice dead calm. "*We can talk about Brookston just as well right here as anywhere else.*"

"*Brookston? You want to talk about Brookston now? Hours from my confirmation? What the hell is wrong with you people?*" She paused and her voice got angrier. "*I gave your agents this information twenty-four hours ago. Why wait till now to bring this to me?*"

"*My agents?*"

"*Monk and Sands, the agents handling my investigation. They must have reported it to you by now.*" Her voice turned icy. "*I cannot imagine why you're talking to me about it tonight . . . and here. Since when does the bureau conduct business like this in an automobile?*"

"*You're fortunate we're in this car. If I had my way, we'd be talking in a jail cell.*"

"*Are you crazy? Do you have any idea who I am?*"

"*Fortunately I do. What you are is a baby killer, Judge. A murderer. Not a goddamned thing more than that.*"

A pause.

"*This meeting is over,*" Brenda Thompson said. I saw her car door swing open before she said, "*I'm leaving. I want you out of this car when I get back.*"

"*Close the goddamned door!*" Finnerty shouted. "*This meeting isn't over until I say it is.*"

The door swung closed again. I could hear the solid clunk as it engaged the latch.

"*I didn't kill anyone,*" she said, breathing hard. "*What I did became legal a few weeks later. I've already told your people about it,"* she repeated. *"You've already told the president. He hasn't said a word to me."*

"Nobody told the president anything, Judge. Nobody will tell him now. Not now, not ever."

"Than what's the point?" She paused again. *"You can't be serious. This can't be what I think it is."*

"It would be a mistake to believe that."

"You don't know me very well, do you, Finnerty? How could you imagine I'd allow you to blackmail me like this?" She paused again, just barely this time. *"The president will have my letter of resignation in the morning."*

"He will not. I will destroy you if you tell him."

"You've already destroyed me. You've made sure I'll never be a Supreme Court justice."

"When I'm finished you won't be any kind of judge at all. You'll have to move to the Third World to keep people from pointing and staring at you."

"And the alternative is what? Waiting around for your next order?"

"You're a quick study."

"I'll see you in hell first."

"You can do that. Of course you can, but you'd be over-reacting, Judge. You'll never see me in person again, never even talk to me. When it's necessary to enlist your help, you'll know it without me having to tell you."

She said nothing. The silence grew until Finnerty broke it again.

"In fact, we're finished here tonight," he said, *"and you'll feel differently in the morning. Trust me, Judge. In the morning you will understand."*

THIRTY-SIX

IT WAS PRETTY DAMNED QUIET IN THE VAN AFTERWARD.

Even though we'd known it was going to happen, exactly how Kevin Finnerty was going to extort the judge, the reality of his crime had been infinitely more brutal than we'd expected.

But we didn't have long to think about it before Finnerty was back in his own car. Before he could move, we heard the sound of his car phone ringing. I glanced at Lisa. The microphone behind his backseat hadn't been a total waste after all.

Our eyes were riveted on his car as we listened.

"You found what?" he barked into the phone. *"How long's it been under there?"*

We couldn't hear the other voice, but there wasn't much doubt whose it was . . . or what he'd found.

"But that's ridiculous. My car is alarmed to make sure that doesn't happen . . . that nobody can plant a bug in it. Who in the hell would have been able to . . ."

His voice died in midsentence.

I heard him toss the phone aside. I could see him twisting and turning as he looked through the car. I saw his door open, the ADIC hurry around and open the passenger door, crouch while he searched that side. He left the door open and stepped to the back door, yanked it open, crawled into the backseat. A moment later we heard the harsh sound of a hand closing over the head of our microphone. Then a single sharp curse word. Then nothing.

I turned to my team. No one said a word. I grabbed my phone and called Brodsky. No answer. I tried again, just to make sure. Still nothing. I chewed the inside of my cheek, troubled, but only for a moment. We didn't need to worry about him. Besides, Vincent Wax's whereabouts no longer concerned me. I might not know where the killer was at the moment, but it wouldn't be long before I did.

I started for the front seat, then stopped and turned back to Gerard.

"Your man can go home," I told him. "No more need for high-tech. From here on in, it's going to be about as low-tech as it gets."

He nodded, then climbed down out of the van just as my phone rang.

"This is no good," Brodsky told me. "I haven't seen Wax since he stuck his van in the garage downstairs. No way to tell if he's even here anymore . . . and it's too damned dark and wet . . . I have to keep my window rolled down to see anything at all. I can't stand out on the sidewalk either. If he's still around, he's sure to spot me."

"Burn off," I told him. "We don't need to be on Wax anymore. I've got a better way to find him."

"Where do you want me?"

"Head toward the house. Get me on the phone when you're in the area."

"I'm on my—"

His voice stopped in a strangled gasp. The hair on my neck stood up as I stared at the phone.

"Brodsky? What the hell's going on?"

He didn't answer, but suddenly he was screaming in pain.

"Brodsky!" I shouted. *"Damn it, Brodsky, talk to me!"*

I pressed the phone to my ear. I heard the crashing sounds of two big men locked in combat, then a loud thump as the phone hit the floorboard.

I spun toward Lisa. "Wax has Brodsky! At the apartment! Call 911 . . . *now!*"

I reached for the ignition key, but pulled back. Patrol cars were everywhere in that section of Washington. M.P.D. would be there before we could go five blocks. Whatever was going down over there, we couldn't do a damn thing to stop it.

I snatched the phone to my ear again. The fighting had stopped. Now they were talking. And that was even worse.

". . . know what the fuck you're talking about!" Brodsky croaked, his voice virtually gone. "Who the hell *are* you?"

I heard the unmistakable cough of a silenced automatic, followed by a scream that seemed to wrap its icy hands around my throat.

"*Brodsky!*" I yelled. "*Wax, you son of a bitch! Don't do this. You want me, come and get me . . . but don't do this!*"

I heard moaning, a half sob of pain. Wax—it couldn't be anybody else—had shot Brodsky. From the sound of his cries, in the gut, maybe a kneecap. The pain had to be mind-numbing.

"Let's try it again, Brodsky," Wax said. "Where are they going? What are they going to do?"

I could hear Brodsky struggling to respond, gagging on his own blood, sick with pain and fear. What seemed like an hour passed with his gasps for enough air to speak. Then the surprisingly strong sound of his voice.

"Fuck you, Wax." A pause for more air. "All the way to hell!"

There was a second cough, another bullet, but no shriek at all this time. Not a sound.

The three of us didn't speak until we were halfway to Finnerty's house. Brodsky's murder had made the air so heavy it was impossible to speak, difficult even to think. Finally I broke the silence. It was no time to sag, I told Lisa and Gerard. Brodsky was still with us, I said. He'd be there all the way to the end.

They nodded. Professionals often have to wait to grieve,

and they knew that as well as I did. I briefed them on the next phase of the operation, my voice quiet.

"But how can we do that?" Lisa wanted to know. "Go back to Finnerty's house? He's bound to get back there before we do."

I shook my head. "He's not going back there, not yet. There's only one thing that matters to Kevin Finnerty now. And to get that, to get us killed, he needs Vincent Wax more than ever."

"So how do we find them? How do we know Wax won't just split for good?"

"He won't split. Not when he realizes what's at stake, what his part in this whole thing is going to cost him."

"Finnerty's wife, then," Lisa said. "She's in the house right now, and that's just as bad."

I shook my head. "You saw her, Lisa. We both know what happened when Finnerty left her alone. The second he was gone, she was into the next bottle of wine, the one he wouldn't let her have at dinner."

"Good point. You'd have to set off a stick of dynamite to wake her up now."

Gerard broke in. "What can I do to help?"

I gestured toward the equipment behind us in the working compartment.

"Get back there and start making copies of what we just heard. Two copies, save the original for your own files. And hurry, Gerard. From here on in, the only thing that counts is speed."

Twenty minutes later, I pulled the French van into Finnerty's circular driveway. Lisa and I got out to make our entry. There was no way I was going to leave her out here on the street without me, but I also knew she wasn't about to let me go back into the house without her. Besides, I needed her to operate the bureau portable radio she was carrying just in case we needed it. I turned back to Gerard, who'd taken my place behind the wheel.

"Get back out of sight," I told him. "You can watch on the monitors. You'll know when to come back and pick us up."

He nodded and drove off, leaving us standing at the red front door.

I might as well have had a key this time, as quickly as Finnerty's front door fell open under my picks. I pushed the door open and we went through.

Again the alarm tone sounded, even louder in my ears than the first time, but this time exactly the sound I needed to hear. It wouldn't be long until my failure to enter the proper code hit the WMFO switchboard. The phone in the house would ring, I would ignore it, and the office would reach Finnerty on his cell phone or car radio. All I had to do was wait for the ADIC and his goon to come after us.

Not a lot of time, but enough for us to get ready.

The shrill tone ended, Lisa and I both watching the staircase ahead of us for any sign of the wife. The phone rang. Four times before the answering machine picked up. Again we looked for the wife, again she failed to show. Then we hustled toward Finnerty's office down the hall.

Inside the office I took the audio copies Gerard had made on the way over, laid them squarely in the center of Finnerty's desk. Then I moved to the bookcase we'd seen Finnerty swing aside earlier, just before the ADIC entered his vault. I didn't bother trying to find the latch. I had enough adrenaline pumping to make it unnecessary.

I took hold of the bookcase itself with both hands, wrenched it away from the vault door. The latch gave way with a sharp crack, plaster came away with it and fell on the floor at my feet.

I turned to Lisa, motioned for her to follow as I hustled back through the office door and back toward the living room, to the windows we'd be using to spot the man when he showed up.

We'd barely left the office when we heard voices.

Red leader, red six.

Go, red six.

Voices clear enough to be in the next room.

Or outside in the front yard.

I stared at the radio in Lisa's hands. The voices had come from her radio, the FBI radio she'd tuned to a secure channel no one else but the bureau should have been using. My heart began to race, my stomach to tighten. Lisa turned up the volume.

Drive-by negative for vehicles, red leader. Checking nearby streets for bucars.

Ten-four, red six. I'm getting out of my unit, be on my hand-held.

Roger, red leader.

My throat constricted as I admitted my mistake.

I'd known Finnerty would send Vincent Wax.

I couldn't possibly have known he'd send an entire SWAT team.

I stared at Lisa as I tried to figure out why. Surely he wasn't interested in arresting us. Our testimony in court would kill his Brenda Thompson scheme just as dead as if he let us go altogether. He and Wax would end up in the same prison cell.

Red four, red leader.

Go, red leader.

Target inside residence. Prepare for insertion at back door. Victor Whisky on his way. Advise when ready.

Roger, red leader.

I let out the breath I'd been holding. Now it made sense again.

Now I knew exactly what Finnerty was planning.

The SWAT team was only here for one reason. They didn't even know why, not the real reason anyway.

Their job was to prepare for the entry, to surround the house to make sure Lisa and I were trapped inside. To prepare the killing ground for Vincent Wax. The killer would be first through the door. We wouldn't be alive to see the rest of them come in after him.

And that's where Finnerty's plan turned brilliant, although Wax himself probably wouldn't think so.

If Wax made it inside and killed us, Finnerty would win.

If we killed Wax on his way in, the rest of the SWAT team would cut us to ribbons, and that would be even better. Resisting arrest, having killed an FBI agent, we would deserve no less. There wouldn't even be an inquiry into the shooting. Headlines for a day or two—another scandal about wayward FBI agents—but nothing after that. Life for the ADIC would go on without a hitch. Life for my partner and me would not.

"Puller," Lisa said. "What can we do? How can we . . ."

Her voice died as she realized there was no point asking. For all its deadliness, the issue was incredibly simple.

If we ran, Wax would kill us. If we stayed, Wax or the SWAT team would kill us.

And that made our solution just as simple.

We couldn't be inside when they came in.

We couldn't let them see us running away.

Simple.

All we had to do was make it happen.

I visualized the layout of the house, then the big backyard and the chest-high wall surrounding it, finally the trees filling the yard back there. I could see in my mind the opposition. They would follow bureau procedure, bureau rules of engagement. Two men at the back door off the kitchen, two at the front door, two more on the side lawn, outside the French doors in the TV room, probably one or two on the other side of the house next to the garage. We had only one asset, darkness, and it wasn't much.

It was dark in the house. Outside, the night sky bore a crescent of new moon, moving in and out of the gathering clouds above the tops of the trees surrounding the yard. Reaction is always slower than action, and in the dark it would take them fractionally longer to react than for us to act. If worse came to worst, we could try to run for it and hope for the best.

I tried not to picture the last part, Lisa and I sprinting to avoid their bullets, but the scene flooded my mind anyway. I reached to her, touched her arm.

"You ready?" I asked.

She nodded, then opened her jacket to reveal the Sig Sauer in the holster on her belt and I saw that as usual she'd been right inside my head with me.

"Let's do it, Puller," she said. "Let's just get it over with."

THIRTY-SEVEN

RED SIX, RED LEADER. REPORT YOUR STATUS.
Victor Whisky onsite, red leader.
Stand by for insertion, red six. Command code Foxtrot.

I grabbed Lisa's arm and pulled her into the darkness of the TV room. The code wasn't a tough one to break.

Vincent Wax was here and ready. All he was waiting for was the command from Foxtrot. But Foxtrot wouldn't be here, of course. Finnerty wouldn't be anywhere near the scene of our murders.

I reached for the Smith-10 in my belt-holster, pulled the silencer from my jacket pocket, and screwed the noise-suppressor on the end of the barrel. I held the weapon in my hand, nodded at Lisa. She'd already pulled hers. Despite the darkness, I could see her face drawn tight, her dark eyes ready.

A sudden sweep of illumination from a flashlight cut through the windows. We leaped for cover behind the nearest of the leather recliners. A pounding fresh rainstorm battered the roof, a tattoo of noise that made it hard to think. I crept up close to the windows again, peered outside at the downpour exploding against the flagstone terrace. The red team was both tough and professional. Under normal conditions they'd be impossible to beat. But these conditions were no longer normal. In the startling commotion of the storm they were getting less and less normal by the second. No matter how elite the troops outside, no one endures that kind of weather without turning away from it. They wouldn't leave their posts, but they'd be a tick less efficient. If I could come up with one more distraction, we might just have a chance.

I reached for the phone on a small table Lisa was crouched next to, punched 911.

"Police emergency," the operator said.

"This is FBI Assistant Director Kevin Finnerty," I said, then gave the address. "There are strange noises in my yard. I think I see someone out there prowling the house."

I heard the operator issue radio commands to nearby patrol units.

"Responding now, sir," she told me a moment later. "Should only be a couple of minutes. Stay inside and wait for the officers."

I hung up and listened for the reaction. It came even faster than I'd thought. It was astonishing the weight Finnerty carried in this town.

Red leader, red four.

Go, red four.

Locals headed your way, red leader. Bunch of them. Patrol cars, no sirens.

Roger. Stand by.

An instant later a new voice. One I recognized.

Red six from Foxtrot. Foxtrot calling red six.

Red six, go Foxtrot.

Proceed with insertion. Repeat. You will proceed with insertion immediately. Deadly force authority granted.

Shit. Here they come.

Finnerty was nowhere near the house, I was certain, but he knew better than to wait for the police, knew that once the cops showed up it was all over for him. In the cold aftermath of a local police investigation, he wouldn't stand a chance.

I sprinted to the entryway, Lisa on my heels, then knelt

close to one of the narrow windows on either side of the door, exposing just enough of my head to see out.

The visibility was terrible, the storm relentless. Out of the darkness I saw the first of the patrol cars slide to a stop at the end of the circular driveway. Then another one. Then two more. I grabbed the bureau radio from Lisa's hands and raised it to my lips.

"The garage!" I shouted to the red team outside. *"The garage! They're on the roof!"*

I looked through the window and saw what I'd caused.

Confronted by armed men in ninja suits running around the front of the house toward the garage, the local cops were responding exactly as they'd been trained. The noise of the storm was overwhelmed by a roar from the police bullhorn. *"POLICE OFFICERS! STOP RIGHT WHERE YOU ARE! DROP YOUR WEAPONS!"*

The ninjas froze. The cops froze. For a long moment the front yard was a tableau, and exactly what we needed.

We raced back to the French doors in the TV room, but I stopped Lisa before we kept going. I grabbed my credentials with the imbedded gold badge, hooked them over the pocket of my jacket, motioned for Lisa to do the same. Maybe they'd think we were there with them, looking for the same burglars. Wasn't likely we'd fool anybody, but it wouldn't hurt to try. There had to be red team people watching the back yard. Maybe they'd be confused at the sight of our badges. All we'd need was a few seconds, just enough to get over the wall behind the property.

"Don't run!" I told Lisa. "Not until I tell you to!"

We stepped through the French doors. Despite my words to Lisa, the urge to run was overpowering. We didn't. Running away was the surest way to draw fire.

We forced ourselves to walk, guns in hand, just another couple of agents working with the SWAT team, trying to cover the backyard against a possible escape attempt. The back of my head buzzed with the feeling that someone was aiming a weapon at us as we moved toward the chest-high wall at the rear of the back yard. The urge to run grew stronger the closer we got. I kept my hand on Lisa to make sure she didn't.

Ten feet from the wall, a ninja jumped out from behind a tree, aimed an automatic rifle at us.

"Up front!" I shouted at him. "Be careful! Cops everywhere!"

The ninja turned to stare toward the front of the property, took a couple of tentative steps, then turned back to us.

"What the hell? Who *are* you people?"

"WMFO!" I yelled. *"Get your ass back to the house!"*

He was a good soldier, knew a command voice when he heard one. He started to run, then stopped again. He shook his head and started back to us.

But in the instant he'd taken to do it, we raced to the wall and vaulted over it into the gravel alley.

We turned to cross the alley into the woods beyond, but there was a big gray Ford van directly in our way. Next to the driver's-side door, Vincent Wax stood waiting for us.

The gun in his hand looked even bigger than he did.

THIRTY-EIGHT

HE SHOT ME FIRST.

The bullet's impact into my Kevlar vest hurled me backward into the wall.

Before I could get my own gun up, Lisa shot him.

Vincent Wax stared at her for an instant, then down at his shoulder. She fired again; this time I did, too, but we must have hit his own body armor, because Wax showed no reaction at all before leaping into his van. The engine roared, the tires spitting gravel as he raced away.

We started to chase him, but stopped after a few steps. We stared at the van as it approached the end of the alley. I turned to Lisa. I couldn't see her face in the dark, but it had to be filled with the same helpless look, her mind with the same unspoken thought.

We had no car. Wax was getting away and there was no way we could stop him.

I pulled her along with me up the alley toward the street where the van had now disappeared. "C'mon!" I urged. "We still have to get the hell out of here!"

Before we'd taken a step, a second van came skidding around the corner and up the alley toward us. A brown van this time. Our drain-cleaning van, its back door swinging open as it slid to a halt next to us.

"Yes!" I hollered. "God damn it, yes!"

A moment later we were inside. Gerard was behind the wheel.

I shoved him into the passenger seat. "I'll drive!" I turned to Lisa. "Get in the back and buckle up!"

Seconds later we were out of the alley and racing up the street toward Wax. Cars slowed as we passed, the drivers' eyes wide as we swerved to avoid them.

A block and a half later we caught up with Wax.

"Sorry about this, Gerard," I said, then shoved my foot to the floor and rammed the son of a bitch.

The force of the impact drove me back in my seat, then hurled me toward the steering wheel. Thank God there were no air bags.

Up ahead, Vincent Wax slowed for a moment, then accelerated again. The back of his van was bashed in, but it just kept going.

So I smashed him again.

This time he pulled straight sideways and my momentum took us past him. I slowed, stared in the rearview mirror and saw him wobble back into place, behind us now. I could see his empty eyes and his deformed nose as he moved up close, then eased up against my bumper and began to accelerate. *What the hell?* He was *pushing* us! I looked through my windshield and saw what he was trying to do.

Dead ahead was a crowded intersection.

The light was red. Traffic roared by in both directions.

He would push us through the light, directly into that traffic.

I hit the brake pedal with both feet but it was no good. Our lighter van was no match for the power of his overbuilt engine. In another few seconds we'd be at the mercy of drivers who had no way of knowing we were coming, who had no way to stop in time.

I did the only thing I could.

Instead of trying to stop Wax with my brakes, I floored the accelerator. Our van leaped toward the intersection. I wasn't about to let Wax take control. At least this way we'd have a chance.

Seconds later we were in the middle of it.

Two cars and a pickup truck shot past us, horns yelping, voices shouting. From my left a black SUV with huge wheels tipped forward, tires screaming as the astonished driver fought to stop. I stomped the accelerator, trying desperately to outrun him. The SUV skidded sideways as it slid toward us. I threw my weight forward, as though the motion itself could carry us through to the other side. The SUV slewed wildly, grazed our rear bumper as it hurtled past.

A moment later we were on the other side.

I wanted to stop, but in my rearview mirror I could already see Wax making a U-turn and heading the other way. Now trying to get away.

Fuck that, I told myself.

I made my own U-turn just as the light turned green and we went after him.

I floored it again. Our van was wobbling now, from the damage to the front end from bashing Wax, but I caught him at the end of the next block. He accelerated harder but I managed to get up next to him. I swung the van into his door, knocked him toward the curb to his right. He came back at me.

"Hold on, Lisa!" I shouted an instant before he struck.

The impact threw Wax's van back a dozen feet. I caught the reflection of a streetlight off the barrel of the gun he stuck out the window. I hit the brakes. We dropped back as his gun flashed . . . once . . . then a second time. Sparks exploded from the short hood of our van.

"One more time!" Gerard yelled, a long-barreled automatic in his hand. "Get up next to him! Pull your head back and give me a shot!"

I pulled alongside the van. Again Wax's gun jutted from his window. I ducked. From this range Wax couldn't miss. And I wasn't about to wait for Gerard to send a bullet past my nose.

So I lifted the Smith-10 from my lap and killed Wax myself.

Five shots directly into his face.

His weapon tumbled from his hand. He slumped over his steering wheel.

But he didn't die.

I stared at the van but it didn't even waver. I blinked in disbelief.

I couldn't have missed! Not from this range!

Who the hell is this guy?

I mashed the gas pedal, ready to do it again, but before I could get there Wax swerved to the left, directly into our path. I wrenched the wheel to keep away from him, but he careered back the other way this time. His van seemed to accelerate before it struck the curb and flew almost straight upward, then headlong into the high brick wall surrounding one of the estates that dominated the street. A moment later it burst with a tremendous explosion into flames.

My head swiveled to watch as we passed, before I slowed down and managed to bring my own wreck to a stop. I sat for a moment with my head hanging, my body shivering, then turned to Gerard. His face was the same khaki color as the upholstery.

I looked around for Lisa. She stood in the passageway into the back.

"Everyone okay?" I asked.

They nodded.

I started driving again, nursed the van to the next intersection, saw a liquor store on the nearest corner, and pulled off the street into the parking lot. Three college student types came out of the store, looked the van over as they passed, laughing and pointing at the damage.

"We did it," Lisa said after a moment. Her voice was barely audible. "My God, we actually did it."

I shook my head. "Not yet, Lisa. Not quite yet."

"But we have the evidence. We have the audio of Finnerty's meeting with the judge . . . We have audio of his order to Vincent Wax to kill us . . . We heard Wax kill Brodsky, for Christ's sake! We have all the evidence we'll ever need."

"Are you sure about that?"

"How could I not be?"

"Look at it Finnerty's way. His raiding party will testify they caught us together in his house. Finnerty will swear to a jury we resisted arrest when Vincent Wax caught us trying to get away. Then he'll use Wax's death to charge us with murdering a federal officer in the course of a getaway." I stared at her. "That's what the jury will hear. That Special Agent Vincent Wax died in a heroic effort to capture us."

I paused, my throat tightening at the thought of Edward Brodsky.

"And the sheriff?" I said. "There won't be any evidence linking Wax to his murder . . . just what we say about it. And we're the bad guys. After we're arrested, nobody will believe anything we say."

She nodded. "The only bullets recovered from that burned-up van will be yours and Gerard's." She looked at Ziff. "Yours will conveniently disappear. Monk's will turn into evidence at our trial."

We sat in silence for a moment.

"Wait a minute," she said. "What about Gerard's testimony? The video of Finnerty's extortion of Senator Randall. He's got enough to . . ."

She stopped when she saw us staring at her. She looked away, shook her head slowly, then turned back.

"I'm a fool even to bring that up, aren't I? The French government won't be any part of this, will they?"

Gerard didn't bother to answer.

"Damn it," she said. "I know you said we wouldn't get anything admissible in court out of all this, but you didn't tell me we'd end up with nothing at all."

I reached out and touched the back of her hand.

"We don't have much, but it's a lot more than nothing." I paused long enough to hope that I was telling her the truth. "A hell of a lot more than nothing."

THIRTY-NINE

I DIDN'T WASTE A SECOND GUESSING ABOUT WHERE TO FIND Finnerty.

The ADIC was a Hoover man, first, last, and always. Faced with an attack, Finnerty would do just what the Old Man would have done. J. Edgar had set up his fortress long before the Hoover Building came into existence, at the FBI's headquarters in the Department of Justice Building. Kevin Finnerty had built his own fortress at WMFO, and he'd stay there until we were safely in custody . . . or dead.

And he'd never see us coming.

Finnerty was an egomaniac in a world over which he had complete control. He couldn't even comprehend being attacked by his own agents, employees he'd long ago stopped thinking of as equals.

The office was never empty, of course, but it would be damned close to that tonight. Every available agent would be out looking for us. Nobody left but a skeleton crew to handle emergencies, plus the normal support staff working the night shift. Nothing resembling a SWAT team . . . or a red team. They'd be elsewhere, as well, waiting for us to be found.

The rain had turned to a light snowfall as I steered the Caprice down the ramp and into the basement garage at

WMFO. We'd given the drain-cleaning van back to Gerard when we left him out in Kalorama Heights. It was ten-thirty-seven when I parked the bucar. I saw Finnerty's black Marquis in its usual spot next to the elevator doors.

Lisa and I sat for a moment and went through the plan for a final time. Her role was critical, I reminded her again. We'd fail if she didn't play her part to perfection.

"I know, Puller," she told me, her eyes exasperated with my insistence on repeating the same thing over and over again. "Do I need to remind you what I used to do for a living? I know exactly how to do this. I've bullied confessions out of animals who'd rather die than take orders from a woman. Finnerty will cave. I'll make damned sure he does."

I looked at her but didn't say anything. He'd cave all right, but I wasn't about to leave it entirely to her. We would talk all about it afterward, I was sure of that. She was going to have a lot to say afterward.

Upstairs, we came out of the elevator on the top floor and saw that the corridor was deserted. I wasn't surprised, but I knew better than to relax. Just because we couldn't see them didn't mean there weren't people hidden away, ready to respond to Finnerty's call in an instant.

My hand was on the big grip of the Smith-10 on my belt, as we moved into the ADIC's suite of offices at the end of the corridor. I kept my hand on it as we opened his office door and went through.

Kevin Finnerty sat behind his desk.

His eyes came up and widened. His hands lay in the middle of his green blotter, a couple of files to his right, a small stack of paperwork next to them. I watched his hands as he broke the silence.

"You're under arrest," he said. His voice was steady, calm, confident. "Both of you. You will turn over your weapons, credentials, and badges to me immediately. My SWAT team is on its way back here to take you to jail. I won't bother advising you of your rights, you both know them as well as—"

"Shut up, Finnerty!" Lisa shouted. "You will not speak

again until I give you permission. You will keep both hands where I can see them."

Finnerty's eyes bulged, his mouth twisted, but he said nothing.

I stared at his hands as Lisa moved to the television set built into the bookcase to the left of Finnerty's desk, a VCR atop the set. From her purse she pulled two videotapes, copies that Gerard had made in the van on the way to Finnerty's house. She inserted the first tape into the VCR, pushed a couple of buttons, and the TV came to life. On the screen, the image of Finnerty pulling his vault door open and disappearing into it couldn't have been more clear.

Finnerty's head jerked from the screen to me. His mouth opened and closed, but he said nothing. I continued to watch his hands.

Then Lisa played twenty seconds of the Senator Randall tape from the French collection, followed by pictures of the ADIC getting into Judge Brenda Thompson's car and a few moments of the audio of his extortion that Gerard's technician had transferred to videotape to make it easier for us.

The ADIC could no longer remain silent.

"What possible good can this do you?" he demanded. "More evidence against you, is all this is. More evidence to put both of you in prison for the rest of your lives."

"There's not going to be any prison," Lisa told him. "Not for us, not for you."

"What the hell are you talking about?" He shook his head. "You really think you can hurt me? That two useless FBI agents—a *woman*, for Christ's sake—can possibly hurt a man like *me*?"

Lisa came back and stood directly in front of him.

"Here are your orders, Finnerty. You will prepare a signed statement . . . every detail about your secret files. Where you got them. How you've been using them." Her voice rose. "You will expose the rest of your group, identify each of them to us, then use your batphone here to call them and tell them it's over."

Finnerty's gray eyes darkened with rage. Hearing such

demands from an ordinary FBI agent was killing him. Taking orders from a woman would destroy every last vestige of his self-control.

Lisa continued, her voice sharp as she commanded him to obey. "You will admit to the extortion of Judge Brenda Thompson and to your blackmailing of Senator Randall."

Sweat began to bead on Finnerty's brow. His hands began to clench and unclench, then move toward his paperwork. Almost, I told myself. My hand returned to the weapon in my holster.

"You will name everyone you've done the same thing to," Lisa went on. "You will give me a letter of resignation, which I will hand-carry directly to the president. You will not return to your office. You will never again enter the Hoover Building for any reason. You will have no contact with any member of the FBI. Finally, you will give us the files in that vault in your home and keep out of our way as we load them up for the White House."

"I'll see you in hell first!" he screamed, spitting with fury, specks of saliva flying with the force of his words.

Lisa reached for a pad of yellow paper on the desktop, tossed it at him. The pad struck Finnerty in the chest and fell into his lap. He left it there, just sat and stared at us.

God damn it, I thought. *What's it going to take to push him over the edge?*

"Start writing!" Lisa shouted. "I don't have all night."

Finnerty's face turned purple. He stared at the stack of paperwork to his right, then reached for it. But he didn't actually touch it. Instead, his right hand fell to his lap, toward the yellow pad still lying there. He grabbed at the pad, but only succeeded in knocking it to the floor. He bent to retrieve it.

I watched his right shoulder, saw it change directions as he grabbed for the weapon I'd known would be on the floor under his feet. When his gun came up toward Lisa I shot him in the face.

There was a sharp cough from my silenced semiautomatic.

And a round red hole in the center of his forehead.

A millisecond later the tumbling bullet took most of his brain and splattered it across the wall to the right of the windows behind him.

A look of immense surprise filled the ADIC's face as his already dead body flew backward against his chair, then collapsed sideways and slid to the floor.

I turned to Lisa. She stared at Finnerty's body for a moment, then at me. I saw in her eyes the questions already forming, but it still wasn't time to answer them.

I slipped around Finnerty's desk, careful to avoid stepping in the blood and gore on the other side, then pulled a pair of needle-nose pliers from my pocket and moved to the wall. I found my bullet quickly, covered in the worst of the goo running down the wall, used the pliers to tug it out of the crater it had formed. I dropped the messy and misshapen slug into my pocket, used the pliers again to pick up the Sig Sauer nine-millimeter that had fallen from Finnerty's hand as he died.

I pulled a handkerchief from my jacket, used it to hold the Sig while I transferred the silencer from my gun to his, then aimed his weapon directly into the same crater from which I'd pulled my own bullet. I squeezed the trigger. Another cough. This time I left the bullet in the wall. I knelt on one knee and replaced the Sig next to Finnerty's hand, stepped carefully back around the desk and rejoined Lisa.

Her eyes couldn't seem to leave the carnage, especially the bloody gun on the floor.

"That . . ." she said. "This won't . . ."

"Later," I told her. "It's time to leave."

The snow had turned serious by the time we came back up out of the garage. I turned the wipers on to brush it back, but it was already sticking to the ground outside. Lisa didn't say a word until we were two blocks away from WMFO, when she turned to me and ordered me to stop the car.

"I saw what you did," she told me when I pulled to the curb. "I know exactly what you did."

I said nothing.

"You used me. You used me to execute him. You lied to me to get me to help you. You knew what he'd do when I yelled my orders at him, that he would rather die than take that kind of abuse from a woman. That he'd never confess, that he'd . . ."

She stopped talking, then reached for the door handle and opened the door.

"Lisa," I said. "You had to know. You had to know there couldn't be a trial. Not for us, not for him." I touched her arm. "We all knew that. Gerard, Brodsky, all of us. And you did, too."

She shook my hand away, slid out of the car, turned back to me. Snowflakes began to cover her head and shoulders as she spoke.

"You can't *possibly* think this will work," she said. "That we're going to fool *anybody* with that phony suicide." She paused. "And Christ, Puller, our fingerprints are all over this thing, and I don't mean real prints. You used bureau equipment. The bug in Finnerty's car, the bugs in his house. How long is it going to take for them to come get us?"

"Nobody's coming. Nobody's going to come."

She stared at me.

"Think about it, Lisa. Think about a trial, ours *or* Finnerty's. What the bureau would have to let the public know in order to prosecute any of us. What the public would force Congress to do about it." I shook my head. "Just think about it."

"But you murdered him," she said. "*We* murdered him."

"He killed himself."

"Brodsky knew, Gerard Ziff knew. You used me," she repeated, "all of you."

"We used each other, all of us. Each of us gets something out of this, you included. Don't pretend you don't know that."

She shook her head, her eyes downcast. She spoke without looking at me.

"Maybe I did," she said. "Maybe I'm no better than you

are . . . than any of you are." She looked at me. "But I do know one thing. I've got to go away from you until I know for sure."

She turned and started to leave.

"Lisa," I called to her, "don't do this. At least let me give you a ride home. At least give me a chance to help you understand."

She looked back at me and shook her head.

"I don't need a ride, Puller," she said. "Right now I'd rather use a taxi."

I opened my mouth to argue, but she'd already turned and walked away into the storm.

FORTY

SUPER BOWL SUNDAY CAME TO A FREDERICKSBURG BURIED by the same snowstorm that had started the night I killed Finnerty. Snow had continued to fall all that night and into the following week. I welcomed it, found myself hoping it would never go away.

For me it was like a shroud, a funerary blanket to hide the gruesome events of the past few weeks, as well as a clean base on which to make a brand-new start. A new start I had to make soon, I kept telling myself, but one I just couldn't force myself to accept.

The problem was Lisa. She'd gone away that night, and I hadn't seen or talked to her since. She'd gone on leave after the shooting and got herself reassigned to the Baltimore office when she came back. And I couldn't seem to move beyond her loss, couldn't make myself stop missing her so much I simply didn't care about anything else. Even the Super Bowl, and the five-thousand dollars I'd had to bet just to get her out of my mind long enough to watch it.

As I'd told Lisa, there wasn't even a ripple in our lives following the ADIC's death. Finnerty hadn't bothered to tell anyone he'd suspended us. Lisa had gone away for a week, I'd gone straight back to the office and my SPIN squad. And the cover-up had begun. This time it was the Hoover Building using Quantico rules.

News of Finnerty's "suicide" had been all over the radio and TV an hour after we'd left him. Information like that was impossible even for FBI Headquarters to keep under wraps. Brenda Thompson would have heard it before she went to bed for the night, at which point she must have decided his insanity had killed him, that she was free to continue with her own dream. And she would be free, I knew. Free from Kevin Finnerty, at least, and maybe even from her long-ago nightmare in Brookston.

Then the Hoover Building would have gone to work on the real problem, how to save itself from extinction, should the truth ever become known.

Orders would have been given immediately following the discovery of the ADIC's body. The instant the director had been shown the videotapes we'd left in Finnerty's office, specially trained agents would have raced to the ADIC's home, into his office, where they would have found copies of the same thing, along with the ripped-away bookcase and the secret vault. It wouldn't have taken them a half-hour to blow the vault door off, to get inside and find the evidence of Finnerty's treachery.

They would have searched the rest of the house and found my bugs, my official bureau bugs. They'd have figured out what had been done, and, more importantly, who'd done it. We hadn't left any fingerprints, but they would know. Fortunately for us, they wouldn't want to know. Still didn't want to know.

The Hoover Building didn't give a damn about Kevin Finnerty. All they cared about was that his crimes had been kept in house. By leaving a trail of bread crumbs back to WMFO I'd given them exactly what they needed. We are a family, after all. As long as the dirty laundry stays hidden, everything's okay.

And the cover-up would include the murders, as well— Vincent Wax's slaughter of three good people, his attempts to kill Lisa and me. I could barely make myself think about Brodsky. How we'd started together, the respect that had developed between us, the growing friendship I was looking forward to enjoying in the future. I wondered when that particular lump in my throat would finally go away.

Bottom line, none of this would ever make the papers or TV. The public would never have a clue, but each of them— the sheriff, Jabalah Abahd, and Pastor Johnson—had been avenged, and that's all that really mattered.

The rule of law is a majestic concept, but it's most majestic when you don't look too hard at it. Sometimes the law doesn't work at all, and when it doesn't—when it can't even be allowed to try—someone has to step up. This time that someone turned out to be me, but I knew better than to feel like a hero. Heroes are supposed to be selfless. In a perfect world of altruistic justice, my motives would have been perfectly clean, but perfect worlds are hard to find.

To make what I'd done altruistic, I shouldn't have gotten anything back, but I did. And I don't mean such nebulous things as a better society or a more peaceful world. I mean pretty damned earthbound things like Lisa and I keeping our jobs. Like eliminating—at least for now—the dreaded polygraph the ADIC sooner or later would have forced on me. With Finnerty dead I was safe from bureau lie detection long enough for Dr. Chen to turn me into the android I'd have to become to get into the counterterrorism program where I belonged.

I thought for a moment about the French government's belief that Finnerty and Wax were not the only two involved, that there were other FBI agents providing the information the ADIC had been using. Angry people who might very well want to come after Lisa and me to avenge his death, or continue their master's work with a new set of secret files.

It could be true—most likely it was true—but I knew better than to worry about it. Finnerty had been the ideologue, the Hoover disciple. With him gone, his gang would disappear back into their holes. As for Vincent Wax, he was nothing but muscle, and nobody ever cared about hired help. As a matter of fact, Finnerty's cabal would be damn happy Wax was no longer around to cause them trouble.

As Finnerty had known she would, Brenda Thompson had been okayed by the Judiciary Committee on Friday morning, then confirmed by the entire Senate after lunch. Madam Justice Thompson's swearing-in ceremony the following Wednesday had drawn hundreds of well-wishers to the Supreme Court building, including our director and the president of the United States.

I was happy for her.

Justice Thompson wasn't the first member of the high court with a history, and she wouldn't be the last. She would take her place alongside her just-as-imperfect brethren, to continue a long line of magnificent jurists with their own human frailties. As a man with one or two smudges on his own escutcheon, I was happy the nation's highest court wasn't filled with angels.

I stared past the TV and out the window.

Nearly six o'clock and the evening sky was already dark, just as clear as it had been every night since I'd killed Finnerty. The moon was bright enough to cast shadows on the snow. Carl Sandburg wrote about the grass that covers the battlefields of Austerlitz and Waterloo, the turf that hides the bleeding wounds of war. From the dome I couldn't see our hometown battlefield, across the meadows under Marye's Heights, but under the snow there was grass on that horrific ground as well. The snow made it look even more benign than Sandburg's grass, and I was counting on the snow to do the same thing for me that it had done for those mangled soldiers.

I looked at my watch. Kickoff in three minutes. It was time to turn off my mind long enough to enjoy the game, to fully enjoy the money I had riding on the outcome.

I rose from the couch and went to the kitchen, grabbed a couple of Sam Adamses, a bag of Ruffles, and a tub of chemically enhanced cheese dip, took them back to the coffee table in front of the couch. I sat again and stared at the food and drink, then admitted there was one more thing I had to get out of the way before the game.

Annie Fisher.

I hadn't seen or heard from her since the day I left her drying out in my bed. She'd always accused me of being a pathological caregiver, and—at least in her case—it was hard to deny. We'd parted badly and I couldn't stand to leave it that way.

She answered after the first ring.

"Annie," I said.

"Puller."

I waited for more, but there wasn't any.

"I feel bad, Annie . . . about the way it ended."

"Why does it have to end?"

"Don't you think we're past that point?"

"So why are you calling?"

"To reassure you, I guess. That I'm always here, that I'll always be here for you. That I'm a friend you can count on, no matter what."

She laughed, but there wasn't any humor in it.

"Tell you what, Puller. I'm up to my ass in friends right now, but should there be an opening, you'll be the first one I call."

Then the sound of her slamming the phone in my ear.

I hung up, looked out the window. I had to be crazy. Even to me, my words had sounded both lame and terrible at the same time. I'd have said the same thing in her place.

I grabbed my beer and took a long swallow. Balls. My mojo was leaking fast. I couldn't love Annie, I couldn't stop loving Lisa. What the hell's the matter with you? I asked myself. *You've got everything you need. Super Bowl . . . beer . . . chips and dip. If you had a baseball cap to turn backward, you'd have it all.*

On the screen, the Dallas kicker was teeing up the ball to start the game. I reached for a chip, dipped it, then dropped it back into the dip when my telephone rang. I scowled at it. Obviously Annie wasn't finished with me. The sarcasm hadn't done it for her. Luckily, I'd turned down the volume on the answering machine to keep from being disturbed during the game. She could vent into the machine but I didn't have to listen.

The Dallas kicker gathered himself and the crowd turned silent.

"Come on, Denver," I said out loud to the waiting Broncos. "I need this game . . . gotta have this game. Don't make me beg."

The kicker lofted the ball into the San Diego sky. It came down at the goal line, to Jamal Edwards, the Broncos' fastest man, the man who was going to help turn my five grand into ten. Ten thousand dollars for my Visa card debt to Pinewood Manor. Ten K to keep the pastor away a while longer.

Edwards tucked the ball, started to his left, then cut back up the center. My heart stopped for an instant as he broke past the wedge and into the clear before being dragged down by the kicker himself. Christ, I thought. Christ. A good omen. A great omen.

The network went to commercial, to a whole string of the brand-new commercials that often turned out better than the game itself. I took the opportunity to listen to Annie's message on my machine. I leaned to my left and punched the play button, then stiffened as I heard the caller's voice. I stared at the machine as my last partner came straight to the point.

"We have to talk," Lisa said. "Not about Finnerty—you were right about what we had to do—but about us." She paused. "I'm here, Puller, is what I'm trying to say. Call me when you get the chance."

She hung up and I continued to stare at the machine. On the TV screen, the game was back. I turned to it.

Bronco quarterback Phil Danders took the first snap of the game, dropped back two steps, and fired a pass over the middle, good for a dozen yards and a first down. I watched it like a man watching a dream, seeing it, knowing how good it was for the bet I'd made, but somehow at the same time detached. The second play was a screen pass, good for another twenty.

I rose to my feet and pointed the clicker at the TV, turned it off. I reached for the telephone but pulled my hand back. I only needed one thing, and it sure as hell wasn't a phone conversation.

The snowplow had been early this morning, I remembered. To avoid getting stuck in my driveway I'd left the Caprice on the street last night. There'd be no problem making it to I-95 North, and the rest of the way to Alexandria would be a snap.

Read on for an excerpt from
Gene Riehl's next novel

SLEEPER

*Coming soon in hardcover
from St. Martin's Press*

*April, 1992
Paris, France*

Samantha Williamson wasn't born to be an assassin.

She was never meant to be a whore either, or an art thief,
or a terrorist.

And she wasn't any of those things until the day Pyongyang decided it was time to begin her training. American-
born Samantha had just turned sixteen. For all but the first
forty-eight hours of her life, she'd been called Sung Kim,
and she had no awareness of ever having been anyone else.

Paris was unusually warm that day, especially for so early
in spring. Tourists jammed the Rive Gauche, the sidewalks
of the Rue Montgolfier a crawling throng of visitors from all
over the world. At her table in the Salon de Thé—one of the
most popular of the dozens of outdoor cafes along the
street—Sung Kim reached across and touched her mother's
hand.

"How's your tea, Mom?" she asked, in the flawless English she'd been taught by the parents who'd adopted her,
before they'd allowed her to speak even a single word of Korean.

"Fine, sweetheart," her mother answered in English, but

her eyes stayed every bit as sad as they'd been all day. She squeezed Sung Kim's hand hard enough to make her wince. "You're so special, my darling," she told her daughter. "You will always be special to me."

Sung Kim looked more closely at her mother, puzzled by the somber tone of her voice, but she had no problem with the words themselves. Her parents had been telling her how special she was since she was old enough to understand the word, and by the time she was twelve she'd decided to believe it. Now, as a full-blown teenager, she was tall, leggy, model-slim, and utterly convinced her life would never be anything but perfect.

Like this trip to Paris, for example, and this flawless day.

Across the street, the Seine glittered like a ribbon of satin under the afternoon sun. The tea was somehow sweeter today, almost as satisfying as the crunch of her teeth into the Brie-slathered hard rolls brought by an over-attentive waiter who didn't bother to hide the longing in his gaze at every part of Sung Kim's body.

She'd been to Paris before, of course. Her adoptive parents had made sure she would grow up knowing all about the world outside North Korea. It was an important part of her education, an invaluable preparation for the college years she would spend in America. And it was pretty much the same for her classmates back home, as well. All ten of the *Ipyanghan*, the "adopted children," spent their school holidays in the most glamorous cities in the world. Like Sung Kim, they'd all been told the same lie: that they'd been abandoned at birth by Americans too obsessed with wealth to be bothered by unwanted children. Like Sung Kim, they would never know the truth about the kidnappings. She took her eyes off the crowded sidewalk and looked at her mother again.

"What's the matter, Mom? Are you feeling okay?"

Her mother nodded. "Just tired, honey." Her smile was even smaller this time. "I think the trip's beginning to catch up to me."

Her mom's pretty face, narrow with a strong chin and

dark brown eyes, looked so morose Sung Kim wanted to stretch out and hug her.

She turned to her father. She was lucky to have been adopted by someone so kind and so generous. Sure he was strict, but all fathers were. She wasn't the only one of the *Ipyanghan* who hardly ever got to leave the compound in which they all lived back home, the two-square-mile, walled enclosure near the palace that set the elite apart from the rest of Pyongyang. Her dad's vigilance was just another sign of his love for her. Even here, in the safety of Paris, he couldn't seem to relax. Across the table his strong square features were frowning, his eyes scanning back and forth, up and down the street, as though he were waiting for someone to join them. Sung Kim couldn't see his feet, but she could hear the nervous tapping of one of his shoes against the pavement.

"Having a good time, Dad?" she asked him.

He nodded but said nothing. Her father had a great sense of humor, but she couldn't remember him smiling since the day they'd arrived.

"Hey," she said. "I'm a big girl now, and I'm perfectly safe here." She glanced over her shoulder toward the kitchen, then made a mock-serious face at her dad. "The waiter's the only one you've got to look out for."

This time he did manage to smile, but his eyes never left the street.

Sung Kim followed his gaze but couldn't tell what he was looking at. The street was busy, clogged with the Mercedes taxicabs that flooded Paris. From the sidewalk she heard a number of languages. French, of course, but German, too, in addition to Italian, Japanese, and English.

It wasn't hard to pick out the Americans.

All you had to do was listen.

It wasn't only their distinctive English—the same English Sung Kim spoke—it was the way they talked. Overly loud, aggressive, obnoxious. We own the world, their manner shouted, and we'll act any damned way we want to.

Sung Kim turned back to her mom, but a sudden commo-

tion over her right shoulder brought her eyes back around to
the sidewalk. Two men had pushed their way right up to their
table and stood staring at the three of them. Short men in
American clothing, tan slacks and flowered shirts not tucked
in. The heavier of the two was carrying a newspaper.

"No!" Sung Kim's dad shouted as the man raised the
hand carrying the newspaper. She heard what sounded like a
sharp cough and her father fell back in his chair.

"*Dad!*" she screamed, as she started for him.

Before she got there, Sung Kim heard a second cough.
She swung back toward her mother just in time to see her
mom's body slump sideways.

Now the man with the newspaper turned to Sung Kim.

Her voice sounded distant in her ears. "Please," she heard
herself saying. "Dear God, please."

The man shook his head. "God? This hasn't got anything
to do with God."

He lifted the paper. Sung Kim stared at him, frozen as she
realized she was about to die.

But suddenly a third man darted from the crowd and
crashed headlong into the shooter, knocking him sideways,
slamming the newspaper and gun out of his hand. Sung Kim
saw the black steel pistol clatter along the sidewalk. The
shooter's partner pulled the gunman to his feet, and they
raced off into the mob.

Sung Kim couldn't make herself move. Or look at her
parents. She tried to form a thought but couldn't. A moment
later, the man who'd saved her life grabbed her arm and
yanked her toward the street.

"Quickly," he said in Korean. "We cannot stay here."

"But . . . ," Sung Kim said. "I can't . . ." She tried to pull
the man's hand away. "My parents," she said. "I can't leave
my mom and—"

"Now!" He jerked harder on her arm. "The Americans
are monsters. They murdered your parents. They won't quit
until they kill you, too."

Sung Kim pried at his fingers but he was too strong.

"No!" she hollered, as he dragged her toward a waiting taxi. "You can't make me . . ."

Her voice died as he pulled the taxi door open and shoved her inside. The Mercedes accelerated hard. Sung Kim swung around in the seat, desperate to see her parents. The crowd had finally realized what had happened. A tall woman was the first to reach her mom, to extend her hand and close Sung Kim's mother's eyes. Sung Kim stared at the tall woman until the Mercedes turned the next corner. Her shoulders slumped as she began to cry.

Back at the Salon de Thé, the tall woman stepped into the street to make sure the Mercedes was out of sight before she turned back to Sung Kim's parents.

"Okay," she said in English. "They're gone."

Sung Kim's mother rose from the chair first, followed by her husband. They came around and stood facing the crowd, which had grown even larger as word of the shooting raced up and down the street. The tall woman smiled at the astonished faces around them.

"Sorry if we startled you," she said in French. "But your reaction will make the movie all the better."

She turned toward Sung Kim's parents and began to applaud. A teenager in the crowd started to clap as well, and suddenly everyone was doing so. Sung Kim's parents bowed, but her mother couldn't help looking up the street, at the corner where the Mercedes had disappeared.

September, 1997
Buenos Aires, Argentina

Tonight Sung Kim was a whore.

And quivering with impatience to get on with her mission.

At twenty-one, she was well aware of her position in the

spotlight. As the first of the *Ipyanghan* considered by Division 39 of the Central Workers Party to be ready for relocation to America, the success of Pyongyang's "sleeper" program would be judged by her performance here. For five years she'd been studying fine art, psychology, and a number of languages at Kim Il Sung University. Away from the campus, her training had been every bit as good. She'd learned her tradecraft from world-class murderers and saboteurs, from cat-burglars and prostitutes, all of them disaffected Americans from every level of criminality in the United States, and now it was time to see how it worked in the real world.

By ten o'clock that night, Buenos Aires was ready to party. The street called Macacha Guemes was bursting into life. A stream of diminutive Fiat Uno taxicabs arrived and departed from the wide sidewalk in front of the Hilton Hotel toward which Sung Kim strolled. Groups of expensively clothed young Argentinians strolled toward the hotel as well. With their slicked-back hair, silk turtleneck shirts, and linen jackets, the men looked like movie stars, but it was the women who made Sung Kim shake her head. It was hard to disguise yourself as a prostitute these days. Despite her micro-mini leather skirt, the four-inch spikes on her come-fuck-me pumps, her "big hair" curly brown wig, and the huge shoulder bag swinging against her hip, she didn't look all that different from the women around her.

But different enough, she discovered a few moments later as she approached the two-story-high glass entrance to the hotel.

"*Dios mio!*" a slouching man in a cheap suit said as he blocked her way on the sidewalk. "*¿Tienes algo para mi?*"

Sung Kim laughed. Did she have something for him? "*Lo siento, chico,*" she told him. Sorry, pal. "*Puede ser la proxima.*" Maybe next time.

He stepped aside as she pushed past him and continued into the entrance to the hotel. The doorman in his blue blazer and gray slacks looked her up and down but only for a moment. This was Buenos Aires, after all, and the Hilton was a popular hotel for businessmen from all over the world. Sung Kim wasn't the only hooker expected here tonight. He held the door open. She tossed her head as she passed and caught him grinning.

She crossed the enormous lobby, glancing up at the glass roof of the hotel, seven stories above. The place was really quite elegant. Had to be costing Kwon Jong a fortune to stay here. Money he'd stolen from his own government, her government. Money that could have bought food for the starving children who lay dying all over Pyongyang. The thought darkened her mood and made her even more eager to get to him.

Kwon was in Suite 491, she'd been told, along with his bodyguards, and they were staying in tonight. Her contact in Buenos Aires had checked only ten minutes ago. At the bank of elevators on the left side of the lobby, she pushed the UP button, and a door to her right slid open almost immediately. There were two men in the elevator, both much shorter than she. She stepped in and pushed the button for the fourth floor. She could feel the two men staring at her legs. One of them broke the silence.

"Christ," he said in semi-slurred English to his companion. "I wouldn't mind having those legs wrapped around my neck."

In your dreams, Sung Kim thought, although she knew better than to say it out loud. Later, when the cops talked to these two fools, she didn't want them remembering the Argentinian whore who spoke idiomatic English.

The elevator arrived at the fourth floor and she got out. She could hear the two men talking about her ass as the doors slid shut. In the hallway, her eyes turned hard. Suddenly she could hear the words of her trainer as clearly as if he were standing next to her.

In fast, Sung Kim. Out fast. No mercy.

She read the sign opposite the elevator. Suite 491 was to her left and would be near the end of the corridor. She kicked her ridiculous shoes off and headed in that direction. As she passed the rooms on both sides, she could hear the muted sounds of television but nothing else, until the soft scrape of a door opening behind her brought her to a dead stop. Sung Kim whirled, one hand reaching for the weapon in her shoulder bag, but stopped when she saw a little girl with huge brown eyes staring at her. A moment later, an adult arm reached out and snatched the child back into the room. Sung Kim's heartbeat took a moment to steady again, as she turned and continued toward the end of the hallway.

Suite 491 would be on her left, Sung Kim saw, as she passed 481. The fifth door on her left. She stopped for a moment to reach into her shoulder bag and withdraw the Beretta 92FS nine-millimeter pistol with three-inch silencer she'd chosen for tonight. She held the brutish black weapon close to her body, out of sight of anyone who might step out into the hall, then advanced toward the door.

At the door she tapped softly. *"La camarera,"* she said. The maid. *"Esta listo su traje."* Your suit is pressed and ready.

There was no answer. Sung Kim knocked again, but as she did so, she heard a door opening behind her, then a rush of footsteps. She pivoted toward the sound but wasn't able to completely face the bear of a man hurtling toward her before he kicked her in the back, a blow that sent her flying into the wall to the left of the door. The Beretta spun from her hand and arced through the air before tumbling to the floor a dozen feet away. Her shoulder bag slid off as she crashed to the carpet, but she jumped instantly to her feet to face the man shuffling toward her.

She stepped back against the wall to give herself room, and an instant to assess the danger. The man was half a head taller and at least a hundred pounds heavier. He wasn't Korean. Her contact had been wrong about something else as well. There wasn't supposed to be another hotel room involved. The two bodyguards were never supposed to leave Kwon Jong alone. Which meant the other one had to be close by.

The big man bent his knees for an instant, then sprang at her with amazing speed, his hands up, an eager smile on his face. His right fist shot toward her head, all his body weight behind the punch, but Sung Kim deflected the blow. As his fist passed her head, she used both hands to grab his shirt, to pull him toward her in a classic *akido* response. Off balance now, he had no strength to resist as she pivoted and moved her shoulder under his body, used the momentum of his superior weight to throw him over her and onto the floor. He fell hard but was up in a flash and facing her again. His smile got bigger now, as he appeared to relish the idea of her worthiness as an opponent.

She took a fighting stance, feet shoulder-width apart, her body turned until her right shoulder was facing him, "blading" herself to present a smaller target. He did the same, then advanced toward her more slowly this time. She waited for him to attack, to give her an idea of how he'd been trained, to reveal a vulnerability she might use. He approached to within kicking distance and raised his knee, preparing for a snap kick. Sung Kim waited for the twitch of movement that would send his foot flicking toward her head. He kicked but she danced out of range. He shuffled forward and tried again—like a boxer using his jab to measure the distance—but again she moved away. His smile seemed a little more forced now.

He was using a mixture of *hopkido* and *akido*, Sung Kim decided. A combination of fists and feet. But he had a problem with his arms. Both times he'd kicked at her, his arms had gone wide in an attempt to maintain balance. Not as wide as an amateur, but a dangerous flaw anyway.

Now he was as bladed as she was. She slid toward him, inviting another kick, her eyes locked on his midsection, waiting for him to telegraph which leg he'd use. He rocked back, "unweighting" his front leg, but the instant his foot swung toward her, his arms went wide. Now his fists were useless. She slipped into his body, inside the effective arc of his kick, then used both hands to parry his thigh and throw his leg past her. The movement served to cock her right arm for her own strike. She crouched slightly and felt the energy gathering in her legs. *All power comes from the ground.* She fired the elbow up and out, directly into the base of the giant's nose. In the quiet of the hallway, she could hear the cartilage tearing away as it slid upward into the sinus cavity above his eyes. He staggered back, his hands on his face, trying to stop the blood that was pouring through his fingers, and Sung Kim slid her foot behind his ankle. He tripped over her foot, twisted as he fell, and crashed on his stomach. Before he could turn over and continue fighting, she leaped on him, all her weight on her knees as she drove them into his back. He grunted as the air rushed from his lungs. She reached for his head, one hand grabbing his greasy brown hair, the other gripping his chin. She pulled his head back, then wrenched his chin around and back toward her. The sound of the bones in his neck breaking echoed in the corridor. His body seemed to deflate as she let go of his head and watched it bounce against the floor.

She was up in an instant, her eyes searching for the Beretta, but she heard the knob turning on Kwon Jong's door before she had a chance to start for the pistol. She grabbed for her shoulder bag instead, managed to pull out her knife just as the door swung open and the second bodyguard stepped into the doorway. Sung Kim brought the stiletto up as hard as she could. The point of the blade struck just below his sternum and traveled from there directly into his heart. He frowned for an instant before falling. Sung Kim stepped up close, left the knife in him as she caught his body and pushed it back into the room.

She had to hurry now.

She hadn't made much noise, but that didn't mean somebody hadn't called hotel security. Or that Kwon himself hadn't loaded up a shotgun and lay waiting for her inside the suite.

She darted back into the hallway and scooped up the Beretta before returning to the doorway. Holding the weapon with two hands, she stepped through. The living room of the suite was deserted. She glanced at the couch and chairs, at the computer work station near the glass doors out to the balcony, then to her right. Through the open door, she saw a bedroom. She crept through the door and swept the room with the Beretta. It was empty. She retreated through the door and stepped across the living room to the closed door on the left side of the suite. She paused outside the door for an instant, then turned the knob and burst through.

Kwon Jong sat upright on the king-size bed. He was wearing a white hotel bathrobe and holding a small revolver. His hands trembled as he tried to train the weapon on her. Sung Kim swung the Beretta into place and fired. The silenced pistol coughed quietly. Kwon's round face was expressionless, as a crimson-black hole appeared in the center of his forehead.